Earth in the Year 2042:
A Four-Part Invention

BEN BOVA
FREDERIK POHL
JERRY POURNELLE
CHARLES SHEFFIELD

An AvoNova Book

William Morrow and Company, Inc.
New York

AVON BOOKS
A division of
The Hearst Corporation
1350 Avenue of the Americas
New York, New York 10019

Introduction copyright © 1994 by Charles Sheffield; "2042: A Cautiously Pessimistic View" copyright © 1994 by Ben Bova; "Thy Kingdom Come" copyright © 1993 by Ben Bova; "A Visit to Belindia" copyright © 1994 Frederik Pohl; "What Dreams Remain" copyright © 1994 by Frederik Pohl; "Report on Planet Earth" copyright © 1994 by Charles Sheffield; "The Price of Civilization" copyright © 1994 by Charles Sheffield; "Democracy in America in the Year 2042" copyright © 1994 by Jerry Pournelle; "Higher Education" copyright © 1994 by Jerry Pournelle and Charles Sheffield.
Published by arrangement with the authors
Library of Congress Catalog Card Number: 93-43202
ISBN: 0-688-13173-5

Library of Congress Cataloging in Publication Data:
    Future quartet : Charles Sheffield . . . [et al.].
        p. cm.
        1. Science fiction, American. 2. Twenty-first century—Fiction.
    3. Twenty-first century. I. Sheffield, Charles.
    PS648.S3F9 1994   93-43202
    813'.0876208—dc20   CIP

First Morrow/AvoNova Printing: April 1994

AVONOVA TRADEMARK REG U.S. PAT. OFF. AND IN OTHER COUNTRIES, MARCA REGISTRADA, HECHO EN U.S.A.

Printed in the U.S.A.

ARC 10 9 8 7 6 5 4 3 2 1

CONTENTS

INTRODUCTION
by Charles Sheffield

2042 A.D.: in the year two-thousand-and-forty-two, my youngest child will be the same age as I am now.

This sounds like the beginning of one of those brain-teasing problems, beloved of algebra teachers and psychologists, that invite you at the end to calculate the age of someone's maternal grandmother. It is not. It is a simple and true statement, whose purpose is to point out that the year 2042 is *real*, as real as 1942, as real as 1992, as real as today. Our sons and daughters and grandchildren will be alive in 2042, as we are alive in 1992 and our grandparents were alive fifty years ago.

And because we are parents, we have to wonder about that world of fifty years from now, whether or not we expect to be here to enjoy it ourselves. Fifty years on: it seems so far off. What will life be *like* in 2042? What things will be the same? What will have changed beyond recognition, socially and tech-nologically? How do we even approach the problem of *making* such projections?

In the fall of 1990, the magazine *THE WORLD & I* came to me with this very problem. They wanted to explore the possible worlds of 2042, fifty years from the five hundredth anniversary of Columbus's first voyage to the New World. They recognized that *any* effort like this was difficult and dangerous. (*Whether there be prophecies, they shall fail—Isaiah, xiii, 2*). Projections made fifty years ago contained no mention of computers, nuclear energy, jet aircraft, electronic mail, communications and weather satellites, or any other form of space exploration; no mention of antibiotics, CAT scans, laser surgery, DNA structure, gene mapping or gene modification; no mention of global warming or global nuclear war, oil shortages and gluts, acid rain, disappearing forests, or environmental pollution; nothing of the breakup of the British Empire, or the decline of Communism.

The magazine wanted something more than the short-term and half-baked prophecies of psychics—the newspaper predictions that appear every year, concentrate on personalities more than events, and are unfailingly wrong. However, *THE WORLD & I* also recognized the limitations of even the best specialists in any field, whose projections seldom take account of technology interactions or social implications. How could one define a *plausible* and *whole* future?

I suggested my own preferred (and perhaps biased) way to address the problem of projection. Take the technology forecasts of top specialists in rapidly changing fields: computers and artificial intelligence, material sciences, communications and transportation, biomedical research, environmental change, the uses of oceans and space. Give all those forecasts to a select group of four people, used to thinking about the future in social terms as well as technological ones. Ask each of them to provide an integrated scenario, in which all the projected developments of science and technology would be melded with social variables. However, ask that the scenarios be generated *independently*, so that no one would know what the other three were saying.

And finally, to make sure that the results span a

range of possible futures, ask each of the four to make a different assumption about how nice or nasty our future world might be: one future should be very bad, one very good, and a couple in between.

The result was four speculative essays, deliberately ranging from dystopian to utopian. Those essays will be found here. But then, because the four scenario writers are as comfortable writing fiction as fact, another tempting thought was almost inevitable: Here we have four intriguing descriptions of our world, fifty years on. Within those futures there will be people, just like us, with their own pleasures and problems and preoccupations. Wouldn't it be wonderful to have a matched set of four new *stories*, written by our same four essayists, each taking place in a private vision of the future?

You are holding the result. And it is full of surprises, as the future is always filled with surprises. For in the best of times there will be individual misery, just as a fortunate few will find prosperity and happiness in the worst of times.

Will the world resemble any of the word pictures painted here? It could. As Dennis Gabor, the inventor of holography, remarked thirty years ago: *The future cannot be predicted; but futures can be invented.* But will it?

That depends on us. Here are four possible futures. Now we must decide which one we will choose to invent.

2042: A CAUTIOUSLY PESSIMISTIC VIEW

by Ben Bova

Address by the Hon. Chiblum C. Lee, Chairman of the World Council, 2 February 2042

My fellow citizens of the world:

It is both an honor and a grave responsibility to assume the task of chairman of this newly formed World Council. The burdens that face us are immense, as you are all aware. Our resources seem barely adequate to deal with the massive dislocations forced upon the world's people by population growth and climate shift.

Famine stalks much of the southern hemisphere. Even in the industrialized nations, life expectancies are declining. Civilization stands on the brink of a precipice, in danger of a fall from which it may never recover.

If I may have your indulgence for a few moments, I want to review the most significant problems that beset us. You are all as familiar with them as I am, I realize. But I want to demonstrate, if I can, how the interrelated nature of these problems has created a negative synergy that actually makes their totality much more difficult to solve than they would be as individual predicaments.

First, and foremost, is the continued explosive growth of world population. Ten point seven billion human beings occupy Planet Earth, according to this morning's computer monitoring data. More than sixty percent of them live in urban areas. Cities all across the world are bursting with overpopulation that is outstripping their transportation facilities, their water supplies, and their food and waste removal systems. From New York to São Paulo, from Cairo to Tokyo, the great cities of the world have become festering ghettos rife with crime, drugs, and despair.

By today's end, some three hundred thousand additional babies will have been born. Each of these human beings requires food, shelter, education, and a means of self-support. Each of these factors, in turn, demands a share of the planet's natural resources and energy. As long as population continues to grow unchecked, all our efforts to increase the Earth's productivity will continue to be swallowed up by the rising tide of hungry mouths.

Exacerbating this problem of population is the problem of climate shift. It is as if the punishment for the sins of our fathers has been visited upon us. Two and a half centuries of industrialization have so polluted the atmosphere of our world that global temperatures have risen into true greenhouse levels. Lands that were once fertile and abundant are turning into deserts. Sea levels are rising all around the world, threatening inundations that will force the relocation of hundreds of millions of families. Annual monsoons and tropical storms have increased in ferocity, as almost everyone who lives in a coastal area knows, to his or her sorrow.

The seven-decade-long Petroleum Wars have come to an end, at last, thanks in large part to the dedicated men and women of the International Peacekeeping Force—although perhaps even larger thanks should go to the scientists and engineers who have given us practical and efficient nuclear fusion power.

I want to dwell a moment on the IPF. When it was created, more than a generation ago, most of the world viewed the Peacekeepers with intense skepticism, if not outright hostility. An international organization dedicated to the prevention of war, authorized by the old United Nations to serve as a standing army—small but highly mobile—armed with the most modern and sophisticated defensive weapons that science can produce. It was unprecedented, even though *ad hoc* peacekeeping forces had been assembled by the UN as early as 1950!

To the astonishment of almost everyone, including many here in this great assembly hall this morning, the International Peacekeeping Force has worked. The Peacekeepers did not prevent aggressors from launching attacks on their neighbors—at first. But slowly, the world's national leaders learned that *any* attack by *any* nation upon any other nation would swiftly be met by powerful defensive forces, in the name of the united human race. Gradually the International Peacekeeping Force convinced would-be aggressors that the price for military assault was higher than any possible reward might be.

The Peacekeepers can serve as a model of how we can work together for the betterment of the human race. They have been able virtually to eliminate the scourge of war; we must work together to eliminate the potential causes of future strife.

The Petroleum Wars, of course, were not entirely military in character. Economic warfare, political maneuvering, even public-relations tactics, were all a part of this seventy-year-long struggle. Much like the old Cold War between the North Atlantic nations and the former Soviet Union, the Petroleum Wars were fought at many levels. They have exacted a terrible toll of human lives wasted, resources squandered, and environmental degradation.

As I said, today we stand at the edge of a precipice.

The human race has reached a turning point, one of those moments in history where the decisions we make now will determine the fate of humankind for centuries to come—perhaps forever. I see the fundamental problem that faces us as nothing less than the choice between the survival of civilization or its extinction—perhaps forever, certainly for longer than the lifetime of any human being alive today.

Our civilization has achieved great things, technologically. We can fly through space and build habitats at the bottom of the ocean. Our medical sciences have extended the average life expectancy in the industrialized nations to the point where difficult legal and ethical questions are being argued over the state's right to impose a limit on human life spans, as opposed to the individual's right not only to live for many more decades than a century, but to have one's body preserved at the point of death in the hopes of being revived at a later time, cured of the "fatal" disease, and then resume living.

But these wonderful achievements have been restricted to the rich alone. The overwhelming majority of the world's peoples are poor. They live and mate and die as they have for untold generations. Their numbers grow almost exponentially. And each generation they grow poorer, both in absolute terms and in relation to the growing wealth of the rich. Meanwhile the rich control their family sizes; the wealthy nations have stabilized their population growth and erected virtually impassable barriers against immigration, to prevent poor people from entering their countries.

How long can this planet continue to exist with a steadily growing population of extremely poor people and a small, stable population of extremely wealthy people? How long can we have one-quarter of the world's people consume ninety percent of its natural resources and energy, while the other three-quarters try to eke out a precarious living in growing squalor, misery, and frustration?

As an American president said nearly two hundred years ago, "A house divided against itself cannot stand."

The Petroleum Wars were a symptom of this fundamental problem. Behind the politics and the military combat was the desperation of poor people struggling to obtain some scant slice of the world's riches. The Wars have ended, but the underlying problem remains. If we fail to solve it, new fighting will break out: revolutions and terrorism that even the Peacekeepers will be helpless against.

Let me emphasize this point: Unless we achieve some means to alleviate the poverty and hunger that haunt three-quarters of the world's population, our civilization will crumble and collapse into a new Dark Age of incessant warfare and chaos. The rich will be swept under by the growing tide of the desperately poor. The world's population problem will be solved by the Four Horsemen of antiquity: Famine, Disease, War, and Death.

I will not accept such an end to our noble dreams of freedom and plenty for all. I believe that we can and we will solve the problems that beset us, no matter how difficult they are or how agonizing the solutions may be. It is the sacred duty of this World Council to find these solutions, and to implement them.

We have the tools. We have the knowledge, the technology, the understanding to build a new world society that is fair, and free, and flourishing. But do we have the will, the courage, to create fundamental changes in the world's existing political and economic structures?

That is for you to decide. This World Council is a recognition by all the nations of the world that the old order must be replaced by something new. National efforts have not solved the world's problems. Not even multinational efforts have been effective. The problems we face are global; our solutions must be global as well.

How do we narrow the vast and growing gap between the rich and the poor? How can we avert the famines and end the poverty that already hold in their pitiless grasp three out of every four human beings on Earth?

I can see two possible approaches: coercion or cooperation. Of these two, I much prefer cooperation. But allow me to say a few words about the concept of coercion.

There are two possible ways to use coercive tactics in our attempts to increase the wealth of the poor nations. One: force the rich nations to give up enough of their wealth so that the poor nations may advance economically. Two: force the poor nations to limit their population growth and adjust their economies for long-term growth rather than the stopgap measures they now employ to struggle through their most immediate problems.

I think you can see the difficulties with each of these tactics as well as I. The rich nations will resist a drastic redistribution of wealth. They will fight such measures politically and economically, and, failing all else, they will resort to force of arms. If all—or even most—of the industrialized nations took up arms against our World Council, not even the International Peacekeeping Force could prevent them from sweeping us into the dustbin of history. We cannot coerce the rich nations, but they can coerce us if they so choose.

Coercing the poor may sound easier, but how do we go about enforcing population limits for entire continents? Do we have the right—to say nothing of the power—to enter the bedchambers of three-quarters of the world's peoples and intervene in their most intimate acts? Do we have the moral superiority to tell literally billions of men and women that they must ignore the dictates of their religions and their social customs in the name of *our* vision of what the world should be?

The poor will resist such attempts, if we should be foolish enough to try them. They will not battle us with military weapons. They will simply ignore us and continue to have babies. What would we do then: slaughter the innocents in the name of global economic progress?

My friends, coercion will not work. Not only is it wrong, it is ineffective.

That leaves us with the tactics of cooperation. There is no other choice.

A very wise man once observed, "The problem with the world is not that there are so many poor people; it's that there are not enough rich people." The difference is subtle, perhaps, but very real. We cannot force the rich to give their wealth to the poor. We cannot even expect them voluntarily to give up large portions of their treasure to their needy brothers and sisters.

The alternative, then, is somehow to make the poor richer *without* pauperizing the rich.

As I said a moment ago, I believe that we have the tools to do this. We have a panoply of technologies that can generate abundant wealth, if they are effectively employed. It is up to us, this World Council, to lay out a long-range plan for the effective use of our best and most productive technologies.

Some of you who make up this Council are scientists and engineers. Most of you are not. To all of you, I say that technology—tool-making—is the way human beings adapt to their environment. We do not grow wings, we invent aeroplanes. We do not have the muscular strength of the gorilla nor the fleetness of foot of the antelope. Yet we lift tons of weight at the touch of a button and race across land and sea faster than any gazelle or dolphin.

Yet technology is not, and should not be, an end in

itself. Tool-making for the sake of making tools will never solve our problems. Tool-*using* has been the salvation of the human race time and again, since the Promethean days when our ancestors first tamed fire. Our task is to use the bright, shining tools that the technologists have produced for the betterment of the human race's economic and social condition.

Let me give you an example of how some of our best and most sophisticated tools are being poorly used today.

In the industrialized nations, the work force consists of almost as many robots as human workers. This is especially true in the manufacturing and extractive industries, where robots "man" the factories, the mines, and the farms. A generation ago, when truly useful and adaptable robots began to enter the work force in Europe and North America, there was a great surge of labor unrest. Human workers feared that they would be replaced by robots.

It was the Japanese who showed the way around this problem. In one form or another, human employees formed partnerships both with their robot coworkers and with the owners of the firms that employed them. In essence, the human workers began to draw their incomes not from their own labor, but from the wealth generated by the robots who labored for them. In the United States, for example, employees now buy robots the way they buy shares of corporate stocks. The robot works in place of the human, while the human receives the income that the robot has produced.

This system of employee ownership has allowed ever-more-sophisticated robots to enter the work force of the industrialized nations smoothly, with a minimum of labor strife and a maximum of profitability for employee and employer alike. But the increasingly roboticized work force of the industrialized nations has had devastating effects on the economies of the poorer nations.

Robots in England, for example, now produce clothing more cheaply than the lowest-paid human workers in Angola or Bangladesh. Robots in California do the "stoop labor" of harvesting that was formerly done by migrant farm workers. California grows richer; Mexico grows poorer. Robots are widening the gap between the rich and the poor. Indeed, robots are even replacing domestic servants among the very rich.

Researchers are today developing robots that will rival human thinking power. They enthusiastically report that it will be merely a matter of a decade or so before robots are so intelligent and so flexible that they will be able to replace human workers in virtually every task we now undertake. Perhaps at that time some very intelligent robots will be able to solve all our problems for us, and we poor, slow-witted humans can at last relax and enjoy the fruits of our machines' cogitations. [Pause for laughter.]

But that day is not with us yet. We must face our own problems and produce our own solutions.

Can robots help to make the poor nations wealthier? Can, for example, a team of robots turn a squalid farming village in Guatemala into a thriving and prosperous community? No. Not by themselves. The people of that village are unprepared for such a leap into the modern world. They lack the education and the social framework to deal with machines that move and work and think. Their village, their entire nation, lacks the economic foundation to employ robot labor usefully.

But robots can help the poor nations indirectly by helping to produce the wealth needed to start those nations on the road to riches. It is inevitable, inescapable, that the rich nations must devote some portion of their growing wealth to the salvation of the poor.

I propose that we, the World Council, establish a tax upon all nations, based on the ratio of each individual nation's Gross National Product in comparison to the mean GNP of all the nations. Thus, the very richest nations would pay the largest amount. The very poorest nations would have a negative tax: they would receive income from the tax fund.

The income that any nation receives, however, must be devoted to long-term programs that will improve that nation's economy. Thus the rich nations will pay to make the poor nations richer. In essence, the roboticized work force of the rich nations will help to increase the wealth of the poor.

This proposal smacks of the coercion I spoke against just a moment ago. But I ask the leaders of the rich nations to undertake this small sacrifice willingly. I have no intention of coercing any nation, and this World Council certainly does not have the power to be coercive. We need your cooperation, rich and poor alike.

No one likes to pay taxes. The rich nations may vote against this program. They may even refuse to support it even if the Council passes it. That would mean the dissolution of this World Council and a step backward toward the chaos of previous years. But all the nations that worked so hard and so long to bring about this new World Council of ours have known from the out-set that there would be new taxes to be paid. To quote the vernacular, "There ain't no such thing as a free lunch."

I propose that we set a tax rate that is as low as pos-sible, commensurate with producing a fund that can adequately help the poor. I further propose that we fix this tax rate for five years, so that all the nations can make economic plans that need not fluctuate annually. And, of course, I want to see the best and brightest economists, anthropologists, and business managers put to work to help the poor nations begin to build their economies toward self-sufficiency.

I am not here merely to propose new taxes, how-ever. I realize that if all we intend to do is to shift wealth from the rich to the poor, our efforts will be resisted and ultimately fail. We must, therefore, develop wherever possible the means and the opportunity to generate new wealth. It should be our primary goal to enlarge the human race's supply of real wealth: natural resources, energy, and human potential.

The place to find new resources is on the frontiers of our existing habitat. Obviously, we have physical frontiers in the world's vast oceans and the even vaster deeps of outer space. Yet there are mental frontiers, as well. Research laboratories are frontier country.

Perhaps the best news that we have received in this century is that a practical, efficient nuclear fusion power system has at last been developed to the point where it can leave the laboratory and begin to deliver reliable and safe electrical energy. After nearly a century of research, our scientists and engineers have harnessed the energy of the Sun and the stars themselves. We owe our everlasting thanks to the perseverance of the brilliant men and women who have given us this inestimable gift. In my mind, it ranks with the original gift of fire, back in the mists of prehistoric times.

Nuclear fusion power offers us the opportunity of moving away from all types of fossil fuels, with their inevitable outpouring of greenhouse gases, and away from the highly radioactive fissionable fuels of old-style nuclear power plants, as well. There are many who still fear the idea of nuclear power of any sort. We must convince them that fusion power is far safer than the old fission plants of the twentieth century. The fuel for fusion comes from ordinary water. Its major by-product is helium, an inert gas. There is no buildup of radioactive wastes, although the fusion equipment itself becomes radioactive over the course of its half-century-long useful lifetime.

The fusion process is so energetic that there is enough fusion fuel in an eight-ounce glass of water to equal the energy content of five hundred thousand barrels of petroleum! And less than one percent of the water is consumed! The rest is available for drinking, irrigation, or other uses.

I dwell on the prospects of fusion power because it is the key to the ultimate solution of the tremendous problems we face. With clean, efficient, and ultimately cheap fusion power we will be able to bring safe and reliable energy to the poorest of nations. We will have the energy to desalt seawater economically, in those growing areas where groundwater supplies are either disappearing or have become contaminated. We will have the energy to pump desalted water long distances for irrigation, to counteract the growing desertification of formerly productive farmland.

Another important use for fusion energy will be in recycling waste materials. For fifty years and more we have looked to recycling metals and plastics as a means of cleaning the environment. Recycling has been seen as an alternative to landfills or dumping our garbage into the sea. But recycling requires energy, and our efforts in this environmental-protection area have been limited by the costs of the energy required. Fusion power will make recycling profitable. Moreover, when fusion-driven recycling centers are reducing practically all our waste materials into highly refined elements, we will have opened a new source for raw materials. Recycled metals and chemicals will be cheaper, in many instances, than digging new ores out of the ground or the sea bottom.

Fusion energy can also power our explorations and developments on the ocean floor and in outer space.

But before I turn to these physical frontiers, there is another intellectual frontier that we must consider carefully. I speak now of the tremendous opportunities and problems created by the biological sciences and their offspring biotechnologies.

Biologists have delved into the very core of living

cells. They have learned the secrets of our genes so well that it is possible to extend healthy human life spans far beyond a century. There is even the faint chance of literal immortality glimmering in the latest reports from the research laboratories. With the population problems we already face, we have scant need for longer life spans. Yet, who would reject such an opportunity?

Of more immediate import is the enormous impact that biotechnology is making in agriculture and medicine. New strains of food crops, genetically engineered to withstand drought, heat, frost, insect pests, or other hostile conditions, can greatly increase the world's food supply. Genetically engineered bacteria now "fix" nitrogen for many food crops, eliminating or greatly reducing the need for artificial fertilizers.

These are powerful aids to our efforts to feed the world's hungry people. Yet these advances are not entirely without their risks. The temptation to plant nothing but these new "supercrops" could lead to disaster if some factor has been overlooked and the crops ultimately fail. Diversification must be the watchword among the world's farmers, not uniformity.

Biotechnology, like all technologies, is a two-edged sword. The very breakthroughs that produce cures for genetic diseases such as diabetes and cystic fibrosis are also capable of producing biological agents of unparalleled virulence. Biological warfare weapons have been justly called "the poor man's nuclear bomb." I am not suggesting a Frankenstein scenario, but I do insist that biotechnology laboratories must be under the continuing scrutiny of World Council monitoring agencies, just as nuclear facilities are. The benefits to come from new biological developments are immense; so are the possible dangers. Our aim must be to reap the benefits while minimizing the risks.

Now to the physical frontiers.

We have seen that there are immense resources in

the world's seas: resources of food, energy, and raw materials. We are today consciously reproducing in the oceans the Neolithic Revolution that our prehistoric ancestors produced on land some ten thousand years ago: that is, we are moving from merely gathering food from the sea to deliberately growing food there. Fish farms, algae farms, carefully tended beds for shellfish—these and more can eventually produce far more food, per hectare of sea surface and per calorie of energy input, than farms on land.

There is energy in the sea, as well. By tapping the difference in temperature between the cold deep layers of the ocean and the sun-warmed surface layers, it is possible to produce abundant electrical power without harm to the environment. Thus, industrial facilities and human habitats on the sea can be self-sufficient in energy, and will even be able to sell energy to consumers on land.

Seabed mining is already contributing to the world's supply of important metals such as magnesium, manganese, copper, and molybdenum. Future efforts will bring more of these resources to us, and increase humankind's supply of wealth even more than today.

Outer space is also a source of unimaginable wealth. More energy and raw materials exist in space than our entire planet Earth can provide, by many orders of magnitude. However, the costs of operating in space are still so high as to be prohibitive for all but the most profitable endeavors.

Today, three Solar Power Satellites provide half the electrical energy used by Japan. As large as Manhattan Island, placed in high orbits where sunlight constantly drenches their broad panels of solar cells, they beam energy in the form of microwaves to receiving "antenna farms" built off the coasts of two major Japanese islands, Honshu and Kyushu. A multinational consortium is attempting to raise capital for two more Solar Power Satellites, one each for

Europe and North America. Furthermore, Moonbase Inc. has recently announced plans to build solar-power "farms" on the surface of the Moon and offer the electrical energy they produce to consumers either on Earth or in the growing number of manufacturing and research stations in orbits between the Earth and the Moon.

The old dream of mining the asteroids for their metals and other raw materials has not yet been realized. The asteroids lie twice the distance of Mars, for the most part, and there is as yet no economic necessity to go that far for metals that can be obtained on Earth. Indeed, asteroid mining, if it ever becomes practicable, may threaten the economies of resource-rich nations that depend on exporting raw materials.

However, the space frontier is expanding, steadily if slowly. Thirty-two thousand people are working off-Earth as of this morning's census. Most of them are in near-Earth orbital facilities. Eight thousand are on the Moon, at the various government and private bases established there. And, of course, there are fifty men and women carrying out the continuing exploration of the planet Mars.

Outer space is a harsh and dangerous frontier. It will never serve as an outlet for the Earth's growing population. There will not be mass emigrations to space; not in our lifetime, nor in any foreseeable future. However, space *is* rich in energy and raw materials. And it offers unique environments in which inventive humans can produce goods and services that are impossible to produce on Earth.

The highest-quality metal alloys are manufactured in zero-gravity orbital facilities. The best crystals for our electronics industry are made there, as well. Much of the pharmaceutical industry is moving to space manufacturing facilities, where there is abundant solar energy, the ultraclean environment of high vacuum, and the availability of zero gravity. And a small but apparently lucrative tourist industry has sprung up in Earth orbit—for those few rich enough to afford it.

Outer space, the deep oceans, the research laboratories at universities and corporate centers around the world: these are the frontiers from which we may generate the new wealth that can bring the poor nations out of their deepening crises of poverty and hunger.

But all that we do, all that we hope to achieve, everything we plan will come to naught if the world's climate continues to deteriorate. You know the terrifying facts as well as I do. Every year in this century, thousands of square kilometers of productive land have turned into desert or useless scrubland. More thousands of square kilometers have been inundated by rising sea levels.

The global climate is warming, heated by greenhouse gases that we ourselves produce. For the first time in history, the actions of the human race are overshadowing the natural processes of climate and weather. We are overburdening the atmosphere, the oceans, and the land with our own filth. The result is contaminated drinking water, desertification, and a growing greenhouse warming of the planet.

We must mend our ways. We must reverse the man-made trends that are altering our environment so swiftly that natural processes are being overwhelmed.

We have the tools to accomplish what must be done. As I have pointed out to you, modern technology has given us cheap fusion energy, solar power, and energy from the oceans. All of these systems are essentially renewable and produce no environmentally degrading greenhouse gases. Superconducting motors and batteries, which can be made small and powerful enough to rival existing petroleum-burning engines for automobiles and other forms of transport, can end the smog problems that still plague the world's major cities. Such electrical vehicles will make a huge contribution to lowering the amount of greenhouse gases being pumped into the atmosphere.

Our biotechnologies offer the opportunity of using biological means of increasing farm productivity and controlling insect pests, rather than brute-force methods of artificial fertilizers and pesticides.

We have the tools. Do we have the intelligence and the courage to use them wisely? Military men speak of "friction," meaning the thousand-and-one individual misunderstandings and resistances that arise in the heat of battle. "Friction" is what comes between the general's brilliant plan and the actual outcome of the combat. You and I face "friction," also.

The sad fact is that human beings change their attitudes only slowly.

A villager who owns a petroleum-powered tractor has very little incentive to go into debt for a new electrically powered one, especially if he must learn to deal with superconducting machinery that requires liquid nitrogen.

A corporate executive who oversees the operation of a petrochemical plant is not going to endorse a shift to biotechnology that will replace everything he knows and leave him feeling useless.

A factory worker who controls several robots will not endorse a tax increase that is earmarked for assisting people of different lands, different skin color, and different social values.

And, saddest of all, there are still too many politicians who think nothing of siphoning off funds from aid projects for their own personal use. How many earlier attempts to assist the poor merely served to make certain political leaders rich?

This is the kind of friction we must overcome. As I said earlier, we stand at the edge of a precipice. All of us, rich and poor alike, are staring at the extinction of our civilization. Let there be no mistake about that. We have fouled our environment and overstrained our social systems to the point where civilization's continued existence is very much in doubt. Sooner or later—and I fear it will be sooner than we dare think—the cumulative effects of climate shift, burstingly crowded cities, growing hunger, and poverty will combine to tear apart the very fabric of society. Chaos and bloodshed such as the world has never seen will sweep across the face of the Earth.

Then it will be too late to change. Too late to mend our ways. The bright hopes of our sciences and technologies will have been washed away in blood. Nowhere will there be the energy, the capital, the human brain power to reinvent civilization. Humanity will sink into savagery while the climate continues to deteriorate, fed now by the raging fires of our destroyed cities and the decaying bodies of the dead.

That is the nightmare we must avoid. Our policy must point toward the good dream of a free, fair, and flourishing world society, where we fight with all our strength and all our wisdom against humankind's ancient and remorseless enemies: poverty, hunger, ignorance, and despair.

It is far from certain that we can win this battle. But we must try, for if we do not, then the end of civilization is at hand and the legacy we give to our children will be endless savagery and pain.

THY KINGDOM COME

by Ben Bova

Audio transcript of testimony of Salvatore (Vic) Passalacqua

I knew it wouldn't be easy, but I figured I hadda at least try. Y'know? The [deleted] Controllers had grabbed her in one of their swoops and I hadda get her back before they scrambled her [deleted] brains with their [deleted] sizzlers.

Her name? Oh yeah, I forgot you're tapin' all this. How do I look? Not bad for a guy goin' on twenty, huh? Yeah, yeah. Her name's Jade Diamond, keenest-looking piece of—no, that ain't her real name. 'Course not. Her real name was Juanita Dominguez. I knew her before she changed it. And her eyes. Like I said, she was real beautiful. Naturally. Without the implants and the eye job. They changed her eyes 'cause most of the big spenders are Japs.

Anyway, she was supposed t'be protected just like all the hookers. Except that the [deleted] [deleted] Controllers don't take nobody's payoffs—that's what they say, at least.

So there was Jade in the holdin' jug down at City Hall and here was me makin' a living out of old TV sets and tape players, anything to do with electrical stuff. Where?

23

In the junkyards, where else? You don't think I stole anything, do you? Why would I have to risk my butt goin' into the tracts and breakin' into peoples' houses when they throw away their stuff every year and it all winds up in the junkyards.

Yeah, I know the stuff is all supposed to be recycled. That's what I do. I recycle it before the [deleted] recyclers get their [deleted] claws on it.

Look, you wanna know about the Chairman and Jade and me or you wanna talk about business?

Okay. I was in love with Jade, that's why I did what I did. Sure, I knew she was a pro. You'd be too of you'd grown up in the city. We don't exist, y'know. Not legally. No records for any of us, not even the [deleted] police bother to keep records on us anymore. Not unless we done somethin' out in the tracts. As far as your [deleted] mother-[deleted] computer files are concerned, we weren't even born. So of course we don't die. If we don't bury our own, the [deleted] sanitation robots just dump our bodies into a pit and bulldoze 'em over. After they've taken out all the organs they wanna use for transplants, that is. And we sure don't get nuthin from your sweetheart of a government while we're alive. Nuthin but grief. Lemme tell ya—

Okay. Okay. Jade and the Chairman.

None of it would've happened if the Controllers hadn't picked up Jade. I guess they picked her up and the other girls 'cause the Chairman was comin' to Philly to make a speech and they wanted the streets to look clean and decent. First time I saw a sanitation robot actually cleanin' the [deleted] street. First time in my life! I swear.

Anyway, there Jade was in the tank and here I was at the junkyard and all I could think of was gettin' Jade out. I knew I needed help, so first thing in the morning I went to Big Lou.

His name's kind of a joke. You know? Like, he's even shorter than me, and I been called a runt all my life. His face is all screwed up, too, like it was burned with acid or somethin' when he was a kid. Tough face. Tough man. I was really scared of Big Lou but I wanted to get Jade outta the tank so bad I went to him anyway.

The sun was just comin' up when I got to the old school building where Big Lou had his office. He wasn't there that early. So I stooged around out in the street until he arrived in his car. It was polished so hard it looked brand-new. Yeah, a regular automobile, with a driver. What's it run on? How the hell would I know? Gasoline, I guess. Maybe one of those fancy other fuels, I don't know.

At first Lou told me to get lost, like I figured he would. I was just small-time, a junkyard dog without the teeth, far as he was concerned. See, I never wanted to be any bigger. I just wanted to live and let live. I got no hatred for nobody.

But while I'm beggin' Big Lou for some help to spring Jade, he gets a phone call. Yeah, he had a regular office in the old school building in our neighborhood. I know, they shut down all the schools years ago, before I was even born. They're supposed to be abandoned, boarded up. Hell, most of 'em were burned down long ago. But not this one. It's still got a pretty good roof and office space and bathroom, if you know how to turn the water on. And electricity. Okay, sure, all the windows were smashed out in the old classrooms and the rest of the building's a mess. But Lou's office was okay. Clean and even warm in the winter. And nobody touched his windows, believe me.

Y'know, down in South Philly, from what I hear—Oh yeah, you people don't know Philly that well, do you? Where you from, New York? Washington? Overseas? What?

Okay, okay. So you ask the questions and I do the answerin'. Okay. Just curious. Where was I?

Big Lou, right. He had an office in the old school building. Yeah, he had electricity. Didn't I tell ya that already? There was a couple TVs in the office and a computer on his desk. And he had a fancy telephone, too. I had put it together myself, I recognized it soon as I saw it. Damned phone had its own computer chips: memory, hunt-and-track, fax—the works. I had sold it to Lou for half a peanut; cost me more to put it together than he paid for it. But when you sell to Big Lou you sell at his price. Besides, who the [deleted] else did I know who could use a phone like that?

Anyway, I'm sittin' there in front of his desk. Big desk. You could hold a dance on it. I had figured that Big Lou could talk to a couple people, put a little money in the right hands, and Jade could get out of the tank before the [deleted] Controllers fried her brains and sent her off to Canada or someplace.

Lou gets this phone call. I sit and wait while he talks. No, I don't know who called him. And he didn't really do much talkin'. He just sort of grunted every now and then or said, "Yeah, I see. I gotcha." His voice is kinda like a diesel truck in low gear, like whatever burned his face burned the inside of his throat, too.

Then he puts down the phone and smiles at me. Smiles. From a face like his it was like a flock of roaches crawlin' over you.

"I got good news for you, Vic," he says. "I'm gonna help you get your spiff outta the tank." All with that smile. Scared the [deleted] outta me.

"The hearings for all the bimbos they rounded up are three o'clock this afternoon. You be there. We're gonna make a commotion for you. You grab your [deleted] and get out fast. Unnerstand me?"

I didn't like the sound of that word *commotion*. I wasn't sure what it meant, not then, but I figured it would mean trouble. All I wanted was for Big Lou to buy Jade's way out. Now it sounded like there was goin' to be a fight.

Don't get me wrong. I've had my share of fights. I'm on the small side and I'm sure no jock, but you can't even exist in the city if you can't protect yourself. But I didn't like the idea of a fight with the city police. They like to beat up on guys. And they carry guns. And who knew what in hell the Controllers carried?

"You unnerstand me?" Big Lou repeated. He didn't raise his voice much, just enough to make me know he wanted the right answer outta me.

"Yeah," I said. My voice damned near cracked. "Sure. And thanks." I got up and scooted for the door.

Before I got to it, though, Big Lou said, "There's a favor you can do for me, kid."

"Sure, Lou," I said. "Tonight, tomorrow, when? You name it."

"Now," he said.

"But Jade—"

"You'll be done in plenty time to get to City Hall by three."

I didn't argue. It wouldn't have done me no good. Or Jade.

What he wanted was a fancy electronic gizmo that I had to put together for him. I knew it was important to him because he told one of his goons—a guy with shoulders comin' straight out of his ears, no neck at all, so help me—to drive me all the way downtown to the old Navy base. It had been abandoned before I was born, of course, but it was still a treasure island of good stuff. Or so I had been told all my life. I had never even got as far as the electrified fence the Feds had put up all around the base, let alone inside the base itself. You had to go through South Philly to get to the base, and a guy alone don't get through South Philly. Not in one piece, anyway.

But now here I was bein' taken down to that fence and right through it, in a real working automobile, no less! The car was dead gray with government numbers stenciled on the driver's door. But the driver was Big Lou's goon. And Little Lou sat on the backseat with me.

Little Lou was a real pain in the ass. Some people said he really was Big Lou's son. But he sure didn't look like

Big Lou. Little Lou was only a couple years older than me and he was twice Big Lou's size, big and hard with muscles all over. Good-lookin' guy, too. Handsome, like a video star. Even if he hadn't been a big shot he could've had any girl he wanted just by smilin' at her.

He was smart. And strong. But he was ugly inside. He had a nasty streak a mile and half wide. He knew I wanted to be called Vic. I hate the name my mother gave me: Salvatore. Little Lou always called me Sal. Or sometimes Sally. He knew there wasn't a damned thing I could do about it.

I tried to keep our talk strictly on the business at hand. And one eye on my wristwatch. It was an electronic beauty that I had rebuilt myself; kept perfect time, long as I could scrounge a battery for it every year or so. I kept it in an old scratched up case with a crummy rusted band so nobody like Little Lou would see how great it was and take it off me.

It was noon when we passed through a gate in the Navy base fence. The gate was wide open. No guard. Nobody anywhere in sight.

"So what's this gizmo I'm supposed to put together for you?" I asked Little Lou.

He gave me a lazy smile. "You'll see. We got a man here with all the pieces, but he don't know how to put 'em together right."

"What's the thing supposed to do?"

His smile went bigger. "Set off a bomb."

"A bomb?"

He laughed at how my voice squeaked. "That's right. A bomb. And it's gotta go off at just the right instant. Or else."

"I—" I had to swallow. Hard. "I never worked with bombs."

"You don't have to. All you gotta do is put together the gizmo that sets the bomb off."

Well, they took me to a big building on the base. No, I don't remember seein' any number or name on the building. It looked like a great big tin shed to me. Half fallin' down. Walls slanting. Holes in the roof, I could see once we got inside. Pigeon crap all over the place. Everything stunk of rust and rot. But there were rows and rows of shelves in there, stacked right up to the roof. Most of 'em were bare, but some still had electronic parts in their cartons, brand-new, still wrapped in plastic, never been used before. My eyes damn' near popped.

And there was a guy there sittin' in a wheelchair next to a long bench covered with switches and batteries and circuit boards and all kinds of stuff. Older guy. Hair like a wire brush, a couple days' beard on his face, grayer than his hair. One of his eyes was swollen purple and his lip was puffed up too, like somebody'd been sluggin' him. Nice guy, beatin' on a wheelchair case.

I got the picture right away. They had wanted this guy to make their gizmo for them and he couldn't do it. Little Lou or one of the others had smacked the poor slob around. They always figured that if you hit a guy hard enough he would do what you wanted. But this poor bastard didn't know how to make the gizmo they wanted. He had been a sailor, from the looks of him: face like leather and tattoos on his arms. But something had crippled his legs and now he was workin' for Big Lou and Little Lou and takin' a beating because they wanted him to do somethin' he just didn't know how to do.

He told me what they wanted. Through his swollen, split lips he sounded strange, like he had been born someplace far away where they talk different from us. The gizmo was a kind of a radar, but not like they use in kitchen radar ranges. This one sent out a microwave beam that sensed the approach of a ship or a plane. What Little Lou wanted was to set off his bomb when whatever it is he wanted to blow up was a certain distance away.

Electronics is easy. I heard that they used to send guys to school for years at a time to learn how to build electronic stuff. I could never understand why. All the stuff is pretty much the same. A resistor is a resistor. A power cell is a power cell. You find out what the gizmo is supposed to do and you put together the pieces that'll do it. Simple.

I had Little Lou's gizmo put together by one o'clock. Two hours to go before I hadda be in City Hall to take Jade away from the Controllers.

"Nice work, Sal," Little Lou said to me. He knew it got under my skin.

"Call me Vic," I said.

"Sure," he said. "Sally."

That was Little Lou. If I pushed it he would've smacked me in the mouth. And laughed.

"I got to get up to City Hall now," I said.

"Yeah, I know. Hot for that little [deleted], ain'tcha?"

I didn't answer. Little Lou was the kind who'd take your girl away from you just for the hell of it. Whether she wanted to or not. And there'd be nuthin I could do about it. So I just kept my mouth zipped.

He walked me out to the car. It was hot outside; July hot. Muggy, too. "You start walkin' now, you'll probably just make it to City Hall on time."

"Walk?" I squawked. "Ain't you gonna drive me?" I was sweatin' already in that hot sun.

"Why should I?" He laughed as he put the gizmo in the car's trunk. "I got what I want."

He shut the trunk lid real careful, gently, like maybe the bomb was in there too. Then he got into the car's backseat, leaving me standin' out in the afternoon sun feelin' hot and sweaty and stupid. But there wasn't a damned thing I could do about it.

Finally Lou laughed and popped the back door open. "Come on in, Sally. You look like you're gonna bust into tears any minute."

I felt pretty [deleted] grateful to him. Walkin' the few miles uptown to City Hall wouldn't have been no easy trick. The gangs in South Philly shoot first and ask questions afterward when a stranger tries to go through their turf.

About halfway there, though, Little Lou lets me know why he's bein' so generous.

"Tonight," he says, "nine o'clock sharp. You be at the old Thirtieth Street Station."

"Me? Why? What for?"

"Two reasons. First we gotta test the gizmo you made. Then we gotta hook it up to the bomb. If it works right."

He wasn't smilin' any more. I was scared of workin' with a bomb, lemme tell you. But not as scared as I was at the thought of what Little Lou'd do to me if the gizmo didn't work right.

So I got to City Hall in plenty time okay. It's a big ugly pile of gray stone, half fallin' apart. A windowsill had crumbled out a couple months ago, just dropped out of its wall and fell to the street. Solid hunk of stone, musta weighed a couple tons. It was still there, stickin' through the pavement like an unexploded bomb. I wondered what would happen if the statue of Billy Penn, up at the top of the Hall's tower, ever came loose. Be like a [deleted] atomic bomb hittin' the street.

Usually City Hall is a good place to avoid. Nobody there but the suits who run what's left of the city and the oinks who guard 'em.

Oinks? Pigs. Helmet-heads. Bruisers. Cops. Police. There are worse names for them, too, y'know.

Well, anyway, this particular afternoon City Hall is a busy place. Sanitation robots chuggin' and scrubbin' all over the place. A squad of guys in soldier uniforms and polished helmets goin' through some kind of drill routine in the center courtyard. Even a crew of guys with a truck and a crane tryin' to tug that windowsill outta the pavement. Might as well be tryin' to lift the [deleted] Rock of Gibraltar, I thought.

They were goin' through all this because the Chairman of the World Council was comin' to give a speech over at Independence Hall. Fourth of July and all that crap. Everybody knew that as soon as the Chairman's speech was over and he was on his way back to New York or wherever he stayed, Philly would go back to bein' half-empty, half-dead. The sanitation robots would go back to the housing tracts out in the suburbs and Philly would be left to itself, dirty and hot and nasty as hell.

I felt a little edgy actually goin' *inside* City Hall. But I told myself, what the hell, they got nuthin on me. I'm not wanted for any crime or anything. I don't even exist, as far as their computers are concerned. Still, when I saw these guys in suits and ties and all I felt pretty crummy. Like I should have found a shower someplace or at least a comb.

I didn't like to ask nobody for directions, but once I was inside the Hall I didn't have a [deleted] idea of where I should go. I picked out a woman, dressed real neat in kind of a suit but with a skirt instead of pants. Even wore a tie. No tits to speak of, but her hair was a nice shade of yellow, like those girls you see in TV commercials.

She kind of wrinkled her nose at me, but she pointed up a flight of stone stairs. I went up and got lost again right away. Then I saw an oink—a woman, though—and asked her. She eyed me up and down like she was thinkin' how much fun it'd be to bash me on the head with her billy. But instead she told me how to find the courtroom. She talked real slow, like I was brain-damaged or something. Or maybe she was, come to think of it.

I went down the hall and saw the big double-doored entrance to the courtroom. A pair of oinks stood on either side of it, fully armed and helmeted. A lot of people were streamin' through, all of them well dressed, a lot of them carrying cameras or laptop computers. Lots of really great stuff, if only I could get my hands on it.

Then I saw a men's room across the corridor and I ducked inside. A couple homeless guys had made a camp in the stalls for themselves. The sinks had been freshly cleaned up, though, and the place didn't smell too bad. I washed my face and hands and tried to comb my hair a little with my fingers. Still looked pretty messy, but what the hell.

Taking a deep breath, I marched across the corridor and through the double doors, right past the oinks. I didn't look at them, just kept my eyes straight ahead.

And then I saw Jade.

They had her in a kind of a pen made of polished wood railings up to about waist level and thick shatterproof glass from there to the ceiling. She was in there with maybe three dozen other pros, most of 'em lookin' pretty tired and sleazy, I gotta admit. But not Jade. She looked kind of scared, wide-eyed, you know. But as beautiful and fresh as a flower in the middle of a garbage heap. I wanted to wave to her, yell to her so she'd notice me. But I didn't dare.

You gotta understand, I was in love with Jade. But she couldn't be in love with me. Not in her business. Her pimp would beat the hell out of any of his whores who took up with anybody except himself. I had known her since we were kids together runnin' along the alleys and raiding garbage cans, keepin' one jump ahead of the dog packs. Back when her name was still Juanita. Before she had her eyes changed. I had kissed her exactly once, when we was both twelve years old. The next day she turned her first trick and went pro.

But I had a plan. For the past five years I had been savin' up whatever cash I could raise. Usually, you know, I'd get paid for my work in food or drugs or other stuff to barter off. But once in a while somebody'd actually give me money. What? Naw, I never did much drugs; screwed up my head too much. I usually traded whatever [deleted] I came across. I seen what that stuff does to people; makes 'em real psycho.

Anyway, sometimes I'd get real money. That's when I'd sneak out to the housing tracts where they had automated bank machines and deposit my cash in the bank. All strictly legitimate. The bank didn't care where the money came from. I never had to deal with a living human being. All I had to do to open the account was to pick up a social security number, which I got from a wallet I had found in one of the junkyards when I was ten, eleven years old. Even that young, I knew that card was better than gold.

So I had stashed away damn' near a thousand dollars over the years. One day I would use that money to take Jade outta the city, out of her life. We'd buy a house out in the tracts and start to live like decent people. Once I had enough money.

But then the [deleted] Controllers had arrested Jade. What I heard about the Controllers scared the [deleted] outta me. They were bigger than the city oinks, bigger even than the state police or the National Guard. They could put you in what they called International Detainment Centers, all the way out in Wyoming or Canada or wherever the hell they pleased. They could scramble your brains with some super electronic stuff that would turn you into a zombie.

That's what they were goin' to do to Jade. If I let them.

I sat in the last row of benches. The trials of the pros were already goin' on. Each one took only a couple minutes. The judge sat up on his high bench at the front of the courtroom, lookin' sour and cranky in his black robe. A clerk called out one of the girls' names. The girl would be led out of the holding pen by a pair of women oinks and stood up in a little railed platform. The clerk would say that the girl had been arrested for prostitution and some other stuff I couldn't understand because he was mumblin' more than speakin' out loud.

The judge would ask the girl how she pleaded: guilty or innocent. The girl would say, "Innocent, your honor." The judge would turn to a table full of well-dressed suits who had a bunch of laptops in front of them. They would peck on their computers. The judge would stare into the screen of his computer, up on the desk he was sittin' at.

Then he'd say, "Guilty as charged. Sentenced to indeterminate detention. Next case." And he'd smack his gavel on the desk top.

I remember seein' some old videos where they had lawyers arguin' and a bunch of people called a jury who said whether the person was guilty or innocent. None of that here. Just name, charge, plea, and "Guilty as charged." Then—*wham!*—the gavel smack and the next case. Jade wouldn't have a chance.

And neither did I, from the looks of it. How could I get her away from those oinks, out from behind that bulletproof glass? Where was this commotion Big Lou promised, whatever it was supposed to be?

They were almost halfway through the whole gang of girls, just whippin' them past the judge, bang, bang, bang. Jade's turn was comin' close; just two girls ahead of her. Then the doors right behind me smack open and in clumps some big guy in heavy boots and some weird kind of rubbery uniform with a kind of astronaut-type helmet and a visor so dark I couldn't make out his face even though I was only a couple feet away from him.

"Clear this courtroom!" he yells, in a deep booming voice. "There's been a toxic spill from the cleanup crew upstairs. Get out before the fumes reach this level!"

Everybody jumps to their feet and pushes for the door. Not me. I start jumpin' over the benches to get up front, where Jade is. I see the judge scramble for his own little doorway up there, pullin' his robe up almost to his waist so he could move faster. The clerks and the guys with the laptops are makin' their way back toward the corridor. As I passed them I saw the two oinks openin' the glass door to the holding pen and startin' to hustle the girls out toward a door in the back wall.

I shot past like a cruise missile and grabbed Jade's wrist. Before the oinks could react I was draggin' her up the two steps to the same door the judge had used.

"Vic!" she gulped as I slammed the door shut and clicked its lock.

I said something brilliant like, "Come on."

"What're you doing? Where're we going?"

"Takin' you outta here."

Jade seemed scared, confused, but she came along with me all right. The judge was nowhere in sight, just his robe thrown on the floor. Somebody was poundin' on the door we had just come through and yellin' the way oinks do. There was another door to the room and the judge had left it half-open. I had no way of knowin' if that toxic spill was real or not, but I knew that the oinks would be after us either way so I dashed for the door, Jade's wrist still in my grip.

"You're crazy," she said, kind of breathless. But she came right along with me. And she smiled at me as she said it. If I hadn't been so wound tight I would've kissed her right there and then.

Instead we pounded down this empty corridor and found an elevator marked JUDGES ONLY. I leaned on the button. Somebody appeared at the far end of the corridor, a guy in a business suit.

"Hey, you kids," he yelled, kind of angry, "you're not allowed to use that elevator."

Just then the doors slid open. "Emergency!" I yelled back and pulled Jade inside.

When we got down to the street level everything seemed normal. Nobody was runnin' or shoutin'. I guessed that the toxic spill was a phony. I couldn't imagine Big Lou doin' something like that just for me, but maybe he needed his bomb gizmo bad enough after all. Anyway, I told Jade to act normal and we just walked out into the central courtyard nice and easy, me in my shabby jeans and sneakers and her in her workin' clothes: spike heels, microskirt, skintight blouse. They had washed off her makeup and her hair looked kind of draggled, but she was still beautiful enough to make even the women out there turn and stare at her.

The work crew was still tryin' to tug that fallen windowsill outta the cement when we walked past. I steered Jade toward the boarded-up entrance to the old subway.

"We're not going down there!" she said when I pushed a couple boards loose.

"Sure as hell are," I said.

"But—"

"Hey you!" yelled a guy in a soldier uniform.

"Come on!" I tugged at Jade's wrist and we started down the dark stairway underground.

The steps were slippery, slimy. It was dark as hell down there and it stunk of [urine]. The air was chilly and kind of wet; gave you the shakes. I could feel Jade trembling in my grip. With my other hand I fished a penlight outta my pocket. What? I always keep a light on me. And make sure the batteries are good, too. You never know when you're gonna need a light; trouble don't always come at high noon, y'know.

"Vic, I don't like this," Jade said.

"I don't either, honey, but we gotta get away. This is the best way to do it." I clicked on my penlight; it threw a feeble circle of light on the filthy, littered tiled floor. "See, it ain't so bad, is it?"

Jade was right in a way. The subway tunnels really were dangerous. We had heard stories since we were little kids about the hordes of rats livin' down there. And other things, monsters that crawled outta the sewers, people who lived down there in the dark for so long they'd gone blind—but they could find you in the dark and when they did they ate you raw, like animals.

I was kind of shakin' myself, thinkin' about all that. But I wasn't gonna let Jade be taken away by the Controllers and I wasn't gonna play with no bombs for Little Lou or Big Lou or anybody. I was takin' Jade and myself outta the city altogether, across the bridge and out into the housing tracts on the other side of the river. I'd take my money from the bank and find a place for us to live and get a regular job someplace and start to be a real person. The two of us. Jade and me.

Okay, maybe it was just a dream. But I wanted to make my dream come true. Wanted it so bad I was willin' to face anything.

Well, there ain't no sense tellin' you about every step of the way we took in the subway tunnels. There were rats, plenty of 'em, some big as dogs, but they stayed away from us as long as the penlight worked. We could see their red eyes burnin' in the dark, though, and hear them makin' their screechy little rat noises, like they was talkin' to each other. Jade had a tough time walkin' on those spike-heel shoes of hers, but she wouldn't go barefoot in the sloppy goo we hadda walk through. My own sneaks were soaked through with the muck; it made my feet burn.

Jade screamed a couple times, once when she stumbled on something squishy that turned out to be a real dog that must've died only a few hours earlier. It was half eaten away already.

No monsters from the sewers, though. And if there was any blind cannibals runnin' around down there, we didn't see them. The rats were enough, believe me. I felt like they were all around us, watchin', waitin' until the batteries in my light gave out. And then they'd swarm us under and do to us what they had started to do to that dog.

All the subway tunnels meet under the City Hall, and I sure as hell hoped I had picked the right one, the one that goes out to the river. After hours and hours, I noticed that the tunnel seemed to be slantin' upwards. I even thought I saw some light up ahead.

Sure enough, the tracks ran up and onto the Ben Franklin Bridge that crossed the Delaware. It was already night, and drizzling a cold misty rain out there. No wind, not even a breath of air movin'. And no noise. Silence. Everything was still as death. It was kinda creepy, y'know. I been on that bridge lotsa times; up that high there was always a breeze, at least. But not that night.

At least we were out of the tunnel. On the other side of that bridge was the housing tracts, the land where people could lead decent lives, safe from the city.

I knew the bridge was barricaded and the barricades were rigged with electronic chips that spotted anybody tryin' to get through. Those people in the tracts didn't like havin' people from the city comin' over to visit. Not unless they drove cars that gave out the right electronic ID signals. But I had gotten past the barricades before. It took a bit of climbin', but it could be done. Jade could take off her spike heels now and climb with me.

But in front of the barricade was a car. A dead gray four-door with government numbers stenciled on the driver's door. Only the guys standin' beside the car weren't government. They were Little Lou and his goon driver.

Lou was leanin' against the hood, lookin' relaxed in a sharp suit and open-collar shirt. His hair was slicked back and when he saw Jade, he smiled with all his teeth.

"Where you goin', Sal?" he asked, real quiet, calm.

I had to think damned fast. "I thought we was in the tunnel for the Station! I must've got mixed up."

"You sure did."

Lou nodded to the goon, who opened the rear door of the car. I started for it, head hung low. He had outsmarted me.

"Not you, stupid," Lou snarled at me. "You sit up front with Rollo." He made a little half bow at Jade, smilin' again. "You sit in back with me, spiff."

Jade got into the car and scrunched herself into the corner of the backseat, as far away from Little Lou as she could. I sat up front, half-twisted around in the seat so I could watch Lou. Rollo was so big his elbow kept nudgin' me every time he turned the steering wheel.

"You was supposed to be at the Thirtieth Street Station at nine o'clock," Little Lou said to me. But his eyes were on Jade, who was starin' off at nothing.

I looked at my wristwatch. "Hell, Lou, it's only seven-thirty."

"Yeah, but you were headin' in the wrong direction. A guy could lose some of his fingers that way. Or get his legs broke."

"I just got mixed up down in the tunnels," I said, tryin' to make it sound real.

"You're a mixed-up kid, Sally. Maybe a few whacks on your thick skull will straighten you out."

There wasn't much I could say. If Little Lou was waitin' for me at the bridge he had me all figured out. I just hoped he really needed me enough to keep me in one piece so I could set up his bomb gizmo for him. What would happen after that, I didn't know and I didn't want to think about.

We drove through the dead empty city for a dozen blocks or so. I had turned around in my seat and was lookin' ahead out the windshield. Everything was dark. Not a light in any window, not a street lamp lit. I knew people lived in those buildings. They were supposed to be abandoned, condemned. But nobody bothered to tear them down; that would cost the taxpayers too much. And the people who didn't exist, the people whose names had been erased from the government's computers, they lived there and died there and had babies there. I was one of those babies. So was Jade.

"Are those tits real?" I heard Lou ask.

Through the side view mirror I saw Jade turn her face to him. Without a smile, with her face perfectly blank, she took his hand and placed it on her boob.

"What do you think?" she asked Lou.

He grinned at her. She smiled back at him. I wanted to kill him. I knew what Jade was doin': tryin' to keep Lou happy so he wouldn't be sore at me. She was protectin' me while I sat there helpless and the dirty [deleted] [deleted] bastard climbed all over her.

"Thirtieth Street Station comin' up," said Rollo. His voice was high and thin, almost like a girl's. But I bet that anybody who laughed at his voice got his own windpipe whacked inside out.

Lou sat up straight on the backseat and ran a hand through his hair. Jade edged away from him, her face blank once again.

"Okay, Sally, you little [deleted]. Here's where you earn your keep. Or I break your balls for good."

Lou, Rollo, and me got out of the car. Lou ducked his head through the open rear door and told Jade, "You come too, cute stuff. We'll finish what we started when this is over."

Jade glanced at me as she came out of the car. Lou grabbed her by the wrist, like he owned her.

If Lou had been by himself I would have jumped him. He was bigger then me, yeah, and probably a lot tougher. But I was desperate. And I had the blade I always carried taped just above my right ankle. It was little, but I kept it razor sharp. Lou was gonna take Jade away from me. Oh, I guess he'd let her come back to me when he was finished with her, maybe. But who knew when? Or even if. I had only used that blade when I needed to protect myself. Would I have the guts to cut Lou if I could get him in a one-on-one?

But Lou wasn't alone. Rollo was as big as that damned City Hall windowsill. There was no way I could handle him unless I had a machine gun or a rocket launcher or something like that. I was desperate, all right. But not crazy.

The Station was all lit up. Cleaning crews and robots were crawlin' all over the old building, but I didn't see any oinks or soldiers. Later I found out that they would be pourin' into the area in the morning. The Chairman was due to arrive at 11:00 A.M.

Lou took me and Jade to a panel truck marked PUBLIC WORKS DEPARTMENT. Two other guys was already sittin' up front. And there was my gizmo, sittin' on the bare metal floor. All by itself. No bomb in sight. That made me feel better, a little.

They hustled us into the truck and made me sit on the floor, big Rollo between me and the back door and Lou across from me. He made Jade sit beside him. She kept her legs pressed tight together. We drove off.

"Where we goin'?" I asked.

Lou said, "There's a maintenance train comin' down the track in half an hour. You set up your gizmo where we tell you to and we see if it can spot the train at the right distance away and send the signal that it's supposed to send."

"What're you guys gonna do, blow up the Chairman?"

I got a backhand smack in the face for that. So I shut my mouth and did what they told me, all the while tryin' to figure out how in hell I could get Jade and me outta this. I didn't come up with any answers, none at all.

When the truck stopped Rollo got out first, then Lou shoved me through the back door. The other two guys stayed in their seats up front. Lou pushed the gizmo across the truck's floor toward me. It was heavy enough so I needed both hands.

"Don't drop it, [deleted]head," Lou growled.

"Why don't we let Rollo carry it?" I said.

Lou just laughed. Then he helped Jade out the back door. I thought he helped her too damned much, had his hands all over her.

We was parked maybe ten blocks away from the station. Its lights glowed in the misty drizzle that was still comin' down, the only lights in the whole [deleted] city, far as I could see. Some of the people livin' in the buildings all around there had electricity, I knew. Hell, I had wired a lot of 'em up. But they kept their windows covered; didn't wanna let nobody know they was in there. Scared of gangs roamin' through the streets at night.

All those suits and oinks and everybody who had been at City Hall was all safe in their homes in the tracts by now. Nobody in the city except the people who didn't exist, like Jade and me. And the rats who had business in the dark, like Little Lou.

I saw why Lou didn't want Rollo to carry the gizmo. The big guy walked straight up to a steel grate set into the pavement. It must have weighed a couple hundred pounds, at least, but he lifted it right up, rusty hinges squealin' like mad. I saw the rungs of a metal ladder goin' down. Lou shone a flashlight on them. They had been cleaned off.

Rollo took the gizmo off me and tucked it under one arm. I followed him down the ladder. Down at the bottom there were three other guys waitin'. Guys like I had never seen before. Foreigners. Dark skin, eyes like coals. One of them had a big dark droopy moustache, but his long hair was streaked with gray. They were all kind of short, my height, but very solid. Their suits looked funny, like they had been made by tailors who didn't know the right way to cut a suit.

The two clean-shaven ones were carryin' automatic rifles, mean-looking things with curved magazines. Their jackets bulged; extra ammunition clips, I figured. They looked younger than the guy with the moustache; tough, hard, all business.

"This is the device?" asked the one with the moustache. He said "thees" instead of "this."

Lou nodded. "We're gonna test it, make sure it works right."

"Bueno."

We were in a kind of—whattaya call it, an alcove?— yeah, an alcove cut into the side of the train tunnel. The kind where work crews could stay when a train comes past. This wasn't one of the old city subways; it was the tunnel that the trains from other cities used, back when there had been trains runnin'. The Chairman was comin' in on a train the next morning, and these guys wanted to blow it up. Or so I thought.

Rollo carried the gizmo down to the side of the tracks. For an instant I almost panicked; I realized that we needed a power pack. Then I saw that there was one already sittin' there on the filthy bricks of the tunnel floor. I hooked it up, takin' my time; no sense lettin' them know how easy this all was.

"Snap it up," Lou hissed at me. "The train's comin'."

"Okay, okay," I said.

The guy with the moustache knelt beside me and took a little metal box from his pocket. "This is the detonator," he said. His voice sounded sad, almost like he was about to cry. "Your device must make its relay click at the proper moment. Do you know how to connect the two of them together?"

I nodded and took the detonator from him.

"Tomorrow, the detonator will be placed some distance from your triggering device."

"How'll they be connected then?" I asked.

"By a wire."

"That's okay, then." I figured that if they had tried somethin' fancy like a radio link, in this old tunnel they might get all kinds of interference or echoes. A hard-wire connection was a helluva lot surer. And safer.

It only took me a couple minutes to connect his detonator to my radar gizmo, but Lou was fidgetin' every second of the time. I never seen him lookin' nervous or flustered before. He was always the coolest of the cool, never a hair out of place. Now he was half jumpin' up and down, lookin' up the tunnel and grumblin' that the train was comin' and I was gonna miss it. I had to work real hard to keep a straight face. Little Lou uptight; that was somethin' to grin about.

Okay, so I had everything ready in plenty time. The maintenance train musta been doin' two miles an hour, max, scrapin' down the tracks and scoopin' up most of the garbage in the tunnel as it dragged along. I turned on my gizmo. The readout numbers on the little red window started tickin' down slowly. When they reached the number already set on the other window beside it, the relay on the detonator clicked.

"Bueno," said Moustache, still kneeling beside me. He didn't sound happy or nuthin. Just, "Bueno." Flat as a pancake.

I looked over at Jade, standin' with Rollo and the other strangers off by the tunnel wall, and I smiled at her.

"Does that mean it works okay?" I asked. I knew the answer but I wanted him to say it so Little Lou could hear it. Lou was bendin' down between the two of us.

"Yes," he said, in that sad, heavy voice of his. "It works perfectly." He said each word carefully, like he wasn't sure he had his English right.

I got to my feet and said to Lou, "Okay. I done my part. Now Jade and me can go, right?"

"No one leaves this tunnel," said Moustache. Still sad, but real strong, like he meant it. He had unbuttoned his suit jacket and I could see the butt of a heavy black revolver stickin' out of a shoulder holster. [Deleted], it would've taken my both hands just to hold that pistol up, let alone fire it off.

"Hey, now wait a minute—" I started to say.

Lou grabbed me by the shoulder and spun me around, his fist raised to smack me a good one. Moustache grabbed his upraised arm and held it in midair. Just held it there. He must've been pretty strong to do that.

"There is no need for that," he said to Lou, low and firm. "There will be enough violence in the morning."

Lou pulled his arm away, his face red and nasty. Moustache turned to me and almost smiled. Kind of apologetic, he said, "It is necessary for you and your lady to remain here until the operation is concluded. For security reasons. Do you understand?"

I nodded. Sure I understood. What I was startin' to wonder about, though, was whether these guys would let us live after their "operation" was finished. I knew Lou was goin' to want to take Jade with him. If these foreigners didn't whack me tomorrow, probably Lou would. Then he'd have Jade all to himself for as long as he wanted her.

So we sat on the crummy tunnel floor alongside the tracks and waited. The foreigners had some sandwiches and coffee with them. Moustache offered a sandwich to Jade, real polite, and one to me. It was greasy and spiced hot enough to scorch my mouth. They all laughed at me when I grabbed for the coffee and burned my mouth even more 'cause it was so hot.

I tried to sleep but couldn't. I saw that the two younger guys had curled up right there on the floor, sleepin' like babies, with their rifles in their arms. Lou took Jade off down the tunnel a ways, where it was dark, far enough so I couldn't see them or even hear them. I sat and watched Rollo, hopin' he'd nod off long enough for me to follow Lou down the tunnel and slice his throat open. But Rollo just sat a few feet away from me, his chin on his knees and his eyes on me. Big as a [deleted] elephant.

Moustache wasn't sleepin' either. I went over to where he was sittin' with his back against the wall.

"Why's the Chairman comin' in on a train?" I asked him, hunkering down beside him. "There ain't been a train through here since before I was born."

Moustache gave me his sad smile. "It is a gesture. He is a man given to gestures."

I couldn't figure out what the hell he meant by that.

"Why do you want to whack him?" I asked.

"Whack?" He looked puzzled.

"Kill him."

His eyes went wide, a little. "Kill him? We do not intend to assassinate the Chairman." He shook his head. "No, it is not so simple as that."

"Then what?"

He shook his head again. "It is none of your affair. The less you know about it the better off you will be."

"Yeah," I said. "Until this thing is over and Lou whacks me."

He shrugged. "That is your problem. Not mine."

A lot of help he was.

My wristwatch said 7:27 A.M. when Lou came walkin' back up the track toward us. His hair was mussed and he had his suit jacket thrown over one shoulder. He grinned at me. Jade came followin' behind him, her face absolutely blank, starin' straight ahead. I figured she was tryin' *not* to see me.

What the hell, I thought. Why don't I kill the mother-[deleted] [deleted] right now. Stick my blade in his nuts and twist it hard before Rollo gets a chance to move. They was gonna whack me afterward anyway. I knew it.

I was even startin' to pull up my pants leg when I felt Moustache's hand on my shoulder. "No," he whispered.

I must have looked pretty sore to him. He said, low and soft, "I am a man of honor. I will see to it that you and the girl go free after our operation is concluded. You can trust me."

Lou had already passed me by then. Rollo got up on his feet, towerin' over us all like a mountain. I let my pants leg slide down to my ankle again. I just hoped Lou and Rollo didn't notice what I had started to do.

A little while later three more guys came down the same ladder we had used, two of them carryin' big leather suitcases, the third carryin' a little metal case and climbin' down so careful that I figured he had the bomb in it. They were foreigners too, but they looked different from Moustache and his men. They had dark skins, all right, but a different kind of dark. And they were taller, slimmer, with big hooked noses like eagles' beaks. Like Moustache and his men, they were wearin' regular suits. But they looked like they were uncomfortable in them, like these weren't the kind of clothes they usually wore.

Anyway, after talkin' a few minutes with Moustache they went up the tracks with the little metal case. They came back again without it, but trailin' a spool of wire. Which they connected to my radar gizmo. I noticed that the detonator was gone; they had taken it with the bomb,

I figured. Then they set the gizmo right in the middle of the tracks and waited.

"Won't the oinks see it there?" I asked Moustache. "The police," I added before he could ask what oinks meant.

In that sad way of his he said, "Your Mr. Lou has been well paid to see to it that the security guards do not come down the tunnel this far." He kind of sighed. "It always surprises me to see how well bribery works on little men."

Bought off the security guards? I wondered if even Big Lou could cover all the Federal oinks that must be coverin' the Chairman. I mean, this guy was the Chairman of the World Council. They must be protectin' him like they protect the president or some of those video stars.

Moustache must've understood the puzzled look on my face. "There is a full security guard on the train itself, and entire platoons of soldiers at the station. The responsibility for checking the security of the tunnel was given to your city police force. That is why we decided to do our work here. This is the weak link in their preparations."

He talked like a general. Or at least, the way I thought a general would talk. No, I never did get his name. Nobody spoke to him by his name; nobody I could understand, at least. I did find out later on that he had another half-dozen men farther down the tunnel, also waitin' for the train. Twelve guys altogether. Fourteen, if you count Little Lou and Rollo.

Okay, so the time finally comes. Little Lou is almost hoppin' outta his skin he's so wired up. Jade was sittin' as far back in the alcove as she could, legs tucked up under her, still starin' off into space and seeing nuthin. I started to wonder what Lou had done to her, then tried to stop thinkin' about it. Didn't work.

Moustache is as calm as a guy can be, talkin' in his own language to his two men. The other three strangers are bendin' over their suitcases, and I see they're takin' out all kinds of stuff. I'm not sure what most of it was, but they had little round gray things about the size of baseballs, weird-lookin' kinds of guns—I guess they were guns, they looked kind of like pistols—and finally they pulled out some rubbery gas masks and handed two of 'em to Moustache's men.

Lou and Rollo both are lookin' down the track toward the station, and I see they both have pistols in their hands. Rollo's hands are so big his pistol looks like a toy. Little Lou is sweatin'; I can see the beads comin' down his face, he's so [deleted] scared. I keep myself from laughin' out loud at him. He's worried that the oinks he bought off won't stay bought. Be just like them to take his money and then double-cross him by doin' their job right anyway.

But then I figured that maybe Big Lou was the one who paid off the oinks. Screwin' Little Lou is one thing; if they mess around with Big Lou they'd regret it for as long as they lived. And so would their families.

Moustache sends off all five of the strangers up the track. I wonder how close to the bomb they can get without bein' blown up themselves. I wonder if the bomb will bring down the roof of the whole [deleted] tunnel and bury all of us right where we are. I wonder about Moustache sayin' they ain't tryin' to whack the Chairman. What're they gonna do, then?

I didn't have to wait long to find out.

Moustache is starin' hard at his wristwatch, that big pistol in his other hand. I hear a dull *whump* kind of noise. He looks up, runs out to the middle of the tracks. I go to Jade, who's gotten to her feet. Lou and Rollo are still starin' down the track toward the station; Moustache is lookin' the other way, toward where the train is comin' from. Nobody's watchin' us.

"Come on," I whisper to Jade. "Now's our chance."

But she won't move from where she's standing.

"Come on!" I say.

"I can't," she tells me.

"It's now or never!"

"Vic, I can't," she says. I see tears in her eyes. "I promised him."

"[Deleted] Lou!" I say. "I love you and you're comin' with me."

But she pulls back. "I love you too, Vic. But if I go with you Lou will hunt us down and kill you."

"He's gonna kill me anyway!" I'm tryin' to keep whispering. It's makin' my throat raw.

"No, he told me he'd let you alone if I stayed with him. He swore it."

"And you believe that mother-[deleted] lying [deleted]?"

Just then we hear gunfire and guys yelling. Sounds like a little war goin' on up the track: automatic rifles goin' *pop-pop-pop*. Heavier sounds. Somebody screamin' like his guts've been shot out.

Moustache yells to Lou and Rollo, "Quickly! Follow me!" Then he waves at me and Jade with that big pistol. "You too! Come!"

So with Moustache in front of us and Lou and Rollo behind, we go runnin' up the track. There's a train stopped up there, a train like I never seen before. Like it's from Mars or someplace: all shinin' and smooth with curves more like an airplane than any train I ever saw. Not that I ever saw any, except in pictures or videos, y'know.

I see a hole in the ground that's still smokin'. The track is tore up. That was where the bomb was. It was just a little bomb, after all. Just enough to tear up the track and make the train stop.

We run past that and past the shining engine. Even in the shadows of the tunnel it seemed to shine, like it was brand-new. Not a scratch or a mark on it. No graffiti, even. Where I come from, we don't see much that's new. It was beautiful, all right.

Anyway, there are three cars behind the engine. They all look spiffy too, but a couple windows on the first car were busted out, shattered. The car in the middle had a blue flag painted on its side, a flag I never seen before.

Moustache climbs up onto the first car and we're right behind him. We push through the doors. There's a bunch of dead bodies inside. Flopped on the floor, twisted across the seats. Not regular seats, like rows. These seats were more like big easy chairs that could swivel around, one next to each window. You could see there'd been plenty of bullets flyin' around; the bodies was tore up pretty bad, lots of blood. I heard Jade suck in her breath like she was gonna scream, but then she got control of herself. I almost wanted to scream myself; some of those bodies looked pretty damned bad.

One of the tall guys came through the door up at the other end of the car. He had his gas mask pushed up on top of his head. His rifle was slung over his shoulder, makin' his suit jacket bunch up so I could see a pistol stuck in the belt of his pants. He looked kind of sick, or maybe that was the way he looked when he was mad.

Moustache went up and talked with him for a minute, lookin' kind of pale himself. Lou told Rollo to pick up all the loose hardware layin' around the car. What? Hardware. Guns. Must of been six or eight of 'em on the floor or still in the grip of the dead guys. Oh yeah, two of the dead ones were women, by the way. Far as I remember, neither one of 'em had a gun in her hand.

We got through the connecting doors and into the middle car. Not everybody in there is dead. Only a couple guys in blue suits that Moustache's men are already draggin' down into the third car, at the end of the train.

There was one guy alive in there, a little guy no bigger than me with eyes like Jade's. Otherwise he looked like a regular American. I mean his skin wasn't dark even though it wasn't exactly light like mine. And the suit he was wearin' was a regular suit, light gray. Right away I figured he was the Chairman of the World Council.

C. C. Lee.

He was sittin' there, his face frozen with no expression on it, almost like Jade's when Little Lou had been pawin' her. I looked at him real close and saw his eyes weren't exactly like Jade's; they were real oriental eyes, I guess. Hard to tell how old he was; his hair was all dark, not a speck of gray in it, but he didn't look young, y'know what I mean? Straight hair, combed straight back from his forehead. Kinda high forehead, come to think of it. Maybe he was startin' to go bald.

Anyway, Moustache sat down in the chair next to his and swiveled it around so they were facin' each other. Jade and I stood in the aisle between the rows of chairs. The others moved out to the other two cars.

"This is not what I wanted," Moustache said. He talked in English, with that accent of his.

"It is what you should have expected," said the Chairman. His English was perfect, just like a newscaster on TV.

"I regret the killing."

"Of course you do."

"But it was necessary."

The Chairman looked at Moustache, *really* looked at him, right into his eyes like he was tryin' to bore through his skull.

"Necessary? To kill sixteen men and women? How many of your own have been killed?"

"Four," said Moustache. "Including my brother."

The Chairman blinked. "I am sorry for that," he said, almost in a whisper.

"He knew the risks. Our cause is desperate."

"Your cause is doomed. What can you possibly hope to achieve by this action?"

"Freedom for the political prisoners in my country. An end to the dictatorship."

"By kidnapping me?"

"We will hold you hostage until the political prisoners are freed," said Moustache. "The people will see that we have the power to bend the dictator to our will. They will rebel. There will be revolution—"

The Chairman shook his head like a tired, tired man. "Blood and more blood. And in the end, who is the winner? Even if you become the new head of your nation, do you really think that you will be better than the dictator who now resides in the presidential palace?"

"Yes! Of course! How can you ask such a question of me? I have dedicated my life to overthrowing the tyrant!"

"Yes, I know. I understand. Just as Fidel did. Just as Yeltsin did. Yet, if the people are not prepared to govern themselves they end up with another tyrant, no matter how pure his motives were at the start."

Moustache gave him a look that would have peeled paint off a wall. "You dare say that to me?"

The Chairman made a little shrug. "It is the truth. You should not be angered by the truth."

Moustache jumped to his feet, yelling, "The truth is that you are our hostage and you will remain our hostage until our demands have been met!" Then he stomped up the aisle toward the front car.

I told Jade to stay there and hustled after Moustache. I caught up with him in between the two cars, out on the platform connecting them.

"Hey, wait a minute, willya?"

He whirled around, his eyes still burnin' with fury.

"Uh, excuse me," I said, tryin' to calm him down a little, "but you said it'd be okay for us to leave once the job was over, remember?"

The anger went out of his face. He made a strange expression, like he didn't know whether to laugh or cry. "The job is far from over, I fear."

"But I did what you wanted—"

He put a hand on my shoulder. "We had intended to take the Chairman off the train and drive him to a helicopter pad we had prepared for this operation. Unfortunately, the truck we had stationed at the emergency exit from the tunnel has already been seized by your soldiers. We are trapped here in this tunnel, in this train. The Chairman is our prisoner, but we are prisoners, too."

"[Deleted] H. [deleted] on a crutch!" I yelled.

"Yes," he said. "Indeed."

"Whattaya gonna do?"

"Negotiate."

"What?"

"As long as we hold the Chairman we are safe. They dare not attack us for fear of harming him."

"But we can't get out?"

"Not unless they allow us to get out."

I got this empty feeling in my gut, like I was fallin' off a roof or something. I guess I was really scared.

Moustache went through the door to the car up front. I went back into the middle car. Jade was sittin' where Moustache had been. She was talkin' with the Chairman.

"I had wanted to bring a message of hope to the people of America, particularly to the disenfranchised and the poverty classes of the dying cities," he was tellin' her. "That is why I agreed to make this speech in Philadelphia on the anniversary of the Declaration of Independence."

"Hope?" I snapped, ploppin' myself down in the chair across the aisle from the two of them. "What hope?"

He didn't answer me for a second or two. He just looked at me, like he was studyin' me. His eyes were a kind of soft brown, gentle.

"Do you know how many people there are like you in the world?" he asked. Before I could think of anything to say he went on, "Of the more than ten billion human beings on Earth, three-quarters of them live in poverty."

"So what's that to me?" I said, tryin' to make it sound tough.

"You are one of them. So is this pretty young woman here."

"So?"

He kind of slumped back in his seat. "The World Council was formed to help solve the problems of poverty. It is my task as Chairman to lead the way."

I laughed out loud at him. "You ain't leadin' any way. You're stuck here, just like we are."

"For the moment."

Jade said, "We could all be killed, couldn't we?"

I knew she was right, but I said, "Not as long as we got this guy. They won't try nuthin as long as the Chairman's our hostage."

The Chairman's eyebrows went up a fraction. "You are part of this plot? From what your friend here has told me, you were forced to help these terrorists."

"Yeah. Well, that don't matter much now, does it?" I said, still tryin' to sound tough. "We're all stuck in this together."

"Exactly correct!" says the Chairman, like I had given the right answer on a quiz show. "We are all in this together. Not merely this"—and he swung his arms around to take in the train car—"but we are all in the global situation together."

"What do you mean?" Jade asked. She was lookin' at him in a way I'd never seen her look before. I guess it was respect. Like Big Lou wants people to behave toward him. Only Jade was doin' it on her own, without being forced or threatened.

"We are all part of the global situation," the Chairman repeated. He was lookin' at her but I got the feeling he was talkin' to me. "What happens to you has an effect all around the world."

"Bull[deleted]," I said.

He actually smiled at me. "I know it is hard for you to accept. But it is true. We are all linked together on the great wheel of life. What happens to a rice farmer in Bangladesh, what happens to a stockbroker in Geneva—each affects the other, each affects every person on Earth."

"Bull[deleted]," I said again.

"You do not believe it?"

"Hell no."

"Yet what you have done over the past twenty-four hours has brought you together with the Chairman of the World Council, hasn't it?"

"Yeah. And maybe we'll all get killed together."

That didn't stop him for even a half a second. "Or maybe we will all change the world together."

"Change it?" Jade asked. "How?"

"For the better, one hopes."

"Yeah, sure. We're gonna change the world," I said. "Jade and me, we don't even [deleted] exist, far as that world out there's concerned! They don't want no part of us!"

"But you do exist, in reality," he said, completely unflustered by me yellin' at him. "And once we are out of this mess, the world out there will have to admit your existence. They will have to notice you."

"The only notice they'll ever take of the likes of Jade and me is to dump our bodies in a [deleted] open pit and bulldoze us over."

"Hey, stop the yellin'!" Little Lou hollered from the front end of the car. He had just come in, with Rollo right behind him like a Saint Bernard dog. Lou looked uptight. His jacket was gone, his shirt wrinkled and dark with sweat under the armpits. His hair was mussed, too. He was not happy with the way things were goin'. Rollo looked like he always looked: big, dumb, and mean.

Moustache pushed past the two of them. Jade got up from her chair and came to sit next to me. Moustache took the chair and leaned his elbows on his knees, putting his face a couple inches away from the Chairman's.

"The situation is delicate," he said.

The Chairman didn't make any answer at all.

"We are unfortunately cut off here in the tunnel. The security forces reacted much more quickly than we had anticipated. They are now threatening to storm the train and kill us all. Only by assuring them that you are alive and unharmed have I persuaded them not to do so."

The Chairman still didn't budge.

Moustache took in a deep breath, like a sigh. "Now the chief of your own security forces wants to make certain that you are alive and well. He demands that you speak to him." Moustache pulled a palm-sized radio from his jacket pocket.

The Chairman made no move to take it from his hand.

"Please," said Moustache, holding the radio out to him.

"No," the Chairman said.

"But you must."

"No."

We all kind of froze. Everybody except Little Lou. He stepped between Moustache and the Chairman and whacked the Chairman in the mouth so hard it knocked him out of his chair. Then he kicked him in the ribs hard enough to lift him right off the floor. He was aimin' another kick when I went nuts.

I don't know why, maybe it was like watchin' a guy beat up on a kitten or some other helpless thing. I knew the Chairman was just gonna lay there on the floor while Lou kicked all his ribs in and none of these other clowns would do a thing to help him and I just kind of went nuts. I didn't think about it; if I had I would've just stayed tight in my chair and minded my own [deleted] business.

But I didn't. I couldn't. Before I even knew I was doin' it I jumped on Lou's back, wrapped my legs around him, and started poundin' on his head with both my fists. If I'd wanted to really hurt him I woulda taken out my blade and slit his [deleted] throat. I didn't even think of that. All I wanted was for the big [deleted] to leave the Chairman alone.

So I'm bangin' on Lou's head, he's yellin' and swingin' around, tryin' to get me off him. And then something explodes in the back of my head and everything goes black.

When I wake up, I'm seein' double. Two Chairmen, two Jades. But nobody else.

"That was a very brave thing you did," says the Chairmen.

I'm layin' flat on my back. Jade is bendin' over me, two of her kind of fadin' in and out, blurry-like. The Chairman is sittin' on the floor beside me, both his arms wrapped around his chest. Otherwise the car is empty. Everybody else is gone.

"What happened?" I said.

"Rollo knocked you out," Jade answered.

I shoulda guessed that. Musta hit me like a truck. I tried to sit up but I was so woozy the whole [deleted] car started whirlin' around.

"Lay still," Jade said. Her voice was soft and sweet. I thought I saw tears in her eyes, but I was still seein' double so it was hard to tell.

"You okay?" I asked the Chairman.

"Yes, thanks to you." His lip was split and his face was kinda pale, like it was hurtin' him to breathe.

"Where'd they go?"

"They are in the rear car," the Chairman said. "More of them in the front. We are all trapped here. The Council's security forces have sealed off this tunnel. American Army troops have taken over the station and are patrolling the streets above us."

"But they won't make a move on us because Moustache says he'll whack you if they do."

The Chairman nodded. And winced. "We are their hostages. He is trying to convince them that he has not already killed me."

"Why didn't ya talk to your people on the radio?" I asked him. "Lou woulda beat you to death."

He almost smiled, split lip and all. "They can't afford to kill me. Your friend Lou is a barbarian. Even Moustache, as you call him, would have stopped him if you hadn't."

"So I got slugged for nuthin."

"You were very brave," said the Chairman. "I appreciate what you did very much. To risk one's life for the sake of another—that is true heroism."

"You're a hero," Jade said. And she really did smile. Like the sun shinin' through clouds. Like the sky turnin' clean blue after a storm.

I reached for her hand and she took mine and squeezed it. Her hand felt warm and good. I mean, don't get me wrong, I busted my cherry when I was twelve years old. Had my first case of clap not much later. I ain't no Romeo like Little Lou, but I got my share. But Jade, she was special. I didn't wanna just screw her; I wanted to live with her, make a home with her, even have kids with her. Yeah, I know she was fixed so she couldn't have kids. They do that to the pros. But I thought maybe we could find a doctor someplace who could make her okay again.

But first I hadda get her outta her life before she came down with somethin' that'd kill her or got herself knocked off by some weirdo. Okay, it was crazy. Stupid. I know. But that's how I felt about her. And I don't give a [deleted] what you say; I know she felt that way about me, too. I know. In spite of everything.

Anyway, there I was, layin' on the floor of the train car and holdin' on to Jade's hand like I was hangin' off the edge of a ninety-nine-story building. I asked the Chairman, "So what happens now?"

He started to shrug but the pain in his ribs stopped him. "I don't really know."

"I still don't see why you wouldn't talk to your people on the radio."

"We do not make deals with terrorists. I know that every government official of the past seventy-five years has said that and then gone on to negotiate when their own citizens have been taken hostage. You must remember that the World Council is very new. Our authority is more moral than military or even financial—"

"I don't unnerstand a word you're saying," I told him.

He looked kinda surprised. Then he said, "Let me put it this way: We do not deal with terrorists. That is the official policy of the World Council. How would it look if I, the Chairman himself, broke our own rules and tried to negotiate my way out of this?"

"Beats gettin' killed," I said.

"Does it?"

"Hell, yeah! You want Lou to go back to work on you?"

He closed his eyes for a second. "I am prepared to die. I don't want to, but if it comes to that—it comes to that."

"And what about us? What about Jade and me?"

"There's no reason for them to kill you."

"Who the [deleted] needs a reason? Lou wants to whack me, he's gonna whack me!"

"That . . . is unfortunate."

It sure the [deleted] was. For a couple minutes none of us said anything. Finally curiosity got to me.

"What's this all about, anyway? Why's Moustache want to take you hostage? What's in it for him? Who're those other guys with him? What the hell's goin' on around here?"

So he told me. I didn't understand most of it. Somethin' about some country I never heard of before, in South America I think he said. Moustache is the leader of some underground gang that's tryin' to knock off their government. The Chairman told me that their president is a real piece of [deleted]. No freedom for nobody. Everybody's gotta do what he says or he whacks 'em. Tortures people. Takes everybody's money for himself. Sounds like Big Lou's favorite wet dream.

So Moustache and his people want the World Council to get rid of this bastard. The World Council can't do that, accordin' to what the Chairman told me. "We are not permitted to interfere in the internal affairs of any nation." That's the way he put it. And besides, this dictator was legally elected. Okay, maybe the people had to vote for him or get shot, but they did vote for him.

And guess who Moustache wants to make president if and when the dictator gets pushed out? Good old Moustache himself. Who else?

So the Chairman tells Moustache he can't do nuthin for him. So Moustache decides to kidnap the Chairman and hold him until the World Council does what he wants. Or somethin' like that. Other guys from other countries who also want pretty much the same kind of thing from the World Council join Moustache's operation. Arabs or Kurds or somethin', I forget which. So they kidnap the Chairman. Big [deleted] deal.

So there we are, stuck in the train in the tunnel. They got him, but the U.S. Army and god knows what the [deleted] else has got us trapped in the tunnel. Stand-off.

By the time he had finished tellin' me this whole story—and it was a lot longer than what I just told you—I was feelin' strong enough to sit up. At least the room wasn't spinnin' around no more and I wasn't seein' double.

"So what happens now?" I asked the Chairman.

"We wait and see."

I saw a junkyard dog once, a real four-legged dog, get his paw caught in a trap the junk dealer had set for guys like me who like to sneak in at night and steal stuff. Poor damned dog was stuck there all night long, yowlin' and cryin'. Dealer wouldn't come out. Not in the dark. He was scared that if his dog was in trouble it meant a gang of guys was out there waitin' to whack him.

I felt like that dog. Trapped. Bleedin' to death. Knowin' there was help not far away, but the help never came. Not in time. By morning the dog had died. The rats were already gnawin' on him when the sun came up.

"You're just gonna sit here?" I asked him.

"There's nothing else we can do."

I knew that. But I still didn't like it.

The Chairman put out his hand and rested it on my shoulder. "You may not realize it, my young friend, but

merely by sitting here you are fighting a battle against
the enemies of humankind."

I wanted to say bull[deleted] to him again, but I kept
my mouth shut.

It was Jade who asked, "What do you mean?"

"This man you call Moustache. The men with him.
Your friends Lou and Rollo—"

"They ain't no friends of mine," I growled.

"I know." He smiled at me, kind of a shy smile. "I was
making a small joke."

"Nuthin funny about those guys."

"Yes, of course. Moustache and Lou and the rest of
them, they are the old way of living. The way of violence. The way of brute force. The way of death. What
the human race needs, what the *people* want, is a better
way, a way of sharing, of cooperation, of the strength
that comes from recognizing that we must all help one
another—"

I was about to puke in his face when he smiled at me
again and said, "—just the way you tried to help me when
Lou was beating me."

That took the air outta me. I mumbled, "Lotta good it
did either one of us."

"Have you ever thought about leading a better life than
the one you now live?" he asked.

"Well, yeah," I said, glancin' at Jade. "Sure. Who
doesn't?"

"There are Indians living in the mountains of Moustache's country who also have a dream of living better.
And nomads starving in man-made deserts. And fishermen's families dying because the sea has become so
polluted that the fish have all died off. They also dream
of a better life."

"I don't care about no fishermen or Indians," I said.
"They don't mean nuthin to me."

"But they do! Whether you know it or not, they are
part of you. We are all bound together on this world of
ours."

"Bull[deleted]." It just popped out. I mean, I kinda liked the guy but he kept talkin' this crazy stuff.

"Listen to what he's trying to tell us," Jade said. That surprised me, her tellin' me what to do.

"The reason the World Council was created, the reason it exists and I serve as its Chairman, is to help everyone on Earth to live a better life. Everyone! All ten billions of us."

"How're you going to do that?" Jade asked. She was lookin' at the Chairman now with her eyes wide. She wasn't holdin' my hand anymore.

"There's no simple answer," he said. "It will take hard work, for decades, for generations. It will take the cooperation of all the nations of the world, the rich and the poor alike."

"You're dreamin'," I said. "The United States is one of the richest countries in the whole [deleted] world and we still got people livin' like rats, people like me and Jade and who knows how many others."

"Yes, I understand," he said. "We are trying to convince your government to change its attitude about you, to admit that the problem exists and then take the necessary steps to solve it."

"Yeah, they'll solve the problem. The [deleted] Controllers swoop in and take you away, scramble your brains and turn you into a zombie. You wind up as slave labor in some camp out in the woods."

"Is that what you believe?"

"That's what I know."

"What would you say if I told you that you are wrong?"

"I'd say you're fulla [deleted]."

"Vic!" Jade snapped at me.

But the Chairman just kinda smiled. "When all this is over, I hope you will give me the opportunity to show you how misinformed you are."

"If we're still alive when this is over," I said.

"Yes," he admitted. "There is that."

He was quiet for a minute or so. I didn't like the way Jade was starin' at him, like he was a saint or a video star or somethin'. But I didn't know what I could say that would get her to look back at me.

Finally the Chairman pipes up again. "You know, I was born of a poor family also."

"Yeah, sure," I muttered.

"My grandmother escaped from Vietnam in an open boat with nothing but the clothes on her back and her infant son—my father. They went from Hong Kong to Canada. My grandmother died of pneumonia her first winter in Vancouver. My father was barely two years old."

"You're breakin' my heart," I said. Jade hissed at me.

"My father was raised in an orphanage. When he was fourteen he escaped and made his way into the United States, eventually to Houston, Texas." The Chairman was lookin' at me when he was sayin' this, but it was a funny look, like I wasn't really there and he was seein' things from his own life that'd happened years ago.

"My mother was Mexican. Two illegal immigrants for parents. We moved around a lot: Houston, Galveston, the cotton fields of Texas, the orchards of California. I was picking fruit almost as soon as I learned to walk."

"You never went hungry, didja?" I said.

"I have known hunger. And poverty. And disease. But I have known hope, also. All through my childhood my mother told me that there was a better way of life. Every night she would kneel beside me and say her prayers and tell me that I would live better than she and my father. Even when my father was beaten to death by a gang of drunken rednecks my mother kept telling me to keep my eyes on the stars, to work hard and learn and aim high. She worked very hard herself.

"After my father died we settled in California, in a little city called Modesto, where she worked twelve–fourteen hours a day cleaning peoples' homes by day and office buildings at night. By the time she died, when I was sixteen, she had saved enough money to get me started in college."

"At least you had a mother," I muttered. "I was so young when mine died I don't even remember what she looked like."

"That is very sad," he said. Real soft.

"Yeah."

"I remember the prayer my mother taught me to say: she called it the 'Our Father'."

"*Oracion al Senor*," whispered Jade.

"Yes. Do you know it? And the line that says, 'Thy kingdom come?' That is what we must aim for. That is what we must strive to accomplish: to bring about a new world, a fair and free and flourishing world for everyone. To make this Earth of ours as close to heaven as we can."

"Thy kingdom come," Jade repeated. There were tears in her eyes now, real big ones.

Me, I didn't say nuthin. I kept my mouth shut so hard my teeth hurt. I knew that prayer. The one thing I remember about my mother is her sayin' that prayer to me when I was so little I didn't know what it meant. That's all I can remember about her. And it made me want to cry, too. It got me sore, at the same time. This [deleted] big shot of a Chairman knew just where to put the pressure on me. I sure wasn't gonna start bawlin' in front of him and Jade. Not me.

And I had lied to them. I did remember my mother. Kinda hazy, but I remember what she looked like. She was beautiful. Beautiful and sweet and—I pulled myself up short. Another minute of that kinda thinkin' and I'd be cryin' like a baby.

The Chairman kind of shook himself, like he was comin' out of a blackout or somethin'. He looked at me again. "Education is the key, my young friend," he said to me. "If we are to build a new world, we must educate the people."

"You mean, like school?" I asked him.

"Schooling is only a part of it," he said. "If we survive this, will you allow me to get you started on a decent education?"

"School? Me? You gotta be kiddin'!"

Jade said, "But Vic, he's giving you a chance—"

She never got no farther. Moustache came in, with Lou and Rollo behind him.

Moustache looked funny. Like he was real tired, all wiped out. Or maybe that was how he looked when he was scared. He stood in front of the Chairman, who stayed in his seat lookin' up at him. I kept my eye on Lou; he was watchin' Jade like he was thinkin' what he'd do with her later on. Like he already owned her.

"We are at an impasse," Moustache said to the Chairman. "Your security forces seem perfectly content to sit and wait for us to give up."

"They have standing orders for dealing with terrorists," said the Chairman. "This is not the first time someone has attempted to kidnap a Council member."

"They will not attack us?"

"There is no need to, as long as they are certain you will not harm your hostages."

Moustache said, "We have only one hostage, but a very important one."

"Then all the others who were with me are dead?"

"Unfortunately, yes."

The Chairman seemed to sag back in his seat. "That is truly unfortunate. It means that you will not be allowed to escape. If no one had been killed . . ." His voice trailed off.

"Are you telling me that the troops will risk your life in order to punish us for killing a few of your bodyguards?"

"Yes." The Chairman nodded slowly. "That too is their standard operational procedure. No negotiations with terrorists. And no leniency for murderers."

"They were armed! They killed four of my men!"

"Only six of them were armed. There were nineteen altogether, most of them harmless administrators and my personal aides. Five of them were women."

Moustache sank into the empty chair across the aisle from the Chairman. "It was those Moslem madmen. When the shooting started they killed everyone, indiscriminately."

"They were under your command, were they not?"

"Yes, but not under my control."

"That makes no difference."

"You leave us no course, then, but to use you as a shield to cover our escape."

"The security forces will not allow it. Their orders are quite specific. Their objective is to capture the terrorists, irrespective of what happens to the hostages."

"They will let you be killed?"

"I am already dead, as far as they are concerned."

"You will pardon me if I fail to believe that," Moustache said.

"It doesn't matter what you believe," said the Chairman back to him. "That is our standard operational procedure. It is based on the valid assumption that there are no indispensable men. The Chairman of the World Council can be kidnapped or even assassinated. What difference? Another will take his place. Or hers. You can do what you want to me; it does not matter. Violence will not deter us. Threats will not move us. The work of the Council will go on regardless of the senseless acts of terrorists. All you can do is create martyrs—and damage your own cause by your violence."

Moustache looked up at Lou, who'd been standin' there through all this talk with a kind of wise guy grin on his face.

With a sigh, Moustache said, "We will have to try your way, then."

I got to my feet, facin' Lou. Without even thinkin' about what I was doin'. Like my body reacted without askin' my brain first.

"Don't try to be a hero again, Sal," Lou said to me. And Rollo took a step toward me. But Lou went on, "We ain't gonna use no rough stuff—not unless we got to. We're just gonna sneak him out through the tunnel."

"But the soldiers got the tunnel blocked off," I said. "All the entrances—"

"Not all of 'em," said Lou. "There's a side passage for the electric cables and water pipes and all. It's big enough for maintenance workers to crawl through. So it's big enough for us to get through, too."

Lou yanked a map of the tunnel system outta his back pants pocket. It was all creased up and faded, but Moustache pulled a little folding table outta the wall and Lou spread his map on it. Then he pointed to where we was and where the nearest door to the maintenance tunnel was. Moustache decided that only the six of us would go. The rest of his men would stay with the train and keep the soldiers thinkin' we was all still in there.

While Lou and Moustache were talkin' all this over, Jade leaned over to me and whispered, "Vic, you gotta do something."

"Do? What?"

"You can't let them sneak him outta here! You gotta figure out a way to save him."

"Me? What the [deleted] d'you think I am, Superman?"

She just looked at me with those eyes of hers. Beneath the fancy surgery that had made her Jade Diamond, her deep brown eyes were still Juanita's. I loved her and I'd do anything for her and she knew it.

"You've gotta do something," she whispered.

Yeah. What the whole [deleted] World Council and half the U.S. Army can't do she wants me to do.

So Moustache calls in a couple of his men and gives them their orders. You can see from the looks on their faces that they don't like it. But they don't argue. Not one word. They know they're gonna be left hangin' out to dry, and they take it without a whimper. They must've really believed in what they were doin'.

Me, I'm tryin' to look like I'll do whatever they tell me. Rollo is just waitin' for Lou to give him the word and he'll start poundin' me into hamburger. And I figure Lou will give him the word as soon's we got the Chairman outta this trap and someplace safe. Lou wants Jade, so he'll give me to Rollo to make sure I'm not in his way. Moustache wants the Chairman so he can get what he wants back in his own country.

And the Chairman? What's he want? That's what I was tryin' to figure out. Was he really willin' to get himself smacked around or whacked altogether, just for this dream of his? A better world. A better life for people. Did he mean he could make a better life for Jade and me?

Well, anyway, all these thoughts are spinnin' around in my head worse than when Rollo had slugged me. We get down off the train with Lou in the lead, Moustache with his big pistol in his hand, the Chairman, me, and Jade all in a bunch, and Rollo bringin' up the rear. Lou's kinda feelin' his way through the tunnel, no light 'cause he don't want the soldiers to know we're outta the train.

So we're headin' for this steel door in the side of the tunnel when I accident'ly-on-purpose trip and fall to my knees. Rollo grabs me by the scruff of the neck hard enough to make my eyes pop and just lifts me back on my feet, one hand. But not before I slip my blade outta the tape on my ankle. It's dark so Rollo don't notice; I keep the blade tucked up behind my wrist, see.

All of a sudden my heart's beatin' so hard I figure Rollo can hear it. Or maybe the Army, a couple hundred yards up the tunnel. Half my brain's tellin' me to drop the blade and not get myself in any more trouble than I'm in already. But the other half is tellin' me that I gotta do somethin'. I keep hearin' Jade's voice, keep seein' whatever it was that was in her eyes.

She wants a better life too. And there's no way we can get a better life long as guys like Lou and Rollo can push us around.

So I let myself edge up a little, past Jade and the Chairman, till I'm right behind Moustache. It's real dark but I can just make out that he's got the gun in his right hand.

"Hey! Here it is," Lou says, half whisperin'. "Rollo, come and help me open up this sucker."

Rollo pushes past me like a semitrailer rig passin' a kid on a skateboard. My heart is whammin' so hard now it's hurtin' my ears. Moustache is just standin' there, watchin' Lou and Rollo tryin' to open up that steel door. They're gruntin' like a couple pro wrasslers. It's now or never.

I slash out with the blade and rip Moustache's arm open from elbow to wrist. He grunts and drops the gun and it goes off, *boom!*, so loud that it echoes all the way down the tunnel.

"Run!" I yell to Jade and the Chairman. "Get the [deleted] outta here!"

The Chairman just freezes there for a second but Jade shakes his arm and kind of wakes him up. Then the two of them take off down the tunnel, toward the soldiers. I can't see where the [deleted] gun landed but it don't matter anyway 'cause Lou and Rollo have spun away from the door and they're both comin' right at me. Moustache is holdin' his arm with his left hand and mumblin' something I can't understand.

"You dumb little [deleted]-sucking [deleted]," Lou says. "I'm going to cut off your balls and feed 'em to you one at a time."

I hear a click and see the glint of a blade in Lou's hand. I shoulda known he wouldn't be empty-handed. Rollo is comin' up right beside Lou. He don't need a knife or anything else. I'm so scared I don't know how I didn't [deleted] myself.

But I'm standin' between them and Jade and the Chairman.

"Never mind him," Moustache yells. "Get the Chairman! Quickly, before he makes it to the soldiers!"

Everything happened real fast. Lou tried to get past me and I swiped at him with my blade and then Rollo was all over me. I think I stuck him pretty good but he just about ripped my arm outta my shoulder and I musta blacked out pretty quick after that. Hurt like a bastard. Then I woke up here.

So I'm a big shot hero, huh? Saved the Chairman from the terrorists. He came here himself this morning to thank me. And now that the TV reporters and their cameras are all gone you guys are gonna send me away, right?

Naw, I didn't do anything except set up the gizmo for them. And they made me do that. Okay, so grabbin' Jade outta the tank was a crime. I figured you mother-[deleted] wasn't gonna let me go free.

But what'd they do with Jade? I don't believe that [deleted] [deleted] story the Chairman told me. Jade wouldn't do that. Go to a—what the [deleted] did he call it? Yeah, that's it. A rehabilitation center. She wouldn't leave here on her own. She wouldn't leave me. They musta forced her, right. The [deleted] Controllers must be scramblin' her brains right now, right? The [deleted] [deleted] bastards.

Yeah, sure, they're makin' a new woman outta her. And they wouldn't do nuthin to her unless she agreed to it. Sure. Just like she agreed to have her eyes changed. Big Lou said to change 'em and she agreed or she got her [deleted] busted.

You bastards took Jade away and don't try to tell me different. She wouldn't leave me. I know she wouldn't. You took her away, you and that [deleted] gook of a Chairman.

Naw, I don't care what happens to me. What the [deleted] do I care? I got no life now. I can't go back to the neighborhood. Sure, you nailed Little Lou and Big Lou and everybody in between. So what? You think that's the end of it? Whoever's taken Big Lou's place will kick my balls in soon's I show up back on the street again. They know I saved the Chairman. They know I went against Big Lou. They won't give me no chance to go against them. Not a chance.

Sure, yeah, you'll take care of me. You'll scramble my brains and turn me into some [deleted] zombie. I'll be choppin' trees out West, huh? Freezin' my butt in some labor camp. Big [deleted] deal.

I know I got no choice. All I want is to find Jade and take her away with me someplace where we can live decent. Naw, I don't give a [deleted] what happened to Moustache. Or the dictator back in his country. Makes no difference to me. All I want is Jade. Where is she? What've you [deleted] bastards done with her?

Note: Juanita Dominguez (Jade Diamond) graduated from the Aspen Rehabilitation Center and is now a freshman at the University of Colorado, where she is studying law under a grant from the World Council.

Salvatore (Vic) Passalacqua was remanded to the Drexel Hill Remedial School to begin a course of education that would eventually allow him to maximize his natural talent for electronics. He was a troublesome student, despite every effort at counseling and rehabilitation. After seven weeks at the school he escaped. Presumably he made his way back to the neighborhood in Philadelphia where he had come from. His record was erased from the computer files. He is presumed dead.

A VISIT TO BELINDIA

by Frederik Pohl

Of your four prognosticators, I am the one who has been chosen to give you the worst-case out-look for the year 2042 A.D. It's not an enjoyable task—no one likes to be the bearer of evil tid-ings—but unfortunately it's not a difficult one. In fact, it is deplorably easy. In order to predict a pretty gloomy 21st Century all a futurologist has to do is to assume that the human race will go right on doing the things it has been doing all along.

This is the story of a man named Benjamin Brown. He was born in the year 1938, died in 1992, and was born again in the year 2042 A.D.

That last statement is not quite literally true. Ben Brown wasn't really "born" again in 2042, of course. That just happened to be the year when the cryonicists were finally able to take him out of the freezer, replace the cancer-ridden pancreas that had killed him in the first place (at the same time performing quite a few other nips, tucks, and replacements in order to take care of other problems that would probably have killed him not much later), and wake him up to tell him that his gamble with cryonic suspension had paid off.

73

Nevertheless, the fact of the matter was that Ben Brown was alive and well in the middle of the 21st Century, and if he wasn't really "reborn" what he was was certainly good enough for him . . . at least at first.

The most important cause for rejoicing, of course, was simply that he was alive. Not only that, he wasn't even in pain; he was comfortable, and he was well fed, and when he looked out the window of his hospital room he could see the wonderful world of 2042 spread out before him. Well, not the whole world, of course, but he could at least see the hospital grounds, and they were bright with flowers and fountains, and everything beautifully green.

True, there were some things that puzzled him. There seemed to be a glass roof over the hospital gardens, and he wondered why that was necessary. Then there was the question of the hospital orderlies. When, in the old days, Ben thought about the world he hoped to awaken into, he expected that menial work would be performed by smart machines, maybe even robots. These weren't anything like that. They were just ordinary people. You might even say they were a little less than ordinary, since the orderlies were generally not very big or very strong. They didn't even appear to be very well fed—or so it seemed to Ben, when he noticed that whenever he happened not to eat some rolls, or piece of fruit, that came with his hospital meals, one of the attendants was sure furtively to slip it into a pocket. And the television set in his room was not what he had expected, either. It had a big screen, and it was certainly in brilliant color, but it was just as flat as the ones he had owned back in 1992. (Whatever had happened to 3-D television?) And, although his hospital set had more channels to explore than he had time to look at them, they all appeared to be showing the same old movies and sitcoms. He couldn't find a single news program to give him an idea of what his wonderful new world was really like.

But when he tried to talk to his doctor about it, she just smiled. "You've got a lot to catch up on, Mr. Brown," she told him, "but it could be pretty disorienting if you tried to catch up on it on your own. So we've, well, limited your access to news. For your own good. We have a staff of counselors right here in the hospital who will help you through the reorientation period. And actually," she went on, looking at his chart, "I see that you're about due for your counseling anyway, because it's about time we started to think of getting you out of here."

That was the kind of news that made Ben forget his questions. "You mean I'm completely cured?" he asked, as astonished as he was delighted.

"Oh, you've been cured for some time," the doctor said, still smiling. "You're even just about healed from all the surgery. We did that for your own good, too; there wasn't any reason to put you through the postoperative pain, so we kept you sedated while your body repaired itself. No, Mr. Brown, we're just about through with you. I'll make an appointment for you with one of our counselors, and I'm sure he'll answer all your questions."

The counselor was a young man with a thick brown beard, and the first thing he said wasn't an answer. It was a question. He studied Ben Brown for a moment, and then asked, "Did you ever hear of Belindia, Mr. Brown?"

"Is it a country in Africa?" Ben guessed, pretty much at random, but anxious to be obliging to this young man.

"Not exactly—or, yes, there's a lot of Belindia in Africa, in fact more there than anywhere else. But not the way you mean. Belindia is really the whole world now. The word 'Belindia' was what people used to call Brazil, back in your time. They looked on Brazil as two countries that happened to be occupying the same space, you see. There was a Brazil of the small well-to-do class, who lived at the same standard as, say, Belgium; and at the same time there was the Brazil that was made up of the much larger number of poor people, whose standard of living was down around the level of India's. Belgium plus India: Belindia."

Ben frowned. "That's not the way it was supposed to go!" he objected. "I remember very well that we were trying to cut down on the difference between rich and poor even in my time."

"Did it seem that way to you? Oh, yes, I know that there were all sorts of Wars on Poverty and Plans to help what you seemed to call 'Third World' countries. They must have sounded really nice and—what was the word you people used? 'Caring'? I suppose they were even intended that way. But they never worked, you know. Not even in your time. All through the last part of the 20th Century the rich kept getting richer and the poor kept getting poorer. Not just here. Not just in Brazil, either, but all over the world."

"That's shocking!" Brown burst out.

"It was inevitable," the counselor corrected. "Think about all of human history. How did poor people ever get rich? There were only a few ways: by going out to make their fortunes in virgin lands, like the American pioneers; or by finding jobs in new industries and growing with them. But that couldn't happen anymore. The poor people couldn't go out to colonize new lands, because there weren't any."

"Not even in space? Not even in—" Brown scowled, trying to remember some of the things that he had read about in *Time* and *Newsweek* in his former lifetime. "Not even, you know, artificial floating islands on the ocean?"

The counselor looked astonished. "Of course not, Mr. Brown. The rich countries didn't need to spend money on creating new living space by building space habitats or floating islands. They didn't have any population problem. And the poor countries, of course, couldn't possibly build them, because they didn't have the money."

"No new industries, either? But I remember distinctly that science and technology were going great guns in 1992! There were all sorts of wonderful new possibilities coming out of the laboratories every day! Electronics, quantum-effect devices, fusion power, robots, space manufacturing—"

He stopped, because the counselor's expression had hardened. "Yes," the counselor said stiffly, "those technological possibilities certainly did exist. They still do, for that matter—if we can ever get them out of the laboratory. But if you want to convert these possibilities into something real it takes money, too, Mr. Brown, doesn't it? Money for research and engineering and development. And there wasn't much of that, because you people soaked all the spare cash up, didn't you?"

"What are you talking about?"

The counselor was definitely controlling his anger now. "I mean," he said, "that you squandered your capital, didn't you? Your governments spent all their money on what you called 'pork barrel' projects—weapons you didn't need, support programs that enriched a few people at the cost of everyone else, dams and canals that served no purpose—and sometimes had to be put back to the state of nature in the end. You used up all your money on things that didn't matter, and so there was nothing left for research—"

Brown held up his hand. "I know all about the federal deficits," he said gruffly. "Heaven knows, I had to pay the taxes to pay the interest on what the government had borrowed, and, yes, it did mean cutting back on government financing of research."

"Not just research! You let the whole country fall apart, Mr. Brown—didn't maintain the bridges and tunnels, let the sewer systems and the water supplies in the big cities decay—why, by the beginning of this century the biggest new item in the federal budget was trying to keep the infrastructure from collapsing completely. Not even counting the interest on the debt you'd accumulated. So there was even less money for research and development."

Ben Brown was looking as resentful as the counselor. "All right, maybe the government ran out of money. But what about private industry? They were the ones who did the development work that made scientific ideas turn into things that people could build and use!"

"Yes, it was supposed to work that way," the counselor agreed. "But do you remember junk bonds, Mr. Brown? Do you remember leveraged corporate takeovers? All through the 1980s, especially, there was an orgy of takeovers, with one corporation, or one group of financiers, buying up the stock of another. Of course, they had to pay for the stock. And of course they didn't have that kind of capital, or didn't want to risk it if they did, so they did the buying with borrowed money."

"Well, sure they did! What's wrong with that?" Ben demanded.

"Just that the only way they could borrow the money was by paying high interest rates—which meant they were mortgaging the profits of the corporations they took over to pay the interest on the loans. It didn't make any difference whether the money came from banks, or savings and loans, or junk bonds sold directly to the public—the interest still had to be paid. And the only way it could be paid was for the corporations that were taken over to keep on making those profits—no matter what happened."

"That's what companies are in business for, to make profits," Ben said stubbornly.

"Actually," the counselor sighed, "that's only partly true. Corporations aren't supposed just to throw off a profit *now*. They're supposed to *keep on* making profits—which means they're supposed to invest in new plants when they're needed, and to plan for the future. To invest in research and development."

"Sure," Ben agreed. "Are you telling me they didn't do that?"

"How could they, Mr. Brown? When they had to churn out a profit every year, just to pay off those takeover debts? As soon as there was the slightest downturn in the economy—and there had to be a downturn, with all the savings and loan and bank failures, and the federal debt that kept growing—something had to be done to keep the profits coming. And the only thing that was in the power of the managements to change was to 'cut out frills' in their expenses. And the first 'frill' to go was their investment in research for the future . . . so, naturally, there were still more pressures on them in future years."

"They shouldn't have let that happen!" Ben declared. "They should have planned for the future!"

"Oh, yes," the counselor said sorrowfully, "they certainly should have done that, but they didn't. So we never did get all those wonderful new technologies you were talking about . . . except in a few areas, anyway."

Ben brightened. "So there's some good news?"

"Of course there is. How do you think we were able to fix your pancreatic cancer? Medicine's a lot better than it was in your time—they kept funding that kind of research right up to the end, because naturally the people who could make the decisions about such things knew that their own lives were directly affected. And then—" The counselor smiled again, but not happily. "Then there was the other kind of research, the kind people could do in their own basements and garages. We surely had a vast outpouring of new kinds of recreational drugs."

Ben gasped. "You mean *dope*?"

The counselor nodded. "Narcotics, Mr. Brown. Things that you could smoke or swallow or inject into yourself to make yourself crazy. The demand kept getting bigger and bigger, and so the drug dealers kept coming up with new products. The fastest-growing industry in the world, at the end of the 20th Century, was narcotics of a thousand different kinds ... and then, of course, there was what you did to the climate."

Ben was getting angry himself now. "Come off it," he snapped. "What's wrong with the climate? I've looked out the window, things look pretty good—"

"In this complex, of course. Under the dome."

Ben remembered the puzzling glass roof over the hospital grounds. He said, backing away, "Anyway, the climate's an act of God, isn't it? You can't blame that on my generation."

"Who else is there to blame, Mr. Brown?" the counselor asked reasonably. "You people knew in the late 1980s that you were destroying the ozone layer with chlorofluorocarbons—"

"You mean those CFC things the scientists talked about. Sure. But we passed laws to stop that."

"You passed laws to stop *some* uses of them in *some* countries," the counselor corrected. "Then you replaced them with other chemicals that also destroyed the ozone layer—just more slowly—but you increased the volume of those every year, so the damage to the ozone layer kept getting worse even in the countries that pretended to be taking steps. And most of the world kept right on using the old ones ... and you took your time about it all, too, didn't you? So by the time anything *serious* was done it was too little, too late, as you used to say. Because all the time you were stalling and hoping that you wouldn't have to bother, the CFCs were building up in the lower atmosphere. It took fifty or more years for the things to seep slowly up into the stratosphere where they did the damage. Good heavens, man," the counselor said sharply, "we haven't hit the worst of it *yet*! The stuff you were pouring into the atmosphere fifty years ago is *still* destroying ozone now, and we're all feeling the effects. Skin cancers, cataracts, damage to crops— they're all still getting worse. Along with the acid rain. Along with the wastage and destruction of water supplies—the whole Ogalalla aquifer is bone-dry now, because you pumped it out to grow the wrong crops in the wrong place, so now the Great American Desert is a desert again. Along with the global warming. . . ."

He stopped himself, breathing hard. "Sorry," he apologized. "I know you didn't mean any of this to happen. But you didn't do anything to stop it, either, did you?" He was silent for a moment. So was Ben Brown, because he couldn't think of anything to say.

Then the counselor managed a smile. "Anyway," he said, "that's the world you people left us. Belindia. A few million people in the world who live pretty well, under our domes—and a couple billion who, well, don't live very well at all."

Ben Brown's mood had suddenly become a lot less cheerful. "Well," he said, "that's all history, I guess. There's nothing I can do about it now. . . . But I'm alive!"

"You certainly are, Mr. Brown," the counselor agreed. "And you're just about ready to be discharged. About the only thing left for us to do is to discuss your bill."

Ben blinked at him. "My bill? But I put three hundred thousand dollars in escrow to cover all the expenses. That was my whole estate!"

"Of course you did, Mr. Brown. And it very nearly covered everything. But costs have gone up, you know. And you required a lot of special treatment. . . ." He looked at his monitor, thinking for a moment. Then he smiled.

"Actually," he said, "your outstanding debt balance is only about eight thousand dollars. I think we can overlook that. So you can leave as soon as you like— before the end of the day, anyway, so you won't run up any additional charges—"

"But I'll be broke!" Ben bleated.

"Well, of course," the counselor said patiently. "You'll be in the Indian portion of Belindia, Mr. Brown. There's no help for that . . . but at least you'll be alive!" he finished.

And did not add, *If you can call that living.*

WHAT DREAMS REMAIN

by Frederik Pohl

1 ⸺

When Jake Bailey met Sarella Simpson Grant it was probably the luckiest thing that ever happened to him, although he didn't recognize it at the time and he surely would have given you an argument about it later on. Jake wasn't used to recognizing good luck. He kept on looking for it, because he surely needed some, but it was a long time since he'd found anything but bad.

As a matter of fact, looking for some kind of a lucky break was what he was doing in the little town of Citriola, Florida, that night. He wasn't supposed to be there. He didn't have a job, and therefore he didn't have a residence permit, and therefore he would be in bad trouble, the beating-up-behind-the-police-station kind of bad trouble, if the town's Citizen Patrol Corps caught him there. But, hell, he thought, it was New Year's Eve. The cops would be too busy rounding up their resident drunks and stopping fights to check papers, probably.

And there was always the chance that Jake could get to one of the resident drunks before the cops did.

What he would do then he had not spelled out for himself. Something like helping the drunk get safely home, he thought, and then probably getting some kind of a reward from the grateful citizen, or the grateful citizen's wife. A meal, anyway. Maybe some money. Maybe even a friendship. Maybe even the kind of friendship that would lead to the offer of a *job*. At least some kind of breakthrough that would give him some hope of getting out of his miserable vagrant existence, back into the employed and regularly fed and decently housed life he deserved.

What he got, instead, was a gang fight.

He was making his way down one of the residential streets on the outskirts of Citriola, run-down dark houses with the remnants of Christmas decorations still in their windows, when he noticed somebody else was skulking along behind him. He couldn't make out who the person was. A bunch of celebrators were singing and drinking under a streetlight at the corner. Another bunch came yelling and laughing around the corner behind him. While he was peering at the other person, just to make sure that it wasn't a cop, he got the really bad news.

The two groups unfortunately didn't like each other.

As soon as they recognized each other the trouble started. In seconds handguns and assault weapons were popping away and all the bystanders were hitting the ground.

There was only one thing to do then. Jake ran. The other person ran, too, along with him—out of the street, between houses, to get as far as they could from the wildly flying bullets, but also because they heard the sirens of the National Guard coming toward the scene, and neither of them had any legitimate business in Citriola in the first place. They didn't ask questions. They just ran like hell.

Jake hadn't even known that the stranger he'd run with had been a girl until they were huddled together under an oleander bush half a mile away, waiting for the commotion to die down. Then she put her head out to stare, and looked at him, and shook her head and grinned. "It must be after midnight by now," she said. "Happy 2042, whoever you are."

The thing about Jake Bailey was that he hadn't always been a vagrant. There was a time when he'd had a pretty good job up around Boston. He worked as what they called an "electronics engineer"—it only meant that he tended the hardware at a cable TV station, but he had a Cambridge residence permit and an apartment of his own—well, almost his own. He had to share the three rooms with four other people, to be sure, and of course in the streets around the apartment building you had the firefights among the kid gangs to contend with two or three times a week, as well as the dope pushers and the hookers and the police patrols in their armored cars, but you could stand that. It could've been worse. Cambridge wasn't like downtown Boston. And there was always food on the table and his own bed at night and his own job at the cable TV system to go to in the morning.

It wasn't Jake Bailey's fault that the job disappeared when the creaky old satellite that fed their programming finally died. It wasn't even his fault that there weren't any other jobs to be had for electronics engineers, but he paid the price anyway. Boston/Cambridge had no room for the jobless. Neither did Providence, nor Hartford, nor old New York, dying on the vine, its water system finally irrevocably collapsed, its subways breaking down, its tall buildings dry above the first three or four stories and inhabited only by squatters who were no longer even worth anybody's trouble to throw out.

So Jake worked his way on down the coast, out of one winter's freezing gales and through one summer's alternation of burning droughts and torrential hurricanes. The place he sought was never there. Washington might have been good, if he'd known more about guns than about microchips and circuit boards. There were jobs in Washington. But you had to be a fighter to be taken on with the guards who ringed the enclave around the old White House and Capitol, or even to lead the rebellious masses who kept the protected governmental enclave in a state of siege, and Jake Bailey didn't want to fight. Then he heard that there were jobs in Georgia. When he got there he found that that was true enough, where the people were desperately trying to rebuild new generating capacity after the Savannah River catastrophe, but who wanted to stay where every bite of potato or peach you put in your mouth was laced with the deadly residual cesium-137 it picked up from the soil? And then all that was left to try was Florida; and that was where he met Sarella Simpson Grant.

Three weeks after that first meeting, Jake still didn't know what to make of Sarella. He hadn't planned on hooking up with anybody else. It was hard enough to get by alone when you didn't have either a job or a residence permit. But they had been together ever since, and how long the relationship was going to last Jake had not decided.

He didn't particularly want to leave Citriola, although there weren't any jobs there, either. The old juice-processing plants had gone bust when everything else did, decades earlier, right after the big bank collapses around the turn of the century, but at least Florida was warm. And as long as he was going to stay in that vicinity, there were definite advantages to staying tight with Sarella Simpson Grant. She knew the town. She was smart about avoiding the sections where the gangs would make trouble—usually—and she was pretty enough, and young enough, to talk some of the householders into giving them enough work for a meal, and sometimes even for a place to sleep in the back of an old garage. She was easy to get along with, mostly, and certainly she was good in bed— well, would have been, if the two of them had ever had a real bed to share together; but good enough in whatever corner of abandoned shed or backseat of rusted-out car

they found to sleep in. She talked a lot, too—about everything except why she had those funny little tattoos on the
backs of her hands. That she wouldn't discuss; but she
loved to talk about the old days, when everybody had
cars that worked, and color TVs, new ones coming out
every year even if they didn't live on a Reservation, and
people did wonderful things like sending human beings
to the Moon on rocket ships that had been launched
from old Cape Kennedy just across the peninsula and
there was a *purpose* to life . . . the days she herself had
certainly never experienced, because they had been well
and truly over when her own parents were barely born.

Though Bailey was twice her age—nearly forty to her
barely nineteen—he hadn't been born yet in those wonder days, either, but he had lived long enough to be sure
those days were never coming back. Not Sarella. All this
kind of dead-broke, dead-end life was temporary, she
swore to him. The good times would come again. All
they had to do was manage to stay alive until they did.

It was that kind of talk from Sarella that cheered Jake
Bailey up . . . when it didn't drive him crazy. So every
morning they would clean themselves up the best they
could and trudge into the suburbs of Citriola (floppy sun
hats in their hands and their sunglasses off, so they
would look as safe and unthreatening as possible) until
they found someone who wanted windows washed or
trash hauled to the recycling dumpsters or the kudzu
chopped out of what was intended to be a vegetable garden—who wanted anything done that the householders
were unwilling to do for themselves because doing that
kind of work meant saying outside in the lethal ozone-
free sunlight.

Sometimes they even got one of those jobs, because
Citriola was a relatively prosperous little town as towns
went in those days. You couldn't live *in* Citriola without
papers and a real job, but as long as you didn't attract
too much attention from Citriola's Guard they would let
you hang around.

When that happened they at least had something that passed for a meal, handed out to them at the back steps. If they were specially lucky sometimes they might even get some extra food that the householder was getting ready to throw away anyway, and then they could take that back to wherever they were sleeping and actually have a kind of breakfast the next morning. And at least one day a week, when they'd managed to put aside enough so that they could go a day without a handout, they didn't stop at the row houses in the suburbs. On those days they went right in to what was left of Citriola's business district, or out to the few companies that managed to hang on in what had once been Citriola's industrial park, and tried to get a *real* job.

They never had yet. But Sarella was sure that someday they might.

Jake had never had a girl like her. He didn't understand her, or her unquenchable optimism about the future. Or her secretiveness—like the way that, now and then, she would go off on some private and unexplained business of her own for a few hours—but probably that didn't matter, he had decided. If she hadn't told him everything there was to tell about herself, well, he hadn't told her all his own secrets, either.

But there was no permanent commitment between them, not spoken, not even implied. Jake always kept the escape hatch open in his mind. The time might come when it would be possible for one of them to escape into the real world of people-with-jobs—but not two. Then, if he ever had to choose between Sarella and a job, he knew it would be good-bye, Sarella.

That was the way it was with Jake Bailey, right up to the night he became a looter.

Jake hadn't intended to become a looter. It was Sarella's idea, and she certainly hadn't said anything about looting on the way out there. They had been making their usual rounds in the town of Citriola, with discouraging results.

They had no luck that day, no jobs, no handouts, a bad day all around. And then, when the two of them were hiking out of the town at sundown, as they had to be because they didn't have residence permits, she clapped her hands and looked up at him.

"I've got an idea, hon. Let's see if they're hiring any guards at the storehouses."

"We applied there two days ago," he reminded her.

"That was two days ago, hon. I hear they got a big new shipment of salvaged parts today. Don't you think they're going to want extra watchmen to keep an eye on them?"

"No," he said, but he didn't have any better ideas, and so the two of them took the old Interstate southward out of the town of Citriola in the gathering dusk, aware of the eyes that watched from every occupied window to make sure they were on their way. They took the three-mile hike along the old Interstate, swatting at mosquitoes, stumbling over the cracks in the concrete, sweating. Before long the only light they had left was the little sliver of moon, setting as they walked, and Jake wondered why he was doing this. But Sarella had seemed *confident.*

He asked himself again why he stayed with her. It wasn't that he was in love with her, though the sex was certainly a plus. It was partly that, curiously, she was one of the few other vagabonds who didn't seem to be a doper—at least, her nose didn't run and there were no needle tracks on any of the parts of her body he had seen, which was by now most of them. Mostly it was just that Sarella never seemed to be in doubt about what to do next.

While Jake Bailey was in doubt quite often, in the dubious world he had been born into.

To say that Sarella didn't have many doubts was not to say that she was always right. She wasn't even always consistent; and a mile from the storehouse, its floodlights already haloing the tree line ahead of them, she proved that again. She stopped suddenly, with an expression of dawning realization that struck Jake as maybe a little too theatrical to be real, and said, "Oh, shit, hon."

"Shit what?"

"Shit I just happened to think. This is a waste of time. The personnel office'll be closed by now."

He slap-rubbed the back of his neck, hoping to catch a mosquito or two under his palm and get the satisfaction of rolling a soft, juicy body into pulp while he waited for Sarella's next idea.

When it came he didn't like it. "Why don't we just see if there's anything left in those houses?" she said.

Naturally he told her that was a stupid idea. If they were caught that would be called *looting*, and who wanted to have to spend his next couple of months in a workgang under the deadly sun, doing whatever miserable task the workgangs were ordered to do that week? But naturally he did what she said anyway, for the same reason he almost always did as Sarella suggested. Her ideas might not always pan out, but at least she kept thinking of them. And Jake's own ideas had run out.

When they had climbed out of the old roadside drainage ditch, scummy with algae and buzzing with the night's crop of new mosquitoes, Jake paused to look around. "Which house should we try?" he asked.

Sarella looked around. There were four houses ranged around a cul-de-sac, none of them inhabited for a long time. They had been nice houses at one time, not the cookie-cutter things the builders had thrown up by the thousand all over Florida, each one with its breezeway and its crabgrass lawn; these had been owned by people rich enough to pay for full basements and acre plots, carved out of what had once been an orange grove. They weren't nice houses anymore, though. One of them had burned at some time or another, and none of them still had a roof.

"That one," she said, pointing to the nearest. "You go in and scout it out. I'll stay out here to warn you in case anybody comes by."

"Who would come by?" Jake asked reasonably.

"In *case*, hon," she said. "You take the flashlight. And, listen, if you can find a crowbar or something, be sure to rip out the skirting and see if there's anything behind it; people sometimes hid things there."

The house was dark, damp, and smelling of rot and mold. It had been hit by at least a dozen hurricanes over the past forty years, since the weather got so bad, and undoubtedly it had been looted many times before Jake Bailey ever saw it. Its location made it a prime target; it was the kind of place the well-to-do looked for, not in the town of Citriola, exactly, so the householders didn't have to mingle with the masses, but close enough to drive into when they chose to. When they still had cars, at least.

It wasn't that far from various parts of civilization. Out of one window Jake could see the orange skyglow of Citriola, out of another the brighter, nearer floodlights of the warehouses, and beyond them the more distant effulgence that was the rich people's Reservation. But there was no light at all in the house except what the stars gave him through the holes in the roof.

What Jake wished for was a flashlight, but that was just a dream. What he had was matches, and a hoarded copy of the *Citriola Sun-Times*, and he squandered a couple of sheets on a torch to get his bearings.

What he saw wasn't promising. At one time this place had been an expensive five-bedroom split-level with a full and finished basement. It wasn't much now. The only furnishings left were a couple of couches and stuffed chairs, moldering with damp, and some heaps that might once have been abandoned clothing. Sarella's idea of ripping out the skirting around the floors might have been a good one, but someone had been there first; the Sheetrock of the walls themselves had been pulled away, and if there had ever been anything hidden there it was long gone. The kitchen and the baths had been stripped bare, with even the pipes and the electric wiring carted away.

Remained the basement.

Jake peered down the dark steps. His paper torch told him nothing, and it was beginning to burn his fingers. He doused it, found a piece of wood, and tossed it down the stairs. It hit with a faint thud, but not a splash, so Jake started down, carefully testing each step before he put his weight on it because that wood had probably been wet since before he was born and surely rot had at least begun.

The floor was squishy mud, but it didn't come over his shoes. When he had another clump of papers burning he looked around.

There wasn't much left. The ceiling panels that had held recessed lighting were yawning, their compact fluorescents long looted away, and the little closet where the water-softener tank had been stored was missing not only the tank but all its plumbing as well. Over in a corner he saw the rusted wreck of a rowing machine and some crumpled sheet metal in the mud that might once have been a microwave. That was all. Just about everything else that the house's owners had bought and put down there for the embellishment of their soft and privileged old lives, if it was movable at all, had been taken away.

It had been a pretty room once. Jake was surprised to see a painting on the wall—a mural, actually. It was faded and parts of it were covered over by spreading fungus from the damp, but he could recognize the subject. At one time it had been a painting of a Shuttle or some other kind of ancient spacecraft, flames billowing from its base as it took off from a launchpad at Canaveral. It was the kind of thing he thought Sarella would like to see, because she was so crazy about the subject; maybe he would call her down before he left, he thought, but meanwhile there was business.

He found a door that separated the playroom from the

unfinished part of the cellar. Jake was surprised that no one had taken the door off its hinges and carried it away, but when he touched it he saw why. It was worthless. It was made out of fiberboard composition rather than wood, and covered with fungus besides.

As he passed through he kicked something in the greasy mud, and discovered it was a ball peen hammer. The head was rusted and the handle cracked from decades of soaking, but it was still perhaps useful for something. He held on to it, peering around. There had been food here once, on shelves lining a wall. There still was food, or its remains—home-canned vegetables, they looked like, in mason jars, but certainly nothing worth taking; no previous looter had been willing to risk the botulism they were likely to contain, and Jake Bailey wasn't either. A sodden pile in one corner turned out to be books; the long-gone owners of the house had evidently been readers. Bailey would have liked to have the books, even though most of them were paperbacked fiction, but every one was soaked and bloated. And, as he turned back toward the stairway, he heard the sirens outside. And a moment later the stomping of heavy boots over his head, and the cellar door wrenched open, and he saw flashlights shining down the stairs, and the voice of a man shouting down at him, angry, peremptory:

"Police! You! Come up out of there, hands on your head. Move it!"

And when he came blinking up out of the cellar there were four of them in Guard uniforms, all with guns, and all pointed at him. A pair of black-and-white Guard cars were on the lawn, hydrogen motors running, headlights pointed at the house. And of Sarella Simpson Grant there was no sign at all.

2 ———

The jail was in an underground room. It wasn't really a jail, but it served the purpose well enough; it was certainly not a place you could easily get out of. Once it had been the safe-deposit vaults of a little bank, from the days when every little shopping center had its branch bank or S&L. The building hadn't been used as a bank for a long time. Now nothing was left of the safe-deposit boxes but yawning holes, and a dozen canvas cots were lined against the walls for the prisoners. Most of the cots were vacant; besides Bailey himself there were only three others, all men, none known to him.

When the guards woke them up to feed them breakfast—hot milky coffee and a single slice of dry bread apiece—and shuttle them upstairs to the courtroom, Bailey wondered what had happened to Sarella, but not for long. He had more urgent things to worry about.

Being arrested was nothing new to Jake Bailey. He'd been arrested before. But all the other times had been for nothing more than vagrancy, picked up by some community's bum's-rush squad and carried to the outskirts with a warning not to come back. This was different. What he was charged with this time was *looting*. It was a felony, and when you got caught in the commission of a crime it was serious. It was the kind of thing you didn't want on your record. It could tip the balance the wrong way when, and if, The Job finally came along, because with all the unemployed engineers around, what sort of idiot, or saint, would hire one with a criminal record?

He had plenty of time to think about it, because once they were in the courtroom they had nothing to do but wait. For hours—first for the courtroom officially to open for the day, and then for the magistrate who would hear their cases to get around to showing up.

The courtroom wasn't really a courtroom, either. It was just the banking floor of the old building, with tellers' cages still in place, but the best thing about it was that it still had air-conditioning that, miraculously, still worked. Jake Bailey had not been in an air-conditioned place for more than a year. It was an almost-forgotten pleasure. He wouldn't have minded the wait in this dry, cool place, except that the cops wouldn't give them anything to eat and there was no toilet on the premises that they would let the prisoners use.

The room had other amenities, though not for the prisoners. There was a big coffee urn, and next to it a stack of white foam-plastic cups that looked to Bailey as though they had never been used before. There was a plate of sweet rolls, and there were five or six men and women, some in uniform, drinking coffee and chatting with each other, next to the window where the air conditioner was humming away. They had the well-fed and relaxed air of people who had jobs and therefore didn't have any obligation to work at them. Bailey knew that they had to be court officials and lawyers, but they never looked in the direction of the prisoners manacled on their backless wooden bench.

There was one other person in the room, and when the group by the air conditioner looked at anyone, she was it. She was Reservation. She sat by herself, laughing and whispering into a portable telephone—a telephone that evidently *worked*—and she was not only beautiful, she wore diamonds in her earlobes and a bigger one on her finger.

"Oh, shit," the prisoner next to Bailey whispered despairingly. He was a pale, plump little man, whose name was Becker. He was looking at the woman too. "It's Mrs. Hegemeyer," he said, as though that explained something, but he never had a chance to explain what. One of the cops looked up warningly and the man shut up.

Bailey didn't stop looking at the woman; she was by all odds the most interesting thing to see in the courtroom. When he contrasted her with Sarella, the differences leaped out at him. Sarella had looked—well, *used*. Not older. Just more worn. Sarella was no more than nineteen, but her hair was a tangle, her face was scorched by the sun no matter how much cream she had spread on it, her sweat-stained khakis looked as though they had originally been made for a much larger person, and a male one, and they had.

The Reservation woman was much older. For that matter, she was probably older than Bailey himself, he judged, forty at least. But there wasn't a line on her face, her hair was perfectly coiffed, and there was nothing about her anywhere to suggest that she had ever known a moment's worry in her life. She probably hadn't. What did the people in the Reservations have to worry about? They were *rich*. Rich enough so that they never had to worry about being caught out in the noonday ultraviolet, or whether they could afford food from the damaged farms for their children, or whether the next tropical storm would do to their homes what had been done to the one he had been caught in. Reservations people didn't need to leave their domed, controlled enclaves. What outside interests they might have were taken care of by the people they hired for the work, like the rent-a-cops in their various incarnations, Citizen Patrol in the town, National Guard outside it, as well as the prosecuting lawyers—and, if he ever showed up, the magistrate.

So what was this woman from the Reservation doing here?

When the magistrate came in he apologized profusely. Not to the prisoners, of course. Not even to the functionaries hanging around the air conditioner, but to the woman from the Reservation. She was the first one the judge saw and he bustled over to her immediately. "I'm sorry to

keep you waiting, Mrs. Hegemeyer," he said, all but bow-
ing to her. "I had no idea you were going to be here. I certainly wouldn't have done that if anyone had told me—"

She took her mouth away from the telephone long
enough to say—patient, but not very patient—"Just get
on with it."

"Of course, Mrs. Hegemeyer. You there!" he said, calling severely to the lawyers. "Let's get this court in session."

That was when one of the lawyer women came hurrying over to the prisoners' bench, glancing at a pad in
her hand. "Jacob Bailey?" she called, looking around the
group of men.

Bailey raised his hand. She gave him a quick analytical
look, to see how much trouble he was worth, decided not
much. "All right, Bailey," she said, reading from the pad,
"I'm your public defender. I guess you know you're in the
deep shit. Officer Marquez caught you coming out of an
abandoned house carrying stolen goods to the amount of
more than ten dollars, which constitutes—"

"Hey," he said. "It was a beat-up old hammer. It wasn't
worth fifty cents."

She looked at him impatiently. "That's just a techni-
cality. It doesn't make any difference how much the
stuff's worth. It's still looting, but that's only the first
part of it. You were threatening the arresting officer with
a weapon—"

He gaped at her. "The *hammer*?"

"Whatever it was. You threatened him with it."

"Oh, the hell I did. I just had it in my hand because I
found it there."

"His word against yours, Bailey," she said, "and he has
witnesses." She thought for a moment, but not very hard,
then made her decision. "Looks open and shut to me.
We'll plead you guilty and get it over with."

"*No*," Jake said.

"What? You got some other idea? Look, the judge is
going to convict you anyway, so let's not irritate him.

I won't call any witnesses. All you have to do is just—what?"

Bailey was shaking his head. "Put me on the stand."

"What for?" she asked, genuinely puzzled.

"Because I didn't really steal anything, and I'm not a vagrant. Not really. I'm an engineer, and I've got a clean record. Let me tell the court."

"Jesus," she said. "The judge hates it when people waste his time."

"And I hate the idea of cleaning up toxic dumps for a couple of months."

She shrugged, already beginning to look around at the other prisoners. "It's your ass, I guess. Now I've got other clients. Peter Corning? Hi, I'm your lawyer. Listen, Corning, it says here you punched Officer Caldwell in the face when he asked to check your ID—"

When the trials began Bailey didn't go first. That honor went to the little man, Ward Becker, as a courtesy to Mrs. Hegemeyer. It turned out that she was the complaining witness against him because he had been caught in possession of something he'd stolen from her, namely a jeweled watch.

The prosecutor only asked her if she recognized the watch. "Of course. It's mine. Can't you see it has my name engraved on the back?"

And Becker's defense attorney only asked her deferentially if she was sure it was Becker who had stolen it. "Who else? He was in and out of the house all the time, because he was my father's valet."

Then it was the defendant's turn. As Becker was sworn in, Bailey looked at the man with new contempt. He'd been working in the Reservation, and he jeopardized that job by stealing a watch? However his trial came out, he'd lost.

Predictably the man denied stealing it. "Then how did it turn up in your room?" the prosecutor demanded, and Becker hung his head.

"Somebody must have put it there," he said, and winced when people tittered.

His defense attorney only asked him to repeat that, and then the magistrate cut the questioning short. "We've heard enough," he said, scowling. "Ward Becker, I find you guilty. I'm sorry to say that I can only sentence you to ninety days. That's a pity, because if there's one thing I can't stand it's people who betray the trust of decent citizens who have given them a chance to make something out of themselves, but it's the longest sentence this court is allowed to give. I only hope that you do something wrong in the workgang, because then you'll be back before me and I'll give you more. Ninety days. Bailiff, remove the prisoner." Then, all smiles, "Thank you very much for coming here, Mrs. Hegemeyer."

She wasn't listening. She was at the window, talking irritably on her telephone as she looked out; it had begun to rain.

Then Jake Bailey got his day in court. The arresting officer testified that, yes, he had arrested the vagrant, Jacob Bailey, yes, he had discovered stolen merchandise in his possession. Bailey's lawyer looked at first as though she would not bother to ask any questions, but then bestirred herself. "Why did you go to that house, Officer Marquez?"

"On information received from an informant," the Guard cop said.

The lawyer looked interested. Apparently more from curiosity than any desire to help her client, she asked, "What informant was that?"

The Guard looked annoyed. "We were investigating an attempted break-in at the critical-supplies warehouse," he said. "There's an alarm, see, because that place is full of electronic stuff that you just can't get anymore. We were responding to the alarm when we observed a young woman in the woods. On questioning she said she had been in the company of this defendant and he wanted to loot a house, and she didn't want to do it. So she left him. She told us which house he was robbing."

Thunderstruck, Jake stared at the Guardsman. His lawyer gave him a warning glance, but the judge had become curious. "Is this young woman in the court?"

"No, sir. She must've gone somewhere while we were arresting the defendant."

The judge was scowling. "That's pretty poor police work, Officer Marquez," he said severely, glancing at the woman from the Reservation in the hope that she was observing his diligence. She wasn't. "There's a lot of valuable stuff in those warehouses."

"Yes, sir," the Guard said, abashed. "They didn't get anything, though."

"Well, that's a mercy. Counselor, let's move this thing along."

But Jake was no longer listening. Had Sarella really ratted him out? Why would she do a thing like that? He was actually on the stand himself, being sworn in, before he remembered he had more immediate problems.

He collected his thoughts. "I took the hammer, yes," he said to the prosecutor, "but it was abandoned property. It wasn't theft." He opened his mouth to go on, but the prosecutor stopped him. A new man had entered—an older man, well dressed, who nodded to the magistrate. He didn't speak; he just waited at the door for Mrs. Hegemeyer. Through the glass Bailey saw the man's car, a pale blue sedan, old but beautifully kept.

"Go on," the prosecutor said, after making sure the new arrival didn't want to take part in the proceedings.

"I have no previous police record. I'm not a vagrant, either," Bailey said. "I'm an electrical engineer."

The old man from the Reservation, on the point of leaving with the woman, paused, listening to Bailey.

"Oh, really?" the prosecutor sneered. "And will you tell the court, please, where you are employed?"

"I'm not—at the moment," Bailey admitted. "I worked for Pilgrim Cable, Limited, in the Boston area, until they closed down. I have a letter of recommendation from my superior, which says I was honest, industrious, and proficient." He felt the eyes of the Reservation man watching him. The woman, who was evidently his daughter, was impatient to be off, but he restrained her.

"Then why did you get fired?"

"I wasn't 'fired'. Our satellite died, and the cable company went out of business. Since part of my work was in adapting other kinds of electronic equipment for spare parts, I expect to find another job soon."

"Oh, really?" the prosecutor asked, not very interested; everybody knew that there weren't enough factories producing spare parts for anything anymore, so scavenging was a way of life. "And have you applied for work in this area?"

"I haven't found any openings yet," Bailey admitted; and that was as far as he got. When it came his defense attorney's turn she gave him plenty of time to elaborate on his statements, in spite of reproving glares from the bench, but the results were the same. Three consecutive ninety-day terms: one for looting, one for possession of a weapon, and the final one for attempted assault on the person of Officer Marquez; and the judge didn't even pause to draw breath before calling the next case.

When sentence was passed a cop led Bailey out and trotted him across the parking lot, through the hot, teeming rain, to a warehouse to get his workgang clothes. The pale blue Reservation car was gone, with the old man and his beautiful daughter.

By the time he got to the warehouse Jake was soaked, but not cold. It wasn't air-conditioned here. It wasn't even screened, and the windows were open. Jake was glad enough to be able to see outside, where the free citizens of Citriola were hurrying about their business through the downpour, but the open windows meant that flies and wasps were buzzing around inside and he had to be careful where he sat.

Becker was there before him, naked and looking miserable as a guard in a Smokey the Bear hat knelt before him, strapping something around the man's ankle. "Strip," the cop ordered Bailey, and as Bailey removed each article of clothing the cop ordered him to throw it into a bin.

Naked, he sat beside Becker and got his own anklet. It was a steel band, thoughtfully covered in leather so that it wouldn't cut the flesh too quickly, with a lump under the leather on one side. Bailey studied it thoughtfully. He knew what it was: a radiolocator. It snapped on solidly and locked. There was only one way to get it off without a key—by cutting through the steel—and as long as he wore it someone at a console somewhere within a twenty-mile radius would always know exactly where he was. It would, he thought, be difficult to escape from the workgang.

Becker was leaning dismally back against a standpipe, listening to the sound of rainwater from the roof gurgling into the shed's cistern. "Stuck," he said, to himself as much as to Bailey. "I'm stuck here, and it's all Quinn Parkinson's fault."

"Who's Parkinson?" Bailey asked, not so much because he cared as to find out if the guard was going to forbid them to talk here.

"The man from the Reservation, didn't you see him? That bitch Phyllis Hegemeyer's father. I was a good servant to the bastard, but he framed me, and now what am I going to do?"

The guard stretched and yawned, listening without much interest. He unwrapped a stick of gum before he answered. "What you men are going to do," he said, "is cut brush at Camp Three. You're lucky that's all it is right now; last month they were trying to clean up a toxic waste dump. Camp Three's about twelve miles from here, so you better rest up for the walk. Oh," he added, reminding himself, "you might as well get your clothes while we're waiting for the next good man to get sentenced. Come on over here."

The uniform was heavy-duty khaki, and it was all dyed orange—orange pants, orange shirt, floppy orange hat. The sizes were only approximate, and none of it was new: some of the orange was faded, some bright and newly redyed. But there was a pair of boots for each man, calf-length and sturdy. They weren't ordinary boots. Each one had a kind of blister on the outer side of the right ankle to accommodate the radiolocator.

"Make sure they fit," the guard ordered. "You're gonna do a lot of walking in them, and they don't like it at Three if foot trouble slows you down."

"What about our personal stuff?" Bailey asked.

The guard shrugged. "When you finish doing your time you can come back and look for it," he said. "Now just take it easy until the rest of the men get here. There's two more to get convicted before we take you out to the camp."

"Are you sure about that?" Bailey asked curiously. "I mean, doesn't anybody ever get acquitted?"

The guard looked at him in astonishment. "Now, why would the judge ever acquit anybody, when we've got all that cleanup work to do?"

3 ———

Life in Camp Three wasn't a vacation. But it wasn't hell, either. Jake Bailey had had worse. At least here you got fed.

Camp Three had started out as a truck stop along the old Interstate, and the rusted shells of the gas and diesel pumps were still there. Of course the underground tanks were long empty of fuel. No tourists drove up any more to refill on the way to their winter week of bird-watching or

collecting shells on Sanibel Island, because there weren't
any more tourists. The stripped-down shell of the cafeteria where the tourists had fed their kids and bought
their souvenir baseball caps had been turned into the
barracks for the Camp Three guards. The old toilets still
worked, some of them—for the guards. The prisoners
weren't that lucky. The prisoners had no running water,
and only an outdoor privy; they slept in metal bunks,
four high, in what had once been the repair area, and
they didn't sleep long.

What you did on a workgang was work, and the kind
of work you did was the kind nobody else was willing
to do.

That meant cleanup, because in the good old days
people had had some bad old habits, and their consequences were still around. Once there had been a
paper mill just off the Interstate. It had taken the pine
trees and chopped them and pulped them and bleached
them into white newsprint to feed the hungry presses
of the country's newspapers, and in the process they
had poured acid liquor into the ground. The newspapers
were gone. The mill was a burned-out ruin. The waste
remained, laced with poisonous dioxins. Somebody had
to clean it up.

That was what prisoners were for. But the good part,
maybe the only good part, the thing that kept it from
being pure hell, was that Camp Three's prisoners were
spared the worst part of the cleanup. They didn't have
to dig out the worst contaminated soil and pile it in
wagons to be hauled away. That was reserved for the
serious prisoners in Camp One, the murders and rapists,
the ones who had tried to kidnap Reservation people
for ransom—and, worst of all, the ones who had stolen
"strategic" goods to sell on the black market. The Camp
One prisoners were the ones who were likely to die on
the job. The Camp Three prisoners, who mostly cleared
away the brush so the hard-time prisoners could get to
the poisons, only almost died.

Still, cutting undergrowth in the swampy fields was about as hard as work could get. Bailey's clothes were soaked with sweat in a minute; they were a personal prison, but he didn't take them off. He knew that much. The clothes were all that kept the ultraviolet that leaked through the tattered ozone layer from burning him black.

The hours were long. They were rousted out at daybreak, and the sun had set over the Gulf of Mexico before the overseer let them heave the last bundles into the horse-drawn wagons and then trudge the mile back to Camp Three.

That was when one of the guards came up to Jake Bailey, his eyes invisible behind his mirrorshades, his over-and-under shotgun in the crook of his arm. "You two," he ordered. "Fall out."

The man next to Bailey was Becker. "Oh, shit," he muttered out of the side of his mouth. He had taken off his shirt and wrapped it around his waist. His torso was glistening with sweat. The guard turned his shades on Jake for a moment, then turned to Becker. "Put that shirt back on," he ordered. "Jesus, you guys. You're turning red already."

"Sorry, sir," Becker said abjectly, already struggling with the sleeves, but the guard was studying Bailey again. Jake knew the man's name. It was Mr. Lavalette, easily recognizable because he was the only black guard, said to be the least mean of them.

"You Bailey?" he demanded.

"That's right," Jake said, and tardily remembered to add, "sir."

"Well, hell, Bailey. What's the matter with you? Don't you have sun-goggles?"

"I did have. They took them away from me . . . sir."

"You'll get cataracts, boy. How you going to work for us if you get cataracts?" Mr. Lavalette shook his head, studying Bailey. Then he said, "Come around after chow.

I'll see if I can find you some glasses. Now you two better double-time it, the column's way ahead of you."

When they got back to the compound the men lined up to fill their tin cups from the camp's drinking water faucet. Becker was looking at Jake Bailey with respect.

"Did you ever know Lavalette? Before, I mean?"

Jake shook his head.

Becker looked unconvinced. "Well, look, if you get those glasses from him, see if you can get some sunburn cream, okay? I could use it."

Jake didn't say yes. He didn't say no, either; the fact was that he wasn't particularly sympathetic to Becker. The man had his troubles, but who didn't?

But after they'd trotted back from their dinner—horse stew, somebody said, but at least it was meat—the little man flung himself faceup on his bed, shivering as though with cold. On the way out Jake Bailey tarried to look at him. "You all right?" he asked.

Becker opened his eyes long enough to glare at him. "How could I be all right?" he demanded.

"Do you want anything? A drink of water, maybe?"

"What I want," Becker said, "is to get back on the Reservation where I belong. I was a damn good valet, Bailey, kept that shit Parkinson's clothes neat, cleaned up after him, made sure his fucking bath was just the right temperature. Then he went and framed me. I never *saw* the fucking watch."

Jake started to turn away. He was tired of Becker's complaints, and he had his own full quota of subjects for brooding about—starting with why Sarella Simpson Grant had ratted him out. But the little man was in pain. Bailey paused to give him a chance to talk. "Why would he do that?"

"Why do those fuckers do anything? He *said* I was looking at his private files. I wasn't! I don't even know how to run his goddamn computer, I just saw it was on when I came into the room and I was trying to turn it off to save it—those things wear out, you know."

Bailey stared at him. "Even on the Reservation?"

"Where've you been, Bailey? The factories are breaking down, didn't you know that? And they can't get replacements. Only—" he fell back, staring bemused at the bottom of Bailey's bunk—"only it's so *nice* there, Bailey. No bugs. No sunburn. Clean water that doesn't taste salty, and food you wouldn't believe. Of course, they don't give that to the servants, but those fuckers never eat everything they get, and there's plenty left over after every meal." He flopped over. "Leave me alone, Bailey," he wailed. "I got nothing to live for anymore."

When Jake Bailey knocked on the door of the guards' quarters a guard he didn't know poked his head out and barked at him. "What the fuck are you doing out of your barracks?"

"Mr. Lavalette told me to come see him, sir."

The man looked at him suspiciously, then said, "Wait over there."

"Over there" was outside the guards' little yard, the one that had the electronic bug-zapper that killed off all the mosquitoes. Most of them, anyway. Bailey still slapped at a few, but he was wearing his work clothes and the only exposed flesh was his face and hands.

It was warm and clear—quiet, too, except for the croak of frogs along the stream that flowed through the camp, and an occasional rumble of a belated horse-drawn produce wagon heading to supply the Reservation farther along the Interstate. There was no moon, and the camp floodlights were turned off to save energy—they weren't needed, because no convict would get very far at night with the radiolocator on his ankle. Bailey could see the thousands of Floridian stars, and the smaller number of things that were not stars because they were moving.

Bailey stared at them longingly, because he knew what they were. They were space satellites, or pieces of them, left over from the days when human beings could send rockets off the Earth to Low Earth Orbit or even off to the Moon, the planets. One of those satellites—well, one like them, anyway, though in remote geostationary orbit and thus too distant to be seen with the naked eye—had perhaps been the very satellite that had fed his cable network in Boston.

The door to the guards' quarters opened. Mr. Lavalette was standing there squinting out into the darkness. Bailey turned toward him, and the old man walked toward him. "Here," he said, handing something to Bailey. It was a pair of sunglasses. "They aren't the best," he said, sounding almost apologetic, "but at least they'll save your eyes a little."

Bailey saw that the guard had told the truth. The olive green lenses were a funny teardrop shape, and there had been gold glitter on the frames once. Women's glasses, and so old that one earpiece had been mended with surgical tape . . . but a lot better than nothing at all.

"Thank you, sir," he mumbled, and turned to go. Lavalette stopped him.

He squinted up at the sky, seeming to be in the mood for conversation. "That's a military spy satellite up there," he said, pointing. "Do you see it, the one that's moving east? It's still working, sort of, though it's pretty nearly half a century old now. It runs by solar power, and as long as the sun shines it'll keep generating electricity."

"I know what photovoltaics are," Bailey said. "I used to work for a cable station up north."

Lavalette nodded. "Yes, I heard that," he said. "You were an electronics engineer, right?"

Jake blinked at the man. Was it possible that Mr. Lavalette cared enough about his prisoners to take a personal interest in each of them? He confessed, "Well, not really. I mean, I had the training, but there wasn't much demand for designing new systems. Most of what I did was scavenging old parts to keep our receivers going, and making sure the parts we had in storage didn't deteriorate."

Lavalette nodded noncommittally. "Don't give up hope," he advised. "Somebody's going to need those skills, sometime. Now you better get back to your quarters before lights-out."

The next day was Sunday. It wasn't a day off—there weren't any days off on the workgang—but when it came time for the lunch break the prisoners were marched back to camp for other duties. Some of them were nasty—shoveling out the contents of the inmates' privy, to be shipped off to spread on some reclaimed land—and some were coveted, like cleaning the guards' quarters. Jake Bailey got an intermediate job when he and two others were put to unloading a truck that had pulled in from the Interstate. Its cargo was hams—not very appetizing hams, Jake thought; the reason Camp Three got them was that they had been rejected by the people at the Reservation, because they were kind of greenish around the edges and smelling unappetizing. But the cooks would cut those parts off, no doubt—Bailey hoped.

When their chores were done, the prisoners were free for the rest of the day. Most of the men went to swim in the creek; it was their only chance to bathe, or wash their stinking uniforms.

The sun was still too high for Jake Bailey. He thought of going into the water fully dressed, as many of the men had done—the uniforms would dry quickly as soon as they came out—but decided to wait. He sat under the shade of an ancient orange tree, listening to the gossip of other inmates. The big news was that there had been a successful raid on the storehouses. The old Cuban named Ronaldo—once an independent farmer, now jailed for the crime of digging an unauthorized well to irrigate his tiny sweet potato fields—had it direct from the driver of the ham truck: the raiders had disconnected the alarm system, overpowered the guards, and got away with a truckload of parts, more valuable than gold. "But what'll they do with them?" one of the prisoners asked curiously.

Becker answered for the Cuban. "Sell them to somebody on the Reservation," he said wisely.

Bailey frowned at him. "But that's who owned them in the first place," he objected.

"To some *different* person," Becker explained. "They're always stealing from each other there. Jesus, how do you think they stay there? Inside the Reservation they're all friendly and sweet, but there's not one of them that wouldn't steal his own brother's capital if he thought he could get away with it."

Ronaldo shook his head. "I would not do this," he said seriously.

"You don't know what you'd do," Becker told him. "If you ever saw the inside of the Reservation you'd do *anything* to stay there. Why, do you know, they have stores there where you can buy any kind of food—and toasters, air conditioners, all sorts of liquor—anything you would ever want, they have it there. Only they're hard to get, with so many of the factories closed down, so they buy up everything they can get their hands on."

"What was it like, on the Reservation?" one of the prisoners asked, and Becker began to tell him. In detail.

That was when Bailey got up and strolled away. He didn't want to hear about the heaven he could never hope to enter. Bailey hoped—still hoped—that one day he would get the job he was entitled to, his conviction for looting notwithstanding—after all, who kept records these days? How would any employer ever find out, unless he told them? But that was the limit of his dream. Living inside a Reservation was more than he had ever hoped for, because that was for the rich. And if Jake Bailey knew anything for sure, it was that he would never be rich.

Bailey pulled his floppy orange hat closer over his eyes and walked down to the bank of the stream, where it entered the culvert that went under the old Interstate.

There were occasional cars and trucks going by, sometimes the people in the cars peering out curiously at the prisoners. A dozen of the men were still in the water, but most of them were sensibly trying to stay under the shade of the few orange trees that lined it. This whole area had been an orange grove once, Bailey knew. Now it was in a state of decay. Many of the trees had been winter-killed in the deadly frosts that had caught the growers unaware; somehow, nobody had guessed that the violent weather that followed the global warming would include abnormal freezes, as weather patterns changed and cold air pushed unpredictably down from the north. And, of course, the juice plants had closed down in the general financial panics.

Bailey tried to imagine what the world had been like in those days. He had no personal memories of the great crashes; he'd been barely born in those early days of the 21st Century, when junk bonds and go-go banking had finally eaten out the health of the American financial system. Not just America, either; it was troubles at home that had made foreign investors take their money out of U.S. stocks and bonds; the Dow had dropped two thousand points in a single month. His parents had survived, somehow, long enough to put their one son through school—but by then it was the climate and the ultraviolet that had become the biggest enemies.

Bailey thought that his father had been glad enough to die. He didn't blame him, either.

"How's it going, Bailey?" a voice asked from behind him.

He turned in surprise and found that Mr. Lavalette was sitting on a camp stool under the same tree, watching the men in the water, his over-and-under gun in his lap.

When he saw Bailey looking curiously at him he patted the weapon. "In case I see a gator," he said briefly. Then he saw the expression on Bailey's face and laughed. "They probably won't come around with all these people," he said, "but you never know with a gator. Anyway, when you get a chance to shoot a gator you want to take it. You can always sell the hide, and the tails are good eating. Those glasses I gave you doing any good?"

"Oh, yes, sir," Bailey said, touching the silly things. "Thank you, sir."

Lavalette nodded, studying Bailey. "Let me see your hands," he ordered.

Bailey displayed them. They were dark brown now, almost the color of Mr. Lavalette's own skin; the burn had turned into tan.

"You ought to have gloves," Mr. Lavalette said. Bailey didn't see any point in answering that, and the guard nodded. "I'll see what I can do. For now, keep your hands in your pockets as much as you can when you're not working," Mr. Lavalette advised, talking to Bailey but still watching the stream. Half a dozen of the men had gathered under one of the trees, pointing up into it. Mr. Lavalette frowned, then shrugged. "I guess they're after the oranges, but the fruit's not ripe yet," he said, and turned his mirrorshades toward Bailey.

"What are you going to do when you get out of here, Bailey?" he asked.

"Get a job if I can," Bailey said promptly. "Maybe not around here. There's not much doing in electronics here, outside of the Reservation, anyway."

Mr. Lavalette shook his head. "There's not much doing in electronics anywhere," he said. "How about some other kind of job? Do you know what Becker used to do?"

"He was some kind of servant in the Reservation."

Mr. Lavalette nodded. "You could probably do that kind of thing, Bailey. He was a valet. Do you know what that is? It just means he sort of took care of Mr. Quinn Parkinson."

"I saw him," Bailey remembered. "In the courtroom."

Mr. Lavalette did not seem surprised. "Parkinson's a good man," he told Jake. "You could do a lot worse than work for him. You get a job like that," he said, "and maybe the work isn't much fun, but you get to live in the Reservation. Did you ever think of that?"

Bailey looked at the impenetrable shades, wondering if the old man was making fun of him. Did he ever think of that? What human being outside the Reservation had ever failed to think of what it would be like to get a job inside, where the air was always gentle and the food was fine and everything was always *clean*?

The other thing on his mind was that Becker, at least, had not shared the guard's high opinion of Quinn Parkinson. He was too intelligent to mention that, though, and so he just said cautiously, "I did hope, once, that I could get a job fixing things for them."

"That too, maybe," Mr. Lavalette agreed, "but the important thing is to get in in the first place, isn't it? Even as a valet."

"Sure," Bailey said bitterly. "After I finish working out my three ninety-day stretches here."

Mr. Lavalette's mirrorshades turned toward him for a moment, as though studying Bailey's face. "Oh," the guard said vaguely, "you never know."

He seemed content to leave it at that for the moment. Bailey wished he could see the man's eyes. Mr. Lavalette seemed like a fairly decent person, for a guard, but he was still a guard. You couldn't tell what he was thinking behind the shades. It was always possible, Bailey thought, that the man was trying to sucker him into some impermissible behavior. The camp had its quotas to meet, after all, and to meet them it needed a constant supply of convicts. The men said the guards were always trying to get some luckless convict to commit some infraction of the rules so they could send him back to the judge and tack on another ninety days. Mr. Lavalette wouldn't be doing that to him, of course, Bailey reasoned; there wasn't any point to it, not now, not so early in his first term, with the sentences the judge had already laid on him keeping him there for months to come.

But you never could tell, could you? Bailey had just about made up his mind that it was time for him to move away from this threateningly friendly guard when Mr. Lavalette said suddenly:

"This is hurricane weather, they say. You know, I miss the way we always used to know about that sort of thing. You're too young to remember when we had weather satellites that watched the clouds forming all over the world, and airplanes that flew right into the storms to measure wind velocities and temperatures. Those days, we could track them from the minute they started getting organized, way out off the coast of Africa."

"Those were the good old days, all right," Jake agreed, finding himself more and more ill at ease. It seemed that Lavalette had something on his mind, but what was it?

Lavalette paused, the mirrorshades turned toward the creek. Two or three of the prisoners were starting to climb into one of the old trees, but they weren't doing anything prohibited so Mr. Lavalette relaxed again. "Yes, the good old days," he went on meditatively. "When we had a space program. When I was a kid I hoped I might get into the astronaut program. Well, that didn't work out, but I managed to get a job on the security staff, you know, keeping an eye on the liquid gases and fuel when all that terrorist stuff was going on. When they closed the Cape down I stayed on, hoping they'd start up again somehow—"

"They *can't*," Bailey said, startled.

"Never say 'never'," Lavallette said strongly. "I admit things don't look real good, but there's a lot of us that haven't quit hoping." He turned the mirrorshades on Bailey for a moment, as though deciding what to say next. "You know what happened to screw things up, I guess."

"Well, everybody does, don't they, Mr. Lavalette? There was too much junk in Low Earth Orbit. It reached critical mass, with all those pieces of old satellites and stuff crashing into each other. Now people can't launch anything at all and hope it'll survive. I guess we're out of space forever."

"No! That isn't true, Bailey! Someday some of those old things will decay out of orbit, and then it'll be possible again."

"That would be nice," Jake offered, beginning to wish strongly he could get away.

The mirrorshades turned toward him. "You know," he said, "there's a lot of people that blame everybody over fifty these days. Especially scientists. They figure we're responsible, somehow, for the way the world is."

"Well," Bailey began, meaning to say, naturally enough, "Well, you are, aren't you?"—because if it wasn't the people who were alive in the days the world was trashed, who was it who did the trashing?

Fortunately for Jake Bailey, he stopped himself before the words came out of his mouth, because there was no sense antagonizing somebody who had given him a pair of sunglasses and might yet produce work gloves, or even something more valuable.

The old man seemed willing to change the subject, anyway. He stood up, peering toward the river. "Listen, Bailey," he said, "it looks like the men are mostly out of the water now, and I've got to pee. Keep an eye on them for me till I get back, will you? If any of them go back in you tell them I said to stay out because of gators?"

"Right," Bailey said promptly.

He got up and strolled around, needing to think. What was the old fart getting at? There was no real chance, Bailey was sure, that a broken-down workgang guard would have any way of getting him into the Reservation. But Mr. Lavalette had seemed to have something on his mind. . . .

Meanwhile, it paid to do what Mr. Lavalette had asked, so Bailey kept an eye on the water. It was true that most of the men were on the bank of the stream now, staring up at the men in the lower branches of the old tree.

A couple of them had rolled paper and sticks together to make a torch and were trying to get it lit—for what purpose Bailey couldn't imagine.

Bailey stood on the bank of the stream, looking up and down, and not just for alligators. In the still shallows along the far bank, under the thick mat of water hyacinth, there were water snakes; if you had to choose between a gator taking your leg off and a snakebite, you might prefer the snake, but you wouldn't really welcome either.

Bailey couldn't make much sense out of the old black man's behavior. It could be, he thought, that Mr. Lavalette was interested in something other than Bailey's future—like, for instance, his ass; it wouldn't be the first time that a guard relieved the tedium of his work by buggering an occasional convict. But Mr. Lavalette didn't seem like that kind. What he seemed like was that nearly extinct species, the sort of human being who went out of his way to do favors for people who had no way of reciprocating them—in a world where that sort of behavior had gone out of fashion.

The important thing was that Mr. Lavalette was a man who did favors.

Bailey tried to remember what little he had ever known about the space program. In the old days, before he was born, people had spent important money sending astronomical satellites up into orbit so they could study the stars. Bailey had heard some of the names, and knew that they came in many varieties. There had been "optical" satellites that were like giant telescopes, to begin with, just like the telescopes that still existed, probably, somewhere, on the surface of the Earth—except that these were out in space, so there were no clouds to get in the way of what they saw, and not even the thick, damp air of Earth itself to blur their images. But that wasn't all. There had been satellites that looked at the universe in different wavelengths—infrared satellites, ultraviolet satellites, satellites that could detect gamma radiation and X rays and God knew what other kinds. You could probably see some of those old satellites with the naked eye, if you knew where to look, because some of them were still up there. Not working any more, no. Most had been destroyed in collisions, and the rest had simply worn out.

That phase of human history was over. It was a pity in a way, Bailey thought, because while they were putting satellites up in orbit there was plenty of work for electronics engineers, and not just the kind of work Bailey had always done—when he had had any at all to do—simply trying to patch together old generators and appliances to keep them running a little longer.

Bailey turned around, startled, as he heard Mr. Lavalette yelling.

The guard wasn't yelling at him. The old man was running down toward the riverbank, his hat flying off his head, shouting at the men in the tree. "Get the hell out of there! Those bees will eat you alive!"

A little late, Bailey saw what the men had been doing. Someone had spotted a hive of wild bees in the tree, and someone else had thought a little honey would be worth having to supplement their camp food. That was a mistake. The men were jumping out of the tree in panic, and around them there was a haze of angry insects—not just the ordinary bees that farmers had cultivated for hundreds of years, but the Africanized ones that had taken over from the gentler Italian bees years before. The men were screaming and running now, and Mr. Lavalette was still running toward them.

That was another mistake.

For a minute, Jake Bailey thought of trying to help the old man, or even his fellow convicts. But what would be the point? The bees were following everything that moved anywhere near them. Bailey didn't debate more than a second. He turned and—not running, not attracting their attention—went back inside the screened barracks to wait them out.

*   *   *

None of the convicts were killed by the stings, but the men who had taken off their jackets and hats were so severely bitten that, an hour later, a bus pulled into the camp to take them away to the hospital.

The bus took Mr. Lavalette, too. He hadn't received as many stings as some of the others, but he was a lot older than they were. Bailey caught a glimpse of him as he was loaded into the bus and didn't want to see any more.

It wasn't until the least damaged of the beestung prisoners were brought back that Bailey was startled by hearing the news.

Mr. Lavalette had been arrested at the hospital.

Some essential materials had been stolen from his previous place of employment at the Cape, and he was charged with the theft. There was a chance that he might someday get back to Camp Three, or someplace like it, but he would not be a guard anymore. He would be an inmate.

4 ———

The next morning the air was sultry and the winds were gusting; the hurricane was not far off. While the convicts were slopping down their breakfast—ham soup, and sour-tasting—the guards were wrangling over whether it was worthwhile going out to the workpoint. There was no vote. The head guard simply cut off debate and ordered everyone onto the road.

The convict cooks hadn't cut the spoiled parts off the hams, and all the way out to the workpoint Bailey wished he hadn't eaten it. By the time they got there the head guard was in a fury because half the workgang was falling out to retreat behind a bush to deal with their diarrhea.

The only good thing about the day was that it was short. By ten in the morning the head guard came out of the shelter, shouting orders: "Pack it in! We're going back to secure the station." The hurricane was on its way.

The hurricane had a name. It was called Hurricane Ben, which meant it was the second that had come boiling across the South Atlantic toward the Americas in this year of 2042. (But of course it was still early January.) Not every hurricane's track took it through Central Florida, of course; some headed straight into the Gulf of Mexico, where coastal Texas was drowned out two or three times each year, or up the coast past Hatteras, or sometimes even harmlessly out into the ocean itself, where no one was at risk except for ships at sea and, maybe, the island of Bermuda.

Still, Florida got enough. The old truck stop had been battered by twenty or thirty major storms in the past dozen years. Most of what wind damage could do, wind damage had already done. Nevertheless, there were vehicles to be driven into their sheds and pieces of equipment to be lugged indoors, and the sheets of hoarded plywood from the last storm once more to be tacked up over the remaining plate glass windows of the old coffee shop. The prisoners did the windows first, because those were the hardest to handle in the gathering winds. By the time they got the last spare tire and wheelbarrow put away, rain was pelting down, the parking lot was a sea of mud, and the wind was howling louder than Jake Bailey had ever heard it before.

They huddled in their barracks, eating the sandwiches and coffee that were the last meal they would get that day. There wasn't much talk—the noise of the wind and the banging of tree branches and bits of debris against the buildings drowned out normal conversation—and what talk there was was about other storms. Bailey listened, but had little to offer. Of course Boston had not been

spared in some of the storms that clung to the coast, and
Cape Cod had been devastated a dozen times. But some of
these men were from Florida itself—one from Key West,
now an island again since the last couple of hurricanes
had destroyed several of the bridges that linked it to
the mainland; one from Orlando, where he had seen
Disney's Epcot dome blown away one summer afternoon.
Ronaldo Fiera was from Cuba—its cane fields drowned
in repeated floodings, the people without housing; Pete
Corning had spent one summer in New Orleans, where
the old cemeteries had become shallow lakes, with the
mausoleums of the dead sticking up out of the water.
Only Becker had ridden out storms in the dome of the
Reservation, where—he said—you'd hardly know it was
raining at all.

You know it here, Bailey thought. Over the scream of
the wind he could hear all that banging and clattering,
and the building seemed to shake. He wondered if the
roof would come off. It wasn't a particularly worrisome
thought; what did he have to lose?

Then there was a sudden loud bang and crash, nearby.
Ronaldo Fiera risked opening the door a crack, holding
it with all his strength to keep the wind from pulling
it out of his grasp. "It's that fucking sign!" he reported
wonderingly. "Smashed right into the guardhouse!" The
old Phillips 66 sign had finally lost its battles with the
elements; and when it was torn off its rusted hinges what
it had hit was the one remaining plate glass window of
the coffee shop, splintering the plywood shield and shat-
tering the glass.

Ronaldo pulled the door shut and stood with his back
against it. "Oh, shit," he groaned. "Next thing you know
those fuckers will be in here to get us out to put some
ply back, so their goddamn bedding won't get wet."

And, as a matter of fact, they did; and then Jake Bailey
found out what it was like to try to get another sheet of
plywood in place in the teeth of a hundred-mile-an-hour
Class A+ storm.

What the storm was doing to the old truck stop didn't matter, though. It was doing even more to the habitations of far more important people than a gang of convicts, for the hurricane had spawned half a dozen tornadoes in its passing.

So the next morning the convicts didn't go to the workstation. At daybreak the guards got them up for a cold breakfast, and then a twenty-minute wait in the hot, bright morning. There was hardly a cloud in the sky, and Bailey was beginning to wish they'd stayed inside the barracks, away from the burning rays, when an old flatbed truck grunted up from the Interstate. "Everybody on!" bawled the head guard. "You're going to do some emergency work in Citriola."

One tornado had gone through the northwestern corner of the town. When Bailey first saw it he thought it was a normal city street, surprising only in that there were only half a dozen trucks and wagons parked along it, none of them moving. Then he realized that it cut diagonally through seven or eight blocks of small homes. On each side of the swath roofs were gone, windows were blown out, structures were flattened, trees lay across buildings. But in the direct track of the tornado the ground had been sucked clean.

It was what was in the wrecked buildings that the convicts were there to deal with. Each of the tiny bungalows had held four, five, up to a dozen human beings of all ages, but the structures had been flimsy to begin with and most of them had already been searched for casualties. It was the handful of five- and six-story apartment buildings that were the worst. Each one had contained more than a hundred people. Some of the people were still inside. Some of those were still alive.

There wasn't much in the way of heavy machinery to help out, but there was little use even for what was there. Collapsed roofs had pinned people inside, and every time someone moved a beam or a panel of ceiling tile the debris shifted; all too often then there was a scream or a moan from underneath.

When there were no sounds left to hear inside the first apartment building Bailey was sent to, his whole crew was moved to what looked like another, but wasn't. Once this structure had been residential; now it was a hospital, and the patients included the whole spectrum of the disabled of 2042 A.D. There had to be four or five hundred patients in the building, six or eight of them packed into each apartment-sized room, their cots almost touching each other. These were the solar-radiation blinded, their eyes milky with cataracts; the weak and skeletal cancer-stricken with their suppurating skin sores; the victims of malaria and cholera and all the other ills global warming had brought to America. The blind needed only to be led to safety, and most of them were out already. Most of the others needed to be carried. There weren't enough stretchers, and so Bailey found himself climbing down tottering stairways open to the sun, where a wall had been torn away, with a moaning terminal case on his back.

There were more rescue people working here, strangers. In his concentration on the job at hand Bailey did not notice at first that some of them were convicts, too, but not like himself. These men wore leg irons instead of radiolocators. Clearly they were not from Camp Three.

Ten minutes later, on the top floor of the hospital, the rescue workers were ordered to halt while others shored up a tottering wall. Bailey stood by a blown-out window, trying to nibble a splinter out of his hand, Ronaldo next to him. "Ronaldo? Who are those guys with the leg irons?"

"Convicts from Camp Two," Ronaldo said. "Give thanks to God you aren't there. You wouldn't like what they have to do."

"It's worse than cutting brush?"

Ronaldo laughed. "They get put on cleanup," he said. "Toxic wastes, chemical spills—you know the old nuclear power plant on the coast? It hasn't operated for twenty years, but there's still all that spent fuel around it, and the casings have rusted open and the floods have washed the stuff around."

"Jesus," Bailey said. He had heard about the nuke. In one of the floods the nuclear power plant had been inundated—ruining the generators, yes, but that was not the worst part; the stored nuclear fuel had been drowned out, too, and radioactive wastes had soaked the whole catchment area.

"Bailey?"

Bailey turned. Ronaldo was staring down out the window. "What?"

"That woman down there—she was waving a minute ago. I think she was trying to get your attention. Do you know who she is?"

Bailey looked. He did know her. She was wearing clean clothes, her hair was neatly brushed, she looked healthier and plumper than when he had seen her last . . . but there wasn't any doubt about it. It was Sarella.

When he got to the street again there was no sign of her, and no time to look. It was nearly dark before the last casualty was extracted from the last wrecked building; Bailey had no doubt there were still human beings buried in some of the wreckage, but not any more living ones.

The prisoners were at last lined up to be fed. It was soup and bread, the soup thin and the bread hard, but delicious. Bailey sat on the curb, clearing shattered glass out of his way, and attacked his meal. He was almost finished when he realized that the man next to him was wearing leg irons.

The man leaned back wearily, rubbing his hand over his face. Bailey caught a glimpse of tiny tattoos on his hand—a design that Bailey recognized, since it was the same short line at the base of each finger he had seen on the hands of Sarella and Mr. Lavalette.

When the man saw that Bailey was looking at his hand he straightened up, peering at Bailey's own hand. Then he looked searchingly at Bailey's face, silent, as though waiting for Bailey to speak.

Puzzled and uncomfortable, Bailey tried conversation—the only kind he could think of: "What are you in for?" It wasn't entirely a social question; he was wondering what part of the criminal code made the difference between being sent with the workgang in the brush and the deadly labor of cleaning up poisons.

"Theft," the man said. He sounded disappointed, though Bailey could not guess why.

"And for that they sentence you to"— Bailey stopped himself from finishing the sentence with "death" and changed it to: —"cleaning up toxic wastes?"

"They said it was strategic materials," the man said wearily. He looked like someone who had been handling poisons; his face was a bloated yellow under the sunburn cream and his eyes watered.

"What kind of strategic materials?" Bailey asked curiously.

"Radio equipment. That's all on the priority list, though God knows what they want to save it for. Anyway, they said I stole some."

Bailey would have asked more, but the guards were moving among them, ordering them to get up. The convicts from the prison were marched away in one direction, the men from the workgangs in another.

When the men from Camp Three got to their truck the head guard was there. "Hold it," he ordered, as the first of them started to board. "First you get strip-searched, because who knows what you animals picked up while you were in those houses? Take 'em off and line up."

While the guards went through the pockets of their clothes, the thirty men stood there, naked, not even allowed to keep their hats, their bare skins exposed to the setting sun. That wasn't the end of it. Townspeople, going about their own business of trying to salvage what they could, watched curiously as, one by one, the men bent over and allowed their rectums to be plumbed by the guards. Ronaldo made a joke of it. "Hey, you doin' anything later tonight, Mr. Carter?" he asked one of the guards, and another prisoner cried:

"You got me, Mr. Bolzman; I've got a refrigerator I stole up there."

Even the guards were snickering, all but the head guard. "Get the fuck on the truck," he ordered. "We'll see how funny it gets tomorrow morning in the brush." And then, as Bailey was climbing onto the flatbed, "Not you."

Bailey stopped, puzzled. "What's going on, Mr. Bolzman?"

"You'll find out when you find out, but you're not going back with us. You go with Mr. di Cortini there."

"Where's he taking me?"

The guard looked disgusted. "Where you got no goddamn right to go, if you ask me. You're going to the Reservation."

5 ⸺

It was fifteen miles from Citriola to the first checkpoint of the Reservation, all highway. Jake Bailey and his guard did it in twenty minutes in the police car—would have done it faster if it hadn't been for the delays where workgangs were clearing downed trees from the road. It wasn't long enough for Bailey to figure out what he was doing there, and his escort had nothing helpful to offer. "They tell me bring you to the Reservation," he said, "and I bring you to the Reservation. Open the window on your side, will you? You don't smell so good."

It was full dark by the time they got to the check-point at the perimeter of the Reservation, guardhouse and gates along the service road, the cleared and wired space that surrounded it brightly floodlit and bare. Even at that hour there was a line of goods wagons waiting to be passed through, food and supplies for the rich people inside the dome, but the camp guard didn't want to wait. He pulled over into the outgoing lane without a pause, stopping right at the guardhouse. "Prisoner for Mr. Parkinson," he explained, leaning across Bailey to talk to the guards. Then it took five minutes of telephoning before they were allowed to travel the remaining mile to the immense, glowing dome of the reservation itself.

Jake Bailey had seen Reservations before—there were a dozen scattered around the Boston area, including the huge Back Bay dome—but only from the outside. His first impression of getting inside one at last was disappoint-ment: a lobby, a man at a desk, furnishings that were more or less new but by no means extravagant.

A tall woman was waiting at the desk. "Jake Bailey?" she asked, looking at him with as much hostility as inter-est. When he nodded she said, "I'm Lisa Sternglass, Mr. Parkinson's administrative assistant. Mr. Parkinson had to go out of town, so I'll have to orient you." She turned to the camp guard. "Mr. Parkinson asked for this man two days ago," she said, sounding even more hostile.

The guard gave Bailey an angry look, as though it was his fault. "I'm sorry, but we had this storm—"

"I know about the storm. All right, you can go; I'll take responsibility for—this person." She didn't wait for the guard to leave, but turned to Bailey. "Mr. Parkinson is considering offering you a job," she said. "Let's review your résumé."

And they did, the woman preempting the desk to check everything Bailey said against the computer. It was all there, Bailey saw: his school records, his family credit history—good enough, at least until his parents died—his three years with the cable station in Massachusetts.

"Very well," she said when she was through—sounding, Jake thought, reluctant. "Your record's no worse than we expected, I suppose. You'll have to have a physical, of course, and you'll have to get rid of those disgusting clothes. Come along with me."

She took him to another room where he was stripped and given a shower. The physical was quick—blood samples, and a medical tech feeding them into an analyzer—and then they reset the radiolocator on his ankle. When he had clean clothes he rejoined her where she was sitting before another workstation, busy at work.

"You passed your physical. When Mr. Parkinson returns he'll make the final decision as to whether or not he will accept you," she informed Bailey. "If he does, you'll be on trial, of course. While you're working for Mr. Parkinson you will be paid sixty cues a month in cash, as well as your housing and food. If you are satisfactory to Mr. Parkinson you may be kept on permanently, but that will depend entirely on how well you carry out your duties."

It did not even occur to Bailey to think of refusing—even to consider the question of whether he had a right to refuse. He simply said, "What kind of job is that? I assume it's something to do with electronics—?"

She looked at him curiously. "Electronics? Of course not. Mr. Parkinson is hiring you as his valet."

There wasn't really much need for a man like Parkinson, who lived alone, to have a valet. There wasn't much need for him to have two maids, either, not to mention a housekeeper, a butler, a cook, and a kitchen boy as well. (*Household* staff. Mrs. Sternglass and her two assistants were not counted there.) There wasn't any really pressing need for most of those people, either, because there were machines to do almost everything that had to be done to make Parkinson's life clean, pleasant, and effortless. Jake Bailey concluded that people like Parkinson were never really happy with mechanical servants, when they could have human beings to carry out their wishes instead.

Bailey did not complain. He went to bed, in a nicer room than he had ever occupied before, late that night; and he got up early the next morning, because he wanted the time to learn his duties. Claire, the chambermaid, showed him around. Mr. Parkinson didn't have a closet for his clothes; he had two airy and well-lighted rooms for them, where trousers, slacks, jackets, suits, and clothing of all kind hung, clean and neatly pressed, on revolving chain racks; there were formal clothes for evening wear and tuxedos (in three colors) for the slightly less formal; there were business suits and casual suits; golfing clothes and exercise clothes and riding clothes; and that did not begin to take in the underwear and socks and body linen of all kinds, not to mention shirt studs, cummerbunds, cravats, scarves, and accessories of every imaginable variety. There seemed to be at least a dozen of everything and it would be Bailey's job, Claire informed him, to select the right outfit every time Mr. Parkinson desired a change, and then to help him into it.

"That's it? Just get the man into his clothes?" Bailey asked wonderingly.

Claire giggled. "What your job is is whatever he tells you to do," she said, "but getting him dressed is part of it, all right. That's why you get to live in the condo, you know. So you can be there at any hour of the day or night for him." She looked at his expression and giggled again. "It's not so bad," she said. "It's only four of us that live in; the rest have to stay in the servants' apartments, and they're not as nice. They're underground, you know, and sometimes they're damp when the groundwater seeps in."

She paused for a moment, looking at him thoughtfully. "I'm one of the live-ins," she said. "By the way, are you married? No, I thought not. Well, I hope you last longer than the last four or five."

"You mean Becker?"

"For one," she said. "They've been coming and going like a parade. Come on, let me show you around the house before Mr. Parkinson gets back."

There were sixteen rooms in Mr. Parkinson's condo, counting the little suite set aside for the four live-in servants, of whom Bailey was to be one. Bailey saw them all.

Parkinson was obviously a man of eclectic tastes. The walls of his condo were covered with works of art, and they were of all kinds. Bailey knew little of art, but he could tell that many of these were original paintings by names he recognized—Mondrian and Winslow Homer, Picasso prints and Japanese netsuke carvings. If there was one dominating trait of Parkinson's collection it was space. The man seemed to be as much of a space fan as Sarella Simpson Grant had been. One whole wall was a mural of the surface of the Moon, and there were paintings of strange planets and suns, unrecognizable to Bailey, mostly signed by someone named Bonestell.

When Claire allowed him a peek inside Parkinson's study he saw more of the same. "I'm not supposed to go in here," she said, "except to clean up, and I can only do that when Mrs. Canaris is with me. Mr. Parkinson keeps this place private, but I guess you can look."

Bailey looked. What he saw was a large room with a fireplace (a fireplace!), and a bank of computer screens that surrounded a leather-topped desk (leather!). But there too were also models of spaceships and launch vehicles, and a large globe, lighted from within, that was not of the Earth. "That's Mars," Claire said, sounding proprietary. "I guess you could say that's Mr. Parkinson's hobby." Then she lifted her head at a sound Bailey hadn't heard. "The door," she said.

"Mr. Parkinson?" Bailey guessed.

"Oh, no, Banks would have met him if he were back in the dome—or you would have. Let's go see who's visiting."

There were two of the visitors, making themselves

at home in Mr. Parkinson's drawing room—like family. Which they were. Bailey recognized the woman at once. Parkinson's daughter. The woman who had testified against Ward Becker, Mrs. Phyllis Hegemeyer. She was as beautiful and immaculately dressed as ever, though now all she was wearing was a miniskirt and a bright, skimpy sun-top.

The man with her, Claire whispered while waiting her turn to present the new valet, was her husband, Dan Hegemeyer. Hegemeyer didn't get along with his father-in-law, she added, a finger to her lips; Hegemeyer was rich—of course; he was a bona fide resident of the Reservation—but not anywhere near as rich as Mr. Parkinson, and there had been family disagreements over the way in which, Hegemeyer thought, Mr. Parkinson was depleting the family fortune on his hobbies. "He wants to inherit it all, you see," she said. "Come on, she'll want to meet you."

And when Bailey was presented Mrs. Hegemeyer looked at him narrowly. Then she said, "I've seen you before. In court. Oh, God," she said, turning to her husband, "Father's hired himself another thief."

It wasn't Mr. Parkinson's home that astonished Jake Bailey—oh, it was luxurious, of course, but he had never doubted that rich people could afford anything they liked. What was remarkable was the whole Reservation. Inside the dome you would never know that a storm had passed, and if you looked at the people outside, playing tennis, going about their business, whatever that might be, or simply strolling, it was hard to remember that no one did that sort of thing anymore. The people of the Reservation didn't wear long sleeves and floppy hats to protect them from the sun. They didn't need to. The thousands of Buckyball geodesic bits that made up the dome did that for them, each pane coated with something (Claire told Bailey) that cut out the harmful ultraviolet-B radiation. So these people walked about in full sunlight in shorts and scanty tops, bareheaded—bare completely, he saw out one window that looked on a giant swimming pool, when they chose to go into the water.

Of course, Claire pointed out—quite unnecessarily— neither she nor Jake Bailey would ever go in that pool, filled as it was with clean, pure, fresh water. On the other hand, they could have as many showers as they wanted, with the same pure water, because part of their duties was to be, at all times, perfectly clean. Just like Mr. Quinn Parkinson himself. Just like everything inside the Reservation.

It had been a long time since Jake Bailey had had the chance to be really *clean.*

When Claire took him on a quick tour of the outside of Mr. Parkinson's home they didn't go near the pool, but there was plenty to see anyway. Mr. Parkinson had a quarter acre of gardens around his house, and they were rich, luxuriant, and well irrigated with that same pure water. (Jake had a quick, rebellious memory of the old Cuban on the workgang for irrigating his pitiful little plot of yams.) There were boxwood plantings cut in topiary shapes—a shuttle among the dragons and bears; Parkinson's space enthusiasm showing again—but Claire told Jake at once that he wouldn't have to do any gardening. They had, of course, a separate staff to take care of that sort of thing. And then she showed him the front door. It was flanked by two great tall glass cylinders that were fish tanks—a thousand bright orange fish on one side, the other side filled with silver and blue ones. "Of course, we never use this door," she told him. "That's just for company; we use the servants' entrance in the back."

"I wouldn't dream of it," Jake said shortly.

She looked at him, and giggled. "You'll get along here," she predicted. "The work isn't hard. You'll have to watch out for the Hegemeyers, but old Quinn Parkinson is easy enough to get along with, most of the time. And so, you'll find, am I."

*   *   *

When Mr. Parkinson came back Bailey caught only a glimpse of him, for he went directly into his study with Lisa Sternglass. The glimpse was enough to confirm the fact that he was indeed the man Bailey had seen at his trial.

Bailey concentrated on mastering his duties with Parkinson's wardrobe, running through the inventory kept on the household computer system; it showed every garter and collar stud, with data on when it had last been worn and how often. Then he was called in by Mrs. Sternglass, who led him into the study and left him there.

Parkinson looked him over carefully. "Jacob Bailey," he said, and was silent for a moment, as though lost in thought. Then he roused himself. "I'm sorry I wasn't here when you came, but I had some business to attend to over on the coast. Do you want to work for me?"

"Yes, sir," Bailey said immediately.

Parkinson looked dissatisfied. "You don't know me very well yet," he pointed out.

"No, sir," Bailey agreed.

Parkinson looked at him carefully, then nodded. "Yes, I remember you. They convicted you of looting."

Automatically Bailey began: "I didn't really steal anything, Mr. Parkinson—"

But Parkinson waved him to silence. "I know that, and it doesn't make any difference anyway. If you had, who would blame you? Everything around there's abandoned, and if you had found something you would have made better use of it than some dead people. No," he said, smiling affably, "you can forget about that. You're paroled to me now, and I'll get you a full pardon later on—assuming, that is, that you work out here."

"Thank you, sir." Then, greatly daring: "Can I ask a question? Why did you pick me?"

Parkinson shrugged. "Mr. Lavalette mentioned your name to me. He said he didn't think you got a fair shake."

"Oh," Bailey said, marveling—not so much at the information that Mr. Lavalette had put in a good word for him, because the old man was a kindly soul, as that Mr. Lavalette had had any contact with Mr. Parkinson in the first place. He thought of all the things he might say about Mr. Lavalette—that he'd given Bailey sunglasses; that he was less of a monster than the other guards; that the rumor was that he was a thief—and settled on the easiest one. "Mr. Lavalette was very brave," he said.

"You're talking about trying to rescue those idiots from the bees? That was stupid, not brave," Parkinson corrected him. "Anyway he paid for it, and now he's up against some trumped-up charge of theft. I've got my lawyers looking out for him in that matter. Tell me what you did in Boston."

Bailey did his best to keep up with the rapid changes of subject. He explained the cable network, and how it had gone out of business when their satellite finally failed. Parkinson looked somber. "There aren't many of those old satellites left," he sighed. He looked around his office. "You can see that I'm interested in that sort of thing," he said, encompassing the photographs and models.

"Yes, sir."

"Let me show you something," he said, and keyed on his computer. A schematic appeared on the largest screen. "Know what that is?"

"Yes, sir. It's a radio. It looks like the sort of transmitter we had in the satellite, before it died."

"How do you know that?" Parkinson demanded. "You never saw the satellite itself."

"No, sir, but we had to know how it worked. To keep it running, you know. It didn't die all at once; it lost six channels two years ago, and we had to rearrange its feeds."

"Suppose you'd had the actual satellite. Do you think you could have fixed it?"

Jake considered, decided to be truthful. "No, I don't

think so, not at the end. It stopped all at once. We thought it probably got hit by a piece of space junk. Before that, though," he added quickly, trying to divine what Parkinson wanted him to say, "when it first began giving us trouble, yes, then I probably could have fixed it. If I'd been able to get to it. If I'd had spare parts for replacements."

"And you were in charge of spare parts?"

"Yes, sir. Especially the kind you can't get any more. They had to be stored just so, you know. Keep the temperature and humidity just right—I had a hell of a time making sure the air conditioners were always working, you know, they rust up and freeze—"

"Yes, yes, I know." Parkinson picked up a model from his desk and fingered it a moment thoughtfully. "Tell me one more thing, Jake. Are you an honest man?"

Startled, Jake blinked at him. "Honest, sir?"

"Honest *and* idealistic. Do you want to make things better for everybody?"

Jake weighed that question carefully. Honest? Idealistic? As much as anyone, he supposed, which in these times was not all that much. But Parkinson's eyes were on him.

"Yes, sir," he declared. "I certainly would do my best, whenever I could."

It appeared to be the right answer, because Parkinson seemed satisfied. "All right," he said. "I'll talk to you again later."

By the end of his second week Bailey had come to several conclusions about his employer. The first was that Mr. Quinn Parkinson wasn't hard to work for—he didn't seem to mind having to tell Bailey which particular outfit he wanted to wear, or where to find things—and he never raised his voice to Bailey. (How did this square with Becker's report that the man had framed him for theft? Easily enough, Bailey decided; undoubtedly Becker had simply lied.) The second was that Parkinson was not much interested in business. When his managers came in from the field to report progress on the farms and factories Parkinson owned, it was seldom Parkinson himself who talked to them. That sort of thing he left to Lisa Sternglass or one of her helpers, or sometimes to his son-in-law, Dan Hegemeyer.

Parkinson's daughter and son-in-law, however, were a quite different breed. Belowstairs gossip told Bailey much about the couple: Hegemeyer had been one of Parkinson's managers, and when his daughter married him he became a full-fledged Reservation resident.

It was obvious that Parkinson didn't much like his son-in-law. Belowstairs gossip explained that, too. What Dan Hegemeyer wanted most of all was for Parkinson to die before he finished spending his fortune, so he and his wife could inherit it; and Parkinson seemed determined to spend it himself.

"What does the old man spend his money on?" Bailey asked.

"His hobbies," Claire told him. Only Parkinson's hobbies were not limited to collecting art objects and models of spacecraft; according to Claire, he was mad enough to buy the very originals themselves, what was left of them. "He even bought the whole Canaveral operation," she said, sounding almost proud of her employer's obsession. "That's where he was when you came in, making sure all his little toys were all right after Hurricane Ben."

And it was an obsession, Bailey saw that. Mr. Parkinson yearned for the old days. He wanted space travel back.

If Parkinson was easy to get along with, his administrative assistant was not. The woman kept popping up where she wasn't expected—keeping an eye on him, Jake thought, as though he might be planning to steal one of Mr. Parkinson's seven pairs of identical white duck tennis pants. He didn't think the woman liked him.

And so he was surprised when Mrs. Sternglass actually started what seemed to be a casual conversation with him. She entered the room where he was examining the seams of the jacket Parkinson had worn that afternoon, to see if any repairs might someday be needed, and stood silently watching him before she spoke. Then she said, "How do you like your job here?"

Bailey was wary, but thought that the woman was actually trying to be friendly. "Very much, Mrs. Sternglass."

"You've got everything you need? And the work's not too hard?"

"Oh, yes."

She nodded thoughtfully. "You can have this kind of job as long as you live," she said, dangling bait before him, "if you want it. And if you earn it. I'm not just talking about how you do your work. The important thing is loyalty. Mr. Parkinson appreciates loyalty more than anything else. If you're loyal to him, that goes a long way."

"I'm loyal," he assured her, wondering just what it was that he had to be loyal about.

"That's good. That means you don't gossip, doesn't it? Especially to people outside this household—like, for instance, the Hegemeyers' servants?"

"I don't even know any of the Hegemeyers' servants."

"They're a talkative bunch," she informed him disapprovingly. "You'd be well advised to stay away from them."

"Yes, Mrs. Sternglass."

She nodded. "Well," she said, looking at her watch, "the sun is over the yardarm, as they used to say, so it's time to take Mr. Parkinson his cocktail. There's no company today, so he'll have it in his study."

When Bailey brought in the little tray of canapés and the ice bucket Parkinson was sitting hunched over his computer. "Martini, sir?" Bailey asked, and the old man nodded without looking up. Only, as Bailey was getting the shaker and the glass and the precious bottle of Tanqueray out of the cabinet, Parkinson stirred himself.

"Two glasses, Bailey," he ordered. "I don't like to drink alone."

That was a surprise to Bailey, not entirely a welcome one. While he was stirring the drinks Parkinson was playing with his computer, displaying schematics and renderings of all sorts of spacecraft, gazing wistfully at them. "Sit down, Bailey," he said impatiently as Bailey sipped at his drink. "Do you know what these are?"

"Spaceships, sir?"

"*Wonderful* spaceships. Spaceships that never happened to get built," the old man said sourly. "This one's NERVA, that's fusion Orion. Atomic-powered spaceships, Bailey. They could have taken us all over the solar system thirty years ago. Or more. Bailey, I could have been on one of those ships, if they hadn't stopped research."

"It all stopped, sir," Bailey agreed, sipping cautiously at his drink. It tasted good, but the last thing he wanted to do was to let it fuzz up his thinking while he was talking to his boss.

"Oh, hell," Parkinson said, "I'm not talking about the Depression. The reason they didn't build these was that the queers in Washington signed a treaty that said you couldn't have atomic energy in space. Look at this one. Did you ever hear of salt-water rockets?"

"Like ocean water, sir?"

"No, no, a different kind of salt—*uranium* salts. You mixed them with water, you pump them into the reaction chamber, they reach critical mass, they blow and there's your power—all that reaction mass going out your rockets at nuclear-bomb velocities. Of course," Parkinson admitted, holding out his glass for a refill, "you can't use salt-water rockets for takeoff. You don't want radioactive fallout in the atmosphere. But you launch them with chemical rockets, and then you can go fucking anywhere."

"But you can't launch anything anymore, can you?"

"Now, no," the old man said glumly. He didn't have to say why. Everybody knew about the junk barrier in space; ever since the chain reaction that scientists warned about had happened—the pieces of space junk striking each other, splintering each other, filling Low Earth Orbit with four-mile-a-second bits of trash—space launches had become impossible. "But someday we will, Jake, if we have the nerve and the will, and then—"

He tapped the keypad. "Look at this. Did you ever hear of Gerard O'Neill?"

"No, sir," Bailey said, looking at the picture on the screen. It was a cutaway of something that looked like a huge sewer pipe floating in space—"huge" meaning really huge, because inside it there seemed to be houses and farms and parks, all painted onto the inner surface of the cylinder.

"O'Neill was way ahead of his time, Jake. He wanted to build these things. Habitats. Floating in space. Each one an independent world, really—self-sufficient, with a population of a hundred thousand people or so each. In *space*. Where you don't have to worry about what they've done to the fucking climate, or whether you're going to run out of raw materials, or whether you're polluting the Earth—because you're not *on* the Earth any more, do you understand?"

"I think so, sir," Bailey lied.

Parkinson sighed and turned off the screen. He took another drink of his martini and changed the subject. "My son-in-law thinks this is crazy—if not wicked," Parkinson said, looking sidelong at Bailey.

"But it's wonderful, sir!"

"I wish Dan agreed with you," the old man said gloomily. "Well, Jake, I'm keeping you from your duties, and anyway, those fine martinis have made me want to take a little nap. We'll talk again another time."

They did talk another time—they talked many other times, and always about the same thing. Space. it was a subject that held limitless fascination for Parkinson.

It didn't take Bailey long to realize what his part in these conversations was meant to be. Parkinson was a missionary in the holy cause of space exploration. Bailey was his superstition-bound primitive. It was Bailey's job to see the light. He did as he was expected to do. He became a convert. He learned the vocabulary of the space fanatic—easy enough to do, because the old man threw the resources of his library open to his valet, and it was all there. Bailey read himself to sleep every night with bound volumes of *The Journal of the British Interplanetary Society* and the books of people like Carl Sagan and Ben Bova and Robert Jastrow, and, above all, Gerard O'Neill.

In China, many years ago, such converts were called "rice Christians." Jake Bailey was the most fervent rice Christian in the Reservation.

The old man was pleased.

Claire was pleased, too, and told Bailey so. "You're smart," she said, admiring him—rather openly admiring him, in fact, and not just for his rapid acquisition of space lore. "You're the first one that he's really taken a shine too."

As it had become clear to Bailey that Claire's duties sometimes included a spell in Mr. Parkinson's bed, he was cautious with her. "I know he didn't like Becker much."

"Oh, Becker," she said contemptuously. "He was so

damn *earnest*. He really thought that everybody in the Reservation had a duty to conserve all our resources and not waste anything, not even thought, on idle dreams— not that there's any reason he shouldn't think that," she added, "because we're all entitled to our private opinions, aren't we? But he told Mr. Parkinson what his opinions were. Bad mistake. I'm glad to see you're smarter than that."

Jake ignored the implied criticism—or compliment. "I thought Becker got fired for stealing," he said.

"Well, that, too, I guess. But the big thing was he didn't think the way he was supposed to. Or at least act as though he did. Like you."

Which caused Bailey a problem. Claire was, after all, a nice enough–looking young woman who made it clear that she liked him, and their bedrooms were only a step apart. Bailey thought quite often of taking that step, but there was a risk involved in getting too close to his employer's now-and-then bedmate. As well as the risk of encouraging a woman who had seen through his conversion. A little later, maybe, Bailey told himself. It had been a long time since the faithless Sarella, but he could stand its being a little longer. When he was a little more secure in the best job he was ever likely to have— maybe then, he thought, maybe then he would see if that admiration in Claire's eyes translated into eagerness in bed.

But not now.

Phyllis Hegemeyer was always coming around, some- times with her husband. Then there would be a boring dinner, with Mr. Parkinson drinking heavily and nobody having a good time. And sometimes it was just the daugh- ter coming over by herself. Then she and her father would be in the study for an hour or more, and every- body in the house could hear their raised voices; and sometimes she would leave looking triumphant (because she'd got a little more money out of the old man) and sometimes glowering, because she hadn't.

Apart from that sort of thing, the job was actually rather fun. It wasn't just taking care of Mr. Parkinson's clothes and personal needs. It took Jake all over the Reservation—to the shops, where he was dazzled every time at the quality and variety of the goods that were on sale for the fortunate residents of the Reservation, to the park, and the theater. To all sorts of marvels, though not the swimming pool. Jake wished for that to be added to his catalogue of pleasures. He could almost feel how wonderful it was to go naked in the open, with the deadly solar radiations screened out by the dome and only the gentle warmth on his skin. But it remained only imagination.

Of course, if he were actually a *tenant* of the Reservation— But that would never happen. He put that dream out of his mind.

Or tried to.

Then one day Parkinson called him in and said, "Let's see what kind of an electrical engineer you are. My daughter says she's having a problem with her computer. Would you like to go over and take a look at it?"

"I'm sure she has her own technicians," Bailey said, surprised.

"She asked for you. The way it is," the old man said frankly, "when she asks for something, I find that it's easier to just do what she asks, you know. So go ahead. She'll be waiting for you."

Bailey had expected that the home of the Hegemeyers would be handsome, because that was how the owners lived in the Reservation, but he had not expected it to be *that* handsome. It was Parkinson who had the money, after all. His daughter and son-in-law lived only on Parkinson's charity. They didn't *need* a bigger home— as they might have, Bailey thought, if Phyllis Hegemeyer had had grandchildren for the old man—but their place was both larger and a whole lot more opulent than Parkinson's own.

The first thing that happened was that Phyllis Hege-meyer herself conducted Bailey to the study, looking him over carefully. "I hope you're honest," she said. "The last houseman of my father's here tried to steal my jewelry."

"Yes, ma'am," Bailey said, looking over the computer. He saw no purpose in mentioning to her that Becker had claimed he had been framed. The second thing that happened was that Phyllis took a seat in the study to watch him—making sure he didn't steal after all, Bailey supposed—until her husband came in and sat next to her.

Surely they didn't *both* need to watch him? And then, when he ran a couple of test programs through, the third thing was that as far as Bailey could tell there was nothing much wrong with the computer at all. It was a patchwork of modules, like every other computer; screens and computer body and modem and all from different models, coaxed to run together by someone more skilled than himself. But it did work. He ran a diagnostic, and that turned out clean; he asked them for one of their own programs, which turned out to be a spreadsheet of investments and earnings reports—numbers that dazzled Bailey by their size, though he knew how relatively poor the Hegemeyers were—and that came clean, too. "I don't see anything wrong," he reported.

Hegemeyer looked at his wife. "The keypad sticks sometimes," she said.

"I could clean it, I suppose," Bailey said.

"Then do it," Hegemeyer ordered. "How are you getting along with the old man?"

"Mr. Parkinson is a very considerate employer," Bailey said, and hoped it would be let go at that, but it wasn't. All the time he was degreasing the pad and checking the individual keys they were chattering at him, wanting to know how Parkinson spent his time—by which they meant how he spent his *money*—and whether Bailey thought the old man was not, perhaps, just possibly beginning to, well, *fail*.

It was a disagreeable hour for Bailey, mostly because he wasn't sure just what was happening. If these people wanted to pick his brains—and that was most likely, because there hadn't been any other real reason to get him there—they went about it in a particularly clumsy way. And when he told Parkinson about their questions the old man only nodded.

"They think I'm wasting their money," he said. "Only it isn't theirs, is it? It's mine, as long as I'm alive, or they can't have me declared incompetent. You've done well, Jake. Maybe it's time for you to do something more important."

But he didn't say what that "more important" thing might be. Nobody said anything at all, and even Claire, when Bailey tried to get some sort of clue from her, just shook her head. "He might have something about business in mind. Maybe. I don't know anything about Mr. Parkinson's business, though, do I?" And then she stretched and yawned, not unaware that her breasts showed off handsomely when she stretched, and added artlessly, "He's going to be out late tonight, I think."

"I've got to go to the store," Bailey said. He took his time there, too, picking out several new ties and a couple of frilled shirts for his employer to wear at that night's dinner. There had been a distinct implied invitation from Claire. Maybe, Jake thought, it was getting toward time to see just how far the invitation extended.

The thought gave him a pleasurable glow. When, back in Parkinson's condo, he caught a glimpse of Claire dusting in the hallway, he greeted her with a broad smile.

To his surprise, she gave him a frosty look in return. Wondering just what he had done, he put the new garments away in Parkinson's dressing room, and headed for his own.

His shower was running. Someone was taking a bath in his private room.

The only possibility he could think of was Claire, giving up on subtlety and taking matters into her own hands after all, but when he pulled the curtain back the woman inside was someone quite different.

She looked at him welcomingly. "Hello, Jake. Glad to see me? Hand me a towel, will you?" said Sarella Simpson Grant.

7 ———

The first question Jake Bailey asked his once (and perhaps still?) girlfriend, Sarella, was more complicated than he had expected.

He didn't think it would be, because the question was simple enough. It was just, "What are you doing here?"

The complications were that that question turned out to have several answers. The first answer was, "Getting cleaned up—thank God!" and that was true enough, because Sarella dried herself and pulled fresh new store-bought clothes out of her knapsack and put them on. The second was, "I've come to take you for a ride," and that was a surprise, too, because the ride was in a helicopter. *Mr. Parkinson's* helicopter. Waiting for them in the hot sun on the pad outside the dome, with a pair of big and mean-looking men, the pilot and the copilot, who expected them, and shepherded them aboard as soon as they crossed the hot little landing pad, and made sure they were strapped in. And then took off into the burning Florida sky with a jolt and a rocking of the ship and a storm of dust below them without another word, just as though Sarella had every right to call on them for taxi service.

"But I do have that right, hon," she told Bailey cheerfully, shouting over the noise of the helicopter. "Mr. Parkinson said it was all right. In fact, it was his idea." She studied him for a moment across the aisle between the seats, then gave him the third answer. "It's because he wants you to see for yourself what your *real* job can be."

"Real job?" Bailey demanded, but Sarella, smiling, only told him to wait and see. He tried a different tack. "I didn't know you knew Mr. Parkinson."

"Well, I didn't. Not personally. Not until now. But he's a wonderful man, hon. He wants to do something for the whole human race. Imagine! With his money!"

"Do what?"

But the answer was just another "Wait and see"— delivered sweetly and smilingly, and confidently. "Enjoy the ride," she advised. "Have you ever been in a helicopter before?"

He hadn't—how could he have, with helicopters scarce and the fuel they took even scarcer? He peered out through the sunproofed windows at the ground below, some of it jungle, some of it another kind of jungle, subtropical vegetation reclaiming old housing tracts, with the roofless split-levels almost invisible now under kudzu and creepers and brush. He did enjoy the ride, of course. For that matter he was (he discovered) pleased to see Sarella again, a lot more so than he would have guessed. He spent as much time looking at her, and thinking about her, as he did looking out the window, for he hardly recognized the tough partner in crime in this buoyant young creature. She seemed even younger than her real (and very young) age now. Not just younger, either, but, well, more vulnerable. She was flushed and excited as she leaned over the aisle to tap his arm. She was pointing downward, and when he looked he saw they were passing over the ruin of some huge old amusement park, a moldering storybook castle, a spiderweb trail of weed-choked canals that had once been a tourist ride.

And then, as the helicopter twisted in its flight, he caught a glimpse of some other towers, far ahead.

He leaned over to Sarella. "Is that where we're going?" he asked.

She nodded proudly. "The Cape," she said.

They landed on the cracked concrete of the widest roadway Jake Bailey had ever seen, a few hundred yards from the only vehicle in the world that could need that wide a road. It was rusted and most of its huge tires were flat, but Bailey knew what it was. He had seen its picture in a dozen different magazines from Mr. Parkinson's collection: it was a transporter, meant to take spacecraft from the distant, immense Vehicle Assembly Building (once taller than most skyscrapers, but now a crumpled shell) to one of the launchpads scattered around the complex. The launch towers still rose over their pads and flame pits. Whether they were rusted and useless Bailey could not tell at this distance, but they looked sound enough.

"Don't forget your hat and glasses," Sarella ordered, as the copilot came back to open the door for them. When Bailey had them on, and the lightweight pullover the copilot handed him, too, to protect his bare arms against the sun, he jumped out and stared around.

"It's the spaceport," he said, as though there had been any doubt.

"Mr. Parkinson's spaceport," Sarella said, half laughing. "Isn't it wonderful, hon? He *owns* it."

"Why?" Bailey asked. It was a very reasonable question.

"Because it's not just a game with him," she explained, looking at the copilot for confirmation. "It's real. It's going to happen, Jake hon. Not just now—"

"You damn bet it won't be now," Bailey said, staring at the ruin of the transporter.

"Oh, sure," she said loftily, "most of this stuff is in bad shape now. Hurricane Ben knocked down another piece of the VAB, but that doesn't matter. You'll see." She bit her lip, then said, "It means something, Jake, don't you see? It means the future for all of us."

He stared at her, and at the copilot who stood beside her. "You mean he thinks he can *launch* something?"

"He *knows* that, Jake," she said serenely. "We all do. I do. Mr. Parkinson does. Your friend Mr. Lavalette, he does, too, and there are lots more of us, and we've been working a long time." She laughed at the expression on his face. "Oh, hon, trust me! It's really going to happen. Not this year. Not even ten years from now, maybe, but someday; and when the day comes we'll be ready. Come on. We'll show you."

By the time they had marched a hundred yards along the old roadway a three-wheeled guard car had come speeding along to intercept them, with a pair of armed rent-a-cops. The copilot of the helicopter waved to them as the driver leaned out, one hand on the window (Bailey saw that that guard wore the same cryptic tattoo as Sarella herself), and the guards nodded and got out.

"Come on," Sarella said encouragingly. "Get in the car so you can take the tour. We're going to those ware-houses over there, but first I want you to look at Launch Complex Five."

The copilot drove them, leaving the guards talking on their commsets—asking to be picked up, no doubt. Bailey was staring at Sarella. The woman, he decided, was insane. If all the reading he had done in Mr. Parkinson's library had taught him anything, it had convinced him that getting back into space was no longer possible at all. Where were they going to get the raw materials? How could they build all the equipment?

Then the copilot stopped at the base of a launch tower, and there was no rust there. "This is the one we'll use," Sarella said confidently. "Someday. You can see it's been kept up. Mr. Parkinson was worried about it when Hurricane Ben hit, but he flew right down to check it out and—well, you see."

Bailey did see. Someone had put a lot of work in on this old tower. Then they pulled up between two large, low warehouses, and Sarella led him to the door.

There were guards there, too, big men with guns, but they opened the heavy door for the travelers to let them out of the searing sun and the soggy Atlantic wind; inside the building it was cool and quiet. Bailey wondered where they had got the air-conditioning to insure climate control, but there was no doubt it was there, and working.

He saw that the guards, like Sarella, had those little tattoos on the backs of their hands, like little numerals at the base of each finger. Bailey pointed them out. "What are the five little ones for?"

"They aren't ones, hon," she said, tolerant, "they're the letter 'L'. Lower-case 'L', do you see? Five of them. And they mean—?"

He pondered for a second, then had it. "L-5," he said.

"That's it," she said, glancing at the copilot, who had never let them get far away—saying nothing, watching carefully. "That's what we are, Jakey. We're the people who are going to put a real L-5 habitat in space— someday—and this is where we're going to put the stuff together."

"But," he began, and went on thinking of "buts" for her. And one after another she answered every objection. But you couldn't build a habitat and then launch it? No, of course not; the habitat would have to be assembled in space; but here they had all the components they would need. But there was no launch vehicle to get all that material into Low Earth Orbit! No, not yet, but there were two complete Shuttles in storage on the Air Force base a few dozen miles south along the coast; they would need refurbishing and repair, sure, but when the time came they could be put in commission in a matter of weeks. But two Shuttle loads wouldn't do the job, would they? No. Of course not; but each time a Shuttle landed it would be repaired and relaunched with another load.

It would take twenty launches, they estimated—but then they would have a station in space, and then the real work could start.

It was madness. Bailey told her so, over and over, while the copilot listened and scowled. But then there was the evidence of his eyes.

For the warehouses were filled with millions of dollars' worth of matériel, scrounged, saved, stolen, carefully preserved for years; this was no recent whim of Parkinson's; the man had to have been working on it, with plenty of help, for many years. There were acres of sheet metal and tons of specialized steel, all the kinds of steel that would build a shell in space. There were miles of fiber-optic cable and huge bolts of photovoltaic film. There were computer chassis and spare parts, microchips, X-ray etchers—there was more material there than Bailey had ever seen before, and all carefully preserved. When you looked at this accumulation it was almost possible to believe.

"Well?" asked Sarella Simpson Grant.

They were standing at the door. "I don't know," Bailey said honestly. "You said I had a job here. What is it?"

"To help, hon," she said. "Do whatever has to be done. Keep the parts operational. Steal more, when we need them. Whatever it takes to help us get back into space."

By the time they were on their way back, it was already growing dark. The pilot was flying the helicopter alone, because the copilot was standing near them, next to the open door, looking meditatively down at the seven or eight hundred feet that separated them from the jungle below.

"You said something about stealing," Bailey said to Sarella.

"You bet. How else could we get all that stuff? Oh, Mr. Parkinson bought a lot of it, as much as he could, but even Mr. Parkinson doesn't have *that* much money."

She thought for a minute. "Besides," she said, "some of that stuff other people want to use."

"Like for generating electricity?" Bailey hazarded. "Instead of running those old power plants?" He shook his head. "Seems to me that if Parkinson's so hot for the human race, why then shouldn't he be taking more care of the environment? Like," he said, waving around at the helicopter they were riding, "not burning up all this fuel for joyriding."

Sarella glanced at the copilot, who was listening intently. "But it's too late to worry about that kind of thing now, isn't it, hon? That's why Mr. Parkinson wants to go into space; we've wrecked this world, now we can build better ones." She shrugged. "There it is. What do you think? You know all this has to be a secret, hon."

Bailey grinned at her. "I sort of figured that out, yes."

"Well, then? We want you with us. He's trusting you, Jake. *I'm* trusting you. Will you join us?"

"Do I have to get tattooed?"

"Damn it, hon! Don't crap around. What do you say?"

Jake thought for a moment, but not very long. He thought of his life on the Reservation, he thought of the dream of building a better world in some other place— and he looked at the copilot, waiting stony-faced by the open helicopter door.

He nodded. "I'm in," he said.

She looked at him penetratingly. "You promise?"

"I promise," he said. "I'll keep your secrets, and I'll do whatever I'm asked to do."

She looked at him thoughtfully, then turned and glanced at the copilot. He nodded back, then crawled back into the right-hand seat.

It seemed to Bailey that Sarella was waiting to be kissed, just to seal the bargain, or not just to seal the bargain but because she thought that was a good idea anyhow. So he unstrapped himself and crossed the aisle and did it. Then, perched on the arm of her seat, he looked down at her.

"Suppose I hadn't promised?" he asked.

She looked flustered. "Oh, but I knew you would, hon."
Then, "I guess we can close that door now," she said.

8 ———

When they got back Sarella led the way immediately to
Mr. Parkinson's study. The butler nodded them past,
though Bailey caught a glimpse of Claire's hostile eyes
from the end of the passageway.

Mr. Parkinson greeted them nervously and didn't relax
until they were all seated and he had brought out the
martini mixings again. This time he did the honors himself, serving his valet. "I've had my eye on you, Jake," he
said, pouring a refill, "ever since that day in the court.
Mr. Lavalette gave you a good report, and Sarella—well,"
he said, beaming, "you know what *she* would have said
about you. But I wasn't really sure that she was looking
at you with the eyes of reason, rather than love."

"Thank you for giving me this chance, sir," Bailey
said.

"No, no! Just call me Quinn, Jake, all right? When
we're alone, anyway. Now, here's what we're going to
do. That storehouse outside of Citriola? We got some
good stuff out of it the other day, but it's packed with
data-processing hardware that we still want. So we're
going to make another try soon—"

And would have gone on indefinitely, if Sarella hadn't
coughed and looked at her watch. And then, of course,
they wound up in Bailey's bedroom, and then in Bailey's
bed, and it was a very pleasing evening for Jake Bailey;
and then, when he was sure she was asleep, he got up and
silently dressed and let himself out the servants' door.

*   *   *

No one was awake at the Hegemeyer residence, not even their butler. When the butler finally did come to the door, wearing a robe and a murderous expression, it took all Bailey's persuasion to get him to wake up his master.

"You goddamn *better* have a good reason," Dan Hegemeyer growled as he lurched into his drawing room. The butler had already begun to pour the black coffee that Hegemeyer had demanded.

"I think I do," Bailey said, and waited, looking significantly at the butler, until the man had withdrawn. "The thing is, I understand there's a reward for turning in resource thieves."

"That's a matter for the civil authorities," Hegemeyer growled blackly.

"I understand that, Mr. Hegemeyer. The trouble is, then they confiscate the criminal's possessions, don't they? So then the criminal is punished, but so are his innocent heirs. I thought maybe if I came to you quietly—and we worked out some other way of handling the reward—"

Hegemeyer was wide-awake now. He studied Bailey over his coffee cup. "You're talking about my father-in-law." Bailey shrugged. "But if you could prove it on him, it would still go public."

"I think," Bailey said, "that if you were the one to provide the evidence, then the courts might understand that you and your good wife shouldn't be penalized. Especially if you made it clear that poor Mr. Parkinson is, well, showing the effects of his age. He might not even get a jail sentence."

Hegemeyer brushed off the question of what would happen to his father-in-law. "What evidence are you talking about?" he demanded.

"Oh, there'll be *evidence*. I'll need some equipment—a recorder I can wear under my shirt, a camera, that kind of thing—and I'll need a little time. But I can promise the evidence will be there." He coughed. "And then," he said, "there's only the question of the reward to be decided, you see. Rather quickly, please, because I'd like to get back before anyone notices I was gone."

"Ten percent," Hegemeyer snapped, suddenly looking eager.

"I was thinking twenty percent," Bailey said. "In writing. Irrevocably. I'm afraid it will have to be at least that much, you see, because that's what I'll need to become a resident here myself."

Hegemeyer stared at him for a moment, then rang for the butler. "Get my lawyers over here," he ordered. "Right away. This gentleman and I have some documents to sign."

REPORT ON PLANET EARTH
A fifty-year retrospective for 2042 A.D.

by Charles Sheffield

The young have dreams;
the old have nightmares.

THE PAST.

They said it could only get worse.

The professional futurists, peering into their cloudy crystal balls back in the 1990s, could see many ways for the world to go downhill. Worse than that, the decline that they perceived would continue as far in the future as they dared to look.

The bogeymen of our grandfathers and grandmothers came in two main categories. First, there were impending shortages. The world would run out of many basic materials in the next half century; cheap oil would disappear by about 2030, natural gas by 2050, coal low enough in sulfur to be burned without polluting the air beyond tolerance would be gone by 2090. On the minerals side, although there was enough iron for centuries, lead would show a severe shortage by 2040, and copper by 2050.

Even more alarming, perhaps because less obviously a resource until recent times, the world's need for

155

fresh water would exceed fresh water production by 2020 or earlier. The world's tropical forests would be gone by that date, and the great boreal forests of the northern hemisphere would be in decline because of acid rain and the *Waldsterben* that by the mid-1980s was already affecting half the woods of Europe. In train with forest clearing and with overproduction from agricultural lands would come the loss of topsoil, and the decline in the total available area of arable lands. Food production potential would diminish.

Removal of forest cover, especially tropical forests, led to another and irretrievable loss: of *species*. Of the roughly five million total different types of plants and animals on Earth in 1990, about three-quarters of the species were to be found only in the tropics. In the decade from 1990 to 2000, about a million species became extinct. Another two million would go by 2020.

The projected shortages were alarming. The world would run short of many things. But perhaps more frightening was the second class of problem: the projected *surpluses*. Air pollution by nitrogen and sulfur oxides was on the increase. More and more water supplies were contaminated by harmful toxins. The loss of the world's forests would decrease the capacity to remove carbon dioxide from the air by photosynthesis. But at the same time the burning of fossil fuels would increase the level of atmospheric carbon dioxide. The globe would retain more solar heat, to induce an overall "global warming" of anything from one to five degrees Celsius. The polar ice caps would melt. Sea levels would rise, to inundate the world's coastal plains. Arable land, and cities, would vanish. The most pessimistic of the end-of-the-century seers thought it not impossible that Earth might move away from its eons-old stable heat balance, and suffer a runaway heat-death that would transform the planet into a hot and lifeless hell like the planet Venus.

All these ominous changes and trends, shortages and surpluses, were driven by one overriding "surplus." The world's population, which had been a mere billion in the year 1800, had increased to two billion by 1930, four billion by 1975, and six and a half billion by the year 2000. Projections for 2050 ranged from a low of eight and a half billion, to a frightening fifteen billion or more.

Our grandparents examined the trends, and made their gloomy projections. A world of desperate shortages, diminishing options, and degraded lifestyle seemed inevitable for all but a fortunate few. By 2042, or much earlier, starvation and deprivation would be the norm.

What they could not see, although with the benefit of hindsight we can discern them clearly, were the seeds, vigorously sprouting, that would transform the world before the middle of the next century.

THE TIME OF CHANGE.

In any era since civilization first developed on Earth, it is likely that people have looked back on the half century immediately before their own time, and concluded that those fifty years were uniquely important in the world's history. This tendency toward "temporal chauvinism" should perhaps be deplored; and yet we cannot help indulging in it, and asserting that the period between the year 2000 and today has truly been the most critical ever for humanity. For it is now true that for perhaps the first time in the whole of human history, the future looks bright.

The most important event of the past fifty years has arguably been not change, but *constancy*. And for the first constancy, we humans can take no scrap of credit. The stability of the vast self-regulating entity that forms Earth's biosphere has proved to be truly extraordinary. Any increase in carbon dioxide levels is followed, almost at once, by an even stronger increase in plant activity. As the burning of fossil fuels released carbon dioxide into the air, plants gobbled it up as fast as it could be produced. They increased their own growth rates even faster. During the last decade of the twentieth century and the first of the present one, plant growth everywhere showed increased vigor. The level of available biomass, for food, fiber, and fuel, increased. Just as important, stimulation of plant root activity accelerated the availability of humus and the renewal of topsoil.

The stability of the biosphere was due to Gaia, not *homo sapiens*. So was the vast and interconnected nature of Earth's total genetic pool, which makes the loss of even two and a half million species apparently of minimal practical significance. We can, however, take credit for the second great constancy. Basic materials did not and have not come into short supply, and it is humanity's own creations that must be thanked for this.

The first attempts to make robots, in the latter half of the previous century, were discouraging. Perhaps this was because, following popular fiction, computer-controlled devices were perceived as *servants*, functioning to perform such tasks as housecleaning and maintenance. It took a long time to realize that a human household is a vastly complex operating environment, intolerant of optimum performance, compared to the uniformity of a deep mine, a water filtration plant, or an ocean floor. Beginning with the remotely operated deep-sea submersibles of the 1980s, such as ALVIN, robots in the 1990s and early 2000s began to be employed in every structured environment that is difficult and dangerous for a human, and in every situation where tasks can be clearly defined: examples include mining for low-yield metals, for low-sulfur coal, and for iron ore, on land, and for the increasingly important metal, manganese, in the deep sea. Smart robots also permitted the mining of ores far poorer than those traditionally of economic value. Real material shortages are still a problem for the future, but that future is in the twenty-second century.

Increased use of specialized robots has also decreased failure levels. To give one example, robot coal miners, designed for this job alone, are able to sense ambient levels of methane directly and continuously, so that underground explosions have become a part of mining's primitive past. Miniaturized miners, a few micrometers across, also monitor sulfur levels in coal directly, and separate it out, while smart sensors in the support beams of the mines report continuously on stress and movement levels.

Even smaller specialized robots, at the molecular level in size, remove toxins from our air and water, at efficiency levels undreamed of in twentieth century "scrubbers" and filtration units. Since production plants and transportation systems are now obliged to take at least ninety percent of the air and water they use from their own effluents, recycling has become close to perfect.

As our unpaid and unsleeping robots have decreased the cost of raw materials, so also have they decreased the cost of refining and of manufacturing production. This, together with the development of increasingly robust and versatile plastics and ceramics, has lowered the final consumer cost of manufacturing. In terms of buying power, finished products are far cheaper than they were half a century ago. Since the early 2000s, robots have replaced humans in manufacturing, where robotic elements now run all factories, and in the agriculture of staple products, where high levels of judgment are not required. The danger and tedium of twentieth century factory or agricultural duties would be deemed totally intolerable by today's workers.

Robots, and robot control of operations, today are everywhere—or almost everywhere. The general-purpose household robot, flexible in tasking and safe in all circumstances, has proven vastly difficult to develop. Only recently, in the past ten years, have robots smart enough to simulate and interact with human activities over a broad range been evolved.

Humans can also take credit for the third great change of the first half of this century: widespread starvation, for so long the specter looking over our shoulder, has left the scene.

Starvation was banished by three changes. First, recombinant DNA methods allowed Earth's scientists to build super-plants, ones which can thrive with high productivity in areas too saline, too cold, or too arid for earlier natural plant forms. Half a century ago, only 15 million square kilometers of the world's 150 million kilometers of land were cultivated for food and fiber, and three-quarters of the whole was judged unusable. Today, over 40 million square kilometers of land are in flourishing cultivation, while the water demand for irrigation has been more than halved.

Second, wholly artificial food production from raw materials, dreamed of for centuries, became practical in the 2020s. It has never been wholly accepted or generally popular, and individuals claim to know the difference between real and synthetic foods (although double-blind taste tests show that they are deceiving themselves). But natural foodstuffs are preferred, and some individuals even grow some of their own food and make their own wine, although these cost vastly more than purchased products. However, artificially produced food stands as a bulwark against true shortages, and is available everywhere in time of need.

These two developments, of artificial food and of super-plants, would have been meaningless had Earth's population continued its blind and insensate increase. That it did not is due to one simple biological advance, already on the horizon more than half a century ago. This was flexible and foolproof contraception, and associated fertility control.

Although religious debate did not end in the 1990s (and has not fully ended today), pills for contraception, the direct descendants of the antiprogestin pill of the 1980s, had by 2010 become cheap, safe, and ubiquitous. This put the choice of family size, firmly and finally, into the hands of the people who bore the children: the women. In a single generation, families of more than four children became the exception. By 2020, two children per family was, as it is now, the norm.

Today's world population, of nine billion, is even showing signs of a slight downturn. For the first time in two and a half centuries, ever since Malthus made his ominous prediction, the diapason of population growth is not sounding through the whole of human affairs. The Right to Bear Children, like the Right to Bear Arms, is an ongoing argument; but it has become less bitter since the average family size has decreased. The future no longer holds out to us a prospect of universal malnutrition.

THE QUALITY OF LIFE.

Life at its most primitive is very simple: a sufficiency of food, clothing, and shelter.

Once these are satisfied, however, our demands become more complex. We begin to ask for more.

High on that list of increased demands comes our own health. Just as so many of life's joys and miseries depend on small things, a large number of those small things relate to how we are feeling, day by day. And when we do not feel good, we have come to expect that to change.

As the first half of the twenty-first century nears its close, we have become accustomed to noninvasive medical diagnosis, and to minimally invasive medical treatment. We expect that external imaging sensors, and internal "insensible" sensors, will tell us what is wrong with us. We expect that drugs, increasingly, will cure us. If we now consider it an inconvenience to swallow a pill-sized object, one containing its own sensors and able to be guided internally to any point of the human body without being felt by the patient, we are ready to faint at the idea of the old discomforts and dreads: the drawing of blood, the catheters, the proctoscopies, the biopsies. Death, or even cure, used to be accompanied by a thousand indignities. That is no longer considered tolerable.

And drugs are able, more and more, to cure us. All immunological functions are now understood, one by-product of the genome mapping that was well underway half a century ago. Cancer, the "big problem" of former times, is an immunological deficiency disease that is now completely curable; just as important, so are a hundred other ailments, as "insignificant" (except to the victim) as asthma, hay fever, and hyperallergic reaction to everything from foods to dust.

The growth process is understood also, for nerve, organ, and muscle cells. At its most spectacular, this has made possible the end of paraplegia, and the replacement of eyes, limbs, and internal organs; at a lesser level, it has allowed the removal of the curse of being freakishly taller, shorter, fatter, or thinner than the rest of humanity.

Another important contributor to the enjoyment of life is the amount of available leisure time; or, to invert that thought, any undesired arduous labor and wasted time diminishes life's pleasure.

The shrinking need for human labor as a result of computers and widespread automation was predicted in the 1950s, but its social implications were misread completely. People foresaw massive unemployment. Instead we have moved through this century to today's ten-hour work week, with positions shared by ten or more individuals who are on duty consecutively through the week. Although there is thus seven-day-a-week service for everything, it is a rare individual who works for more than two days of those, and then it is from choice, not necessity. The move to the two-day work week, plus vastly improved and widespread electronic communications and the freedom to work from one's home, has also made the words "rush hour" as much an anachronism as "computer error." The Robotic Revolution has proved to be rather like the Industrial Revolution, which at its outset forced lives of appalling toil on the less fortunate of the industrial nations, but ultimately provided their descendants with vastly increased leisure and personal freedom.

Two other phrases, now also anachronisms, were used frequently during the last half of the previous century. The story of the improved quality of life of the past fifty years would be incomplete without them. We are referring to *civilian murder*, and *global war*.

The former dwindled to its present negligible level when a basic distinction was drawn between the right to *bear* arms, and the right to *manufacture* arms. The first still exists, but strict curtailment of the second has led to a far safer world. Access to weapons able to kill many people quickly is now tightly controlled.

As for global war, this was already declining as a central concern by the 1990s. It finally vanished as a direct consequence of the world's increasing economic interdependence, with regional specialization on particular products. As the world's population became psychologically unwilling to endure the loss of available products, a reluctance to cut off the supply of those products increased. We now take for granted our year-round access to produce of all nations, just as we take for granted our seven-day-a-week, twenty-four-hour-a-day access to services.

THE FUTURE.

Certainly, we do not live in Paradise. There is still aggression, there are some holdout diseases.

And finally, there is still death. Human maximal life expectancy has not increased, although with new drugs and new protocols we have come to expect a healthy old age, with a thousand times as many centenarians—*vigorous* centenarians—as half a century ago.

For the average human, the world today *is* Paradise, compared with every earlier age. Yet we recognize it as an incomplete paradise.

Some of our still-sought changes are elusive, or may never happen. The world remains a Tower of Babel, with all attempts to create a universal language unsuccessful. However, the fact that eighty-five percent of the people in the world have a working knowledge of English makes that less of a worry.

Universal literacy still eludes us. Worse than that, we are divided more than ever into the *can reads* and the *can't reads*, a division more devastating to the latter group than anything of race or heredity.

The long-promised cornucopia of space still withholds its bounty. Three-quarters of a century ago it was seen as the place where earth's energy supply would be generated by sunlight, and beamed down as microwaves to the surface. Now we realize the historical inevitability of increased *energy density*, which has been a theme through all human history as animal, human, and wind power have given way to water, steam, chemical, and, finally, nuclear power. Humanity will never return to a major dependence on the diffuse natural fusion energy of the sun, now that controlled and economical man-made fusion energy is (at last!) a reality.

Half a century ago space, like the oceans, was also seen as a some-time utopia for human habitation. Today it still holds that future prospect; but for everyday life, earth orbit is the place where we put the dirtiest and most dangerous of human activities. For above all else, space is an *insulator*, a barrier against toxins of all kinds. We have at last learned the lesson of the Middle Ages; the privy and the well should not drain into each other.

We are still struggling to evolve the "ideal" political system for human affairs. The Individualist Movement is having the formative effect on this century that Democracy and Communism had on the nineteenth and the twentieth, but it is an unfinished story. We still yearn for a system which sets great controls on rash and harmful actions, but few controls on benevolent ones.

The central ideas of Individualism are possible only because computers have changed the old economic imperative of mass production. The guiding industrial principle, *Every one the same*, which favored the production of millions of identical copies, gave way early in this century to the principle, *Every one different*. With computer control, there is no increased cost for tuning products to individual tastes, and bigger potential markets. We are still working out the social and political consequences of this new production world. For example, houses are now mass-produced in central locations, yet infinitely varied. But we have not been able to define the optimal city size. Meanwhile, cities have been shrinking without formal controls, with more and more at about thirty thousand people. This is tiny by twentieth century standards, yet services are available within them at unprecedented levels.

Not everything looks like progress. The right to individual choices is more important today than ever before, and this century has seen the development of a new "Bill of Rights," which provides increased right to individual views, and more right to individual lifestyle. Like it or not, that right includes the freedom to abuse one's own body. People still do so, with a variety of drugs and other excesses. However, this is done only by individual desire. If the life of man is still, as Thomas Hobbes proclaimed, nasty, brutish, and short, it is so more from *choice* than from necessity. We have not reached the end of human frailty, and perhaps we never will.

Finally, we have not reached the end of science and technology, or even the beginning of the end. The understanding of the uses of silicon, which promises to dominate the world of inorganic structures as carbon dominates the world of organic structures, now seems to us to be in its infancy. Nanotechnology, with molecule-sized, human-designed machines employed everywhere from the inside of our own bodies to the deep interior of the Earth and the farthest reaches of space, has yet to achieve its perceived potential. The "simple" process of cellular differentiation remains a puzzle. The subnuclear world continues to produce as many surprises as it did half a century ago. And the structure of the cosmos, and its ultimate origin, is still a deep mystery.

We have much to learn. And we expect that much will change in the next fifty years. The words of George Santayana, written nearly a century and a half ago, seem as true today as in 1905: *Those who cannot remember the past are condemned to repeat it.*

Today, however, we add their converse, to warn us and our successors against complacency and rigid thinking: *If you remember the past too well, you will see no way that the future can ever be different.*

THE PRICE OF CIVILIZATION

by Charles Sheffield

Everything turned out all right in the end, but if Beth had just told her father at the beginning what was happening he could have made it a lot easier on her.

Todd would have found a way to explain things, and it would have *stopped*, then and there. He could have persuaded her. He knew he could. But he never had the chance.

It all started with one stupid field trip, no different from dozens Beth had taken at school over the past six years. Her class was driven sixty miles to the Bay, so that they could see the levees and salt farms and the new polders, already covered with sprouting algae. On the way home the skirt of the bus developed a crack. It began to lose air and height. Rather than fray the skirt against the ground, the driver made them transfer to public vehicles for the rest of the way.

No big deal, and in its way quite exciting for Beth. Todd guessed that she had ridden the PV system maybe five times in her life, but never so far and never through the deep basement. When she got home that night, she was full of it.

"You stand at the top of the escalator, and you can't even see the bottom! There's people all the way, riding on every step. And when you get to the platforms and the

169

speed slides, it's *noisy*, everybody talking at once. Even people who don't know each other talk and joke! I think it's a *lot* more fun than surface riding."

"The PV system makes a change, certainly," Todd said. He glanced across at Laura, who smiled and nodded. He didn't think she was really listening. It was the night of the week when she was home for dinner, but as usual her head was still at work.

"If you had to ride the PVs every day, though," he went on, "why, then—"

But Beth was already off in a different direction.

"Daddy, what's *shtupperbait*? Mandy says I'm trailing it, but she wouldn't tell me what it is. And it's not in my dictionary."

Todd wasn't sure how to handle that, but Beth had at last caught her mother's attention.

"You tell Amanda Wescott that she ought to have her mouth washed out with detergent." Laura Prince/Veblen turned to her husband. "And you, Todd, next time you see Gregg Wescott you tell him that his daughter needs talking to. *He's* the one who tells us Mandy's a perfect little lady."

"I'll be seeing him tonight. He's coming over to discuss my idea for a Primera investment."

"Well, then. You tell him."

"Right. I will."

But Todd didn't. He was not good at arguing with Gregg, who was fifteen years older and far more experienced. But it had to be more than years, because Todd couldn't argue with Laura, either, who was his own age exactly. And when Wescott arrived at the Veblen home complex, he didn't give Todd a chance to mention what Mandy had done. He was focused on investment opportunities.

"Forget Primera," he said. "I've got something a whole lot better."

Laura had returned to work, while Beth had retired to her suite. So it was just Todd and Gregg.

"But you were the one who told me about Primera," Todd protested. "You said that the specialty real food market was hot."

"I did, and it was—two years ago, when I told you to go into it. It made financial sense. Not now, though. Do you have an hour to spare? If you do, come with me and I'll show you something."

He knew quite well that Todd had left the evening free, to talk investments. But Todd didn't really want to go out.

"I don't know, Gregg. I told Laura I'd be home if she needed to reach me."

"Call her. I'm sure she'll tell you to protect the family holdings."

Todd didn't make the call. There was no doubt that Gregg was right. Laura had grown up as Laura Prince in a middle-poor background, and she didn't ever intend to go back.

He sighed. "Let me just say good-night to Beth. Then we can go."

He slipped away to her suite. Normally he would not have gone in without permission, but he was in a hurry. He expected to find her in the aquaroom, but she wasn't there—or anywhere else that he looked. He tried her study last. It was empty, although her computer was turned on.

His only reason for going across to it was to see which age-level dictionary was on-line to her. Any full-adult access would have included *shtupperbait* as a defined entry.

Sure enough, she was still connected to a juvenile base. He took the ten seconds necessary to perform a level upgrade, so she could check new words before she went blurting them out and upsetting her mother.

It was while he was waiting for the data base substitution to be made that he actually read what was sitting on the screen.

ELITE *MENU SELECT*: HISTORY OF THE ELITE—NEED
FOR—OPPOSITION TO—DEFINING ACT—GENERAL ACCEP-
TANCE—AMENDMENTS.

He assumed that it was part of a school project, but
something must have made him uneasy because he took
a mental note to find out just what Beth was trying
to find out about the ELitE Act. He also noticed the
little deep-focus card sitting next to the console, with
its image of a smiling youth and the scribbled name
beneath, *Danny*. He made no connection between that
and what was on the computer screen, and other than
wondering why such a handsome, bright-eyed lad had
never been mentioned by Beth, he felt little curiosity.
Beth and Mandy Veblen/Wescott and Chi-Chi Singletary
all had their private crushes on other students. They
were as changeable as the wind, and the girls felt that
parents had no business in that area. Todd rather agreed
with them.

"Find her?" said Gregg when he returned.

"She's in the house somewhere, according to the house
monitor."

Todd again felt a strange unease. But although later
he blamed himself for not following up and seeking out
Beth, he never had reason to change his mind about his
statement. She *must* have been in the house, that night
at least, for that was the same day as the first meeting
with Danny, down on the PV basement platform, and
Todd later confirmed that there had been nothing more
than five minutes of talk and the exchange of names and
pictures between Danny and Beth.

"In the house, but she's vanished." Gregg Wescott
laughed. "Tell me about it. It's the same with Amanda.
Always says she's in and the monitor agrees, but somehow
I can't find her at night. I think she hides on purpose.
Ready? Let's go."

The house system checked the two men out. Gregg
gave the system a forwarding destination for calls.

"Not my house," he said. "What I want to show you is at the Commensal."

That was good, at least so far as Todd was concerned. Gregg's family home was nearly an hour's run, but he time-shared a fifteen-unit Commensal no more than ten minutes away by surface net.

The night was warm for April, and the vehicle top stayed open. The air was unusually clear, with at least a dozen Hilabs visible as bright points of light moving steadily across the southern sky.

"That reminds me," said Gregg. "Laura promised me that the next time she went up, you and I could go along."

It sounded like a change of subject, but Todd knew better. The Neoteen backers were looking for funds. Laura said that everything in the orbiting Neoteen Hilab was fine, and she had been encouraging Gregg to buy in. But there had been rumors of problems. Gregg, cautious and conservative with his money, wanted to go up and see for himself before he made any investment.

"She's lifting again in a couple of days," Todd said. "I'll ask her."

"You'll come?"

"Sure." It was the easy answer, the one that avoided all argument. But later Todd would feel bad about that, too, because he became convinced that he had left Beth at just the wrong time.

Gregg had been counting on the Commensal's being unoccupied at this hour, and it was. The cleaning units had finished work and retreated into their wall receptacles, and the table was completely clear. Gregg went across to his personal floor-to-ceiling locker, opened it, and removed something in a white plastic box.

He moved across to open the chef, keeping his back to Todd and shielding what he was holding. After a couple of minutes of interaction between Gregg and the console, the chef door opened again.

Gregg turned back to Todd, sitting at the table. "How long since you tried Repro?"

"I'm not sure."

"But years at least, right? Okay, now try this." He was holding two plates. "Seem identical, right?"

Todd nodded.

"I'll tell you what you're looking at. One is genuine Primera black Beluga caviar from the Caspian sturgeon farms, refrigerated on the spot and flown twelve thousand kilometers to delight your palate. And one isn't. Now, you tell me which one you like better."

Todd picked up the thin piece of toast, sniffed the lemon juice, and took a mouthful. He chewed slowly, savoring the flavor and in no hurry to swallow. He nodded. It was first-rate.

Gregg handed him a glass of water, and another fragment of dry toast. "Clean your palate, and then try the other."

Todd did, wondering if Gregg was—not for the first time—fooling him by giving him two identical dishes. He ate the second serving of caviar, slowly and thoughtfully.

"They taste almost the same. But that one"—Todd pointed to the first plate—"is just a little bit better."

"I agree. Know why? Because it's a little bit less salty. But that one, the 'inferior' one"—Gregg pointed to the second plate—"that's the Beluga caviar. The one you like better, this one, is Repro. Pure reprocessed shit." He laughed, as Todd put his fingers to his lips. "See what I mean? The Repro people have said there's been a taste breakthrough on synthetics so many times, nobody believes them. But this time there *has* been a breakthrough. Believe me, Todd, someday soon people are going to catch on, and the bottom will fall out of the real food market. When that happens, Primera stock won't be worth transferring."

People still bought real wines, thought Todd, and they certainly couldn't justify the expense for those on grounds of taste. Why should real food be any different? But he didn't want to argue. And Gregg's advice had always worked in the past.

He sighed. "So what do you recommend instead of Primera?"

A big household argument blew up the next day, one that took Todd's mind off any thought of the ELitE or his daughter's perplexing interest in them.

On her next birthday Beth would be old enough for first reconstruction, and she said she wanted a lot of it. She was not satisfied with her nose, her eyelids, her cheekbones, her lips, her chin, her ears . . .

The list was endless, whereas Todd looked at his daughter, and marveled how Laura's strong, slightly angular features and his own rounded nondescript face could have combined to produce such perfection.

Beth was so beautiful. Any change would be a form of despoilment.

Fortunately, Laura agreed completely. "Not one thing," she said. "It's not as though this is the only chance. You can make your list again in three years, when you're fifteen, and then we'll see."

"But my legs—"

"—are still growing, and will be for years and years. I said no, Beth. Do I need to say it again?"

"You don't *want* me to be beautiful." Beth was almost crying as she turned to her father for support. But Todd shook his head, and said, "You *are* beautiful, sweetie. The most gorgeous daughter anybody ever had."

"Other people don't think so!" Beth ran out of the room, leaving Todd to ponder those words. Other people? But two days later he thought he suddenly understood the whole thing.

It was Sunday midday. There had been a high wind on Saturday night, followed by a false entry alarm on the house monitor. Now the sky was black and it was all set for a thunderstorm. Half a dozen flashes and warning rumbles were closing in from the east as Todd went hurrying around the Veblen compound perimeter, trying to check if one of the miniature sensors had been damaged before the coming downpour made his task far more difficult. Near the rear entrance, next to a little sweet-smelling patch of hyacinths, he found Beth sitting on a wooden garden seat. She was giggling, her eyes bright with happiness. Next to her, talking animatedly, sat a tall, serious-faced youth. He looked about three years older than Beth.

Todd was walking on springy grass, and neither of them noticed him until he was a few steps away. Then the boy jerked upright, and Beth followed his startled look.

"Daddy!" She glanced from one to the other, quickly and nervously. "Dad, I want to introduce you to a friend. This is Danny."

"I know it is. I'm Todd Veblen."

"Pleased to meet you." The boy hesitated, but at last he reached out and shook Todd's outstretched hand. "I'm Danny Shawner. You *know*?"

"I saw your picture." Todd felt guilty, admitting to Beth that he had been in her study uninvited; but it was worth it to see the radiant, chin-to-eyebrows blush that lit her face.

"Daddy!" Beth's protest was interrupted by a jagged spear of forked lightning, much closer, followed within a couple of seconds by the thunderclap. Huge raindrops suddenly spattered the garden seat.

"Inside!" shouted Todd, while the rumbles were still going on. He hustled them toward the rear of the house, giving neither Beth nor Danny time to object.

By the time they had covered the forty yards between bench and house, rain was pelting down. Todd headed for the nearest way in, through French windows into the "music room." Todd thought of it like that, because there were a dozen instruments scattered around, both natural and electronic. But no one in the house played any of them.

"Well!" He closed the double doors, as rain sheeted against them. "Just in time."

He stared at Danny. The boy was standing very close to the door, raindrops sending highlights off his thick black hair. "Are you all right?"

Danny's eyes were moving all the time, out at the rain and then back to the musical instruments. "I ought to be getting back home."

"In this! How far do you have to go?"

"A few miles," said Danny vaguely. He glanced beseechingly at Beth. "I shouldn't stay."

"Look, you're very welcome here." Todd waved his arm around the room. "And I'm going." It seemed obvious that he was the cause of the tension—the other two had been perfectly at ease before he arrived. "Make yourself at home, stay as long as you need to, and I'll order you both something to eat."

"I shouldn't." But Danny was staring wide-eyed at the electronic grand, and Todd did not miss that.

"Do you play?"

"Some." It was as though Danny's legs were carrying him across to the instrument against his will, and planting him on the padded seat.

"Then go ahead. I have other things to do." Todd wanted to make it very clear that he was leaving. He went to Danny's side, and again held out his hand. "It was nice meeting you. You are welcome here any time."

There was another moment of uncertainty before Danny Shawner stood up, took Todd's hand, and shook it. "Thank you, Mr. Veblen. But please don't get any food for me. I really have to go, as soon as the rain eases up."

"Which could be hours. I'll order something anyway. Beth will eat it all, even if you don't."

"Daddy! That's *horrible* of you!"

Todd left the room without replying. He closed the door, smiling, and stood outside for quite a while. He was not eavesdropping, at least not to conversation. He was listening to music. It began, hesitantly for the first few seconds, and then confident and glittering, a chromatic and complicated piece. Danny Shawner said he played "some," but the sounds that filled the music room were like nothing produced before inside the Veblen compound.

Todd felt ridiculously pleased with himself. Danny was handsome, and he had talent. But more than that, Todd *liked* him, and had from the moment he saw him. Danny was really personable, in a quiet sort of way. Trust Beth to find, for the first boy that she had a real interest in—and she *did* have an interest in Danny, no doubt about it—somebody out of the usual run.

And yet, when Laura called that night, to say that she would not be home until very late, Todd mentioned nothing to her about Danny Shawner.

Why? He could say that he did not want Laura giving Beth a hard time. But he didn't believe that answer.

It was not until the next morning, during his routine half-yearly physical examination, that Todd had time to ponder the question again.

He had to sit for a full hour in the monitor chamber, naked and as motionless as possible, while the tiny pill-sized internal inspection device that he had swallowed did its work. He could not feel it, but he knew it was wandering along through his body on a programmed route, while the external imagers and chemical sensors monitored his other functions. He was thinking, not for the first time, that people wouldn't always have to put up with this indignity, someday there would be a *civilized* way to perform detailed medical diagnosis; then his mind strayed again to Danny Shawner.

He thought not of Danny's quick intelligence and thoughtful eyes, but of his clothing.

Todd had no particular interest in his own clothes, and he wore whatever the automat put out for him every day. But kids were different. They were strong on cliques and covens and group identifiers. Beth and Amanda and

Chi-Chi put their Lazarus club patches on everything they wore, and the boys Todd knew from their school were no different.

But he had seen nothing on Danny's dark clothes, not one mark to show which societies and associations and clans the youth belonged to.

It was a small thing, but Todd found that it would not leave his mind. He waited impatiently for the examination to be over. As soon as it was finished he swallowed the second pill. This one had been assembled by the on-line patient care clinic in real time, during his examination, and it would correct and balance every minor physiological abnormality or chemical imbalance. Since the readouts showed nothing to require a more substantial treatment, Todd was free to leave.

He took the surface net, not to his home but to his own nearby Commensal. Four other owners were present, but no one was using any of the computers.

Todd signed on and made a general query for the county. He wanted to know how many *Danny Shawners* were listed.

"Are *Daniel Shawner* and *Dan Shawner* acceptable alternate forms for *Danny Shawner?*" asked the search routine.

"Sure."

"There are four entries. Watch for their display."

The information was very limited. Call IDs, but addresses, data receipt points, and all personal data were missing. Todd could not tell which one, if any, was the Danny that he wanted.

He hesitated before he took the next step. At last he entered his Inner Circle code, the sequence of digits that would allow him access to data banks denied to the general public.

Originally he had not wanted to join the Inner Circle at all, but Gregg Wescott and Eileen Veblen/Wescott had reinforced Laura's opinion. "Sure you'll be joining an exclusive club," said Gregg, "and sure, you may never need your membership. But you're a Veblen, dammit, and you deserve something special. There could come a day when you'd regret not having Inner Circle access."

And they had been right. Todd repeated his query, for Dan/Danny/Daniel Shawner. This time the Inner Circle codes could enter protected files and information spilled over the display. He had to take it in sections. Fortunately, subject age was one of the first data items in the file.

Daniel Gerald Shawner. Date of birth, January 28th, 1989. Age, 53 years. Address—

Todd cut it right there. Rejuvenation was coming along, but if there were any technique to make a fifty-three-year-old look like Danny, Eileen Veblen/Wescott would have used it long ago.

Dan Jackson Shawner. Date of birth, July 3d, 2004— Still no good.

Rupert Daniel Xavier Shawner. Date of birth, October 14th, 1944—

Worse and worse, nearly a hundred years old.

Daniel Sims Shawner. Date of birth, February 23d, 2025.

Bingo, thought Todd, just about as old as he looked. But the readout was continuing:

Age, 17 years. Address, 4033 Ridenour Station, Columbia. Access codes—

Columbia. It didn't look right for Danny. That was way over on the other side of the county, in an area that Todd never visited. How could Beth have possibly met Danny, if he came from so far away?

But the display was continuing:—*classification, ELitE. Parents: Arturo Giacomo Shawner, father, classification, ELitE. Mary Lou Draco, mother, classification, ELitE.*

ELitE? No way! That clinched it for Todd. Not one of those "Daniel Shawners" could be Beth's Danny. He must have misheard the name. Had Beth ever spelled it out for him? Maybe it was *Shorner,* or *Schorner.*

Todd tried again, working his way through all the spelling alternatives that he or the computer could think of.

Nothing. He leaned back in his chair. And as he did so, an association finally forced itself into his mind: Beth's computer inquiry about the ELitE, with Danny's picture sitting beside the console.

ELitE. It couldn't be, there was no way that it would happen. They couldn't have even met. (But what about the ride home from the Bay, the one that the school had made through the Public Vehicle system? If Beth had been waiting on the platform, when Danny had happened to come along . . .)

Todd left the Commensal in a trance. He remembered nothing of his journey home. He needed to talk to Beth—talk to her when Laura was not there. But today Laura had said that she might be home early. If she were . . .

Todd ran into the Veblen compound, fast enough to make the house monitor stutter into a HALT AND IDENTIFY command before it matched Todd's template. There was, thank Heaven, no sign of Laura.

"Is my wife home?"

"No, she is not," said the house monitor. "She sent a message for you. She will arrive at 17:00 hours, and she urgently needs to meet with you."

Less than half an hour. "Let me know when she gets here." Todd hurried on, straight into Beth's suite.

He found her there—with Danny Shawner. They were sitting side by side on a couch, looking over one of Beth's old scrapbooks of family events and family history.

Todd jerked to a halt. He had to ask the question—and suddenly he could not find the words. Laura or Gregg would have done it in an instant, without a second thought. But Todd did not want to hurt Beth.

"Hi there." His voice sounded peculiar, even to him. "Hi, Beth. Hi, Danny. Looking at the skeletons in the old family closet, eh?"

"Yes, sir," said Danny. He stood up, still holding the book. "Beth was reading me some old news items about

Stanford Veblen. I had no idea that he was her great-grandfather."

"You've heard of him?" Todd felt the knot in his chest loosen.

"Yes, sir. He's very famous. He was the founder of Angstrom Enterprises, and he developed the first generation of microrobots. But there are things about his life in here"—Danny lifted the scrapbook—"that I'd certainly never heard before. See."

He was holding the book out to Todd, inviting him to read from it.

"I got a bit of grit in my eye," said Todd, "riding in on the net. Itched and hurt like fury, and it's still watering. Would you read that for me?"

He was astonished at his own cunning. But then his heart sank. Danny was hesitating, glancing first at Beth, then at Todd, and back again.

"Go ahead," said Todd. *And I'm praying that you can.* And, when Danny still hesitated, "What's wrong?"

The youth looked again at Beth, his face unhappy. "Well, Mr. Veblen, some of the things in this article are not very nice."

"Oh, that's all right." Beth laughed. "Daddy knows about *them*—the whole family does."

"Very well." Danny nodded, and began to read: " 'An individual of unquestioned genius but equally undeniable eccentricity, Stanford Veblen sometimes sought funding for his audacious enterprises in ways that brand him as a rapscallion of the lowest order. He sold to his own mother large amounts of worthless stock in insolvent corporations, bankrupting her in the process. He drained employee pension funds of companies that he owned. He sought to gain access to the trust fund income established by his uncle for Veblen's own children—' "

Danny stopped. "His own mother? And his own children?"

"That's right." Todd was grinning, but he felt like laughing outright. Danny had read smoothly, flawlessly, effortlessly, without stumbling at all over the longest words. He just *couldn't* be an ELitE. Todd himself would certainly not have read so well.

"My father was one of those children," Todd went on. "But don't worry on our behalf. Stanford *tried* to get his hands on the trust funds, in every way he could think of. But they were tied up way too tight. Beth's right, you see, the whole family knew Stanford was a scoundrel, even then, although no one seems to remember it now."

Danny was staring at Todd's grinning face. He must have sensed something odd in the whole situation. Too late, Todd rubbed at his "injured" eye. But Danny had already laid the book down on a table and was looking at Beth.

"It's nearly five, you know. I ought to be going."

"You can't—not until you play." Beth turned to her father. "He wrote a piece of music, just for me, and he promised to play it today." She touched Danny on the arm, hardly more than the lightest of fingertip contact. "I won't let you go 'til you play."

The expression on her face made Todd delighted and jealous, all at once. How could a smile brim over with such happiness, how could eyes in a human head shine so bright? But that sort of loving look had once been reserved for Todd alone.

"I'll play it just once, then I'll go." Danny turned awkwardly to Todd. "It's nothing much, Mr. Veblen, but I'd be delighted for you to hear it, too."

"I'd love to. But not today, because I have things that must be done before dinner." That was a lie, but no more a lie than the grit in his eye, or Danny's polite invitation to come and listen. Beth's visitor didn't want Todd there when he played for Beth, any more than Beth herself wanted her father present—Todd could see her out of the corner of his eye.

But there was nothing to prevent Todd's listening, without their knowing. He waited until Beth and Danny had left for the music room, then quietly followed. The music that came through the closed door was fierce and urgent, not in the least what Todd thought of as "romantic." And yet it was more than Todd had ever created for anyone, in his whole life.

Beth's a lucky girl, he thought, as he started back to the main atrium of the house. *I don't think she knows how lucky.*

Then he realized that he still had one nagging question: What was Danny's last name? It could not be any of the forms that he and the computer had tried. And where *did* he live? His clothes today had again lacked any form of clan or clique identification.

He could ask Beth, but he didn't want to interrupt. And suppose that she didn't know the answer? There was an easier way. Todd changed direction and headed for Beth's suite.

The deep-focus picture of Danny still sat next to the computer, but now it had its own little frame. Todd picked it up, and walked with it closer to the room's monitor camera.

"Make a copy of this," he said. "I want a full resolution facsimile placed into my private data files. Store it under *Danny.* Then I want a search-and-match for identification of the individual. If necessary, use my Inner Circle access code in the inquiry. I want the results of that in my private data file also."

"Yes, sir," said the house monitor. "It is copied. Search is beginning."

Danny replaced the image exactly where he had found it. Feeling like a sneak thief in his own home, he headed again for the main atrium.

Just in time. Before he got there, the closest speaker of the house monitor spoke to him again. "Your wife has arrived. She is waiting for you."

"Tell her I'll be there in a few seconds." Todd increased speed. For some reason he didn't want Laura wandering the compound, looking for him and possibly running into Beth and Danny.

When he reached the atrium he realized that there was no danger of that. Laura was sitting with her knees tight together and her look-what-you-did-to-me-now expression on her face.

"You are the absolute limit, you know," she said as a greeting. "Where the devil have you been? I tried your club, I tried your office. I tried Gregg, I tried the medical center, I tried your Commensal."

"I was all those places. You must have just missed me each time. What's the problem?"

"This is." Laura held up two thin cards. "Hilab entry permits. You told me that you and Gregg want to go up with me tomorrow. You put me to all the trouble of getting the permits—it's not like going on a tourist ride, you know, these are restricted premises. And then you do not one damn thing to get yourself ready."

"I forgot about it."

"I *know* you forgot. You think that makes me feel any better? You *always* forget. You'd forget your own head if it was loose. Gregg was *really* upset when he found out you'd done nothing." She thrust the cards at Todd. "I've done all I can. If you and Gregg want to go up with me tomorrow, you've got to take care of these, yourselves, before eight o'clock tomorrow morning. That's when you have to leave—*if* you leave."

"I'll do it." Todd grabbed the cards. If they *didn't* leave, he knew he would be blamed by both Laura and Gregg. Why did they always seem to gang up on him?

Todd had expected a busy evening. It was more than busy. It was frantic. He and an irritated Gregg were chasing permits and approvals until well past midnight.

Todd had no chance to take a look at the new information in his private data base until the next morning, moments before they left.

The search-and-match had been successful. The identification had been made. Todd saw Danny's picture and read the screen. He had seen the identification before:

Daniel Sims Shawner. Date of birth, February 23d, 2025. Age, 17 years. Address, 4033 Ridenour Station, Columbia. Access codes, A-L. Classification: ELitE.

Gregg arrived, ready to go, and Laura brought him into the room just as a shocked Todd was clearing the screen. The three of them headed at once for the outbound spaceport.

They must have talked, but Todd had no idea what was said. That single final word, ELitE, roared inside his head and blotted out all external sounds.

Todd wanted to talk about the problem of Beth and Danny. He *needed* to talk about it. But he had no chance to do so until they were strapped in their seats, he next to Gregg, with Laura across the broad aisle and well out of earshot.

The prelaunch announcements had already been scrolled across the individual screens. Now they were being presented again as pure visuals, for the benefit of ELitE passengers. That gave Todd his opening.

He pointed at the Emergency Action cartoon, which showed a little manikin floating down on an escape chute.

"Ever ask yourself what you would do if Amanda went on a date with one of the ELitE?"

Gregg laughed. Given what had happened the previous night, he was in a surprisingly good mood. Having Laura around always seemed to make him effervescent. "Shoot myself, probably. But it's an impossible question, like, what happens when an irresistible force meets an immovable object. Mandy's too smart to do anything like that."

"She might not even know. Know he was ELitE, I mean."

"Well, *I* sure as hell would—I'd check it out, first thing. And that would be the end of *that*." Gregg smacked his hand viciously onto the armrest between the two men, then looked self-consciously at Todd. "Hey, don't misunderstand me. I have nothing *against* the ELitE. I work with them a lot, get on just fine with them. They have as many rights as we do. But hell, I don't have to tell *you* about ELitEs. Your own father was one of the prime architects of the Exempted Literacy Employee Act."

"He was never all that happy with it."

"Well, he should have been. If he were alive today, he could be proud of himself."

There was a period of necessary silence. The vertical ascent had begun, and the passengers were pinned back in their seats by a force of three gravities. It was four more minutes before the pressure eased and Gregg could wave his hand at the window, down toward the fast-receding Earth.

"I don't want to come on like the ancient geezer, but I am a good bit older than you and I remember what it was like *before* the ELitE act was passed. It was *terrible*, hunger and war and violence and instability, everywhere you looked. If Porter Veblen were alive today, he'd have every reason to feel proud of his work. It may not be Paradise on Earth, but anybody from half a century ago would think it is. Nobody's starving, nobody's sick, nobody's scared. There's no war, and almost no murder and violent crime."

"Dad was never convinced that the changes had anything to do with the passing of the ELitE Act. He always said all those things would have arrived anyway with mandatory birth control and stable population."

"Sure. Maybe they would. And maybe they *wouldn't*. Todd, I knew your dad. He was one of the finest, most thoughtful men who ever walked the earth, and that's just the way he *would* talk, giving the credit due to him to someone else. Porter Veblen helped to change the world once, and if he were alive he might have the nerve to change it again. But you find me *anybody* who would be willing to take the risk of going back to the old system."

"Maybe some of the ELitE would."

"They *wouldn't*, you know. That's been established in surveys, time and time again. You're forgetting something, Todd. The ELitE don't read and write, and some of them are pretty damn primitive, but in a lot of ways they're just as smart as we are. They don't want to get closer to us—any more than we want to be closer to them. And they know, as well as we do, that the world tried a hundred different systems in the past. But there's one big difference between all those old societies, and this one. *Ours works.* If you're rational, you choose to stay with what we have now—unless you're *looking* for wars to start up again, or you *want* to see hungry kids or sick men and women."

"Equal opportunity—" Todd said. But the vehicle announcement overrode his voice.

THE FORCES THAT YOU WILL FEEL FOR THE NEXT FEW MINUTES ARE ENTIRELY NORMAL. WE ARE APPROACHING FOUR HUNDRED KILOMETERS. THE ORBITING MOMENTUM BANK WILL BEGIN TO CHANGE OUR MOTION FROM VERTICAL TO HORIZONTAL, AND SET US INTO THE NEOTEEN HILAB RENDEZVOUS TRAJECTORY.

Entirely normal, perhaps, to a seasoned Hilab visitor. But for Todd, the odd combination of linear and circular accelerations left him unable to speak. And by the time it ended, they were moving along in a totally silent free-fall that made private conversation impossible. He noticed that Gregg was looking at him speculatively, and wondered if his own attitude had come across as casual as he would have liked. There was a horrible moment when Gregg turned to Laura, but he merely started to ask her about the agenda when they reached the Neoteen Hilab. Soon after that the protocol of Hilab entry and quarantine made it difficult to think of anything else.

Laura Prince/Veblen was one of the initiators and principals of the Neoteen Project, but that brought her husband and his friend no exemption from Hilab rules. They had signed nondisclosure agreements before they left Earth. Even so, they were deep-scanned on arrival for telemetry or recording devices.

While that was going on, Todd had time to realize just how much he wished that he were back home. So far as he was concerned the whole trip was totally irrelevant, because at Laura's urging the Veblen estate was already as deeply committed to the Neoteen Project as Todd's financial managers thought prudent. No matter how much Todd liked or disliked what he was about to see, there was no way that he could put in additional Veblen capital.

There was also no way that he could get any of his money *out*, even if—an unlikely prospect—Laura would ever agree to let him try.

She knew as well as he did that his investment was at its limit. It was no accident that all her attention was on Gregg Wescott, while Todd was ignored as soon as the facilities inspection began.

"I'm sure you'll want to spend most of your time talking with the Neoteens themselves," she said to Gregg, "but we're going to start with the wombs, because that's where people say we're having problems. As you'll see, they are quite wrong."

So Laura knew about the same rumors that had worried Gregg. Todd trailed behind the other two as they headed for the wombs. Most of the Hilab living quarters were held at a quarter gravity, but the artificial wombs were almost in free-fall—"because it makes no difference," explained Laura over her shoulder, "so long as you're going to be floating in a bath of amniotic fluid."

The wombs ranged along the whole interior side of the toroidal chamber. They were all the same size, each one almost large enough to contain a full-grown adult human curled into the foetal position.

"Not that it's necessary," said Laura. "Not with present plans. Although maybe in a few more years . . . Now, you can't actually *see* inside, of course, because there's no

light source. But the ultrasonics give you all the detail
you need. Look at the screen. These three are second
trimester."

The screens showed three tiny humanoid forms, each
no bigger than Todd's clenched fist. It was astonishing
to think that he had once been that way himself, or
that Beth had once been small and tight-curled just so
inside Laura herself.

Beth. Todd could not control the onward rush of his
thoughts. *Beth. What are you doing, right now?*

But Laura was moving on, too. "Nothing neotenous
about any of those, of course. Or of this group, either,
which is still in the third trimester. But look at *these*." She
had paused by another group of artificial wombs. "They
look the same from the outside, but the babies inside
could never be born to a natural mother. Neoteens, almost
at the end of the fifth trimester. Their heads are twice the
size of a normal woman's expanded birth canal—and the
brain capacity is still growing as fast as ever. See."

The ultrasonics display showed a couple of Neoteens
as big in torso and limbs as a normal six-month-old baby,
but with a much larger head and a massive jaw.

"How long do you keep them inside, before they're
born?" Gregg spoke for the first time since seeing the
wombs. He was fascinated, without any of Todd's sense
of revulsion.

"How long *do* we keep them, or how long *can* we
keep them?" Laura was staring raptly at the screen.
Todd could not recall her ever looking at him with as
much intensity.

"If we want to," she went on, "we can go well into the
eighth trimester inside the womb, with no problems. Of
course, long before that they've been receiving sensor
inputs. We start with the basics—math, music, phon-
ics—at the beginning of the third trimester. Normally, we
remove the babies from the wombs just before the end
of the sixth. That's about ten weeks more, for these two.
They'll be able to read by that time, and they already

have a good working vocabulary. To give you a basis for comparison, if the Neoteens were normal babies, they'd be nine months old by the time they leave the artificial wombs. But that statement doesn't mean much, because a normal baby's brain growth would have slowed down long before that. Our Neoteen's brain will keep growing at full speed for at least another year. It will mass a little more than three kilos when it's done, and that's double an average human brain."

Laura did something to the control panel on the front of each womb. "There. I just told them that we are here. Watch them, now. There are still plenty of Neoteen mysteries, even in the wombs. We still don't know how they're able to move themselves like that when they're floating inside the fluid."

The babies were turning to a heads-up, face-on position on the display, as though staring out at the visitors. The eyes as seen by the ultrasonics were sunken and closed, overshadowed by the big, hairless cranium and the lengthened lower jaw. Todd wondered how much of that was an effect of the imaging system.

"What do you mean, a good working vocabulary?" asked Gregg. He did not seem to feel Todd's uneasiness at what he was seeing. "They can't talk."

"Computer interface." Laura was working again at the panel. "I'm using it to say hello, and then tell them that we're going. Any other messages?" And, as Gregg shook his head, "All right, let's go. It's time for you to meet a couple of Neoteens that you *can* talk to."

Todd had seen the first ads for the Neoteen Hilab before they were released. Laura had filled every output in the compound with them for weeks, inflicting them on Todd and herself at all times of day and in all sorts of environments.

The ads came in two forms, labeled by Laura as "personal" and "abstract." The "abstract" ones contained no sign of Neoteen presence. They showed only a huge variety of new products and inventions raining down out of the open sky, with ridiculously low prices and ridiculously high capabilities. Then the camera angle slowly changed, questing upward until finally the distant origin of the bounty raining onto Earth was revealed. It was a Hilab, with the single word NEOTEEN written on its circular base.

The "personal" ad showed the inside of the Hilab. A dozen kids wearing NEOTEEN as a clan emblem on their sleeveless shirts were whooping it up in riotous invention inside a scientific laboratory. They were laughing, swapping wisecracks, and clearly having a terrific time. But they were also handing what they made to a group of serious, sober adults, and it was clear from the latter's awed and dumbfounded expressions that the gadgets produced so effortlessly were anything but goofy.

Advertisements were advertisements, nothing more. Todd had not expected to find either form of ad within the Neoteen Hilab. Yet what he saw was a curious mixture of two elements of the "personal" ad.

He and Gregg indeed went into a scientific lab, much like the one in the ad. They were introduced to half a dozen children, who were indeed wearing NEOTEEN emblems on their clothes. The youngsters looked no more than six or seven years old, although the sparse hair covering skulls too large for their bodies, together with the thin, delicate limbs, made ages hard to estimate. The lower jaws were oversized, fully as big as they had seemed in the artificial wombs, and their wide-spaced teeth jutted backward behind full lips.

But it was not any abnormality of feature that Todd found so disconcerting. It was the expressions. The faces were those of the *adults* in the ads—serious, brooding, and lacking any trace of carefree childhood.

The Neoteens did not joke. They did not laugh. They wanted to talk about what they were doing, and it was clear at once that they had been told that Gregg was the prime target.

Todd was ignored, until Laura caught his eye and jerked her head for him to follow her outside. "You're bored, Todd," she said, once they had stepped beyond the deep doorway of the lab. "I was afraid you would be. How would you like to be given a tour of the Hilab, while Gregg and I are in there talking?"

Todd nodded. It was not like Laura to be so considerate of his feelings, but he certainly did not want to appear ungrateful. He was handed over at once to a junior and non-Neoteen Hilab staff member. The man at least treated Todd with deference—probably because he knew the Veblen name, or Todd's relationship with Laura.

As the tour began, it occurred to Todd that Laura had been wrong. He had not been bored back there, he had been *disturbed*. The Neoteens might be much smarter than other humans, he was prepared to believe that. But he shuddered at the idea that any child of *his* might ever look as they looked.

On the other hand, they were humans, and not dumb equipment. Once you got over the look of the Neoteens themselves, what they had to say would surely be much more interesting than any Hilab tour.

Todd was already regretting his decision to go along with Laura's suggestion. His guide was taking him past standard life-support systems, laboratories, living quarters, and manufacturing facilities. Todd had no more interest in factories in space than he had in those back on Earth, particularly when much of the equipment had a run-down and seedy look to it. Like most other space structures, this Hilab had probably been underutilized for a long time. Todd guessed that it had been going cheap, which was why Laura and her backers had snapped it up for the Neoteen Project.

The tour seemed to go on forever. The only item that really caught Todd's interest was one that had more to do with Earth than with the Hilab. It was a high resolution point-and-shoot observing instrument, where the operator could specify a location on the surface of the earth. The big telescope would then focus and hold on that target, as long as it was above the horizon. Adaptive optics compensated for atmospheric turbulence, and the picture seemed to be taken from no more than a few hundred feet away.

While the tour guide looked on impassively—probably every visitor from Earth tried to see his own house—Todd compulsively dialed in the coordinates of the Veblen compound.

It was late afternoon there by local Earth time, and sunny. Beth ought to have been home from school for a couple of hours. Todd scanned the garden of the compound. There was no sign of Beth—or of Danny. But they might be inside the house, where remote observation was impossible.

He watched for many minutes, not sure what he was hoping or fearing to see, until the movement of the Hilab in its orbit began carrying him away over the horizon. And then, in the last few moments, when the oblique viewpoint made details much harder to make out, he caught sight of two figures approaching the compound.

Beth and Danny? It had to be, they were just the right relative height, and the taller one was dressed in the usual dark clothes. They were heading for the house.

For the music room. Or—for Beth's suite?

Well, if they were, so what? They were responsible kids, good kids. Both of them. Even if Danny was . . . what he was.

ELitE. *ELitE*. The worry came back, full force.

Todd didn't remember much of the rest of the tour. By the time that his guide left him at the Lab, the Neoteen children had gone and Gregg and Laura were sitting alone, absorbed in conversation. Todd halted before the deep doorway of the room, still full of his own thoughts and reluctant to go in and disturb the other two.

"I was sure you would," Laura was saying.

Gregg nodded. "I know you were, but I don't think I

believed you. *Very* impressive. But there's one question that you never have answered."

"What's that?" Laura caught Gregg's questioning glance. "It's all right, go ahead. The Neoteens are busy, and everyone else around here can be trusted."

"Very well. Let's talk about *failures*. You're trying something that's never been tried before, ever. It's a great experiment, but it is still an experiment. You must have failures."

"We've had deaths, certainly. Miscarriages, accidents."

"Sure. But I don't mean those. Don't play dumb with me, Laura. You know just what I'm getting at. New outsize brains, new in-womb teaching methods, new environment. All the results can't be positive. You must have instabilities. Madness. Maybe dangerous madness."

Laura was nodding quietly. "I won't deny it. But obviously I'm not going to talk about it."

"You need to—if you want an investor."

"Damnation." Laura glared at Gregg. Todd had seen that look often enough, but Gregg didn't blink or back off. Finally it was Laura who snorted and shook her head.

"All right, easy come, easy go. So I lose an investor. But I'll give you your answer—with a question. Why do you think we put the Neoteen Project up here, in a Hilab?"

"I assumed it was for the low gravity. The oversized heads, and the thin bodies—"

"Never. We could provide supports for those back on Earth."

"Cost, then? No, that's ridiculous, it costs *more* up here. What?"

"The *laws*, Gregg. The damned laws, national and international. But they don't apply to the Hilabs. They don't apply to what might happen to some of the Neoteens." Laura laughed, with no trace of humor. "There, are you happy now? You wanted to know, and now you do know. And I lose an investor."

"*Wrong*." Gregg reached out, grabbed Laura's hand,

and shook it. "You found one. Do you know what I look for when I make a financial investment? I look for *commitment*—for people who do what has to be done to make it work. Even if that means hardship for some."

"Hardship? That's a nice word for it. Isn't this the same Gregg Wescott that told me not long ago that we live in Paradise?" But Laura was smiling, really smiling.

"You remember it wrong. Utopia, I said, not Paradise."

"Utopia, Paradise. What's the difference?"

"A big one. You see, Laura, in Paradise *everyone* is happy. In Utopia some people will still be miserable."

Most of the conversation between Gregg and Laura had washed right over Todd, who was absorbed with his own worries. But he caught the last sentence, and he resonated strongly with its last word.

Miserable.

He backed away from the doorway. Gregg was right. If this were Utopia, at least one person in it was totally miserable. Todd did not want to talk to anyone.

And yet Todd *had* to talk. He could not mention the matter to Laura, because although she would certainly *listen*, she would just as certainly not *understand*. To her everything was always black and white, no shades of gray, no room for indecision.

So it had to be Gregg. Gregg was the best listener that Todd knew. But the conversation had to wait, for what felt like forever, until the two of them were on the ship in the descent phase of the return to Earth. Laura had stayed behind, to work in the Hilab for a few more days, and at last Todd was free to voice his worries.

He tried to ease into things gradually. "While you were with the Neoteens," he began, "I used the big onboard telescope. I took a look at the Veblen compound."

"Because you wanted to know what was going on with Beth," said Gregg flatly. "I hope you saw her. You know, she's been on my mind, too, ever since we talked on the way up."

Todd felt dizzy, and it had nothing to do with motion sickness. "On *your* mind? I don't see why."

"You asked me how I would like it if Amanda dated an ELitE. Some people might drop in a question like that as a purely academic notion, but that's not your style. It *is* Beth, isn't it? You think she might be getting interested in one of the ELitE."

"It's worse than that." Todd felt that he was betraying his daughter, but it was too late to stop. "She's seen him already, I don't know how many times. She really likes him."

And then the whole story came bubbling out, from the suspicion of a first meeting down in the PV basement level, through the picture of Danny in her room and the ELitE inquiry on her computer, on to Todd's final confirmation, just before he left for the Neoteen Hilab, that Danny was definitely an ELitE.

Gregg listened to everything without a word. And when Todd finally was done, and asked, "What do you think I ought to do?", Gregg still sat silent for a long time, staring tight-lipped out of the tiny ship window. They were within a hundred kilometers of the surface and feeling the first impulse of the ground laser, but outside there was still nothing to see but open space.

"I know," said Gregg. "I know that I play the older-and-wiser game a fair amount, and it irritates the hell out of you. It would me, too, in your position. But believe me, I try to be your friend. If I tell you to be careful about certain investments, like that one"—Gregg looked straight up, and smiled. The Neoteen Hilab was almost certainly not in that direction, but Todd knew what he meant—"I probably sound pushy and interfering, especially since I'm going to put money into it myself. But what's right for me may not be for you. I try to help."

"I know you do." It was true. Gregg's advice had kept Todd out of trouble a score of times.

"Well, keep that in mind before you decide that I'm sticking my nose in now. And remember, you did ask me." The smile vanished from Gregg's face. "First, let's talk facts. Tell me what you know about Danny Shawner."

"That's one of the reasons I find this whole thing so difficult. He's a really great kid. I like him a lot."

"*Facts*, Todd." Gregg did not raise his voice. "You like him. That's really nice, but it's hardly a fact. ELitEs can be as likable as anyone else. What do you *know* about him?"

Todd thought of the scanty data that he had seen as a result of his data query. "Not much, until I get a better data set. How old he is, where he lives, the names of his parents, that's about it."

"Both ELitEs?"

Todd did not say anything.

"Good enough." Gregg sighed. "Let me tell you something you won't want to hear. You already know *everything*, everything that you need to know about Danny Shawner. You know that he is an ELitE. That's enough. Has Laura met him? Don't even bother to answer that, I'm quite sure she hasn't."

"She hasn't. But Gregg, he's really smart, and he's talented, too. He must be self-taught, but he can read and write better than any non-ELitE you ever met. Better than me."

"I believe you. But that's not the point, is it?"

"And he has terrific musical ability. I feel sure he's brighter than I am."

"Could be. Still irrelevant. Don't fall into the old fallacy, Todd. I've often wondered why you and Laura didn't have another child."

"I'd have loved to. Laura vetoed it."

"Well, if she ever changed her mind, you'd be approved for a second one *instantly*."

"I don't fool myself, Gregg. I'm *not* smart. Laura's the bright one."

"So what? Todd, your cousin is a wonderful woman,

but do you think I married Eileen for her *brains*? She's like you, you've both got it there." Gregg pointed to Todd's crotch. "In the genes. For God's sake, your father was Porter Veblen, and *his* father was Stanford Veblen. They're known through the Seven States, both of them. But Danny Shawner, he's nothing, and his whole family is nothing. Try saying this to the people who share your Commensal: *My daughter, Beth, is the granddaughter of Porter Veblen, and the great-granddaughter of Stanford Veblen. She is dating an ELitE, and she wants to marry him.*"

Todd shook his head.

"Unthinkable? Right. Un*speak*able? Definitely. I agree completely. So you have to ask what it would be like if one of the Bulletins found out that a Veblen was going around with an ELitE kid from an Exempted Literacy Employee family—and that *you* already knew about it, and did nothing. Hell, never mind the Bulletins, think what Laura would say."

Todd thought about it. "She wouldn't *say*. She'd eat my liver."

"So it's obvious what you have to do, isn't it? You have to talk to Beth. You have to tell her she can't see this Danny person any more. Ever. Promise me, Todd. Promise me you'll do that."

They were in the final minutes of descent, riding the laser in to a feathery landing. Todd stared straight ahead. At last he gave a little nod.

"Say it, Todd. Say it out loud."

"I'll do it. I'll talk to her." Gregg was right, of course he was. And saying what must be done somehow made Todd feel better. "I'll tell Beth she can't have anything more to do with Danny."

"Well done." Gregg clapped his hand on Todd's shoulder. "You're a good father, Todd."

"It will be hard. Really hard. On Beth, I mean."

"Of course it will. Hard on you, too. But worth it. Todd, there's one other thing I have to say, and excuse me if

I get personal. I suppose you realize that Beth and this ELitE kid could be having sex?"

"For God's sake, Gregg. Beth's a *child*. She won't be thirteen for another two months."

"So? Did she reach menarche yet?"

"What?"

"Did she have her first period?"

"Long since. According to Laura, it was more than a year ago."

"There you are then. Don't forget you're dealing with ELitEs." Gregg's voice took on a rare hardness. "As they say, 'If she's old enough to bleed, she's old enough to butcher.' Todd, you have to get Beth inoculated."

"Inoculated!"

"You heard me. For your and Laura's sakes, as well as hers. It's not just a matter of diseases. What would you do if Beth became pregnant?"

"I don't know." Beth, his little Beth, pregnant? It was ridiculous! "I can't even imagine it."

"You're probably thinking, no problem, she could always get rid of the foetus."

"I wasn't thinking that at all."

"Laura would think that, as soon as she heard about it. But suppose Beth didn't want to? Suppose she *insisted* on having the baby? You couldn't force her not to, though we can both imagine her life after that. You know what it's like for ELitE and non-ELitE mixtures; they're neither one thing nor the other."

"I know it. Of course I know it."

"But *Beth* doesn't. All she sees is this nice, friendly kid who met her in the PV system and likes to hang around her. She's too young to protect herself—which means you have to protect her. It's your duty, as her father. She has to be inoculated."

"I could never tell her that."

"There's no reason why you should. No reason she'll ever know about it."

"The doctors—"

"You don't need a physician, not for a simple inoculation. All it takes is a two-second skin spray, you can use it on her at home when she's asleep. If you do what I did for Mandy, and get one that lasts just a couple of years, it will keep her from getting pregnant until she's old enough to make the right decisions for herself."

"The *standard* inoculation kit?"

But Gregg had paused, as though thinking about something else. "Don't ever forget you're a Veblen," he said abruptly. "We have to protect the family name. I'll get the kit for you. That way there's no danger Beth might see the transaction log."

The ship had touched down, gently. Todd had not even noticed the final stages of descent, but suddenly the port buildings were visible outside the little windows, and the doors were already cranking open.

Gregg stood up, stretching luxuriously. Todd remained in his seat.

"What about Laura?" he said. "What do you think I ought to tell her?"

"Everything. But not yet. Do that *after* Beth's been inoculated, and after she stops seeing the ELitE. Then Laura will tell you that you did all the right things."

Gregg made it sound easy. To him, or to Laura, it probably *was* easy. You did what had to be done, and said what had to be said, fast and efficient, and that was that.

Gregg had the inoculation kit the next day, so that Todd could use it before Laura returned. It was as easy to administer as Gregg had promised. Todd applied it that same night, as soon as Beth was soundly asleep. The spray was almost invisible, vanishing at once into the hollow of her neck just below the collarbone. Beth did not move.

But the rest of it was not so easy. Todd made sure that he was in the dining room the next morning when Beth came down for breakfast. He stood behind her as she waited for the chef to open and deliver her order, and he struggled to say the words that he had rehearsed a hundred times.

Beth, you must stop seeing Danny. He's an ELitE, and his kind and ours don't mix. I don't want you to see him anymore.

He opened his mouth.

And could not speak. Beth was singing softly to herself, a breathy little song of youth and happiness in a world where everything was sunny morning. Todd walked behind her as she went to the table, and sat opposite while she ate honey rusks and drank hot tea. When she had finished she smiled at him, deliberately ran a finger around the plate to scoop up warm honey, and placed her sticky fingertip in her mouth.

He sighed. "You're lucky your mother isn't here to see you do that."

She smirked at him. "I know. But you won't tell her, will you?"

She knew him, all too well. He shook his head, and watched as she wandered away out of the dining room. He had missed his chance, and he only dimly understood why. He consoled himself with the thought that it was a Remote day for school. Beth would study at home, so he would have other chances to talk to her.

Todd had those chances, plenty of them. He did not take them. And in mid-afternoon, Danny arrived.

This was surely the right time, the moment when Todd could explain to both of them the hopeless dead-end nature of what they were doing. But Danny was bursting with a new discovery, of an old and wonderful writer whose word magic could carry you away to places you had never been before.

" 'Where but to think is to be full of sorrow, and leaden-eyed despairs, where beauty cannot keep her lustrous eyes, or new love pine at them beyond tomorrow.' Just *listen* to that!"

It meant nothing to Todd; but he heard Beth catch

her breath, and suddenly his own chance to speak had vanished. Soon the two left the atrium together, hardly aware of Todd's existence. When he followed a few minutes later there was no sign of them. The house monitor was unable to tell him where they had gone.

That was his first failure, but not his last. He had breakfast with Beth again the next morning, and spoke to her only about schoolwork. Danny came soon after midday. Todd joined them in the music room, but once the three of them were together it was Todd who seemed like the intruder. The other two were so happy, so deep in conversation, so well suited in interests and personality, so clearly a *couple*.

But Laura would be home in another day. Already she had extended her stay at the Neoteen Hilab longer than usual, to accommodate another brief visit there from Gregg. If she returned, met Danny, and then learned of Todd's promise to Gregg . . .

Todd made up his mind. Next time he saw Danny and Beth he would sit them down, together, and he would tell them. He could not put it off any longer.

The next morning he canceled his plans to go over to the Veblen Center and waited at home. Beth came back from school at three o'clock. She stayed in the atrium, but she said little to Todd. She was obviously waiting, too. As the afternoon wore on she became steadily more restless and dejected.

When the sky light bleeding into the atrium began to fade, Todd went across and put his arm around her. "What's wrong, sweet pea?" He might not be able to talk to Beth about Danny, but he could certainly talk to Beth about Beth.

"Expecting somebody who didn't appear?" he went on, when she did not respond.

"Not really." Beth turned to her father, and laid her head against his chest. "But I was hoping. Danny said he was going to tell his parents about me today. He told me it might get them really angry. He said he'd come over here if he could, but I shouldn't be surprised or upset if he couldn't make it."

Todd squeezed her to him. "Never mind, Beth. He'll be here tomorrow."

But maybe not.

The surge of feeling inside Todd was not sadness or sympathy. It was *relief*. He had overlooked something obvious: Danny Shawner's ELitE family might be just as upset about Danny seeing Beth as Todd was about Beth seeing Danny. If *they* told Danny that ELitE and non-ELitE did not mix, and laid down the law, then Todd's unpalatable chore would be done for him.

He waited with Beth until he felt sure that it was too late for Danny to arrive. Then he went and directed the house monitor to include him on any call to or from Beth. It seemed certain that Danny would try to reach her, and when that happened Todd wanted to speak with both of them.

But Danny did not call. Todd went to bed late, able to relax for the first time in days; because, according to the house monitor, for the past few weeks Danny had always called Beth just before her bedtime, and tonight he had not.

He slept heavily and was jerked to reluctant wakefulness when it was still dark outside, by the insistent voice of the house monitor.

"An incoming call has been received for Beth Veblen, and has been reported to you according to your instructions. Do you wish to continue to receive calls?"

"What time is it?" Todd realized that he had been hearing voices in his sleep, and ignoring them.

"It is 5:11, A.M."

"Patch me in as a listener to the call."

"That is not possible. The call has already ended. It was not recorded."

Todd lay groggy for another few minutes, wondering what was going on. He was brought fully awake when the house monitor said calmly: *"Compound integrity has been breached. Beth Veblen has left by the front entrance and has failed to rearm the security system. Should it remain open?"*

"Rearm." Todd was already out of bed and hurrying into his clothes. "Can you give me a source for the incoming call?"

"That information is not in the general net."

"Use my Inner Circle access code."

"Inner Circle access code activated. The incoming call was from the Ridenour, Columbia, exchange. Do you want the number?"

"No. Give me the address, and tell me the fastest method of travel to get me there. Hard and soft copy outputs. Did Beth ask for any travel instructions?"

"No, she did not."

The call had come from Danny Shawner. Todd was sure of that, even before the confirming address appeared on the screen. He grabbed the plastic card output and headed at top speed for the compound exit. Since he had been provided with the fastest way to reach Ridenour Station, Columbia, and Beth had not, there was a good chance that he could be there before her. But suppose that she had already made the trip before—who knew how many times—and did not even have to worry about directions?

It was still dark outside, and all public lighting had been powered down for the predawn period. Todd did not try to think about where he was heading. His thoughts were with Beth. She was safe enough physically, anywhere and at any hour. But what had Danny told her, to make her leave the compound at once, without telling anyone, in the middle of the night?

He climbed into one of the cars at the compound exit, closed the door, and slipped in the plastic card. The car started at once, heading rapidly east. After a few minutes Todd could see the faint glimmer of false dawn ahead of him.

They were heading for a part of the county where he

had never been before. As the light brightened, Todd could take a good look at his surroundings. Instead of widely spaced and formally structured compounds, open gardenlike developments blended naturally into rolling countryside. When the car turned off the main highway, the signs along the narrow streets were all pictographs, warning or informing in nonverbal messages. The houses on either side were numerous and close spaced, but somehow they did not seem crowded. They looked peaceful and pleasant, still asleep in the early light.

Todd stared at them, and had the incongruous thought that he liked their looks better than his own compound. Of course, the walls and the security systems of the Veblen Compound were an anachronism anyway, a leftover from the bad times thirty years ago, a relic that Todd had never bothered to take out. But the garden atmosphere here was appealing. If the Veblen compound walls were to come down, Beth might like the increased openness, the greater feeling of freedom.

His thoughts dropped back to Earth.

Beth. And this was ELitE country. Todd was an alien here.

"*Destination,*" said the car softly. "*4033, Ridenour Station.*" They were rolling to a silent halt in front of a rambling structure, mostly underground, with its roof windows surrounded by blooming azaleas, and arrays of tulips and hyacinths growing in beds on the roof itself.

Todd scrambled out as the car door opened. He had not known what he would do if he arrived before Beth, but that decision would not have to be made. He saw her red-and-white checkered blouse, bright among the soft green of tall foliage. She must have ridden the fastest PV slides in the deep basement to get here so soon.

Beth was not alone. She was standing facing a man in a dark shirt and pants, and her right arm was held out, pointing at the steps that led down to the entrance of the house. He was shaking his head. Todd assumed that it was Danny, then realized in the next fraction of a second that it could not be. This was a stranger, bowed in the shoulders, shorter than Danny and with dark hair streaked with gray.

The man turned at the sound of the car door. Todd saw a bewildered, haunted face, with something of Danny in the eyes and cheekbones.

"Mr. Shawner?" Todd groped for the first name. "Arturo Shawner?"

At his voice, Beth broke away from the man and flew to his arms.

"Oh, Daddy." Her voice was breaking, her face red and her eyes swollen. "Daddy."

"You are the father?" The man stared at Todd with a changed expression. "Take her away. We did not ask her to come; we did not invite her into our home. He called her, after the second seizure. But we do not want her here."

"Danny—"

"You are too late." The expression was no longer bewildered. It had found something to hold on to, hostility and hatred. "He has—gone. He went very quickly, after the third seizure."

"What happened?"

"I—I struck him." The words forced themselves out, in little bursts of sound. "When—he told me—what he had been—doing with her. I did not hit hard—not hard, not hard at all. But—he fell. He fell. And then a seizure." Arturo Shawner glared at Todd. "For God's sake, go. Take her with you. If it had not been for her, I would not—and my Danny . . ."

A woman was emerging from the sunken door of the house, her face hidden within a white cloth. Arturo Shawner straightened up when he saw her, and suddenly his resemblance to his son was uncanny.

"No, Mary. Do not come out." He took Todd by the arm, and began to push him roughly away from the house. "Go, both of you. We do not want your kind here, to feed on our grief." He was urging Todd and Beth into the car. "Leave us *alone*."

"*Destination?*" said the car softly, as Shawner slammed the door closed.

"Home," said Todd. Beth had her face buried in his jacket. He turned his head as the car started forward. Danny's mother had not retreated, and now she and Arturo Shawner were clinging desperately to each other.

"Beth?" But she would not speak. She shook her head, and kept her face hidden against his chest. He noticed that she was holding a piece of paper in her right hand. When he took it from her she did not resist, or even seem to notice. She was crying, in long, dry sobs that came from deep in her chest.

Todd held her close, while with one hand he slowly unfolded the yellow sheet. He had expected a handwritten note of some kind. Instead it was a scrap of computer printout. He read it, slowly, his own mind a cloud of confusion and speculation.

> *When I no more can see your face,*
> *At midnight or at noon,*
> *I'll find the world a lonely place,*
> *And leave it soon.*
>
> *Eagles in an empty sky*
> *Move but never meet;*
> *My soul will through eternity*
> *Seek memories sweet.*
>
> *And in my thoughts, when you are gone*
> *Love itself will linger on.*

Beside the last two lines of the brief poem, the computer, cold and systematic as ever, had added the printed result of its automatic search routine: "These words cannot be copyrighted. They are a close paraphrase of the final two lines of 'Music, When Soft Voices Die,' a poem by Percy Bysshe Shelley (1792–1822)."

Beth wrote poetry. Had she written this, and brought it with her? Or had Danny himself written the lines, and left them for her as he lay dying? It did not matter. If Danny wrote this, he wrote it *for her*.

Danny, bright-eyed and intense, filled with wonder at the world. Danny, dead at seventeen. No need now for Todd to agonize over what he would say to them, or how he would say it. All his energy must go to comforting Beth. Fortunately that came naturally to him. But there was something else, something that burned and blazed in Todd's mind and would not leave. The car's motor was quiet and the interior compartment soundproof, but he seemed to hear the roaring of engines all the way back home through the waking streets and busy highways.

He led Beth into the compound, handed her over to the home medical unit, and stayed with her until the sedatives and tranquilizers had taken effect. He tucked her into bed with his own hands. After some hesitation he placed the poem on her dressing table. When he was sure that she was asleep he walked slowly back through the house to the atrium.

He sat in his favorite chair, unaware of the passage of time. He was waiting for Laura, but it was no surprise that Gregg Wescott was with her when she arrived. They had returned together from the Neoteen Hilab, and they were both laughing as they came into the room.

At the sight of Gregg's strong, confident face, all Todd's own uncertainties vanished. Todd *knew*. And that knowledge allowed him to speak, to Laura or Gregg or anyone else.

"Beth has been seeing an ELitE," he began. "A young man called Danny Shawner. She met him a few weeks ago."

He did not look at Laura or at Gregg. He went on without giving them time to say anything. "Danny Shawner died this morning. His father said it was the result of a blow. He hit Danny, and later Danny fell down in a seizure, what his father seemed to think was some kind of stroke. But Danny was young and strong and fit, and his father said that he did not hit him hard. A slap on the face or a smack on the head, that wouldn't have killed him—wouldn't even hurt him. Something else caused his seizures."

Todd finally turned to face Gregg Wescott. "I asked you about the inoculation. You told me that it was a standard one. But it wasn't, was it? It was the special one, the one you don't talk about. An Inner Circle inoculation."

Gregg remained quite calm. "Don't pretend, Todd. You knew it. When we first talked about it, I told you we had to protect the Veblen name. You knew what that meant. You knew Shawner was an *ELitE*."

"We're responsible—*I'm* responsible."

"*Wrong*." Wescott came across to where Todd was sitting. He put his hand on Todd's shoulder. "*Shawner* was responsible. The virus is transmitted sexually, and *only* sexually. If he hadn't taken your daughter, hadn't *defiled* your daughter, nothing would have happened to him."

"That sort of inoculation, without our knowledge or approval—"

"I'm sorry, Todd, but it wasn't like that." Wescott glanced at Laura.

"Gregg's right." She came across to stand in front of Todd. "He told me the whole thing, the same day the two of you discussed inoculation. He wasn't betraying you, dear. He just felt that I had to know, and it would be hard for you to tell me. When I heard everything, I agreed with both of you. I told Gregg to go ahead, and get you the inoculation kit."

"The danger—"

"Is nonexistent. Beth had her viral protective shot years and years ago, I made sure of that just in case. She's as immune as any of us."

"And if you're thinking of danger from evidence," added Gregg, "there's no sign of the virus ninety minutes after death. That must have passed long since. Do you know when he died?"

"Early this morning. I was there soon after. Beth was there when it actually happened."

"Oh, my God." Laura jerked forward, closer to Todd. "Beth saw the ELitE *die*?"

"I think so. I think she was with him."

"My poor sweet girl. It must have been terrible for her."

"It was awful. She's in her bed now, sedated."

"I have to see if she needs anything. God, I hope she's all right. That damned ELitE. If anything happens to Beth . . ." Laura hurried out of the atrium.

"Poor Laura. She's really upset about this." Gregg wandered across to the central counter. "And I know you are, too. But it's all over now. You both need to look forward, not back."

"Beth is devastated. Totally heartbroken."

"Of course she is." Gregg was busy, pouring three hefty drinks. "Beth's upset because she's a sweet, caring person. But hey, think positive. She's young, she'll get over this fast. She'll meet other boys. Just you wait, in another few months she'll fall for somebody else—*not* an ELitE, thank God—and you'll never hear one word more about Danny Shawner."

He came back and handed one glass to Todd. "Just now I'm more worried about you, buddy. You don't look good. Here, have a go at this."

"It was a terrible thing."

"I'll never disagree with that. But it was necessary. Civilization doesn't come cheap and easy, ever. If you want things to go on being good for everybody, you have to be ready to pay the price. We normally don't think that way, but today just happened to be your turn to pay."

Gregg went back to the counter and picked up another filled glass. "I'm going to give this to Laura, she can probably use it right now as much as you can. Stay here with your drink. I'll be back in a few minutes to tell you what Laura showed me in the Neoteen Hilab—really interesting stuff. Maybe you ought to try to make a bigger investment there after all."

He hurried off toward Beth's suite. Todd was alone. He sipped from the glass, grimaced at the strength of the drink, and then took a big gulp.

> *Eagles in an empty sky,*
> *Move but never meet.*

It was bad, but it could have been much worse. Suppose that Beth had become pregnant with an ELitE's child? Suppose that Shawner had infected her with some strange ELitE disease—officially there were no natural diseases left in the world, but there were always rumors. Worst of all, suppose that *Beth* had died.

But she hadn't. He had protected her, and now his little girl was safely tucked up in her own bed. She would be sad when she awoke, sure she would. But that just made it so much more important for Todd and Laura to think positively, to find ways of cheering her up over the next few weeks.

They had a wonderful, special daughter; and she was going to grow up smart, beautiful and loved, in a wonderful, beautiful world.

He raised his glass. *Here's to you, Beth, and a long, happy future. And here's to me as well.*

By the time that Gregg returned to the atrium, Todd was full of exciting plans for Beth and had poured himself another drink.

DEMOCRACY
IN AMERICA
IN THE YEAR 2042
by Jerry Pournelle

People often assume that science fiction writers can predict the future. While some of us sometimes pretend to do that, the reality is a bit different. No one can predict *the* future. What "futurists" from Bertrand de Jouvenal's *Futuribles* to pulp science fiction story writers do is attempt to describe a *plausible* future: one that we believe could be, or, at worst, that we can make *you* believe could be whether we believe it or not.

Such projections can be optimistic or pessimistic, and can take into account various trends—or ignore them. In this series, I chose the "cautiously optimistic" scenario. This fits fairly well with my personal view of the world: things do get better, sometimes quite a lot better, but for every several steps forward there is at least one step back, and a couple sideways.

With that in mind, let's examine where cautious optimism might take us in the year 2042.

One trend is clear, both from the projections of the scientists invited to participate here, and from the scientific literature: technology improves by leaps and bounds, and material wealth flows in abundance. For much of the world things are getting better. People live longer and eat better, and have more material

213

possessions; and where they do not, the failure to build a decent life isn't due to technology but to politics.

Indeed, it is clear to me that by 2042 we will certainly have the technical capability to supply every person on Earth with material possessions equivalent to what the average American enjoyed in, say, 1940; and to do that without undue strain.

Energy: there is no energy shortage if we don't want there to be one. Despite the popular myth, no responsible official ever said that nuclear power plants would make electricity "too cheap to meter"; but it is true that Japan and France are greatly reducing the cost of energy to their citizens by constructing nuclear power plants, and other countries are beginning to follow suit. There are some dangers to nuclear power, but they are not insurmountable; while the processing and storage of nuclear wastes is a solved problem. As Gerry O'Neill points out in his paper, we probably do not want to run the Earth exclusively on nuclear power plants; they would be singularly inappropriate for some nations which lack the necessary infrastructure.

However, O'Neill also points out that one doesn't need nuclear energy to supply the energy needs of the world. In addition to nuclear power plants, there are various forms of solar power. These include Ocean Thermal (OTEC) which has been successfully demonstrated off the Kona Coast of Hawaii; ground-based solar; and Space Solar Power Satellites (SSPS). OTEC works well—I do not share Dr. O'Neill's misgivings about "waste heat"—but can only be built in areas fairly remote from where the power is needed. Ground-based solar power is too diffuse and too irregular—not available on cloudy days, nor at night. Space-based solar power systems are quite feasible. For less than the cost of the Persian Gulf War the United States could have built the first of a series of Space Solar Power Satellites; proved the concept; built the first ground stations; and, most importantly, have built the fleet of new generation space transportation systems for lofting the required materials to orbit.

Of course SSPS provides only electrical energy, and most of our economy now demands oil; but this is no real difficulty. We already have alternate ways to distribute energy if we have enough. Almost any stationary oil-burning system can be converted to electricity, provided that we have the electricity. Many mobile systems would work as well or better with electricity than with oil; others can be powered by propane; and as a last resort, we can use electrical energy to make oil, either from shale beds, or if need be from scratch. That latter isn't very efficient, but given SSPS it becomes feasible.

SSPS has a further benefit. One way to reduce the cost of SSPS systems is to use extraterrestrial materials in their construction. It may or may not be possible to build the Silicon or Gallium Arsenide solar electric conversion cells on the Moon, but it is certain that the Moon contains everything needed for the actual structure of the SSPS; thus one benefit of SSPS will be a permanent Lunar Colony.

(Sanity check: the Lunar Society already has the names of over three hundred highly qualified and technically skilled Americans willing to live permanently on the Moon, provided only that the logistics base to put them there and keep them supplied has been built.)

Access to the Moon means access to all the Solar System; and it is easily proved that ninety percent of all the material resources easily available to humanity is not on the Earth. The Moon contains most of the heavy elements—iron, titanium, silicon, aluminum—needed by heavy industry, as well as more-than-abundant supplies of oxygen. It lacks many of the lighter elements, such as carbon, chlorine, and hydrogen. These could be supplied from Earth; but it is more likely that they will be supplied from stations in the Asteroid Belt. The Moon, Mars, and the Asteroids among them contain everything needed for an industrial economy; moreover, any raw materials lacking on Earth can be supplied to Earth.

Moreover, as Dr. O'Neill points out, it is quite feasible to build colonies in space. The late Dandrige Cole once predicted that the majority of humanity would live on space colonies within five hundred years. He may well have been right, assuming that the human race continues to exist for that long.

Some projections of the future raise questions about food production and pollution: will we starve, or so destroy the environment that we cannot live in it?

It seems unlikely. Food and pollution are not primary problems: they are energy problems. Given sufficient energy we can produce as much food as we like, if need be by high-intensity means such as hydroponics and greenhouses. Pollution is similar: given enough energy, pollutants can be transformed into manageable products; if need be, disassembled into their constituent elements.

It's fun to go into the details, but in fact there's no need to do so. On any trend analysis whatever there is no real danger that the world in 2042 will be short of the technology required to produce abundant material goods at reasonable costs, both economic and environmental. This is also the conclusion of all the scientific papers submitted to this project. We have the science and technology necessary that by 2042 we can, if we will, provide luxury for many, plenty for the majority, and enough for all mankind.

Why, then, is our optimism cautious? Why do we feel uneasy when contemplating the future? The Cold War is, if not ended, at least greatly mitigated. Technology pours forth. When we contemplate food, energy, material goods, and even pollution, we have good reason for optimism, but in fact most of us are not optimists; for we see some frightening trends.

First, political: The United States is at present governed by a Congress which has less turnover than the British House of Lords; by a Senate which has fewer new faces after an election than the Supreme Soviet of the USSR. Our politicians pay themselves and their aides more than most of us expect ever to make, while simultaneously exempting themselves from the laws they pass for us to live under. The result is that "We the people" no longer think of "our government"; rather we see "the government." The government in Washington is not "us," it is "them," not "our Congress" but "the Congress." Cynicism abounds.

Meanwhile, our economy gets more and more bogged down in rules and regulations.

Example: after years of study the national commission on acid rain reported that industrial pollution isn't the problem; that most of the acid rain isn't a serious problem anyway; that some lakes are threatened, largely by the runoff from forests which are not allowed to burn naturally (thus converting the tannins and other acidic forest products to smoke); but those lakes can be saved by a few tens of thousands of dollars spent on lime each year.

The report came in; but instead of following the scientific advice, we have brought in a monster political program which will add many billions of dollars to the costs of industry, and which will accomplish almost NOTHING toward ending lake acidity. Few who have taken the trouble to inform themselves on the acid rain situation want the acid rain bill; but the monster has a political life of its own now, and it seems that nothing can be done.

Example: after years of discussion about Global Warming, we now find that the Sun is going into a period of minimum sunspot activity, and we may be threatened, not with Global Warming, but a new Little Ice Age such as the Earth experienced from the fourteenth to the eighteenth centuries. However, although the scientific community has turned away from Global Warming (this year's annual meeting of the American Association for the Advancement of Science had very little on the subject, and none of the highly visible experts who came to last year's meeting), the politicians continue to act as if it's the most important problem facing us. That too has taken on a life of its own.

Example: environmental regulations require pollution controls that make a PERCENTAGE reduction in sulfur content of gases from coal-fired furnaces. The result is that Western coal, which has low sulfur, goes INTO the highly expensive stack gas scrubbers with lower sulfur content than is in the gases from Eastern coal AFTER it comes OUT of its scrubbers. Both scrubbing operations cost the same—are very expensive—but while scrubbing Eastern coal accomplishes something, scrubbing Western coal accomplishes almost nothing. The result does little good for the environment, but a great deal of harm to our productivity.

I could continue; but the trend looks clear. As Tocqueville observed a long time ago, the characteristic disease of democracy is not naked tyranny, but a network of fine regulations. Cicero said much the same thing. The end product is not freedom under law, but regulation upon regulation, so that the world might look like India: democratic in form, but with few individual rights; and because elections always go to the incumbents (and election reforms must be voted in by incumbents who are unlikely to reduce incumbent advantages), changes in the trends seem impossible. The ideal of the rule of law fades like dream stuff.

The second disturbing trend is that politics becomes more important than anything else. On reflection it is not at all clear that who has been elected to public office should affect the life of the citizen more than who has been chosen to head the company he works for, or who has been chosen to head the church he belongs to, or even who has become the head of the local university; but in fact we all know that it's true, that political power "trumps" all others.

Worse, there is the tendency to use political power to destroy one's enemies. Lyn Nofziger was hounded unmercifully after his term as a White House staffer. We can multiply examples; but the institution of "Special Prosecutor" is now standard, and used as a means to attack anyone unfortunate enough to fall into political disfavor. Thus politics has become all-important; yet it becomes dangerous for any but professional politicians to participate, and if the trend continues, the dangers of being on the losing side become greater.

Alas, that can lead to disaster. Imagine a war far away, say in a desert; it is an undeclared war. The Congress reluctantly has gone along with allowing the troops to be sent, but seeks an opportunity to punish political enemies. (This is a fantasy, of course, but bear with me).

There are political restrictions placed on the way the troops are to be used, enough so that the military is unhappy. The military does something unpopular; perhaps a large number of enemy civilians are killed by mistake. A general popular with his troops is hampered by even more regulations and restrictions, and there is a military debacle. The US loses a major battle, and appears to have suffered a significant defeat.

Congress brings the general home. Demagogues howl for blood. Congress and the press declare the general guilty even before he arrives. Blustering speeches are made describing what terrible things will be done to the man.

The general fears for his freedom, defies the Congress, and asks his military comrades to defend him.

Whatever the outcome, the result cannot be good for the republic.

Other scenarios suggest themselves—politicians who are no longer content to lose an election, because they believe that they will be allowed to keep nothing: they will be ruined defending themselves from "special prosecutors," and they may be cast into prisons like common felons. In those circumstances the temptation to use political power to subvert the electoral process and thus retain office may be well-nigh overpowering. After all, if the Congress can have ninety-eight percent reelection . . .

The political trends are disturbing, especially to a student of history; but there is one more frightening still.

In 1982 a Presidential Commission on Education headed by Nobel Prize winner Glenn T. Seaborg concluded that "If a foreign nation had imposed this system of education on the United States, we would rightly consider it an act of war." There have been significant changes in the education system since that report; alas, they are changes for the worse.

In 1991 the United States has a lower literacy rate than Iraq. Colleges teach elementary algebra instead of physics. High schools struggle with illiterate students who know no arithmetic.

In his introduction to a new edition of the classic *Teacher In America* Jacques Barzun says:

"The once proud and efficient public-school system of the United States—especially its unique free high school for all—has turned into a wasteland where violence and vice share the time with ignorance and idleness, besides serving as a battleground for vested interests, social, political, and economic. The new product of that debased system, the functional illiterate, is numbered in millions, while various forms of deceit have become accepted as inevitable—'social promotion' or passing incompetents to the next grade to save face; 'graduating' from 'high school' with eighth-grade reading ability; 'equivalence of credits,' or photography as good as physics; 'certificates of achievement' for those who fail the 'minimum competency' test; and more lately, 'bilingual education', by which the rudiments are supposedly taught in over ninety languages other than English. The old plan and purpose of teaching the young what they truly need to know survives only in the private sector, itself hard-pressed and shrinking in size."*

Indeed, we can wish that in 1994 things were no worse than Barzun describes; but alas, we now have high school graduates who not only cannot read at the eighth-grade level, but cannot read at all.

The fact is that the public school system of the United States has become little more than a vast welfare scheme for credentialed incompetents; and whatever else the system's output, it will not fail to produce a sufficiency of clients for the 'social science' graduates who staff the more traditional welfare systems. Moreover, the trend is down, not up; and every attempt at educational reform runs afoul of the political trends described earlier.

This has serious consequences. To begin with, where will we get the workers who can build the society of peace and plenty described in the first part of this scenario? Indeed, we already project shortages at all levels. The AAAS foresees a serious shortfall of Ph.D scientists. Most industries wonder where they will get their future engineers. At the moment we meet the shortages in part by draining other nations of their best and brightest, and perhaps that will continue; but assuming we produce enough college graduates and Ph.Ds, where will we get the skilled workers for industry?

---

*[Jacques Barzun, Preface to the Liberty Press Edition of *Teacher in America*, 1981; Liberty Press, 7440 North Shadeland Avenue, Indianapolis, Indiana, 46250; p ix.]

Already American industries are finding that in addition to the $50,000 or so in capital required to create a new job, they must also spend another $15,000 or more to educate the new worker to levels that we once expected from high school graduates. The result has serious impact on our competitiveness and productivity. Nor is reform likely: every attempt at "reform" results in even more money being spent on the system. We are, in effect, invited to reward those who failed, and to bribe those who destroyed the system to make it better. This is unlikely to work.

Since this is an optimistic scenario, I am now required to show a way whereby we can overcome the serious difficulties I have projected.

In politics I will merely plead the good sense of the American people. We have had great shifts in political trends in the past, and it is at least possible that we will have another—that the sentiment to "turn the rascals out" will prevail at one or another election, and the newcomers will obey their instructions to dismantle some of the structure of incumbent advantage.

Moreover: although we may debate whether the Cold War is truly over, I think few will dispute that it has wound very far down. For the first time since 1938 the United States is no longer required to be the arsenal of democracy. Few Americans can remember a time when the primary mission of the United States was not to stand as the last defender of Western Civilization; when we could, quite literally, through miscalculation, misadventure, or sheer funk, throw away the last best hope of mankind.

The strain of that period is obvious. In order to hold together the domestic coalition required to fight the Cold War, Americans of what is loosely called "The Right" were required to concede a great deal to "The Left." Concessions included a vast bureaucracy, an enormous welfare system, expensive social programs,

and the general expansion of the function and impor-
tance of government.

Now, suddenly, we can stop and take stock; we
can ask the fundamental question, "What is America
for?" It was once said that "the business of America is
business." Whether or not that is true, it has at least
become possible again.

The optimist, then, need not describe the political
course over the next fifty years; he need only postulate
that the pernicious trends will be reversed, that the
American people will once again get in control of their
government, and, more important, that government
will become the servant of the people rather than the
master.

That does not solve the problem of education. It
takes more than mere reform to rebuild an education
system when the very notion of demanding success
has been lost.

In the twentieth century there have been three
enormous systems organized as government control
monopolies: NASA; the American public school system;
and the Soviet system of agriculture. Each has produced
a few early successes followed by a dismal record of
failure. Each has utterly resisted reform, whether from
within or imposed by external government.

It requires a greater optimist than I am to believe
that any organization will voluntarily give up a
monopoly.

However, I do note one hopeful trend: over the past
few years, large companies have discovered that it is
quite profitable to offer employees day care for their
children. Providing day care decreases absenteeism,
increases productivity, and creates employee loyalty—
sometimes fanatic loyalty. The number of companies
offering day care to children of employees has grown
every year for the past several years.

Postulate, then, that the large companies offer education in addition to child care. Assume further that

they do what school systems do not do: that they demand results; that they simply will not accept excuses for failure. "We hired you to teach the children to read. If you cannot do that, we will find someone who can, for we simply do not believe that our children are inferior and unable to learn."

When I grew up in rural Tennessee our teachers were two-year Normal School graduates; Capleville could not afford four-year college graduate teachers. We had two grades to the room, and about thirty children to the grade; and in Capleville Elementary *every* child could read. Even the village idiot—who was fifteen and still in fifth grade—could *read*, if not well. Moreover, by seventh grade we read a number of important works. It never occurred to anyone that there was a good reason why we shouldn't.

If the large companies start with the attitude that the Capleville School Board must have had when I was growing up, we will soon have students who learn grade school subjects in grade school, middle school subjects in middle school, and on up the ladder. The supply of skilled workers for our industries will be assured.

Of course we can't pretend there won't be problems from having so many of our young people grow up as clients to big companies; but examining that situation is beyond the scope of this scenario.

Meanwhile, small computers have become ubiquitous; and with the computers come networks. Not only can we "commute" by telecommunications, we can also continue education that way. I need not belabor the point: the next century will be marked by an abundance of information. I said in 1977 that by the year 2000 everyone in Western society will be able to get the answer to any question. It seems clear to me that I was wrong only in placing the year so late. We already have electronic networks that provide information for the asking, and we haven't begun to tap the resources we are already technologically capable of. If we can teach the children to read, we can certainly provide them with instruction at every other level.

Thus I have, I hope, shown a plausible path to an optimistic future.

On the other hand, I have left until last what is perhaps the most important difficulty of all: I have said nothing about the wellsprings of morality.

In the past twenty years the United States has waged unrelenting warfare on any sign of Western Judaeo-Christian religion. The symbols of religion are excluded from public property, and no hint of religious origin of "values" may be given in schools. Worse: most schools teach, or attempt to teach, a kind of neutrality among cultures and value systems. This not only tolerates, but makes respectable, practices which were prohibited by law only a few years ago. The moral basis for all law is questioned, and often found wanting. We are, it seems, to produce a nation of ethical philosophers who will reason their way to civilized behavior—and do that in schools that cannot even teach the children to read.

The result is not encouraging. We see TV clips of young people accused of rape and aggravated assault, and whose only apparent remorse is that they were caught. Indeed, they don't even seem particularly unhappy to be in custody, since they apparently know that little will happen to them. We may not yet have produced a generation of barbarians within the gates, but surely it is not mere paranoia to suspect that we will manage that feat rather soon? We have sown the wind; perhaps we will reap the whirlwind.

I raise the question, but I have no real answer. Alas, I am not at all sure I understand how we get from where we are to a generation which obeys the laws, and does not consider it fun to be beastly. I do believe that education will help; and that education provided by the private sector may yet retain some flavor of the moral principles our courts assure us are forbidden by the First Amendment.

One thing is clear: any optimistic projection of the future must assume that the nation—all of Western Civilization—undergoes a revival of morality and finds new wellsprings of moral behavior. Indeed, one might even say that this is the very definition of an optimistic future.

HIGHER EDUCATION

by Jerry Pournelle
and Charles Sheffield

At sixteen, Rick Luban's life was about to end. He didn't know it yet. He thought he was all set for a good time.

The first period had gone no differently from usual. Mr. Hamel had been teaching high school for thirty years—forever, in Rick's eyes. He looked like an old turtle, and like a turtle he had developed his own survival techniques. Nothing got to him; not talking in class, or eating, or farting or sleeping. Gross and direct rudeness or violence, too much even for him to ignore, he passed up the line at once to the principal's office.

Hamel's rule: No fuss, no muss. And if that meant no work and no learning, too, he would settle for it. He usually reached that understanding with a class before the end of its first week.

"Test today." Hamel took no notice of the halfhearted groans. Failing an Act of God, biology tests in his class came every Tuesday and everyone knew it. "Read the questions, mark the answers. You have forty minutes."

More out of boredom than anything else, Rick put on the earphones attached to the desk and slipped the written sheet of questions into the reader.

"Question one," said the voice in his ear. "Five point credit. One of the animals on your screen belongs to a

227

different class from the others. Indicate which one. For assistance on the biological definition of *class*, or for name identification of any of the animals shown, touch the empty box."

The TV screen in front of Rick was divided into six rectangles. The first was empty. The second through sixth showed an ant, a butterfly, a mosquito, a spider, and a caterpillar. They were all in color, and all moved in natural settings.

Rick saw Dim Willy Puntin, Puntin the Pumpkin, reaching out to poke the icon of the caterpillar. It certainly looked grossly different from the other four. Rick snorted to himself. That was just like Hamel, trying a trick question. Rick had hardly been listening to the lesson about larval insect forms, but even a five-year-old knew that caterpillars turned into butterflies; and insects all had six legs.

Rick reached forward to touch the icon of the spider, at the same moment as Juanita Cesaro, two seats in front of him, removed her headset. She raised her hand and then stood up.

Hamel left the raised podium and moved over to her at once. Rick eased the earphones away from his head. Juanita was dim, but she was hot stuff. Half the boys in her year—including Rick—had been through Juanita; but you'd never know it from seeing her in class. She always sat demure and quiet, doing so poorly in every subject that her teachers all had trouble passing her. She *never* caused trouble.

"These." Juanita waved her hand vaguely at the headset, television, and reader. "Not working."

Hamel came around the desk and leaned over to examine the television picture. He was very careful not to touch Juanita, and careful to stand so that this fact would be apparent on the classroom videocamera recording.

Wily old turtle. No sexual harassment charges for you. Rick could see the empty box and the five icons on

Juanita's screen, just like on his own. Another clapped-out reader, it had to be. The readers were junk, breaking down all the time. Even when they worked they would only handle one size of page. School was too cheap to buy decent equipment. Not like the school the telephone company ran. That one had great equipment, but it was just for kids whose mothers worked there. His mother had got herself fired for drugs six weeks after she started with the phone company, so Rick had only been at the company school a little while. That was back in kindergarten, but he still remembered the school.

Hamel had apparently made up his mind about the reader. He was glancing thoughtfully around the class, finally gesturing to a girl at the back. "Belinda. For this period I want you to change seats with Juanita."

As expected. Belinda Jacob was one of three people in the class who could read well enough to handle the test from the printed sheet, without using a reader at all. *So see what reading does for you,* Rick thought, as the two girls changed places. *Not a damn thing.* Belinda was Hamel's star student. She had probably been halfway through her own test before she had to move—and now she was forced to start over, while Juanita would get the benefit of her right answers.

Rick grinned to himself as he settled back to listen to the rest of the questions. Unless Hamel went to the trouble of noting the point where the two had changed over, which wasn't at all likely, Juanita, for the first time in her life, was going to score—on a *test*.

The broken reader was all that the first period could offer to relieve the boredom. That was predictable with Mr. Hamel. Dullness was the rule. What Rick and his friends had been looking forward to for a week was second period. They were supposed to get a new civics teacher then, right out of training.

"Willis Preebane, his name is. An' if I can't have some fun with him, I'm losing my touch," Screw Savage said.

Any one of the three might have offered the same

statement, but Screw had special credibility. He was a school legend. Two years before, by a mixture of near-inaudible insult and off-videocamera dumb insolence, he had made a new teacher take a swing at him on her very first day. She had been fired on the spot. Screw was provided with a groveling apology from Principal Rigden. His parents had sued school and county anyway, and been paid a hefty out-of-court settlement. Now Screw tended to get high grades without ever doing homework or handing in tests.

"But we'd all like to have first go at him," Screw went on, "so we do it fair, an' draw lots."

Rick and the other two were walking between classes, heading for Room 33 with Screw Savage leading the way. The corridors were their usual confusion with backed-up lines in front of the metal and plastique detectors. Hoss Carlin, walking next to Rick, took a step to his left and reached out to brush his fingers over the breasts of a girl walking the other way. She slapped his hand away, but she turned to give him a big smile and said, "See you tonight."

"Watch it, Hoss," Rick warned. "You're in deep shit if they have that on camera."

"Nah." Hoss jerked his head upward. "Checked already."

The ceiling videocamera for the corridor was ruined, lens broken and body a shattered hulk. It was like this all over the school. Every time a corridor camera was repaired, within a day or two it would be smashed.

"Anyway," Hoss went on, "Jackie'd be on my side if they did see me. She'd tell 'em I was swattin' a wasp off her tit or somethin.' "

The three youths were almost at Room 33. Most of the class was already there, standing waiting outside the locked door.

"Mebbe Preebane's not as dumb as you think, Screw," Hoss said. "He knows at least that much. Lockin' the door stops us givin' him a welcome."

"So one of us has to get real inventive once we're

inside." Savage turned around, three toothpicks sticking up from between the knuckles of his closed right fist. "Short one has first go at Papa Willis. Who wants first pick?"

"Me," Hoss said, and grimaced with annoyance when the toothpick he pulled was full-length. "Lucky with women, unlucky in the draw. Go on, Rick. You got a one out of two chance now."

Rick plucked the toothpick from between Savage's first and second finger, and grinned when he saw it was a fragment only an inch and a half long.

"Lucky bastard." Screw opened his hand to reveal a third, full-length toothpick. "You get Preebane all to yourself."

"Aha!" The voice, thin and with a definite lisp, came from behind Rick. "And do I hear thomeone taking my name in vain?"

Rick turned and stared. The man waddling along the corridor was too good to be true. He was pale, short, and grossly overweight. He had watery blue eyes in a pudgy face, and he sported a flat, gingery brown mustache that looked as though it had been poorly dyed and pasted above his full upper lip.

Preebane's very appearance was an opportunity to have fun. If Rick didn't get in quickly, some other class joker certainly would.

In fact, it was already happening. Rick heard a whisper, deliberately loud, from among the group of waiting students: "Quiet now. Here comes our new PE teacher."

Preebane, heading for the classroom door, paused uncertainly. After a moment he decided to pretend he had not heard the comment. He unlocked the door and waved the students inside. Rick, contrary to his natural instincts and usual practice, went to sit in the middle of the first row. Preebane, belly wobbling, moved to stand beneath the videocamera right in front of Rick. He beamed directly at him.

Rick gazed back and waited for inspiration. He, who

usually had a thousand ideas for baiting teachers, suddenly found his mind a blank. Willis Preebane looked like a man who, if goaded to physical violence, would drop dead from the exertion before he could land a blow.

And that voice. "Good morning. I am Mr. Preebane, and I want to welcome you to my class on introductory civics." Or rather, it was "Mr. Pweebane," and "my clath on intwoductory thivicth."

"I told Pwinthipal Wigden of my appwoach, and she agweed with it completely. Begin by forgetting evewything that you have ever been told about the Conthtituthion."

"Done," said a girl's voice from the back of the room, followed by a loud male whisper, "Hire the handicapped."

The others were starting without Rick. He could feel Screw and Hoss glaring accusingly at his back. And still his brain was empty. It was an enormous relief to hear the click of the PA system, right above his head, and a voice saying, "I am delighted to announce that we have been paid an unexpected visit by Congresswoman Pearl, who as I am sure you know serves on our Board of Education. All students and teachers will please assemble at once in the main hall."

Principal Rigden didn't sound delighted to Rick. She sounded ready to shit bricks. But the interruption would give him time to think. He stayed in his seat until everyone except Mr. Preebane had left the room, then he moved out and held the door for the teacher. Preebane nodded his thanks. Rick closed the door; was careful not to lock it; and hurried after the rest of the class ahead of Preebane. He caught up with them as they were filing into the hall.

"What about some action, dipshit?" Screw Savage didn't wait until they were seated. "If I'd known you was goin' to just sit there like a dried-out dog turd, I'd never have held any draw. You can't hang old Willis out to dry, what the hell can you handle?"

"His dick." Hoss stood on the other side of Screw. "He's done it too much and softened his brain."

"Don't you believe it. I know what I'm doing. And it's something special." Rick glared at both of them. "But I need a little bit of help from you. You have to go sit down near the front."

"And where will you be?" Screw sounded suspicious.

"Right at the back. Near the door. The classroom's not locked, Screw. I was last out, I made sure it was that way."

"Ah!" The other two understood at once.

"What do you want us to do?" Hoss asked.

"Wait 'til the principal is ready to introduce Congresswoman Whats-it. It should get real quiet. Then you drop something."

"What?"

"Hell, I dunno. Anything. Anything that makes a decent noise."

Hoss dived into his pocket and came up with a handful of change. "This? People will scrabble around after 'em, too."

"Perfect."

"But the old Rigger will have my ass in a sling for interrupting her."

"For dropping money by accident, and losing some? Don't think so. Anyway, if you're going to help, get going. I can't wait much longer. Have to find a seat near the side door."

Hoss and Screw nodded. Rick turned at once and started easing his way against the main flow of students. The seats at the back, usually filled first, were today half-empty. Everybody wanted to see Principal Rigden wriggle and grovel, the way she always did with Board of Education visitors. Rick sat at the end of a row he had almost to himself, close enough to the open door for a quiet getaway.

He waited impatiently while the stage filled with the senior teachers. Willis Preebane was up there with them— that was surprising for a new and junior staff member. The honor didn't seem to make him comfortable; maybe because his ass would hardly squeeze in between the arms of his chair.

There was one student on the stage, too. Daniel Rackett. As valedictorian (vale-*dickhead*-torian, as Hoss usually put it) Danny would be called upon to say something to welcome their guest. He didn't look comfortable, either. He was peering at the headset that was supposed to read his speech into his ear. From the expression on his face it wasn't working right. Even from the back of the hall Rick could see his Adam's apple bobbing up and down.

Finally Principal Rigden appeared, smiling broadly and leading a large, red-haired woman in a green pantsuit. They moved to two empty chairs at the front of the stage, Congresswoman Pearl sat down, and the principal turned to face the students. "I would like—"

There was the clatter of two dozen small coins falling onto the wooden floor. Some of them were still rolling when Rick quietly rose and slipped out of the side door.

The principal would speak, then Danny Rackett, then the visitor. Rick probably had at least half an hour. But that wasn't long for what he had in mind.

First he headed away from Room 33, keeping his eyes open for working videocameras. The contraceptive dispensers were down by the cafeteria entrance. They needed a student name and ID code before they would operate, but Rick was prepared for that. He entered "Daniel J. Rackett" and "XKY-586", waited as the valedictorian's ID was confirmed, and took the packet of three condoms. He did it twice more. Nine should be enough. If anyone checked today's records, Danny would get quite a reputation.

The corridors were deserted as he hurried back toward Room 33, opened the door, and slipped through. The tricky piece now was to disable the classroom videocamera without being seen by it. The cable ran along the ceiling, well out of reach. Rick scaled the open door and balanced precariously on top of it. He had no knife on him—anything that might form a weapon would never get past the school entrance—but his nail clippers were enough for this job. He crouched on top of the door, reached up, and delicately snipped the thin grey cable.

He lost his balance as he did so and had to jump, but he landed easily. And finally he could close the classroom door. There was no way of locking it from the inside, but he felt a lot safer once it was shut.

He blew up eight of the condoms and tied their ends. They formed great balloons, a couple of feet long and nine or ten inches wide. He taped them all around Preebane's desk, stepped back, and surveyed his work.

It was a start, but it was not enough. He could imagine Screw Savage's sniff and critical comment: "Kindergarten stuff." He had to try for the rest.

Rick went to the door, opened it, and looked along the corridor. He had no idea how much time had passed, but everywhere was still silent and deserted. He left the door unlocked and hurried along to the washroom at the end of the corridor. He placed the end of the remaining condom over a faucet, held it in position, and turned on the water.

It took forever to fill. Rick put in as much water as he dared, until he was sure that the thin skin would burst under the weight. At last he tied off the end. The bloated condom had become amazingly heavy. He cradled it in his arms and headed back to the classroom.

The most difficult part still remained. Somehow he had to balance the monstrous condom right above the door, so that it would burst as the door swung open. And he had to get out, himself, after the trap was set.

It sounded impossible. Rick puzzled over it, increasingly sure that he was running out of time, until at last he realized that he was trying to solve the wrong problem. He didn't have to leave the room at all. There was going to be total confusion after the door was opened. He could

236 Jerry Pournelle and Charles Sheffield

hide behind the desks at the back of the room, and leave when the excitement was over.

He spent ten nervous minutes arranging a harness of tape around the condom, then placed thumbtacks through the ends of the tape. Finally he dragged a chair over to the door and lifted the condom into position. He pushed the pins into the wall and made delicate adjustments. When the door was opened, its rough top had to just scrape the bottom of the condom enough to break it. But the condom felt so distended and tight, he was almost afraid to move it now.

At last he realized that he was doing more harm than good. The changes he was making were loosening both the pins and the tape. He returned the chair to its original position and forced himself to retreat to the back of the room. He found a place which allowed him a narrow view of the door, with a very small chance of his being seen.

And then he waited. And waited.

What could be going on in the hall? There was no way to know how long Congresswoman Pearl would decide to speak. Certainly, Principal Rigden would not dare to interrupt a visitor who was a member of the Board of Education. Suppose that she went on right until lunchtime, and the class did not return to this room?

Rick's legs were stiff and his knees sore from crouching on the hard floor when at last he heard the sound of footsteps clattering along the corridor. He tensed. He had not been able to lock the door, as he had originally intended. Maybe Preebane would notice that.

Apparently not. The metal handle on the inside was turning. The door opened its first inch and Rick heard Preebane's voice saying, "After you, Aunt Delia. I am weally glad that my clath will have you—"

The door swung open. Rick had one glimpse of Willis Preebane, ushering a large, green-clad figure ahead of him into the room. Then the giant condom, scraped by the top of the door, burst with a soft, subdued plop. Water deluged down.

Rick, peering through the narrow slit, had the sudden feeling that the flood had decapitated Congresswoman Pearl. He could see her red hair, sodden with water, lying on the floor.

Then he heard her scream. She clutched at her head. The hair beneath the wig was revealed as short-cropped and grey.

Behind the congresswoman and Preebane, crowding now into the doorway, came Rick's whole class. They were buzzing with excitement and delight. Delia Pearl's secret would be all over the school by lunchtime. Rick saw Screw near the front, standing openmouthed with astonished glee.

He felt a huge satisfaction. He had promised; and he had certainly delivered.

Rick also believed that he was safe from discovery. In the melee that followed, the classroom had been total confusion. No one noticed when he joined the rest— even Hoss and Screw didn't realize that he had been in the room, and they had no idea how he had managed the trick until he explained.

It was a total shock to Rick when he was called out of class right after lunch and taken to Principal Rigden's office.

The principal was there. So was Congresswoman Pearl, the three assistant principals, Willis Preebane, and two other people whom Rick did not recognize.

The congresswoman had managed to dry her wig, and she was wearing it. That was a mistake. After its soaking it looked like a strip of cheap coconut matting wedged down onto her head. Beneath it, her blue eyes glared at Rick with undisguised hatred.

"This is the one?"

"We believe so." Principal Rigden wasted no time on formalities. She turned to Rick. "Ricardo Luban, do you know of the outrage that was perpetrated on Congresswoman Pearl this morning?"

"Yes." Rick felt uneasy, but he could not see how anything could be pinned on him.

"Will you admit that you were responsible for it?"

"I didn't do it."

"Were you in Mr. Preebane's class, before the assembly to greet the congresswoman?"

"Yes."

"And you were the last to leave that class?"

"Yes. I think so."

"Mr. Preebane?" The principal turned her head.

"He was the last. Definitely. He held the door for me."

"Did you?"

"I guess so."

"And you locked the door after you, as you were supposed to?"

"Sure."

Rick felt easier in his mind. They were going to try to prove that he hadn't locked the door. He didn't think they could. And even if they did, that was a long way from proving that he had set the booby trap. But the principal didn't pursue that line. She merely nodded, and asked, "Mr. Preebane tells us that you then went on ahead of him, toward the hall. Is that right?"

"Yes." Rick was uneasy again.

"And you attended the general assembly?"

"Yes."

"And remained there throughout?"

"Yes." If they were going to ask him what happened in the hall, he was on solid ground. Hoss and Screw Savage had briefed him pretty thoroughly over lunch. Danny Rackett's headset hadn't worked right. He had tried to read his speech of welcome from printed sheets, stumbled over every word longer than one syllable, and made an ass of himself until Principal Rigden finally cut him off. She had then made a short speech herself, explaining what a wonderful person the visiting congresswoman was. And finally Congresswoman Pearl had offered her own contribution, telling the audience how pleased she was that her own nephew, Willis Preebane, had decided to teach here, how talented he was, and how lucky the school was to have him. She hoped he would be really happy with his choice.

She had said it all twice, to make sure that the principal and the other teachers got the message, added that she was looking forward to seeing an actual class being taught, and at last sat down.

If Principal Rigden wanted anything more detailed than that, Rick would plead ignorance. He was sure that was all anyone else remembered. Most wouldn't know that much.

"So where did you sit during the assembly?"

The question was totally unexpected. It left Rick floundering.

"I dunno."

"That's silly, of course you remember. Now, where?"

"I guess maybe I was near the back. Near the side door."

"Very good." The principal turned to the screen that covered one wall of her office. "Right here, in fact." She touched the wall. "This is you, is it not?"

The screen showed a videocamera still. The resolution was not good. Rick sitting way at the back of the hall was barely recognizable.

"Yeah, that's me."

Mistake. Should have said maybe, not sure. He thought of changing his story, but it was too late. The picture had flashed off, to be replaced by another, and Principal Rigden was saying, "The first image I showed was taken at the beginning of the assembly. This one was taken close to the end of it. The seat where you were sitting originally is now empty. Where are you sitting now, Ricardo Luban?"

"I moved." Rick spoke automatically, but he knew he was doomed. If they had been able to locate him on the video image . . .

"We are quite sure that you moved." The principal stepped away from the wall screen. "But where did you move to? During the lunch period we managed to identify every student in school today, in both the first and the second picture. I should say, every student except one. You are present in the first image, and absent in the second. Now would you like to confess?"

Rick shook his head. They had him on ice, but he wasn't going to admit it. He would plead innocent today, and tomorrow, and if necessary for the whole of the next two years, until the end of his time in school.

It was with disbelief that he heard Principal Rigden saying, "I quite agree with you, Congresswoman Pearl, and with the other board members. Guilt is established beyond reasonable doubt. Such people have absolutely no place in this school or in our school system. We will take action for expulsion as soon as the necessary signatures can be obtained and the paperwork completed."

"For the final, official decision." Delia Pearl stared stonily at Rick. "But unofficially, pending that decision, expulsion will happen today, and the Welfare Department will be notified today."

"Today?" Principal Rigden hesitated. "Very well. Of course." She turned to Rick. "You are expelled from this school, effective immediately. The final notification will follow in a day or two. Please collect your possessions and leave the premises as soon as possible."

"You can't do that!" Expulsion, for a simple practical joke that had really hurt no one? Rick knew a student who had broken his language teacher's arm, and another who had deliberately run over a science teacher with his car. Explosive booby traps for other teachers had been set, filled with shit or warm tar. But those people had received only trifling punishments.

"I think you must let us decide what we can and cannot do."

"I'll sue. I will."

For a second everyone stared at him. Then they all smiled.

"Sue a Congresswoman?" The Principal laughed aloud. "And what lawyer will take your case? Get out, Luban. Go."

Delia Pearl's mouth twisted with satisfaction, and she turned to Preebane. "Willis, I do not feel that we can trust this young man one little bit. Would you please accompany him when he collects his possessions, and then escort him off the premises."

"Of course." Preebane did not even look to the principal for confirmation.

Rick was led away. He was too dazed to resist. He hardly saw Hoss or Screw or the other members of his class as he picked up his school bag, and he did not say a word when he was escorted to the front door and his ID was canceled from the entry system. He walked out into the afternoon sunlight and stared around him as though he was on an alien planet.

He went to the side of the school, walked out beyond the sports field, and sat on the grass. He was still sitting there when school was released for the day. Occasional students passed by. No one spoke to him. He did not stir or speak to them. Only when a long afternoon shadow fell across him, and silently remained there, did he look up.

It was Mr. Hamel, more like a turtle than ever as he stood motionless with his head pushed slightly forward. He nodded at Rick.

"Caught at last, Luban. And not before time."

"You heard what happened?"

"The whole school heard. Would you like to talk to me about it?" And, when Rick shook his head, "Very well. That is your option." He began to walk away across the grass.

"Wait!" Rick struggled to his feet and hurried after him. "I don't want to talk, but I want to *ask*."

"Better yet. We learn by asking, not by talking." Hamel continued, slowly pacing out of the school grounds and into the street. "So ask."

"Why *me*? I mean, why did the motherfuckers dump on *me* like that? What I did wasn't any big deal compared to the other shit that goes down all the time in this school."

They had come to a bench. Hamel sat down on it and gestured to Rick to join him.

"Must you use that language?"

"What'll you do, expel me? You never heard people talk like that?"

"I hear people talk that way every day," Hamel sighed. "It's unpleasant. Do you want people to wish you were not around them? It's easy enough to do. Or do you want answers."

"Answers. Why'd they dump on *me*?"

"Very well," Hamel said. "Luban, you are not stupid. But you are a fool. For one thing, you consort with people like Savage and Carlin who really are stupid. You are also ignorant, cynical, amoral, and unthinking. Wait a moment." He held up his hand. Rick was starting to stand up. "I am going to answer your question—or rather, I am going to let you answer it. You are—how old? Sixteen? So you have been in the education system for eleven years. And what have you learned?"

"My grades are all right."

"Certainly. Because nothing is required of you. It is easy to hit a target pasted to the end of the rifle. We are also required to help you feel good about yourself. The technical term is to raise your self esteem. While you were in school I could not have spoken to you this way, because you had to be protected from the truth. Now I can. Despite all the work we have done to raise your self esteem, surely you must know you've learned very little."

"I do all right," Rick protested again.

"You do all right. What does that mean? Let us examine what you know.

"You can read short, simple words, but only those you have seen before. You have a reasonable speaking vocabulary, but you cannot read more than half of the words you know. You have a rudimentary knowledge of simple science, and you can do simple arithmetic. I've hammered some biology into your skull, but you know little mathematics, and no economics, geography, history, arts, or languages. You can recite all manner of song and rap lyrics, but no poetry or literature. And you would be little better if you stayed here another two years and graduated."

"Reading from books is a waste of time. Like adding up numbers. I got a calculator that does that. Reading's ancient history. The readers do it for us fine."

"They do when they work, and when you have one available. But you miss a point. A person who cannot *read* can also not *write*. Writing—and revision—is essential for completeness and clarity of expression. But I do not want to digress. You have been in the education system for eleven years. How much, in that time, have you learned about the system itself, and how it works?"

Rick considered the question. He had never had the slightest interest in the education system. Nor did anyone else in his right mind.

"Not much."

"But you have enough information to work things out for yourself. For instance, whom do I work for—to whom do I report?"

"Principal Rigden."

"And to whom does she report?"

"I dunno. I guess, the Board of Education."

"Good enough. There are a couple more layers in there, but that will do. Now another question. How much of the county and state's total budget goes toward education? I don't expect you to know the answer to that, so I will tell you. It is about four-tenths. That's an awful lot of money, a huge vested interest at work. Now, who decides what that amount will be and how it should be allocated?"

"Congress?"

"For all practical purposes. Very good. So let us climb the ladder of our status society. If you play one of your unfunny 'jokes' on a teacher, and are caught, you pay a price. But a teacher, most students are amazed to learn, is the *lowest* form of life in the school system. Do something to the principal, that's worse, and the punishment is more severe. To a Board of Education member, worse yet. And to a *congresswoman*, who is also a member of the Board of Education—"

"I didn't know I was doing nothing to a congresswoman."

"That is the plea of the foolish through all of history: *I didn't know what I was doing.* But I, speaking as a teacher, tell you that I have no sympathy for you. Is it better to insult and offend and diminish me or Willis Preebane, rather than Congresswoman Pearl, simply because the punishment is less? That is the logic of a coward."

"I ain't no coward!"

The sun was setting in their faces, and Hamel shielded his eyes with his hand. Rick could see the deep lines on his cheeks and around his mouth. Hamel seemed ancient, far older than when he was teaching his class, until suddenly he lowered his hand and turned to face Rick. His eyes were alert and astute, changing his whole face.

"You want some good news? Until today you had two more years of schooling here. Did you have any thought of continuing beyond that?"

Rick shook his head. For the past three years he had wanted to finish school and get out of it more than anything. "Mick makes me stay in school because Mom gets the education incentive bonus in the welfare. I'd be long gone if I could."

"So now what happens to you?"

"I don' know. Watch the virtual tube, I guess. Only Mick will kill me. Throw me out on the street anyway. The education incentive was nine forty a month and we only get sixty-two hundred."

"A good part of the money. Of course you don't get the money."

"Naw, Mick takes it. He's gonna hate losin' that nine-forty. Fifteen percent—"

"It is that. You do percentages in your head?"

"Sure, that's easy."

"I see. So now you're out. Suppose you had stayed in. At eighteen, you would graduate. Even with your minimal skills and application, you would receive your diploma. Then you emerge and offer your talents to a waiting world. Did you have any plans as to what you would do?"

"Find a job, I guess. There's supposed to be plenty of jobs around."

"In laundries, or fast food places. Or running a scanner, there are usually jobs in data entry. There is also the Job Corps, makework jobs, cleaning litter from parks. Plenty of those. That sound good?"

"Naw, but there's other stuff."

"Not for you," Hamel said sadly. "The fact is that perhaps two dozen of your classmates will have any skills anyone wishes to pay for. Of course nearly everyone has the grades to go on to junior college."

Rick shuddered.

"You won't learn anything there, of course," Hamel continued. "But it would keep you off the streets, and separate you from the genuinely stupid. Better than nothing, but still pretty much a dead end."

"Education incentive, too. Goes up to a grand a month."

"A thousand a month to stay in junior college for two years. Do you think you would learn anything you could sell?"

"I don't know," Rick protested. He shook his head. "The way you talk, I guess not. So who gets the real jobs?"

"Who do you think? Those who have salable skills. A few of your classmates, perhaps, but mostly students from company schools." Hamel shook his head sadly. "I have lived to see the transformation of the United States from a republic to a feudal aristocracy. Not pretty."

"I don't know what you're talking about."

"No, I don't suppose you do. You ask who gets the jobs. Simple. People with real knowledge and drive. There are jobs for them. Not for an arrogant, semiliterate, unfocused, trouble-making know-nothing. Not for amoral, idle, cynical wasters, which is what you'd be if you stayed here. I told you I had good news, but you may find it hard to see it that way. Here it is: you are fortunate to be expelled from this school. Had you remained you would have wasted another two years, and at the end of it you'd have no more knowledge or capability than you have today."

Rick stood up. "I don't need to take this crap from anybody. I'm going."

"Very well. Going where?"

Rick shook his head. "I dunno, Mick's going to kill me." He knew how it would happen. When they found out that the education incentive would stop, his mother would scream and Mick—Rick's "stepfather," though he certainly wasn't—would tell her to shut her yap. Then they would start in on each other. Finally, when the fight between them cooled off, they would gang up and turn it all on him.

"Going home, I guess. I got a truce with the gangs, but I can't be out after dark unless I pay, and I don't have any money."

"And tomorrow morning, when you get up and school is closed to you?"

"I don't know. Look for a job."

"Selling dope?"

"I don't know, what else is there?"

"Theft. Shoplifting. Working for a pimp. Admittedly those don't pay as well as being a pusher, but they stay out of jail somewhat longer. Live longer too."

Rick knew what that meant. Most rackets were controlled by gangs, or even by adult mobsters. Mick, his current stepfather, claimed to have mob connections, but nobody believed him. Especially not Rick, because Rick had asked about getting set up in a good racket, and Mick kept stalling him off. Rick was sure that Mick didn't know jack shit about real rackets. And if you didn't have connections, you wouldn't last long, either get busted or shot, or maybe both. "All right, I don't know," Rick said.

"I assumed as much. However, I have a suggestion." Mr. Hamel handed Rick a small yellow card. "Can you read what is written there?"

Rick stared at the card in the fading light. "Eight-one-five-two." He paused. The numbers were easy but the words were long and unfamiliar. At last he shook his head. "Not without a reader."

"Then I will tell you. It says, 8152 Chatterjee Boulevard, Suite 500. Can you remember that, and find the place?"

"Sure." Rick stared at the card. "Say it again."

"Yes, 8152 Chatterjee Boulevard, Suite 500."

"Got it." Now that he'd heard the words he could sort of read the card, at least enough to remind him.

"If you go there tomorrow, there is a possibility of useful employment."

"A job?"

"Exactly. Not an easy job, but a worthwhile one. You may keep the card."

Rick studied the words, silently mouthing them to himself. "I know how to get to Chatterjee Boulevard. If I went there tonight, would someone be in Suite 500?"

"I cannot say, but it is not impossible." Hamel stood up. "I must go now. But you have the right idea. Action is usually preferable to inaction."

Rick stood up too. He wanted somehow to thank Mr. Hamel, but he did not know how. "Why are you doing this for me?"

Hamel paused. "Certainly it is not because I like you, Luban. I do not. As I said, you are a fool. And you are—"

"Ignorant, cynical, amoral, and unthinking. I heard you."

"Correct. Did I omit to say lazy? But you are not stupid. You are, I think, basically very intelligent. However, all forms of intelligence and *aptitude tests* that might suggest one student is more able or talented than another were long since judged discriminatory, and banished from our school system. Therefore, I have no objective basis for my conjecture. But I do hate waste. You and your friends have been wasting your lives."

Hamel nodded and started to walk away, a small, stooped figure in the twilight. "Do you think I'll get a job?" Rick called after him.

"I cannot say." Hamel did not pause or turn around. "But if you do, wait a while before you thank me for it."

Mr. Hamel had sensed the truth: Rick could not face going home. The school might not have called his mother, but somebody would have called, and they'd make sure she knew there wouldn't be any more education incentive money. Nine hundred and forty bucks a month. Fifteen percent. He never got any of that money, but it would be his fault they weren't getting it, and they'd make him pay. Mick would wait up for him, drunk or drugged but anyway in a foul temper. If only, when Rick finally had to go to the apartment, he could tell them that he already had some sort of job, some way to bring home some money. . . .

It seemed like the thinnest of straws to grasp at as he descended from the overhead Public Vehicle at the corner of Chatterjee Boulevard and began to walk along toward Number 8152. He had to push his way through crowds of young men and women, standing or wandering aimlessly along the littered street. They were part of the Pool. Not more than one in ten of the Pool would have a job of any kind—ever. Yet most of them had graduated from high school and junior college, and some of them from a real college. Rick had already known most of the things that Mr. Hamel had told him. He had just never thought about them.

They didn't want us to think about them. Rick remembered what Mr. Hamel had said about self esteem. He'd heard some of that before, too, but hadn't understood. *They want us to feel good and not think about the future. It works, too, why should we?*

Number 8152 was a ten-story windowless building, its featureless walls made of grey lightweight carbon composite. Rick waited stoically as his ID was verified by the automatic guard and the card given to him by Mr. Hamel was read. It was close to eight o'clock at night. On the way here he had convinced himself that Suite 500 would be empty.

That conviction grew when he at last stood outside the entrance of the suite. He could see through the shatterproof glass door that it was just one room. It had plenty of computers and displays inside, but no people.

He touched the attention panel anyway, and was astonished when after about ten seconds a woman's voice responded, "You are at an office of Vanguard Mining and Refining. Please identify yourself."

Rick went through the ID process all over again. He showed the little card and stumbled through the explanation that it had been given to him by Mr. Hamel, and why. The woman did not say another word, but at last the door swung open. Rick went in. The door closed behind him and one of the television monitors came alive.

"Sit down right here."

Rick took the only seat near the monitor. Now he could see the woman on the screen. She was small, thin, and sharp-featured, and somehow reminded him of an animal. A rat? No. Not quite.

She was examining something in front of her, not visible to Rick. "You are sixteen years old. You have been expelled from school. And it is eight o'clock, your time. Right?"

Each of the statements was true enough, but taken together they made little sense.

"That's right."

"I want you to tell me exactly why you were expelled from school. Take your time and give as much detail as you can. I'll try not to interrupt. If I do, there will be a delay of about five seconds between what you say, and my comment or question. So you may have to back up occasionally and say things over. Go ahead."

There was a temptation to lie, or put things in a way more favorable to Rick. Some instinct warned him that would be a mistake. He recounted the whole episode, from the arrival of Willis Preebane to Rick's interrogation and expulsion by Principal Rigden. It was difficult to talk about the condoms and the booby trap. After the fact it sounded so stupid and pointless and unfunny. Rick was sure that any hope of employment with Vanguard Mining was evaporating with every word he said. He plowed on, ending with his decision to come to this office tonight even though it was so late.

"Not late where I am," the woman replied. "I got up just two hours ago. But are you tired?"

Just got up. She had to be somewhere on the other side of the Earth! The speech delay must be caused by the satellite link. "I'm not tired."

"Good. Can you read?"

"A little bit." But five seconds was far too long for a satellite link delay. Rick struggled to remember things that had never before been of the slightest interest to him. Radio signals traveled at the speed of light. But how fast did light travel?

"Can you write?"

"Just a few things."

"Hell." The woman's opinion of his reply showed more in her tone of voice than in her comment. "Well, no matter. Anyone can learn to read and write. We'll manage. I want to give you a whole set of things called *aptitude tests*. First, though, we have to deal with a few formalities. You never had tests like this in school, because they're forbidden in public programs. We're a private company but still the tests can't be given to you without suitable consent. In the case of someone like you, less than eighteen years old, that consent has to come from a parent or guardian."

Rick felt an awful sinking feeling. He was going to be sent home after all with nothing to tell except his expulsion from school.

"Problem with that?" The woman must have been studying his face. "Tell you what. Suppose that we give you the tests anyway, see how you do. If the results are good you can get consent later and we'll postdate the tests. If they're not good, we purge the test results from our files and you're no worse off."

What she was suggesting sounded illegal—but if that didn't worry Vanguard Mining, it sure didn't worry Rick. He took a deep breath.

"I'm ready."

"Any last question before we begin?"

Rick shook his head, then changed his mind. "You said you just got up. Is it morning where you are?"

"Morning, afternoon, evening, anything you choose to call it." The woman smiled, to show small, sharp teeth. Rick suddenly caught the right animal resemblance. Not a rat, but a weasel—though he had never actually seen a live weasel. Mr. Hamel had somehow taught Rick more biology than either of them realized.

"I'm on CM-2, one of Vanguard Mining's translunar training stations," the woman went on, "about seven hundred thousand kilometers away from Earth. But the tests will be delivered where you are by a local program.

I'll still be here if you get stuck. Don't call me unless you absolutely have to, though—the tests are timed. Ready to go?"

Rick nodded. His heart was racing and his mouth felt too dry to speak. The woman's picture vanished from the screen and was replaced by a sequence of numbers.

"Good luck," said her disembodied voice. "Do well on your tests—and one day maybe you'll come out here and see this place for yourself."

Seven weeks of mind-numbing briefings, endless questions, and bruising physical tests and conditioning; they were all converging, collapsing now to a single, final minute.

Rick had been strapped into his seat for more than an hour. Next to him sat Deedee Mao, another of Vanguard Mining's recent recruits. Like him she had been expelled from her school at sixteen, but beyond that they had little in common. She was from the East Coast, three thousand miles away from Rick. She was big, loud, and self-confident, just the sort of aggressive female that he hated. They had taken all their courses together, and she and Rick had argued furiously and continuously during the final three weeks; but since boarding the LEO transfer vehicle, neither of them had said a word.

That silence suited Rick. He didn't want to talk to anybody. He could not take his eyes from the changing digits of the display.

Sixty-two—sixty-one. A siren began to wail inside the ship. Only one more minute to lift-off.

He knew, intellectually, that riding the single stage to orbit was not much more dangerous than taking a PV across the city. So why was he gripping the arms of his seat so hard? He tried to move his mind to other things. All he could think of was the bitter memory of his last hours at home.

His stepfather didn't try to hide his relief at getting rid of Rick, the "troublemaker" too bad for even the school system, the extra mouth not even good for the educational incentive. On the first night, when Rick came home and told them that he had done well on the Vanguard Mining tests and needed parental consent to accept a job with them in the Belt, Mick had asked, "When do you go, and how much do they pay to get you?"

No congratulations; no discussion of the job itself, no worry about possible hazards of an off-Earth assignment. No query as to how long it would be before Rick returned. Just, "When do you go?"

His mother had moaned and wept, but she could not keep her eyes away from the credit slip provided by Vanguard Mining—the "sweetener" that expressed the company's financial appreciation of her willingness to sign over to them the parental control of her child.

There was an odd whirring sound and a vibration of the metal surface beneath Rick's feet. The hatch was moving to its final sealed setting. That meant that the lasers were powered up, waiting for their first discharge. The cover beneath the SSTO would have opened, to reveal the ablative layers.

Rick tried to concentrate on factual matters. The first minute would be the most uncomfortable. That's when he and Deedee and fourteen others would feel the highest acceleration. After that the ground lasers would be switched off and the onboard nuclear rocket would cut in. The acceleration force on them would drop to two gees.

Thirty-two, thirty-one, thirty . . .

There were voices in the background. The ground crew for the ship, only five people. Their duties had been explained as part of the "informed consent" briefing.

The moving display in front of him seemed to have slowed, minutes passing between each second. Before he started training, Rick had imagined that travel to and in space would be conducted wearing space suits.

The briefings had taught him that was an idiotic idea, as out-of-date as the notion that aircraft passengers all wore parachutes. Rick was dressed in the same informal uniform of blue shirt and slacks that had become familiar to him since the day he signed up with Vanguard Mining.

Twenty, nineteen, eighteen . . .

Almost as safe as a trip on the PV, the briefings said. But every day the media carried news of PV accidents. The vehicle he was sitting in felt far more vulnerable. Laser power could fail; the nuclear rocket could refuse to cut in; or it could refuse to turn off at the right time and hurtle the passengers away to nowhere. You could sometimes walk away from a PV accident. Had anyone ever walked away from a transfer vehicle failure?

Rick tried to steel himself for anything. He failed. It was with total astonishment that he suddenly felt a hand on his thigh.

You were supposed to keep your arms and hands flat on the padded seat support during launch. Rick turned. Deedee Mao was staring straight ahead of her. Her yellow face was oddly pale and rigid, but her fingers were squeezing and rubbing his leg.

"Wanna get it on when we're on the training station?" She could only be speaking to him, but he could hardly hear her or see her lips moving. "Y'know, in free-fall. I hear it's somethin' special."

It was the worst possible time for a sexual proposition. Even if he had liked Deedee, Rick was far too nervous to feel horny.

But he wasn't going to admit to her or anyone else just how he did feel.

"Sure." His voice sounded like an old man's. He cleared his throat. "Sure." Then he couldn't say any more.

Twelve, eleven, ten . . .

"I'll be in c-cabin t-t—." Deedee's fingers on his thigh were trembling. "Cabin t-t-twenty-eight."

Five, four, three—

"Oh, sweet Lord—"

Her hand was trembling worse. With fear, not passion. Rick felt a strange sympathy. Deedee was looking for distraction, anything to help her through the first seconds of launch.

"She's tracking," a crewman's voice said.

"Mirror's free."

Two, one . . .

Anything. And he needed distraction as much as she did.

Zero.

"Up ship."

As the final digit flickered into sight, Rick broke the rules, too. He lifted his arm from the padded support, and placed his hand on top of Deedee's.

Within half a second he knew that he had made the mistake of the century. Lift had begun. Deedee's hand and his own were suddenly welded together, pressed down by more than five gees of acceleration. His leg was tilted slightly upward and their joined hands inched up his thigh toward his groin.

Rick gasped with pain. If that monster weight kept moving up his body, it would turn him into a eunuch. He tried to lift his hand and arm and found them sheathed in lead. He could not raise his hand, let alone Deedee's. All he could do, with one desperate jerk, was push their hands a couple of inches away along his leg and hold them there.

The pain and pressure was excruciating. Deedee's whole forearm lay across his thigh. He could feel bruises forming there in real time. He sat silent and sweating, pushing and pushing forever, until without warning all weight vanished completely. His stomach at once came free of its moorings and started to float up into his throat, but before he had time to gag he was again pressed back into his seat.

"Power's on."

This time the force was endurable. It had to be the

two gees of the nuclear drive, though compared with the laser-boosted lift-off it felt like nothing.

Rick lifted his hand away from Deedee's, closed his eyes, and relaxed. After a few moments he felt her hand leave his thigh.

"Luban."

"Yeah?" He opened his eyes and glanced across at her. Deedee Mao's smooth yellow face was still pale but now it bore its usual belligerent expression.

"Don't get no funny ideas, Luban."

"Like what?"

"I mean, about what I said back there at lift-off."

"I won't."

"I mean, I was just making conversation."

"Like hell. You were scared white. You should change your name from Deedee to pee-pee. You were ready to pee in your pants."

"Making love to you appeals less than screwing a swamp toad."

"I guess you've tried that. Tough on the toad."

She reached over and grabbed his arm. "Listen, if you want to have this out when we get to the station, that's fine by me. I've eaten smart-ass jerks like you—"

She paused. The steady roar beneath them had ended. Suddenly they were in free-fall, gliding upward in dead silence. Rick once more felt his stomach start to move up his throat.

"—eaten them for breakf—" Deedee couldn't complete the word. Her brown eyes bulged and her mouth clamped shut. She turned away from Rick, reaching forward and trying to hold off long enough to get her suction mask into position.

Rick clenched his own teeth and closed his eyes again. He wished he could close his ears, too. Any smart-ass jerks that Deedee had eaten for breakfast were coming up again, along with everything else; and from the sound of it Deedee was just getting into her stride. Rick didn't want to watch.

Sex in free-fall—or, fighting, or anything else with the possible exception of dying—didn't seem to be in Rick and Deedee's immediate future.

Rick had been told many things about Vanguard Mining's operations, but he lacked the glue to put the pieces together. For instance, he knew from his briefings that franchises for commercial mining of the Belt had bogged down in endless debate within the Council of Nations. That deadlock had continued until the Council's own international (and multilingual) mining effort had ended in disaster, with the loss of all equipment and personnel.

At that point, business interests were suddenly permitted to mine the Belt—and welcome to it. The Council had decided that there was no profit to be made there, although they were more than ready to accept franchise fees. They were astonished when Vanguard Mining's prototype mine and refinery, in 2028, turned out to be profitable. In the sixteen years since then the company had established commercial mining and refining operations on thirty-eight different planetoids out in the Belt.

Rick knew all that. He had also been told, at the time of his first tests by Vanguard, that the woman speaking to him was located on a place called CM-2, in translunar orbit. It never occurred to him to connect those facts until the translunar vehicle carrying the trainees was close enough for Rick to actually see CM-2.

He had been expecting some sleek, clean-lined structure. Instead he found their vehicle was closing on a vast irregular lump of dark rock.

"That thing?" Rick spoke to Deedee, who was standing between him and Jigger Tait, a Vanguard miner who was hitching a ride back from Earth with the trainees. "That can't be the training center."

In the two days since first lift-off, Rick and Deedee had been observing a sort of armed truce. Neither one was sure enough of stomach stability to risk an assertion of superiority. So it was Jigger, big-boned, iron-stomached, unaffected by free-fall, and apparently totally self-confident in every way, who raised his pale eyebrows, sniffed disdainfully, and said, "Don't you guys know *anything*? That's CM-2 out there—commercial mine number two."

"But I thought the mines were all in the Belt."

"They are. But this one has been worked out commercially. When the nickel and iron and platinum and iridium were all gone they attached low-thrust engines and moved it to translunar, so now it's the headquarters for the training school."

"I don't remember that from the briefings." Rick looked questioningly at Deedee, who shook her head.

"Me neither."

"Then you didn't use the browse feature on your reader."

"We weren't told we had to."

Jigger sniffed again. "I'm sure you weren't. But I'll give you some free advice that I had to learn the hard way when I was a trainee: If you only do what you're told to do, you'll soon be in trouble at Vanguard Mining." Jigger lifted from his seat, moving effortlessly in the zero-gee environment. "Okay, kids. Better get your act together and strap in. We'll be docking in a couple more minutes."

He floated away toward the rear of the ship. Rick and Deedee lingered at the screen for a few seconds longer, peering at the object ahead of the transfer vehicle. Now that they were closer they could see how big it was. Each of the wartlike bubbles that covered the surface of the planetoid was actually the exit point for a three-meter mine shaft. The whole object must be riddled with tunnels. CM-2 was more like a whole world than a training station.

The now-familiar warning siren began to wail. Thrust was coming in sixty seconds. Rick led the way back to their seats, striving to mimic the easy free-space motion of Jigger Tait. He couldn't do it. After a few seconds of aimless drifting he was forced to pull himself along using seat backs as handholds. Convinced that Deedee was watching him and laughing, he turned his head. She had just bounced off a wall and was turning end-over-end with a bewildered expression on her face.

One thing about free-fall, Rick thought as they reached CM-2 and went through docking, pressurization, and disembarkation: it made you a lot less likely to laugh at somebody else—because you never knew how soon your turn would come to look like an idiot.

As he left the pressurized dock he turned and caught a glimpse of Earth through the transparent overhead dome. It hung above him, about twice as big as a full Moon.

He halted and stared up at it for a long time. Somewhere on that globe was his school, with Screw and Hoss and Juanita and Jackie, with Mr. Hamel and Mr. Preebane and Principal Rigden. They were seven hundred thousand kilometers away.

They felt more like seven hundred million.

"Let me introduce myself." The man was plump and balding, with fleshy cheeks and drooping jowls. "I'm Turkey Gossage, chief of the training program on CM-2. You can think of me as the principal here—the head teacher. You don't know it yet, but I'm the best thing that ever happened to you."

Rick had taken a position near the back. He craned for a better look. The man in front of the group was dressed in a black tank top and jeans rather than the standard blue jacket and slacks. He scowled aggressively as he stared at them, but his blue eyes were sparkling. There had been a low general mutter from the group, and he was reacting to it.

"You heard me, sweethearts? The best thing. So if you got something to say, get it off your chests now."

No one spoke.

"You, sweetheart." Gossage pointed a finger at a woman in the front row. "I see your mouth moving, but I don't hear you. Don't whisper. Tell all of us."

"Don't you call me sweetheart!" It was Deedee, not much to Rick's surprise. "You can't do that."

"I can't, eh?" Gossage was grinning, but his neck and jowls turned red as turkey wattles. It was suddenly obvious how he got his nickname. "Why not?"

"Because it's degrading, and it's insulting. It's also sexually discriminatory. Do it one more time, and I'll take you to court." Deedee paused.

"You mean you'll sue me?" Gossage grinned again, but now it was unexpectedly friendly. "Sweetheart, that word is music to my ears. It proves we've got innocent new blood out here on CM-2, and it leads me straight in to what I have to say to all of you. Let's get a few things out of the way right now. First, forget the sexual discrimination talk. I call *everyone* sweetheart. You, and bluebeard standing next to you, and the one at the back with the shitface grin on his chops." Gossage was looking right at Rick. Rick stopped smiling.

"Far as I'm concerned," Gossage went on, "you're all sweethearts 'til you prove otherwise. As for suing me, the best of British luck to you. You're not on sue-'em-all Earth now. We got exactly two lawyers out beyond the Moon, and they're up to their asses in mineral depletion allowances and tax codes. If you can afford their time, you don't belong here. And if you did manage to sue, you'd lose for reasons that I'll go into in a minute. So tell me what else is on your mind. You were angry before I ever called you sweetheart."

Deedee shook her head. It was another youth in the second row who spoke up. "What's this *teacher* bullshit? I done with school three months ago. Nuthin' 'bout school in anythin' anybody said to me."

"I see. What's your name?"

"Cokie Mulligan."

"All right, Cokie Mulligan. Nothing about school in anything anybody said to you. Right. You read your contract, did you? The one that you and your parents or guardians signed."

"Sure I did."

"The whole thing?—including the fine print."

Mulligan hesitated. "Yes."

"Then you noticed the place where it says that Vanguard Mining, and in particular its authorized instructors—people like me—are *in loco parentis* to you for the duration of your contract."

"Whaz zat mean?"

"*In loco parentis* means in place of your parents." Turkey Gossage smiled horribly at Mulligan. "So now I'm like your daddy and your mommy, all rolled up into one. And I'm going to take better care of you than they ever did."

Mulligan shook his head. "Maybe. But I don't want no teacher, an' I'm not goin' to no dumb school. I hate school and I'm done school. I never signed up for that."

There was a general mutter of agreement from everyone in the group.

"I see." Turkey Gossage turned, floated across to a chair facing the front of the room, and straddled it with his forearms folded along the back. "What we have here, I suspect, is a simple failure to communicate. It's that hated word, *school*, isn't it? It suggests the wrong thing to all of you, and I shouldn't have used it.

"All right. Let's agree that this isn't a school. Let's say it's a survival course for off-Earth mining operations. The Belt is a dangerous place. You can fuck up big-time out there, eat vacuum, O/D on radiation, blow yourself up, get flattened by an ore crusher, get stranded and starve to death. No legal liability for Vanguard Mining—read your contract. But Vanguard doesn't want you dead, because it cost us money to get you here, and it'll cost more to send you out to the belt. We have an investment in you. So it's my job to make sure that by the time you leave here you know how to *avoid* killing yourself. That means learning a few new rules. Anybody object to the idea of surviving?"

Rick shook his head and glanced around at the others. Everyone was doing the same.

"Good." The smile had never left Turkey Gossage's face. "Now we get down to details. I'm going to give you assignments that have to be completed before bedtime. But before we talk about them I want to talk about you. I'm sure you all think you're hotshots and special and smarter than most people. And you actually are—otherwise you wouldn't be here at all. But smart or not, at the moment you're still zeros. No skills means no value.

"Before we're through here, that will change. You'll have skills. You'll have value. Out here you'll earn that self-esteem they shovel at downers. If you live long enough you'll have a reason to think you're hotshots and special. And it all starts with the assignments. Today it will be reading. All right?"

Nods all round.

"Just one thing." Turkey Gossage was deliberately casual. "I said reading, and I meant reading. By you. Not with a reading machine. There will be times out in the Belt where a knowledge of complex instructions is vital and no electronic readers are available. So you have to be able to read. I'll let you into a big secret, something you'd never be told in an Earth school: reading is easy. Practically everyone can learn to read with a bit of effort. All of you can, or you wouldn't be here. And we won't go too fast at first. Short words, easy sentences." There was a stir at the back of the class. A short-haired and overweight blond girl was moving toward the door.

"Now where are you going?" Gossage did not raise his voice. "Leaving us already?"

She turned angrily at the doorway. "Yes, I am."

"What's your name?"

"I'm Gladys de Witt. I didn't read none when I was in school, and I'm damned if I'm going to start now I'm out of it. Go fuck yourself, Gossage. You think you're the boss, but you're not. You can't stop me leaving. I seen the contract. I don't have to stay. It says you can't use violence on me, neither."

"That's quite true. I can't prevent anyone of you from leaving. I can't be violent with you. And I can't make you complete your assignments." Gossage nodded slowly. "Very true. All I can do, Gladys de Witt, is explain these to you." He held up a handful of small pink cards. "They are meal vouchers. You need one to obtain food from the cafeteria service system. When you complete your assignment satisfactorily—by this evening, or tomorrow morning, or tomorrow midday, or whenever—you will receive one voucher. But if you fail to complete your assignment to my satisfaction, you will not."

"You can't do that to me!"

"I'm afraid I can. Read your contract. Vanguard Mining, *in loco parentis*, decides the manner and extent of trainee nutrition. Now, Gladys. Are you going to leave? Cookie has some oatmeal and vitamin pills, you'll get all of that you want. Or would you like to stay here with the rest of the trainees while I explain today's assignment? Dinner is lasagna with mushrooms, peppers, and garlic bread. The choice is yours."

Turkey Gossage could smile and coax with the best of them, but he was one tough son of a bitch. He hadn't been kidding about the food voucher policy. After a couple of missed meals, even the toughest and most ornery—and hungriest—trainee came into angry line.

Rick observed closely, then put Turkey Gossage into his "handle with care" category. What he couldn't understand, though, was how Gossage had found himself such a pleasant, easygoing—and droolingly sexy—assistant.

Gina Styan was a graduate trainee from three years back, returned for two months to work with Gossage on CM-2 before she went to her post on the newest of the thirty-eight Belt mines. She had a figure that made Juanita Cesaro look like a boy, clear dark skin, and short-cropped black hair that emphasized delicate bone structure and high cheekbones. Those, plus what Rick read as an unmistakable interest in her brown eyes whenever she looked at him, bristled the hair on the back of his neck. The sight of her made him catch his breath.

She had the hots for him, too. He was sure of it. All it would take was a quiet place and an opportunity.

Which seemed to be exactly what CM-2 was designed not to provide. It was just as well that Deedee Mao's lift-off invitation to Cabin Twenty-eight had been bogus, because it now proved to be impossible. She shared Cabin Twenty-eight with three other trainees. Rick was no better off. His cabin had five recruits in it, including Cokie Mulligan, who snored like a saw in free-fall, though he swore he hadn't when he was back on Earth.

It was no better during work periods. The recruits were never out of each other's sight, except when they were busy on their assignments. Then they were permitted the privacy of a single small cubicle. After the first week Rick suspected Turkey Gossage of doing that on purpose. When the only way to be alone was to sit in a little room by yourself and pretend to study, you found yourself actually studying much of the time out of sheer boredom.

Almost against his will, Rick found himself reading. He still wasn't good, and he resented every word, but within a couple of weeks he'd have beaten everybody in his old class and most of his fellow trainees. He was in no hurry to rush on ahead of them. After reading, Turkey Gossage threatened pure and applied mathematics— "the high spot of all your training," as he put it, without convincing anyone.

But all this left Rick's problem with Gina Styan unsolved. How was he ever going to make out with her if they were never alone?

A possible answer came in the third week, when the pure theory of space operations gave way to practical experience. All the trainees had become accustomed to free-fall, so nausea was a thing of the past. But manual work in space was another matter. That took lots of practice.

And practice they were going to get, in assignments that Turkey Gossage described as "Manual coordination and control in a weightless environment." A euphemism, as Rick soon discovered, for unpaid hard labor.

Weightless environment. Moving things around in space, where an object didn't weigh anything, sounded easy as breathing. Nothing to it. Jigger Tait, staying a while on CM-2 with Turkey Gossage before shipping to the Belt again, assured Rick as much. Then he and Rick went together to the deep interior of CM-2 to clear one of the chambers. They moved massive pilings and metal I-beams and irregular chunks of rock.

After four hours of that Rick ached in every bone. His burdens might have no weight, but they still possessed inertia. And inertia was *worse* than weight. Back on Earth, once you had lifted something you could just let it drop and gravity would do the rest. Here you had to start a rock moving, then put in just as much work to stop it.

But Jigger had not been lying. He did the work effortlessly. It was easy as breathing—for him.

Rick wondered how many other half-truths and hidden catches were tucked away in the Vanguard Mining training program. Turkey Gossage was sticking to his policy on the meal vouchers. Rick had handed in his last assignment late, and been handed a meal ticket just before he had to leave with Jigger. It sat burning a hole in his pocket while his stomach growled in protest. He could hardly wait for the word to quit.

But when Jigger Tait told him they were done for the day, Rick still had enough energy and curiosity to notice something when they emerged through the air lock from the planetoid's stony interior. It was a different lock from their entry point and next to it sat another small chamber. It was like no other structure that Rick had seen. There were flat, solid, windowless walls and a massive close-fitting door.

Rick's question produced no more than a shrug and a dismissive "Historical interest only." Jigger Tait would have continued back around the planetoid toward the training facility quarters, but Rick stopped in front of him and swung open the heavy door.

"Hey! Padded floor and walls. What's the deal?"

"Bolt-hole." Jigger followed him inside. The interior lights had come on automatically. "Before the mining produced deep interior tunnels, the miners always faced a radiation danger. Our suits aren't enough to protect us."

"Solar flares?"

"Yeah." Jigger stared at Rick. "I thought you couldn't read."

"Movies. Show it as standard hazard for space travel."

"Well, for once they got it right. If you're out on the surface of an asteroid and a big flare hits, you have three choices: you can move to the interior tunnels, if there are any, or you can head for a special shielded chamber like this one. Me, I'll take this any day. Your own air, see, the interior fills by itself when the door is locked. And there's plenty of reserves of food and drink. Stay here for a week if you had to."

"But there's no air lock."

"There is on the inside. That was put in later. When they built this they figured anyone coming in from space might be in one hell of a hurry."

"You said there are three choices?"

"Sure." Jigger was already moving back through the thick door. "You can stay outside and fry if you want to. Freedom of choice. Isn't that what people back on Earth are all so proud of?"

"Freedom to die?"

"Sure. Most basic right of all." Jigger started around the planetoid, swinging easily along on the fixed network of cables. "Hell, you should be free to die when you want, where you want, how you want. If you're not, your body and your life don't belong to you at all. They belong to your keepers."

"You can die any way you want to?"

"Sure. Anyone works for Vanguard Mining has that right. But dying is a right, not an obligation. So watch your step, Rick. Space is more dangerous than you think."

Rick remembered those words, more or less. But what he thought about a lot more in the next few days was that shielded chamber. Radiation-proof—and soundproof. He visited it a couple more times when he had no other duties. Thick walls, padded floor, and tight-fitting door. Total privacy. Just what he needed.

It took four days before he could trade with Gladys de Witt for her next one-on-one training session with Gina Styan in the interior of CM-2. Fortunately Gladys had her own hot ideas about Jigger Tait. She didn't tell Rick what this particular training was for, and Rick didn't ask. He'd move a lot of rocks for a chance at Gina.

This time his job turned out to be both easier and harder than manual labor. Rick had to learn to operate remote-controlled cutting equipment, and Gina proved to be a hell of a tough teacher. She ran him through scores of operating steps again and again, watching him with that slightly mocking, sexy, and intimate look on her face whenever he messed up a sequence.

"There's a hell of a lot to this." Rick felt obliged to defend himself when the session ended with the cutter under his control waltzing wildly sideways to gouge a hole in the tunnel sidewall. "How long did it take you to remember all the variations?"

"I'm not sure I ever did."

"You have a pictorial prompt in your suit helmet? Then why in hell didn't you give me one?"

"No prompt." Gina waved a small red book at Rick. "The control steps are in here, along with a lot of other stuff. But it's all in words and formulas. Once you can read well—"

"This is really dumb. A few simple pictures, that's all it would take."

"You think so? Listen to this, then you tell me how you would put it into pictures. 'Pressure equalization between old and new drilling is best achieved by releasing stored air into the evacuated chamber. The cutting equipment normally produces a straight cylindrical cavity three meters in diameter, so the volume to be filled is simply $2.25.\pi.L$ cubic meters, where L is the length of the new drilled tunnel in meters.' You know what π is?"

"I think so. I'm not sure." Rick was actually quite sure. Sure he didn't.

"It's a mathematical constant. Draw me a picture of that if you can. Do you know its value?"

Rick shook his head. This wasn't going the way he had imagined it, but he'd bide his time. Let Gina feel superior for the moment. She would find out soon enough who was the real boss.

"Why should I bother to know any of that math stuff? If I ever need it, I'll pull it up on a calculator."

"π is equal to 3.14159." She didn't seem to have heard him. "That's to six significant figures. It's as accurate as you'll probably ever need unless you get into orbit work. You'll have the value of π engraved on your brainstem and your butt before you leave CM-2, along with a lot of other numbers you've never heard of yet. And while we're at it, let me tell you what happens to a calculator or an electronic prompter during a blowout or a big radiation storm: they die, or they become totally unreliable. But this"—Gina held up the red book—"it can stand more radiation, heat, and cold than you can.

By the time a book like this became unusable, you and I would be long dead." She tucked the book into a pocket on her suit. "You'll learn. Let's go."

Rick had learned, at least some things. He had spent many hours studying and committing to memory the network of passages and chambers that crisscrossed the interior of CM-2. Without saying anything to Gina he headed for the surface along a particular set of passages. He emerged, just as planned, right beside the shielded chamber. The door was as he had left it, slightly ajar.

He stopped when he came to it.

"You ever been in one of these before?"

"Ages ago. This, or one just like it." Gina was glancing around her with no particular interest. "I don't know why they keep this place in working order. It has no uses since the interior was excavated."

"It does." Rick swung the heavy door into position and pressed the sealing button. Interior lights came on at once and there was a hiss of released air. He went across and checked that the inner door was also sealed.

"Not needed for radiation protection," he went on, "but it has other uses." He took off his suit helmet and gestured to Gina to do the same.

"You're wasting air." But Gina did not sound much concerned by that, and she followed Rick's lead and removed her own helmet. "Other uses? Like what?"

"Like this." Rick had been sizing up their positions and rehearsing his own next action. He knew the moves and he was pretty experienced, but that had been back on Earth. He had to do things differently in free-fall.

The smart thing was to make the first step one that he knew very well. He was close to the chamber wall. He kicked off from it, drove hard across the room, and pinned Gina against the opposite wall. He had to use both arms and legs to hold her there, but they had finished face-to-face.

"Gina." He spoke in a whisper, though he could have screamed and no one else would have heard a thing.

"Gina, you're really something special. Let's get out of these dumb suits and have some fun." He tried to kiss her, but she turned her head away.

"Dammit, Rick, that's enough fooling. And it's not funny. Let me go."

He almost did. Then he remembered Screw Savage's advice to him and Hoss. "*No* never means no with a woman. They say it because they like to play hard to get, but they really want it bad as you do. You gotta ignore what they *say* and keep chargin'. Go for the gold!"

Rick moved his left arm quickly to turn Gina's head back toward him, pressed his mouth to hers, and started to give her a French kiss. His right hand felt at the same time for her breast.

It was as though he had pressed a starter button. As his fingers met her left nipple through the resilient material of the suit, her right knee pistoned up between his legs. It hit him squarely in the crotch like a bony hammer.

Rick gasped and curled up into a ball, hanging in mid-air. He was sure that the blow had burst his testicles, or driven them right back inside his body. He vaguely heard Gina speak through his fog of pain.

"You little shit! *Nobody* does that to me, *ever*. Apologize." She had him by the ear, pulling it off his head. "Apologize, right now, or I'll really hurt you."

Rick was curled up, forehead close to his knees. He could hardly breathe, and he certainly couldn't apologize. But if he didn't, she might do the same thing to him again.

"Sorry!" It was more a gasp than a word. "Sorry."

"I don't know what made you think I'd be interested in a semiliterate oaf like you, but here's news: I'm not."

She let go of his ear, then clapped his helmet onto his head hard enough to make his ears ring. While he hung dizzy and helpless, she flipped his suit seals into position. "You can find your own way back, dummy, or die trying. I don't much care which."

Rick heard the inner door slam shut and the air lock cycling. He tried to lift his head to see if Gina had gone, until a worse worry took over. Nausea swept over him. He felt ready to vomit—inside his suit.

He swallowed hard, closed his eyes, and fought the urge. The spasm slowly faded. By the time it was over his forehead was beaded with cold sweat and the sickness had been replaced by an agonizing throbbing in his belly and groin.

Fifteen minutes passed before he felt well enough to leave the chamber. Then it was a miserable splay-legged crawl back to the training facilities. He paused before entering.

What had Gina told Turkey Gossage? Surely, the whole horrible episode. Rick was done for. He was going to be kicked out of this place, just as he had been kicked out of school. And where could he go now? Back to join the Pool on Earth?

He couldn't hang around outside forever, and there was no real point in trying to avoid Gossage. Better to get it over with.

Rick eased his way out of his suit and limped to Turkey's office. He didn't see anyone else on the way, and he almost changed his mind when he was right at the entrance. But Gossage had already seen him on the threshold and waved him in.

"You took your time." Gossage nodded to Rick and at once returned his attention to the screen in front of him. "I didn't think you'd make it before I closed for the day. Help yourself to your meal voucher."

Rick, tensed and ready for a storm of anger, stared at Gossage openmouthed. "What did Gina say?"

Turkey really looked at Rick for the first time. "Say? Why, what do you think she said? You did well. I know you rammed the wall with the cutter at the end, but Gina said that the test she gave you was harder than anything in the standard course. So you passed. Now, go and eat. You must be starving."

Rick grabbed the voucher and left before Gossage could ask him anything. But he didn't feel in the least like eating, and still less like going into the cafeteria where he might have to face Gina. He was sore, exhausted, and bewildered. He started for his cabin, knowing that he needed rest. Then he visualized Cokie Mulligan and the other trainees, watching him stagger in and starting the questions.

He couldn't stand that, either. Where could he go?

The only place he could think of was the gym. It should be deserted. There was light centrifugal gravity, and showers. He could examine and bathe his bruised and tender parts, stretch out on a couch, and not move until it was time to wake up and use his meal voucher for breakfast.

He dragged his way toward the outer circle of the training area where the gym was located, thankful that it was a time when few people were about. Safe inside the bathhouse, he removed all his clothes and took a warm bath. He examined himself closely. So far as he could tell everything down there was perfectly normal. He didn't even seem to be swollen, though it felt that way from the inside. Finally he went into the shower, set the water temperature as hot as he could stand, and simply let the steam run over his head and back for a long time.

By the time he dried himself and put on a change of clothing he was feeling human again. He emerged from the shower area and stopped. The gym was no longer deserted. Jigger Tait was running laps, round and round the inside of the big hi-gee wheel. He must have been there for a while, because his blue tee shirt was stained with sweat.

He nodded down at Rick when he caught sight of him and ran around the hoop of the track toward him. "Want to join me?"

Rick shook his head and started toward the exit. But he couldn't help moving in an awkward bowlegged fashion.

"You all right?" Jigger stepped closer.

"Yeah. I'm all right."

"You sure don't look it. You walk like you got a case of hemorrhoids or you just took a dump in your pants. What happened?"

"I just—" Rick paused. He didn't have a lie in his head. Anyway, Jigger would find out soon enough, along with everybody else. He sighed. "I just did something really dumb."

And suddenly it all came spilling out, even worse in retelling than in reality. Jigger stood and listened without saying a word, the sweat cooling on his moon face and steam rising from his damp tee shirt. It was only after Rick told how he had made his move on Gina, and she had kneed him in the testicles, that Jigger shook his head and said, "Wish I'd been there."

"You'd have stopped her?"

"No. I'd have broken you in two." Jigger grabbed Rick by the arm and led him to a pair of rowing machines, the only place where the two of them could sit down facing each other. "How old are you, kid?"

"Sixteen."

"Thought so. Know how old Gina is?"

"Nineteen?"

"She's twenty-two. You're like a baby to her. Hell, you *are* a baby. Back in school you probably felt like a real big shot—I know I did. I'd had girls, busted teachers, the whole bit. But to Gina a kid from Earth is still in diapers. I'd say each year in space, 'specially in the Belt, is like three on Earth. You were a little kid making a pass at a grown-up."

"But she didn't report it to Gossage. And she passed me on the test I took."

"So it didn't really upset her. How'd you feel if a ten-year-old came on strong to you? You'd think it was ludicrous. And you were being tested for proficiency, not maturity. Anyway, believe it or not, Gina likes you.

If she didn't, she'd have ripped your balls off and stuffed them down your throat. Got away with it, too. What ever made you think for one second that she might be interested in you?"

"She looked at me like she was really fond of me."

"Yeah. Know why? Because you remind her of her kid brother. He's back on Earth and going nowhere, just the way she was before she was sent out here. Gina admits it, she used to be a real tearaway. Her parents couldn't do a damn thing with her. But her brother's less of a rebel, and she's afraid he'll just stick in school to the end and finish up in the Pool."

"You don't think she'll tell anyone about what I did?"

"Don't see why she should. But I'll talk to her and make sure."

"Will she listen to you?"

"I think so." Jigger stared at Rick for a second, his head to one side. "You're not too observant, are you? I mean, you've never noticed that Gina and I are an item, have been for a year and a half. That's why I came to CM-2 instead of heading right out for the Belt. That's why I know about her, and what a hellcat she used to be, and all about her kid brother."

Rick gazed at Jigger in horror. He had just remembered what Jigger said about breaking him in two. "I didn't know—I didn't notice. I'm sorry. I mean, if I'd had any idea that you two—"

"You know now. Nothing wrong with feeling horny, either—it means you're physically adjusting to space. But stick to trainees. And don't forget one other thing. California where you came from has the strongest laws in the known universe against sexual harassment and rape, but they still don't work worth a damn. Out here we do things differently. A woman is taught a few tricks so she can look after herself. Deedee and the rest of the women have had special training. Remember that if you want to keep your balls." Jigger stood up from the rowing

machine, came across, and patted Rick on the shoulder.
"And while your jewels are still sore, use what happened
with Gina to remind you of one other thing: If you want
to survive in space, it's not enough to be able to read and
write and calculate. You have to learn to *notice* things—
the sort of stuff you won't find in any book."

Rick skulked for a week. He hid away in the privacy
of the study cubicles, until finally and inevitably he had
the dreaded face-to-face meeting with Gina. She came
into the cafeteria with a group of trainees while he was
taking a hurried meal.

Rick froze. But her casual greeting suggested that
nothing unusual had ever happened between them. Rick
breathed a prayer of thanks and decided that he could
return to a normal life.

He was wrong. That same afternoon he was summoned
to Turkey Gossage's office. Worried again, he was in no
hurry to get there and only a little relieved to find Deedee
Mao arriving at the same time.

Gossage nodded them to seats on the other side of
the circular table that he used as a desk. He went on
studying a monitor, invisible to Rick and Deedee. He
was muttering to himself, until at last he looked up.

"I guess you two think you're real hotshots. Or don't
you know?"

Rick glanced at Deedee. She seemed just as puzzled as
he was.

"I guess not." Gossage was studying their faces. "So
I'll tell you. The pair of you are sitting at the top of the
trainee heap. You've done well. You'll have to fuck up
real bad now to avoid graduating."

Rick's pleasure at that news lasted for only a second, because Turkey was continuing, "Naturally, since
you're such hotshots we want you to have a specially
good chance to make a mess of things. For the pair
of you the training course just moved beyond theory
and supervised instruction. Tomorrow morning you'll

be partners on a practical exercise in space ore mining. And I promise you, it won't be easy. I suggest you spend the rest of today studying the problem. You have until the close of the workday tomorrow to complete the assignment."

Rick and Deedee exchanged grimaces. They had pretty much avoided each other since their first lift-off into orbit. Now they were supposed to cooperate—even *depend* on each other.

"Studying *together*." Gossage had read their faces. "The more you know about each other's strengths and weaknesses, the better. And remember something else: in the real world you don't always get assigned to projects with your best buddies. Go get to work. The universe doesn't care how much people like each other."

The "practical exercise" that Gossage and his staff had prepared did not sound too hard. Rick and Deedee would load a five-hundred-ton ore carrier with low-grade tailings, controlling a semismart mining robot to do all the heavy work. They would fly the carrier to CM-2's refinery, drop off the ore, and return to the mine area on the empty carrier. Their own safe return through CM-2's interior would mark the end of the exercise.

But as Deedee remarked, the devil was in the details. Smartness in a mining robot was a mixed blessing, and the instructions given to it must limit its initiative. That meant learning the interaction manual and understanding the robot's powers and limitations. The ore carrier was no better. Examining its flight path and fuel needs, Rick and Deedee learned that the fuel supply provided for the round trip was barely enough. One mistake, even a small one, would leave them drifting helplessly away from CM-2 and calling for help from an empty carrier. Turkey Gossage, obviously by intention, had provided no precomputed flight trajectory.

Finally there was a hidden variable mentioned nowhere

in the project description: according to training course rumor and legend, Gossage always threw in some extra problem on a practical test, a zinger that could not be predicted ahead of time. You found out about it when it hit you in the face.

Working with Deedee, Rick grudgingly had to admit that she was *smart*. She seemed less cocky and belligerent than he remembered her, and she caught on to new ideas at least as fast as he did. He suspected that in a pinch she could read and remember better. And she never seemed to get tired.

Rick tried to match her. He drove himself harder than ever before, until late at night they found themselves sitting side by side and staring helplessly at a set of schematics. The lines on the screen seemed to blur and curve as Rick watched. The circuit had to be completed correctly before the display would advance but nothing seemed to work.

"It *can't* be that hard," Rick muttered at last.

"It isn't." Deedee sighed and reached forward to turn off the display. "It's us. We've saturated. At least, I have. How about you?"

"An hour ago. I just didn't want to admit it." Rick stood and reached up to rub at his stiffened neck muscles. "Better get some sleep. We've got a big day ahead."

"Yeah." Deedee stretched. "I'm in Cabin Twenty-eight. Wanna get it on? Y'know, in free-fall. I hear it's somethin' special."

Her tone of voice was casual and she wasn't looking at Rick. But she was smiling.

He shook his head. "Better with a swamp toad. God. That was us. Only a couple of months and it seems like ten years ago."

"It *was* ten years. Ten real years." Deedee headed for the exit. "Who said that time proceeds at a uniform rate? Whoever it was, he was crazy."

"Or she was."

"Fair enough. Good night, Rick."

" 'Night, Deedee. Sleep well."

Maybe she did. Rick certainly didn't. He woke long before he needed to, the details of the project swarming through his mind. After half an hour of tossing and turning he rose, dressed, and headed for the cafeteria. He was still ordering a meal when Deedee wandered in. Her face was calm but a little pale.

She came straight up to him. "Anything in the rules that says we can't start early?"

"Nothing I know of."

"Right. Let's get going."

"No." Rick gestured to the place opposite him. "First you eat."

"Hunger sharpens the brain."

"And low blood sugar turns it off." Rick keyed in a huge meal for her, then felt obliged to increase his own order. "We eat. Then we go."

They chewed doggedly, without enjoyment, watching each other's plate until both were empty. By the time they had finished it was close to official breakfast time. Unwilling to talk to other trainees, they hurried out and headed for the lock that led to the interior of CM-2.

The hardest thing of all was to avoid rushing. They put their suits on carefully and checked each other's seals. No little surprises there from Turkey Gossage. But as Deedee pointed out, he was not likely to do anything so obvious.

"Which means if he *did* do something obvious," Rick pointed out, "it *would* surprise us. No assumptions."

"Agreed. No assumptions."

They drifted together through the deep interior of CM-2, heading for the side of the planetoid opposite to the main training facilities. The corridor by now seemed as familiar as home. They did not need to consult maps or tracers. The ore carrier and the mining robot, as promised, were waiting in the main loading chamber.

The tailings had already been sintered to form oddly shaped but identical solid blocks, each weighing half a ton. At a pinch, Rick and Deedee could load each one themselves; but that was a sure way to flunk the exercise.

They put the mining robot through its paces on a dummy run, checking that each movement corresponded exactly to that pictured. Finally, and gingerly, Deedee directed the machine to begin loading. She watched the pickup stage, while Rick counted blocks and monitored their stowing aboard the ore carrier. There were still a hundred more to go when he came out and told Deedee to stop.

"Why? The robot's doing fine."

"Maybe. But we have a problem. The carrier is nearly full. It won't take more than another couple of dozen and we've only loaded nine hundred."

"That can't be right. The carrier is rated for at least five hundred tons cargo mass. Maybe the blocks are heavier than they're supposed to be? Or maybe they're less dense and bigger."

They checked the mass of a sintered block. It was half a ton exactly. Its density was as it should be. Then they crouched in the loading chamber, helmet to helmet, and pored over the electronic and printed manuals. At last Rick sighed. "I get it. I'm a dummy. I should have realized it as soon as the loading started."

Deedee was still staring at the electronic layout diagram of the carrier. "Well, I don't. Everything looks just fine."

"The carrier's fine. The ore blocks are fine, too."

"So what's the problem?"

"It's the *shape* of the blocks. I noticed they looked odd when we first came in. They have the right mass and density but they don't pack tight. There's too much space left between them."

"So what do we do?"

"We look for a better packing arrangement, one that fits the blocks together more tightly."

Ten minutes of useless brainstorming was enough to prove that they would never find the answer by abstract thought. Under Deedee's direction the mining robot began to fit blocks one on another, turning them every way to seek the best fit of the irregular faces. The right answer, when they finally reached it, seemed absolutely obvious. With one particular arrangement the sintered blocks keyed in together tightly and seamlessly.

Then the carrier had to be unloaded, and the whole operation begun over. This time the five hundred tons fitted with room to spare. Deedee came over to watch the last block go in. She ordered the mining robot in on top of it before she closed the hatch.

"Think that was the Gossage surprise?" she said as she followed Rick into the ore carrier's control room.

"The first one, maybe. Nobody said he keeps it to one. There could be another right here."

They examined the carrier's status indicators one by one with enormous care, until at last Deedee shrugged. "We can't stay here forever just looking. Do it, Rick."

Under Rick's nervous control the carrier crept forward out of the loading chamber and into open space. By all Belt standards the journey was a trivial one: a couple of hundred kilometers through unobstructed vacuum, to rendezvous with another body having negligible velocity relative to CM-2. The training facility's refinery was in an essentially identical orbit around the Earth-Moon system.

That fact did not offer Rick any sense of security. He was keyed tighter than he had ever been until at last the carrier was snugly into the refinery's dock. Then it was Deedee's turn. She unloaded the robot and it carried the sintered ore blocks one by one to the refinery's gigantic hopper. They stared at each other as the final block went in.

"Smooth," Deedee said at last.

"Too smooth?"

"There's no such thing."

"You know what I mean." Rick stared at the distant bulk of CM-2, its outside lights clearly visible from the refinery. "Let's get back. If there are surprises here, I don't want to hang around and wait for them to find us."

He checked the fuel as he switched on the drive. More than enough. He could cut off power after a couple of minutes, coast all the rest of the way to CM-2, and finish with a little fuel to spare. And even with the delay in loading they had plenty of time to complete the assignment before the end of the work period. Maybe the only Gossage surprise was the sintered block shape.

That comforting thought was still in his head when he realized that the star field outside was slowly rotating. Instead of heading straight for CM-2 the ore carrier was yawing, turning its blunt prow farther and farther away from the planned heading.

Rick slapped at the controls and turned all thrust power off.

"What's wrong?" Although Rick had not said a word, Deedee caught the urgency of his movement.

"Drive. We're crabbing." Rick was already calling up onto the control display the rear perspective layout of the carrier, to show the six independent but balanced units that provided the ship's drive. "Something's wrong with one of the modules. We're getting no thrust from it."

Deedee was watching the changing starscape in the front port, noting the exact direction of rotation of the ship. "We're tilting to the right and down." She touched her gloved hand to the display, one finger on the stylized image of a module. "If it's a problem with just one thruster, it has to be this one. Any of the others would turn us in a different direction."

"Agreed."

"So turn off the opposite one of the six, directly across from the bad one. Do it, Rick! That will balance us again."

"I can't." Rick gestured at the control panel. "The thrust modules aren't separately controllable. It's all or nothing."

"So what do we do?"

Rick did not answer. He had called up a section of the ship's manual onto the display. More than anything he had ever wanted in his life, he wanted to read that manual. And he couldn't. The words were too long and unfamiliar, the sentences seemed too complex. He strained to understand, willing the words to make sense. And still he couldn't read them. The ship was drifting along, but CM-2 was not directly ahead. Their present course would miss the planetoid.

"Help me, Deedee." Rick was sweating inside his suit. "Help me to figure this out. The manual will tell us what to do. It has to. Help me to read. You read better than me."

"I don't. You know I don't." But Deedee was following Rick's lead, reading each word on the screen aloud, stumbling over the hard ones.

They struggled on, reading in unison, cursing unknown words, correcting each other. Until finally Deedee cried out and pointed at the display, "Att-it-ude. That's what the word is. *Attitude control.* This is the part we want. Come on, Rick. Read it!"

Rick was certainly trying; but he had already discovered that simple need and urgency didn't let you read any faster. They ground on together, word by word, through the next three paragraphs. And at a certain point, groaned in unison.

"It's *obvious!*" Rick slapped his knee with his gloved hand.

"And we're idiots." Deedee repeated the important sentences, gabbling them on the second time through. " 'In the event of thrust module imbalance, the carrier must be returned to the main maintenance facility.'—Yeah. Thanks a lot—'However, should a thrust module fail and a temporary course adjustment be necessary in space, this can easily be performed by the use of minor lateral control jets. These can be used to spin the ship about its long-it-ud-in-al'—hell of a word—'axis, so that the mean thrust is maintained in the desired direction. The same elementary technique can be used to make general direction adjustments, by halting longitudinal rotation after any suitable angle.' Do it, Rick!"

"I am doing it." Rick was already using the lateral thrusters, turning the ship about its main axis to bring the failed thruster module onto the opposite side. "I'm going to have to juggle this. If I thrust too long in the other direction, we'll swing too far and miss the base on the other side."

"Do it in—little bits." The main thrusters fired, this time in a pattern as jerky as Deedee's speech. "We still have plenty of time. Go easy. You can afford to go easy."

"I will go easy. Trust me."

Rick was eyeing CM-2 as it swung back into view in the forward port. Under his control the drive was stuttering uneasily on and off while the ship rotated unevenly about its main axis. He knew exactly where he wanted to go—into the hard-edged aperture that sat like a bullet hole in the planetoid's rugged side. But getting there, exactly there, was another matter. It was another half hour before Rick could turn off all power, shiver in released tension, lift his hands from the controls, and wait for the magnetic arrest system to guide the carrier to a berth within CM-2.

Before the grapple was complete Deedee was out of her seat and heading for the lock. "Come on. We have to go."

"What's the hurry?" Rick was moving more slowly, stretching cramped hands as he eased himself from the pilot's chair. "You said we had plenty of time."

"I lied." Deedee was already in the lock, waiting impatiently. "I didn't want you worrying about time when you were flying the carrier. But it's going to be touch and go."

Rick took a glance at his helmet chronometer and leaped for the lock. "We only have twenty-three minutes left!"

"I know." The lock was cycling. "We can do it, though—so long as we don't meet any more snags."

They flew side by side from the docking berth to the mine entry point to CM-2. "Say, two minutes each end." Rick hit the entry combination. "Twelve minutes to get through the tunnels—that's about as fast as we can go. But we still have a seven-minute cushion." He keyed in the entry combination again. "What's wrong with this thing? It shouldn't take this long."

"The power has been turned off." Deedee pointed to the telltale set in the great door. "And it's too heavy for manual operation."

"Turkey. The bastard. He's screwed us. We can't get in."

"Then we'll have to go around. Or use one of the side tunnels?"

"No good. They all lead outside, not to the training facility."

"That's our answer." Deedee had turned. "We can go right around the outside. Don't waste time with that door, Rick. Come on! We're down to twenty-one minutes."

She led the way, zooming at maximum suit speed for the open entrance of the mine loading chamber. Rick, close behind, did the calculation. They had to make their way right around CM-2 to almost the opposite side of the planetoid. Say, three kilometers. If they could average ten per hour, they would do it. If not . . .

All Rick could think of was that early this morning he had made Deedee sit down and eat breakfast when she was hyped up and raring to go. If they were too late now, it was his fault.

They came to the edge of the loading chamber and burst out from the darkness. As Deedee, still ahead of

Rick, emerged into full sunlight she reversed suit jets and came to an abrupt dead halt.

"Keep going, Dee. I'm right behind you."

But she was not moving. "Listen to your dosimeter, Rick."

He became aware of a tinny rattle in the background. It was his suit's radiation monitor, operating well above the danger level.

"Back inside." And when he hesitated, "We have to, Rick. *Right now.*" She had him by the arm of his suit, towing him. "It must be a solar burst, a sudden one and a big one. We're safe enough as soon as we get some rock shielding around us."

They were already out of sight of the sun. Safe enough. And failed. Rick glanced at his chronometer. Eighteen and a half minutes.

"Deedee, we wouldn't be outside for very long. I'll bet the integrated dose would be small enough, it wouldn't harm us."

"Maybe. But are you sure?"

He wasn't. Worse than that, he didn't know how to make sure. The calculation couldn't be very difficult, no more than a formula and a few simple summations. Jigger would probably have done it in his head. But Rick didn't know how to do it at all. He groaned.

"We're safe enough here." Deedee had misunderstood the reason for his misery. "Rock is a perfect shield."

"I know. I don't want a shield. I want to beat the deadline."

"We can't possibly. A solar storm could last for days, and we have only seventeen minutes left."

Rock is a perfect shield. "Dee, we still have a chance. The sun is shining almost directly into the loading chamber. The training facility is on the opposite side. We can go through a side tunnel to a point where we're out of direct sunlight, then jet the rest of the way outside, shielded by CM-2 itself."

"Sixteen minutes. We'll never do it in time." But she

was following Rick as he plunged back into the dark interior. He picked one side tunnel and went into it without hesitating. Fortunately Deedee didn't ask why Rick knew so well the network of passages and chambers that crisscrossed the interior of CM-2. He certainly wasn't going to mention it or the disastrous episode it had led to with Gina.

The passageways had been designed for mining rather than rapid travel through them. The trip through the interior seemed to take forever. At last Rick and Deedee were at the surface again, about a quarter of the way around the planetoid, but they were running out of time. Five minutes left. A kilometer and a half to go on the outside, hugging close to CM-2 to avoid the solar flare. It didn't sound far. But it meant averaging eighteen kilometers an hour. You couldn't do that. Not in a suit, zooming around the irregular exterior of a planetoid.

Rick knew it. Deedee probably knew it, too. Neither said a word as the final minute flashed past and the deadline was missed. They kept going, bitterly, all the way to the lock that would lead them into the training facility.

As the lock opened, Rick halted. "No good. Six minutes late. Sorry."

"I know." Deedee came to his side, put an arm around him, and hugged him. She leaned her helmet against his as they moved into the lock together. "We gave it our best shot. Nobody can take that away from us."

The lock pressure equalized. They reached up to remove their helmets as the inner door opened—and found themselves staring at the anxious face of Turkey Gossage. Turkey glanced at once at his watch.

"Don't say it." Rick moved out of the lock. "Six minutes late."

"I wasn't going to. Did you come around the outside?"

"Part of the way." Deedee came to stand at Rick's side.

"Let me see your dosimeters so—"

"No problem. We did the first part in the interior, and we only came outside when CM-2 was shielding us from the sun."

"Smart move." Gossage relaxed visibly. "Of course, even in the sun the dose you'd have received in the short time you were there would have been tolerable."

"We weren't sure." Rick was suddenly more tired than he had ever been. "We didn't know how to calculate it."

"I can show you that in five minutes."

"Not today, sir." Rick slumped against the chamber wall and allowed his arms and legs to go limp. "We did our best, we really did."

"And we came so close." Deedee flopped down by Rick's side. "If there had been one less problem to solve—just one."

"I see. Would you agree with that, Luban?" Turkey seemed more amused than sympathetic.

"Yes. But I don't see why it matters."

"It matters very much. To me, at least." Gossage squatted down so that he was facing the two of them. "You see, it's not every day that people mistake me for a deity." And, when Rick and Deedee stared at him with dull and exhausted eyes, "I gave you a test that I thought would stretch you right to your limits. If you did everything right, and fast, and clean, you could make it back before the deadline—just. I rigged the shape of the sintered blocks. I fixed the drive so it would go wonky on the return trip. I turned off the power on the main entry door so you couldn't get back inside and would have to come around the outside. But if there's one thing that even Turkey Gossage can't do, it's to arrange a solar flare for his special convenience. I'd have to be God Almighty to do that. The flare wasn't in my plans, any more than it was in yours."

He reached out, taking Deedee and Rick's right hands in his. "If it hadn't been for the flare, you'd have beaten your deadline with time to spare. That's good enough for me. You did well, better than I expected. You've passed. Now, don't go to sleep on me!"

Rick and Deedee had simultaneously closed their eyes. They showed no sign of opening them again.

"All right." Gossage stood up. He was still holding their hands and his movement lifted them to their feet. "You've passed, the pair of you, but you don't seem to care. Eat and rest, rest and eat. Then things will seem different. We'll talk later about what you'll do when the training course is over." He released them, turned, and headed for the tunnel. As he reached it he added, without turning his head, "Just don't think life is going to be this nice and easy all the time."

The trainees had been bubbling over with excitement for three days. They could hardly wait for graduation. But the ceremony, when it finally came, was another mystery. It represented the culmination of four brutal months of tests, briefings, hectic study, and final practical examination. They had expected—and Rick at least had dreaded—all the pomp and circumstance of a high school graduation ceremony, with robes and pictures and diplomas and celebrities and boring speeches *ad nauseam*.

What Rick got, along with every other graduate of the training program, was one quick handshake from Turkey Gossage.

"What would you do with a certificate if you had one?" Turkey was beaming. "You can't hang it on the wall where you're going—none of you will have a wall."

"Treasure your signature, sir." Gladys de Witt had been forced to perform a southpaw handshake with Turkey. A loose cable had broken her right arm on the final stage of her practical test; but she had finished, flying the ship home to base one-handed. Now she waved her white cast in the air. "Sign this for me instead."

Turkey did so, to enormous applause. As he finished he caught Rick's eye and walked across to him. "No big rush." He spoke softly. "But when you get a free minute you have a visitor. Back in my office."

A visitor? Rick was more than surprised. He was baffled. Everyone he knew on CM-2, including Jigger and Gina, was right there at the graduation ceremony and all set to party.

As soon as he could do it without anyone noticing, he slipped away. He headed for Turkey's office. When he got there he realized that he had been wrong. He did know one other person on CM-2. What he had not known—still did not know—was her name.

The woman nodded to him. In person, the sharp features were much more attractive. Or maybe his standards had changed. Anyway, she no longer made him think of a weasel.

"Congratulations, Rick. You've come a long way from Chatterjee Boulevard. This time I ought to introduce myself. My name is Coral Wogan." She held out her hand. Rick, still baffled, shook it. "At the moment the training course feels like an end to you," she went on. "As it surely should. But it is really a beginning."

"I know that. I have tons to learn. I feel I've just started."

"Which is wonderful, and appropriate." She paused, and Rick realized that Turkey Gossage had come in quietly behind him. "The big question is, what are you going to learn? What should you learn, for a satisfying life. And that leads to the next question: What brings real satisfaction? I would say, the toughest job is also the best job."

Turkey had moved forward and could see Rick's face. "Coral, I know you think you're making sense. But actually you're being as clear as mud. Let me try for a moment."

He turned to Rick. "I've been pumping you up during the training course, telling you that the most challenging job in the solar system is out in the Belt, mining and refining and carrying finished products back to the Earth-Moon system. And that is one hell of a job, no denying it. But it's not the real leading edge. Know what is?"

"Yes, sir. The Jovian system mining expedition. The mission to explore and map the moons of Jupiter."

"Turkey!" Coral Wogan spoke accusingly.

"I didn't, Coral. I swear I didn't say a word." Gossage turned to Rick. "Where did you hear about that?"

"From Jigger and Gina. They've applied. They hope to go as a team." Rick was suddenly filled with enormous excitement. Coral Wogan and Turkey Gossage must be having this conversation with him for a reason. "Sir, can I apply to go?"

"See, Coral? I told you." It was Gossage's turn to sound accusing. He shook his head at Rick. "You could apply, but you'd have no chance. Anyone selected must have at least three years of real Belt experience. If you stay the course, you could apply for the second expedition in five years' time. Ms. Wogan hopes you won't do that, because in five years you could be ready for a different job. Over to you, Coral. This one is your area, not mine."

She nodded. "You see, Rick Luban, the Jovian project may be the most exciting job in the system but it's not the toughest one. The toughest one is to fight a monster that's effectively immortal, a monster with a billion arms and a million times more power than Vanguard Mining. A monster that's not in space, but back on Earth."

"No fancy speeches, Coral." Turkey had read Rick's puzzled look. "Get to the point."

"Right. Do you remember what it was like for you in school before you came to space?"

"Very well."

"Do you think you're smarter now than you were then?"

Rick had to consider that. He wasn't sure just what she was asking. "Smarter, no. My brain's the same. But I know a lot more, and I understand more of what I know."

"Very true. And do you know why that's true? I'll tell you. Back on Earth you were being strangled by the biggest, most inefficient, best-entrenched bureaucratic system in the history of the world. You were in public school, adrift within an education system that has itself lost any interest in the value of knowledge, or truth, or discipline, or self-evaluation. Like all big monopolies, it is more interested in perpetuating and protecting its own territory than in anything else. The men and women who emerge from the school system know less and less—and then wonder why they find themselves unemployable."

"Do you understand all that?" Turkey Gossage showed more interest in Rick's facial expression than in Coral Wogan's flow of words.

"I understand what Ms. Wogan is saying. But I don't know why she's saying it. I mean, you both work for Vanguard Mining. And you train your own people the way you want to."

"We do—by starting over from scratch with good raw material. We can live with that, but it's not the right way. For every bright bored kid like you, Rick, kicked out of the system, another thousand stay inside it and are stifled for life."

"We'd like to change that." Coral Wogan was smiling at Rick in a way that he did not like at all. "We know it's going to take generations, but we want to make a start. And it has to be done from *within*. The toughest, most challenging job in the solar system isn't in the moons of Jupiter. It's to go back down to Earth, infiltrate the education system, and find the children who belong out here. And, eventually, we have to transform and either improve or destroy the whole mess."

"No!" Rick saw in his mind the patient turtle, bowed down by thirty years of frustration and indignity. "If you think I could ever go back to earth and be like Mr. Hamel, to put up with all the bullshit—"

"I don't. Mr. Hamel is someone sympathetic to us, but he is not an activist. We are looking for someone who—"

"No. I'm not interested."

"Told you, Coral. But I promised you a shot." Turkey Gossage came to stand right in front of Rick, shielding him from Coral Wogan. "All right, Rick. The party is starting and you've earned the right to be there. Any statement or question for me or Ms. Wogan before you go?"

"I'd like to find out all I can about the Jovian mining expedition."

"We'll get that for you. I promise. Anything else?"

"No." Rick started for the door, then hesitated. "I'm sorry, Ms. Wogan. I really appreciate being considered. But that sort of thing's not for me."

"I understand. One thing I didn't get to mention is that even if you were interested, we wouldn't think of beginning for another five or six years. You had some of the qualities we need before you left Earth—you knew what it was like to be amoral, cynical, and violent—but anyone who takes this job also needs to be devious and subtle and *very* knowledgeable. That takes time. Is it all right if I ask you again in another five years?"

"Sure. But my answer will be the same." Rick started out of the door, but again he hesitated. "Can I ask one more question?"

"Of course."

"Did you ask anyone else in the training course?"

"One other person. Deedee Mao."

"I see. Can you tell me what she said?"

"Yes. First she said no, no way. No fucking way, to be precise. Then she asked if we had talked to Rick Luban about it. I told her we had not, but we were going to."

"I see. Thank you."

"Thank you, for listening. Now go party." Turkey Gossage waited until Rick was out of sight and out of earshot. "That's it, Coral. Twenty *noes* in a row, and no sign of a *yes*."

"Think I don't realize that?"

"You know why?"

"Because they're young. Because Rick and the rest of them all had terrible experiences in the Earth education system. Because the Belt and Jovian exploration feel far more exciting."

"All those. And one other thing." Gossage came forward to sit at the big round table opposite Coral Wogan. "The trainees haven't watched the Earth system fail, year after year after year. They haven't had the frustration of unlearning lessons in new recruits, before real teaching can begin. The only people who should go down and take on the Earth bureaucracy are ones who have seethed over it and hated it for a long time."

"People like?"

"People like you."

"And you."

"Right. *We* are the ones who know the job needs doing. You and I, and a few others. And we keep trying to talk other people into doing it for us, when we should be starting it ourselves. The trainees don't say it, but underneath they must be thinking, if the job's so all-fired important, why aren't they down there in the trenches, instead of asking us? Well, Coral?"

"No. It's not for me."

"Right. Me neither. But think of the effect on Deedee, and Rick, and all the others, if they found that *you and I* were down there ahead of them, starting the job. What do you say?"

"I say, no way. No fucking way, to quote Deedee Mao. I have a million things to do here."

"Right. Me too. So let's go join the graduation party." Turkey led the way to the door.

As they left the room Coral Wogan said thoughtfully, "I can't go now. I really can't. But in five years' time, or maybe even in one year's time . . ."

Turkey laughed; and then they were gone. The room that formed the nerve center of the training program became silent and empty.

Far away along the corridor the party was at last getting into its stride. From the training room the sound was just a confused hubbub, like the first distant swell of a revolution.